Total Rush

"Deirdre Martin is the reason I read romance novels."
—*The Best Reviews*

"Martin's inventive take on opposites attracting is funny and poignant." —*Booklist*

"Makes you feel like you're flying." —*Rendezvous*

Fair Play

"Martin depicts the worlds of both professional hockey and ethnic Brooklyn with deftness and smart detail. She has an unerring eye for humorous family dynamics." —*Publishers Weekly*

"Makes you feel like you're flying." —*Romance Reviews Today*

Body Check

"Heartwarming." —*Booklist*

"One of the best first novels I have read in a long time."
—*All About Romance* (Desert Isle Keeper)

"You don't have to be a hockey fan to cheer for *Body Check*."
—*The Word on Romance*

"A dazzling debut."

—Millie Criswell, *USA Today* bestselling author

Breakaway

Deirdre Martin

BERKLEY SENSATION, NEW YORK

THE BERKLEY PUBLISHING GROUP
Published by the Penguin Group
Penguin Group (USA) Inc.
375 Hudson Street, New York, New York 10014, USA

Penguin Group (Canada), 90 Eglinton Avenue East, Suite 700, Toronto, Ontario M4P 2Y3, Canada
(a division of Pearson Penguin Canada Inc.)
Penguin Books Ltd., 80 Strand, London WC2R 0RL, England
Penguin Group Ireland, 25 St. Stephen's Green, Dublin 2, Ireland (a division of Penguin Books Ltd.)
Penguin Group (Australia), 250 Camberwell Road, Camberwell, Victoria 3124, Australia
(a division of Pearson Australia Group Pty. Ltd.)
Penguin Books India Pvt. Ltd., 11 Community Centre, Panchsheel Park, New Delhi—110 017, India
Penguin Group (NZ), 67 Apollo Drive, Rosedale, Auckland 0632, New Zealand
(a division of Pearson New Zealand Ltd.)
Penguin Books (South Africa) (Pty.) Ltd., 24 Sturdee Avenue, Rosebank, Johannesburg 2196,
South Africa

Penguin Books Ltd., Registered Offices: 80 Strand, London WC2R 0RL, England

This is a work of fiction. Names, characters, places, and incidents either are the product of the author's imagination or are used fictitiously, and any resemblance to actual persons, living or dead, business establishments, events, or locales is entirely coincidental. The publisher does not have any control over and does not assume any responsibility for author or third-party websites or their content.

BREAKAWAY

A Berkley Sensation Book / published by arrangement with the author

PRINTING HISTORY
Berkley Sensation mass-market edition / February 2012

ISBN: 978-0-425-24368-8   *4767 5870*   *02/12*

BERKLEY SENSATION®
Berkley Sensation Books are published by The Berkley Publishing Group,
a division of Penguin Group (USA) Inc.,
375 Hudson Street, New York, New York 10014.
BERKLEY SENSATION® is a registered trademark of Penguin Group (USA) Inc.
The "B" design is a trademark of Penguin Group (USA) Inc.

PRINTED IN THE UNITED STATES OF AMERICA

10 9 8 7 6 5 4 3 2 1

For my best friend of forty years,
Jane Dashow.

I love you.

Acknowledgments

Special thanks to:
   Jane Dashow, without whose help this book could not have been written.

Additional thanks to:
   My husband, the ever patient Mark Levine.
   My extremely patient editor, Kate Seaver.
   My terrific agent, Miriam Kriss.
   Fatin Soufan, Binnie Braunstein, Eileen Buchholtz, and Dee Tenorio.
   Mom, Dad, Bill, Allison, Frankie, Aine, Sinead, Dave, and Tom.

1

Lord, please don't let there be any truth to the saying, "This is the first day of the rest of your life," thought Erin O'Brien, as she shoved guests' dirty sheets into the massive washer in the basement. Ever since her parents had purchased Ballycraig's sole B and B, she'd come to feel like an indentured servant. Helping her mother run the place was supposed to be temporary until they found "the right kind of help." Apparently, no one in the village was right for catering to the PJ Leary fanatics who made up the bulk of the visitors. Months had crawled by, and Erin was still here, relegated to the less glamorous tasks: laundry, housecleaning, dishes. The worst part was, she did it all for free, out of what mother liked to term "family unity."

Unity? I guess Da and Brian are exempt.

She envied her brother: Brian had left town as soon as he got married, an IT job waiting for him in Liverpool. It was a great career opportunity, except it left their father all alone to run Ballycraig's sole auto shop, which he'd bought from Ned Sykes when the old man retired. For years, her father and brother had worked as mechanics in nearby

Balla. Now, her poor father was working with a very green assistant who'd already come close to crushing himself under a number of cars.

"How's it going down there?" her mother yelled from the top of the basement steps.

"Fine," Erin shouted back, peering up at her mother's creased, anxious face. "Dad did a great job fixing the washer. Could be a second career for him."

"No need to be cheeky."

"I'm not!"

"Nevertheless, watch yourself." Her mother checked her watch. "Christ, the first of the weekend guests will be here in three hours. Would you be a love and go to the supermarket in Moneygall for me?"

Erin's shoulders slumped. "Mam—"

"Asking too much, am I?"

Erin felt guilty. "No, it's just you've more than enough time to go to the market yourself. You'll be back here and baking before they've even arrived."

"Assuming the buses are running on time." She looked fretful. "Normally I wouldn't ask you to shop on such short notice, love. You know that. It's just that I've got so much to do . . ."

God help me, Erin thought. *I really need to get my license. If I don't, I'm always going to be hostage to a bus timetable, or worse.*

"Relax, all right? You know I'll do it."

"You're a good girl, Erin."

"A patsy, more like," Erin grumbled to herself. Her mother was still peering down at her with a distressed expression. "Mam, calm down. I just said I'd do it, so why do you still look so upset? All you achieve by fretting and wringing your hands is driving yourself, and everyone around you, mad. You're going to give yourself a stroke, and for what?"

"I know, I know," her mother agreed distractedly. "It's just that I want it all to be perfect, you know?"

"Perfection doesn't exist."

Her mother snorted. "Oh, so now you're a philosopher, I see. You should be down at the pub with that Holy Trinity of Dimwits, sitting at the bar, each one thinking they're the next Stephen Fry."

The criticism stung, but Erin refrained from saying what she was thinking: *I can never win with you.* She didn't want things to escalate, especially since her mother could go from zero to fifty in the rage department in seconds. Also, that same thought had been running through Erin's head since she was twelve. It would sound pathetic coming from the mouth of a grown woman. Still, she did have a right to defend herself.

"I'm not being philosophical. I'm just trying to point out that you drive yourself mad unnecessarily."

Erin could tell by her mother's lack of response that this conversation was going in one ear and out the other. Her mother had always been anxious, but now she bordered on high-strung. Erin worried that one day, she'd just keel over dead from a stroke.

"I'll leave you a list on the kitchen counter, all right?"

"Sure."

"You're a good girl," her mother repeated.

Too good, Erin thought. She took comfort in knowing her escape plan was firmly in place and that she would, sooner or later, be free. She double-checked behind her to make sure the washer was still tumbling properly and headed up the stairs.

* * *

"Chores" done, Erin went to her room, locking the door behind her. She and her parents now occupied the top floor of the guest house, the sale of their family home and some land having provided the bulk of the money to buy the B and B.

She caught her reflection in the mirror atop the scratched bureau from her childhood. *You're no great shakes,* she told herself. *Nothing special to look at.* But in the career she'd be pursuing, looks didn't matter.

Her eyes traveled the room, caressing the reproductions of some of her favorite artwork that she'd pinned to the walls to help fend off dreariness: Frida Kahlo, the bright reds of Henri Matisse, fields of heart-lifting bright yellow sunflowers by van Gogh, and Irish landscape artist Henry McGrane's gentle impressions of spring. Erin was pursuing an art history degree online with the Open University. Most people would think it impractical, even odd. Erin didn't care: she loved art, and it was something she'd pursued off and on while Rory was away at college. Now that Rory was out of her life, she could do as she wanted, no putting her dreams on hold for that selfish bastard. No one knew she was almost done with her degree but her best friend, Sandra.

Rory Brady. Just thinking about him sometimes made her feel like a twit. Ballycraig's local idiot, that's who she was, too stupid to tell when she was being played. How many times had she replayed their years-long relationship in her mind? Why did she insist on torturing herself? The story always ended the same way: her life in tatters and his looking brighter and brighter, the first Irish-born man playing in the NHL for the New York Blades.

Rory's face swam up in her mind's eye. Her mam had always said he looked like David Beckham, and it was true. If he were a pop star, girls would be breaking into his house just to catch a glimpse of that dirty blond hair and blue eyes. It was a sin that a man should have eyes that beautiful and be such an SOB.

They'd started dating when they were just babies, fourteen years old. It was casual at first, but soon turned serious. Very serious, then committed, even when his family moved to America a year later. They spent eight years of trying to find a place to be alone when his family returned to Ballycraig for the summer, eight years of her arguing with her parents about going to visit him in the States. One memory in particular dashed back at her: It was early evening, and the sky had gone all gray dusk and pink. She and Rory were lounging beneath the big oak tree in Old Man

McDonagh's field, the sun filtering through the latticework of the leaves. *The Lover's Tree*, it was called, because the old man never minded couples loafing beneath it. Rory was leaning back against the tree, and she was stretched out with her head in his lap. It felt like they were in a poem.

Rory looked down at her, smiling. "I was thinking it might be nice if our wedding ceremony was just you and me, and some old padre saying the words in an ancient church, the only light coming from a blaze of candles surrounding us."

Erin settled into his lap dreamily. "That's very romantic."

"And it saves us worrying about a guest list."

Erin clucked her tongue, glancing up at him with affection. "I knew you had an ulterior motive."

"Me? Never." His expression was tender as his large, strong hand brushed against her cheek. "I know it sounds mad, but sometimes I feel like we're already married, we've been together so long."

"Is that your way of telling me you're getting tired of me, Rory Brady?" Erin teased.

"I could never get tired of you."

"Promise?"

He put his hand over his heart. "On my life." His voice, a deep sexy rumble, was charged with emotion as he continued, "You're the only one for me, Erin, and you always have been. Nothing can change that, not even geography. You're going to be my wife."

Erin believed him. Their love was immutable, fixed as law. There was no telling where one left off and the other began. It had always been that way, and always would be.

The memory faded, straight-on narrative returning as if she needed to recount the facts of what happened to make sure it really had happened.

They decided they'd wait to tie the knot until Rory graduated from Cornell and got picked up by a minor hockey team, and then hopefully, the NHL. Which is exactly how it happened.

Except part of it didn't: the wedding. Erin loved him so

blindly, and with such faith, that even after he hadn't come back to Ballycraig for two years running, she still held tightly to their dream. All that rubbish about being in the NHL now and training camp and not having any time to get back home? Deep down, she knew. So when she gave him the ultimatum—either marry me like you said or we're done—she shouldn't have been surprised that he grabbed option B.

Even so, when the crash came, it was no less devastating. She was dragged under by their history together, tormented by every loving thing he'd ever said and done over the years. She'd have donned widow's weeds if she could. It was a lucky thing that she was surrounded by loving family and friends, like Sandra and Rory's former best friend, Jake Fry. Were it not for all of them, especially Jake and Sandra, she'd have spent her life in bed, not caring about anything. She certainly stopped caring about her job in the jewelry store in Crosshaven, quitting a month after Rory dumped her. She couldn't handle dealing with people, especially happy couples who came in looking for wedding rings.

It took her two years to pull herself together, but when she did, she made a promise to herself: never, ever again would she give her hopes and dreams over to a man like Rory Brady.

2

Why didn't I bring a jacket? Walking the twisting hills leading up to her cousin's sheep farm, Erin felt the chill wind pass through her like a ghost. June was technically summer, and summer technically meant sunshine and heat, at least in the rest of the world. But those technicalities didn't count in Ireland. While they did get some lovely bright days and the occasional surprise of warmth, by and large summer was much like the rest of the year: a bit dark and a touch rainy. "Moody," as her dad would say.

Erin paused at the top of the second hill, more to catch her breath than anything else. When she was a girl, she and Sandra used to walk up here, pretending they were queens who ruled the landscape below: the open fields, the ancient, gnarled trees that reminded her of old people's hands. Maybe this was why she liked Henry McGrane's landscapes so much: they brought her back to a time when she was acutely in touch with the beauty that surrounded her.

She'd taken it for granted for many years after she'd grown. It was only when the tourists started pouring in because of PJ Leary that she again saw Ballycraig and its lush surroundings through the eyes of an outsider.

Erin herself had never read PJ's books; she wasn't a huge fan of the fantasy genre. But clearly her literary tastes were in the minority: his first book, *The Wee Ones of Galway*, had sold millions worldwide, as had the subsequent two books in the series. PJ, whom her cousin Liam had known back in New York when the author didn't have two sticks to rub together, was now a very rich man with a fanatical following. Ballycraig was where he made his home, which explained the tours.

A bestselling author in my little town, Erin mused. Who would have ever thought? Certainly not Old Jack at the Oak, who was mystified as to why "those books with that talking salmon shite" had captivated readers around the globe. But Old Jack didn't complain about the business the fanatics were bringing in. No one did. The tourists boosted Ballycraig's economy. Erin could attest to that, spending a good part of her days vacuuming and doing their laundry.

Resuming her walk, Erin reflected on how much she liked PJ. He was down to earth, approachable, and affable up to a point, that point being when fans tramped on private land to get a close-up look at his cottage. Unfortunately, that land had been in the McCafferty family for generations.

Erin's cousin's wife, Aislinn McCafferty, had had to replace many of the small stone walls dividing the pastures with electric fencing. She deeply resented it, but it was the only way to literally shock some sense into the interlopers. Yet there were ways to get around the fencing, and the persistent often did, not realizing what they faced if Aislinn caught sight of them.

Eventually, Erin arrived at what everyone in town called "the driveway of death." Not only was it long and muddy, but it was pitted with potholes the size of meteorites, which Aislinn refused to fill, hoping it would further ward off tourists. How Aislinn's truck hadn't broken an axle was beyond

her. Erin didn't want to think about her cousin Liam maneu-
vering his motorcycle in the mud.

Erin was surprised to see Aislinn rinsing out troughs at
the smaller of the two outbuildings. At this time of day, she
was usually out in the high pasture, herding sheep with her
Border collie, Deenie. Deenie was getting on in years, but
she was as sharp as ever. She moved a bit slower, but it
hadn't affected her ability to herd. Erin dreaded the day
Aislinn had to put Deenie down. It would be like losing a
member of the family.

"Hello, you." Aislinn looked pleased to see her as she
wiped her muddy hands on the front of her jeans. "This is a
surprise. Liam didn't mention anything about you coming."

"I'm here to see Jake, actually."

"Ah." Aislinn looked somewhat surprised. "Does he
know you're coming?"

"He asked me to."

"So you're still mates, then?"

Erin tensed a bit. "Yes."

Jake had been as wounded and angry about Rory's van-
ishing as she had been. One minute, they were thick as
thieves; the next, Rory was giving him the cold shoulder.
Maybe Rory thought he needed to sever all ties to Ballycraig. Or maybe he just couldn't bear to hear Jake tell him
the truth: that he was a selfish jerk.

As far as Erin could see, there was only one problem
with Jake being such a good bloke: over the course of helping her get back on her feet, Jake had fallen for her, hard.
Sandra claimed Jake had always nursed a crush on Erin,
but it didn't matter, because she'd only ever had eyes for
Rory. But Rory was gone, and Jake wasn't, and he'd stood
faithfully by her side through one of the darkest times of
her life. Logic dictated that she should be attracted to him
because he was such a good man, and handsome to boot,
but she wasn't. Still, she tried hard to give it a go. They'd
always got on like a house on fire, but things grew very
awkward very fast. At first Erin rationalized her hesitance

by telling herself this was what happened when good friends transitioned to romance.

But the first time Jake kissed her, she felt nothing, though God knows she wanted to. There was no sizzle and pop, no hungriness for more. Maybe that would come with time, she'd thought, but it soon dawned on her that you couldn't force chemistry: either it was there or it wasn't. For her, it wasn't. And so, she'd gently suggested they go back to being friends.

"Is he up in the high north pasture?" Erin asked.

"He better be," Aislinn replied.

"I'm sure if that's where you want him to be, that's where he is."

Aislinn feigned offense as she readjusted her long red ponytail. "Are you insinuating I'm a tough boss, Erin O'Brien?"

"I'm not insinuating. I know you are."

Aislinn laughed. "My secret's out, then." She paused. "You've been a bit of a stranger."

"My mother believes I'm her personal servant."

Aislinn clucked her tongue. "Still? You've got to start interviewing people yourself or she'll never fill your position. You know that, don't you?"

"Of course I do."

"And it's not like she can't afford to pay someone. Liam says your family is making money hand over fist from these PJ nuts."

"It's true."

"So tell her what the deal is and have done with it." Aislinn squinted, her eyes slowly scouring the surrounding hills. "Shite. I was supposed to be in the south pasture with Alec ten minutes ago." She picked up a half-full bucket of muddy water. "We miss you, Erin," she said with a tinge of sadness. "You know that, don't you? Liam's been feeling a bit put out."

"Then he should pop by the B and B and visit," Erin said with a half smile. "Works two ways, you know." She gave Aislinn a light peck on the cheek. "Give him my love, will you?"

"I will. Someone's got to love him," she joked.

"You don't see me rushing to disagree with you. Take care, Aislinn." Erin crouched down, rubbing her nose against Deenie's. "See you, Deenie." She rose. "I'll come round soon. Promise."

"Good," said Aislinn, looking dead happy. "Now if you'll excuse me, I've got some lovely muck to attend to."

* * *

Erin headed up to the high north pasture, where Jake was running the new Border collie, Jupitus, through a series of commands.

There was no denying he was a handsome man, with lovely thick black hair and soft brown eyes that betrayed every emotion he felt inside. But to her he would always be her mate, that's all. "You're running that poor dog ragged," she noted as she reached him.

Jake grinned. "That's what they like to do: run ragged. If they don't, they go mad."

"So I've heard." Erin felt a twinge of discomfort. "Well, here I am—or to put it in dog language, you called and I came. What's up?"

Jake shielded his eyes against the sun. "A few things."

"That's vague enough to sound serious."

"It's not, really." He paused. "No, that's a lie. It is."

"Go on."

He looked at her. "It's about you and me."

"What about you and me?"

"I know we're great mates and all that, always have been," he began, actually sounding a bit shy. "But I was thinking about, you know, the dating and all that."

Erin kept her tone even. "What about it?"

"I think you pulled the plug prematurely," he declared. "I think you freaked out. You didn't really give it time to develop."

"Jake—"

"Hear me out. 'Love is friendship that catches fire,' isn't that the old saying? You didn't even give us time to light a match."

Erin looked down at the ground guiltily. "It's just not there for me. Plus, I don't want to date anyone right now."

"I'm not *anyone*: I'm the man who knows you best in the world, better than Rory ever did, that's for damn sure."

Erin had never heard him sound so fervent. "And that means what?"

"It means I know your good points and your bad points. I'm not some moony-eyed boy; I'm a man who knows that if you just give me a chance, you could be happy."

"Jake, please." If there were a wall here, Erin would feel smashed up against it.

"I think I deserve another chance, Erin."

"Please don't do this."

"No one else will ever love you as much as I do. Sorry if that sounds like a cliché, love, but it's true."

"I already told you," Erin replied firmly, "I'm not interested in seeing anyone right now. Not you, not even Jesus himself if he came on bended knee."

Jake remained stubborn. "Let me try to change that."

Erin was silent, wishing she could stay that way. But she owed him a response.

"I need to think about this," she said carefully.

"Fair enough. We'll talk soon, yeah?"

"Yeah."

"Look after yourself, then."

"And you as well," Erin replied as she started back down the hill. She had the feeling she'd just made a colossal mistake telling him she'd think things over. It gave him a flicker of hope where none existed. But she couldn't do with bashing him over the head with it. She'd fix it later.

* * *

Some things never change, Rory thought to himself as his gran insisted on pouring him a cup of tea. Though he'd barely just arrived in Ballycraig, from what he could tell, there was still only one church, one pub, and one small store. Bored teenage boys still played football on the green behind the elementary school. He thought how easy it would be to just blend back in to this calm, familiar stasis. His plan was—

"If you stare into space any longer, you're going to hypnotize yourself."

Rory blinked to find his gran squinting at him across the table.

"Sorry."

He did feel a bit hypnotized. He'd never been able to sleep on planes, and though the flight from New York to Galway wasn't that long, it was followed by renting a car and driving up to Ballycraig. He was keeping the car for the summer.

"You should drink more tea," she urged. "It'll pep you right up."

"I prefer coffee."

"You're totally Yankified now. It's sad to see." She pursed her lips, sipping her tea demurely. "Tell me again what excuse you're using to be back here for the summer. Oh, wait, it's coming to me: you're to help Jackson Bell with the football camp, as well as help your poor ole gran with repairs."

"It's true!"

"Not for nothing, but even an eejit could figure out what you're up to. You could have just as easily hired someone here to do the work for me. As for the football camp, you could have just written a check and let Jackson hire someone."

"I started the camp, Gran. Remember?"

"I do. But you stopped giving a tinker's damn about it how many years ago?"

Rory suppressed a smile. On the outside, his gran looked like the stereotypical little old lady: a bit shrunken, a gummy smile, slow moving. But soft-spoken and sweet she was not.

"I don't remember."

His gran looked insulted. "What do you take me for, someone who just fell off the back of the turnip truck?"

"I—"

"You're being here has nothing to do with me and the camp, and everything to do with Erin O'Brien." She sighed heavily. "I love you, son, but you've passed the expiration date on that one. You think that girl is even going to give you the time of day? After what you did to her? If I were her, I'd push you under the wheels of the McCafferty's truck, so I would."

"Thanks, Gran."

"You've always been a bighead, Rory. But acting the swaggering hero returning to town to reclaim his woman isn't going to go down well with anyone."

"I don't really care. And for your info, all I want from Erin is forgiveness."

"And that's it, is it?"

"Yup."

"That lying part of you must come from your mother's side of the family, not the Brady side."

Rory laughed. His gran was right: he was here not only to beg forgiveness but also to reclaim. His mission was to prove to Erin he was worthy of her love and trust. He was going to confess he'd been a total arsehole and that he should never have let her go. He'd been practicing his lines all the way over on the plane: *I was all full of myself, puffed up. And then I realized how hollow it all was without you.*

Rory wasn't going to pretend he didn't love being a professional athlete; he did. It was quite the feather in his cap to be the sole Irish-born player in the NHL, though God knows there were enough Irish American and Irish Canadian players. He felt he'd truly achieved something.

But there was a difference between achievement and contentment. Rory wasn't content, and the worst part was that it was his own fault. He wasn't used to making major mistakes. But that was precisely what he'd done in his personal life.

Rory finished his bread, wiped his mouth, and, to satisfy his grandmother, drank down his tea in one go before rising from the table and kissing her on the top of the head. But before he could leave, her bony hand shot out and she grabbed his wrist. "Don't go swanning into the Oak acting like you own the place. You'll be lucky if they don't break pint glasses over your head."

"As if that'd hurt me," Rory scoffed. "I'm a professional hockey player."

His grandmother released his wrist and, with a disapproving shake of her head, waved him off. *She never changes,* Rory thought, as he started for town. *And thank God for that.*

3

Erin arrived at Sandra's a few minutes early to find her friend settled in nicely on the couch, watching *Top Gear*. Sandra was all dressed up, her makeup flawless. Oona was bent over the refurbished laptop Erin had given her for Christmas; Larry Jr. was watching TV with his mother; and baby Gina, it appeared, was already upstairs asleep.

"There you are," said Sandra with a relieved smile. "I thought you might not come."

Erin was puzzled. "Why wouldn't I come?"

"Thought your mam might have you of slave hours."

"Who's a slave?" Larry Jr. asked.

"Never you mind."

Erin looked at Larry Jr. and Oona, both mesmerized by the respective screens in front of them. "They're turning into zombies, Sandra."

"You 'n' me parked our butts for hours on end in front of the telly and we turned out all right. At least one of us did."

Erin ignored Sandra's self-deprecating remark. "Where's Lucy?"

"Out with her new boyfriend," Oona supplied, her eyes still glued to the computer.

"The last one didn't last very long, did he?" Erin said to Sandra quietly.

"And thank God for that."

"You like this new one?"

Sandra looked appalled. "Bite your tongue. He's a bag o' bones and his head's as empty as a pint glass at closing time."

"He's got a silver skull ring," said Oona, sounding impressed.

"And you, my love, have big ears," Sandra reprimanded affectionately, gesturing for Erin to follow her into the boxy kitchen.

Sandra had never been a great one for cleaning, but in Erin's estimation, it had gotten worse over the years. It wasn't that her house was dirty, per se. It was just overwhelmingly untidy and cluttered.

Erin more than approved of her friend's smart outfit. Sandra was always moaning on and on about how having the kids wrecked her figure, but it wasn't true: she looked fantastic, curves in all the right places, her bobbed brown hair gleaming. Erin hadn't seen her friend turned out like this in a very long time. "You look great."

"Thanks," said Sandra, beaming as she put up the kettle.

Erin was going to ask who the lucky guy was, but noting that Sandra's wedding ring was still on, she realized the only person it could be. "You're not going out with Larry, are you?"

Sandra's smile disappeared. "I knew you'd react this way."

"What way? Shocked that you'd go out with the man you're separated from, who calls you every foul name in the book when he's belted down a few?"

"We're trying to patch things up," Sandra insisted. "Get back the old magic, you know? Rekindle the romance."

Erin stared at her. "I love you, San, but you're an idiot."

"He's the father of my children," Sandra reminded her, smoothing the front of her dress. "You'll understand when you have a family of your own some day."

"And he takes care of his family so well. You've been trying to get out of this poky little place for ages. I don't see how you're going to do that when he can't even hold down a job."

"He's trying. It's not his fault the country's in a recession!"

"I guess that's true," Erin reluctantly conceded, even though she thought it likely that Larry's idea of looking for a job consisted of skimming the want ads while sipping his first beer of the morning.

"Where is Dapper Dan, if I may be so bold as to ask?"

"At his brother, Lance's. He's been living there the past few weeks, trying to get his act together." Sandra looked Erin dead in the eye. "And he has."

Erin counted on her fingers. "I can't keep track now: is it the tenth time he's gotten his act together, or the twentieth?"

"Shut up, Erin."

"At least tell me he's not going to move back in."

Sandra's response was to rattle two boxes of tea. "Barry's or Earl Grey?"

"Barry's."

"So predictable," Sandra teased. "We've not had a good long talk in a few days, you 'n' me."

"I know."

"Fill me in, then. How's Jake?"

Erin sat down, cradling her head in her hands. "I feel terrible. He's such a nice bloke. He helped me out so much after Rory kicked me in the teeth. But I just can't feel anything beyond friendship for him, you know?" Erin looked up at her friend. "What if I'm looking a gift horse in the mouth? What if he's as good as it gets for me?"

Sandra sat down at the kitchen table. "He's not, for the simple reason he wants to live here the rest of his life and you're gettin' your degree and you're outta here, yeah? So it doesn't really matter."

Sandra wet her thumb and rubbed at a smudge of dry jelly on the table. "You know I love Jake to death, but I can't picture ever having sex with him. Can you?"

"I've never really thought about it," said Erin, who was trying hard not to think about it now that Sandra had brought it up.

Sandra glanced furtively toward the living room, then back to Erin. "I know he's good-looking and that, but I bet he's the selfish sort who heaves himself on top of you like a great walrus. Then it's a few pokes and he's done, rolling off you with a burp and a fart until he falls asleep."

"That's not what you thought he'd be like when we were at school!"

"That doesn't count; it was a hundred years ago."

"Well, for all we know, he might be great between the sheets."

"I bet he's no Rory Brady," Sandra said slyly.

"What's that got to do with anything?"

"I'm just sayin' Rory probably ruined you for anyone else. The things you told me—"

Erin could feel her ears turn red. "Shut up, Sandra."

"True love," said Sandra. "Too bad he turned out to be such a shite."

"True love . . . Isn't that what you have with Larry?" Erin lobbed back.

"Yes. But sometimes the flame flickers out for a bit, especially after you have kids. I told you: we're trying to rekindle the romance."

"I hope that means you're going to burn him alive in bed after he falls asleep," Erin mumbled.

"What was that?"

"Nothing."

Sandra looked dubious. "If you say so."

Erin took the opportunity to change the subject. "D'you know what I heard?"

Sandra's eyes lit up. "What?"

Now we're talking. Cut through the everyday dramas and there was nothing better than a good old chin-wag.

"Grace Finnegan has a boyfriend."

Sandra looked appalled. "What? Fintan's body is barely cold!"

Erin frowned. "It has been a year, Sandra."

"She's too old to have a boyfriend. She's sixty-five if she's a day!"

"Well, he's no youngster himself."

"Do we know him?"

"Well, we've seen him. I wouldn't say we know him."

"Quit teasing me!" Sandra begged as she hustled to the whistling kettle.

"It's Wayne Mallory—you know, the fella who supplies her store with produce?"

Sandra's hand flew to her mouth. "Him? Oh, God. The bastard must single-handedly be keeping Viagra in business."

They both laughed.

"I do feel glad for her, though," Erin continued. "Those last years with Fintan's cancer must have been hard."

"True. Grace deserves a healthy man with a big working willie."

Again they were swept away on gales of laughter, same as they'd been doing since they were kids.

Oona popped her head into the kitchen. "What's so funny?"

"Nothing," said Sandra, swiping her eyes. "Go back inside."

Oona opened her mouth to protest, then thought better of it, disappearing with a frown.

"I have some dirt of my own," Sandra confided, pouring the boiling water into the teacups. She was just about to dish when the sound of someone leaning on a car horn pierced the house.

"That'll be Larry," Sandra said, all flustered.

Erin was incredulous. "He's honking for you? He can't even come in and escort his own wife out to the car?"

"He doesn't want to get the kids all worked up."

"Like honking a horn outside the window won't?"

"I told you: if he walks in here, it'll do their heads in."

"When did he get a car?"

"It's not his. He's borrowing it off Lance." Sandra smoothed her skirt, licking her lips nervously. "Do I look all right?"

"Perfect." *Better than that loser deserves.*

"We—I shouldn't be too late."

"I have to be at the B and B by six in the morning, San. If you're not home by then, I'll murther you, as my grand-dad used to say."

"I'll be home, don't worry." She smiled devilishly. "At least I think I will."

"Have him wear a condom, please," Erin requested as Sandra hustled toward her to give her a kiss on the cheek.

"'Course. Thanks for helping me out in a jam. If Lucy gets in after one, tell her she's gonna get a mouthful from me."

"Will do."

Sandra flew out of the kitchen. Erin heard her hurriedly say good-bye to the kids, and then the front door slammed and she was away. *Please, God, let her come to her senses one of these days,* Erin prayed. She finished her tea, then joined Oona and Larry Jr. in the living room. She had a feeling it was going to be a long night.

* * *

Rory took his time sauntering down to the pub. His grand-mother was worried about the rest of the town jumping him when he walked in, but that was the furthest thing from his mind, probably because it was so ridiculous. Four of them could try to take him down, and they'd be the ones to wind up in a ditch moaning in pain, not him. Not only that, but any choice words they threw his way would be a piece of piss compared to the trash talk he'd gotten on the ice. He knew he was a shit for dumping Erin. But at the time, he felt cornered. Never in her life had she given him an ulti-matum, and it caught him unawares. It was the first time she really pushed him, and he reflexively pushed back. And then it was over, all eight years of it.

He was on the High Street now. He remembered walk-ing hand in hand down the street with Erin, proud as could be because the brightest, most beautiful girl in town was his, and always would be. He was suffused with tenderness as he pictured Erin's face: the light splash of

freckles across the bridge of her nose that she'd had since
she was a child, the long raven black hair, the green eyes
flecked with the tiniest bits of gold. He hadn't thought about
what he'd do if she were in the pub, but then again, he didn't
have to. He was Rory Brady. They'd been through thick and
thin for eight long years. The force of history was behind
them, shared memories that only the two of them knew.
He'd win her back. He just had to be patient.

He'd only been with two women since he and Erin split,
neither relationship serious. Not that he didn't have lots
of opportunities. It was unbelievable, the way the women
flocked to him just because he was a professional athlete. It
was the same with footballers in Ireland. When he was
younger, he'd seen guys in pubs who lied through their
teeth, saying they were about to be traded to Real Madrid
or Man United; the girls were on them faster than crows on
roadkill. It had always mystified him—until he made it
into the NHL. Now he understood: it was about power and
status, with a big, heaping side dish of wealth thrown in. But
for all his machismo, meaningless sex had never appealed
to him.

Four years, and nothing in his hometown seemed to
have changed. The rhythm of life was slow; there was never
anything so important that you couldn't stop and make a
cup of tea. He chuckled; that would never happen in New
York. New Yorkers might find it quaint for a minute, but
then they'd see it as counterproductive. You can't do that!
You're wasting time! Valuable time where you could be
working and making lots of money! To which Rory thought,
How much feckin' money do people need? He was grateful
for his salary, but to him, income wasn't the yardstick by
which he measured his success. He measured it by the fact
he'd made it into the NHL. He'd started playing late in
life—when his family had moved to the States—and yet
he'd done it. And now that he was back in Ballycraig, there
was only one other way to measure success: getting Erin
back.

Outside the pub, people were crowding the sidewalk,

chatting and enjoying the cool night air, trying to catch a respite from the bodies packed inside like sardines. The pub door was open: obviously Old Jack had yet to spring for AC. Rory remembered how evil hot it could get inside, even in the dead of winter. It had to be sweltering in there right now.

He casually assessed the knot of people in front of him. Not locals, he could see that right away. Windcheaters, walking shoes, and not one of them with a cig dangling from between their lips. Tourists. Polite, he nodded to them and headed inside.

No one noticed him at first. Maybe it was because he wasn't "swanning in," as his gran said. But then Old Jack clapped eyes on him. One minute the old man was running in ten different directions, filling orders. The next he'd stopped dead, glaring at Rory as if the devil himself had just strolled in for a pint.

"Jesus H Christ," Jack bellowed. "If it isn't the biggest prick in the Western Hemisphere."

Tourists turned to look at Rory. Not one appeared to be offended by Jack's vocabulary; they probably thought it was colorful. Women were indiscreetly checking him out. When Rory ignored them, they went back to chatting with their friends. It was a pity that wasn't the case with the locals: if hostility could be harnessed as electricity, no one in Ballycraig would have to pay a lighting bill for months.

He reached the bar. "Hello, Jack."

Jack was unsmiling. "You can shove your 'hello' up your arse cheeks, Sunny Jim."

Nervous laughter rippled around him, but Rory was unruffled.

"What do you want?" Jack continued, his lips drawn back in a snarl.

"Pint of Guinness, please."

"Not sure I can do that, son. We don't serve the likes of you here."

Jack looked around the pub, hoping everyone saw him as the tough guy he thought he was.

"I said I'd like a pint of Guinness," Rory repeated firmly.

"Yeah? Well I want Angelina Jolie to ride me, but that doesn't mean it's gonna happen."

Sniggers. Then someone he didn't recognize addressed him from behind the bar in an American accent.

"Guinness?"

"Yeah."

The guy nodded curtly and went to pull his beer. It took a second, but then the lightbulb went off above Rory's head: it was Erin's cousin, Liam O'Brien. Hanging out at the Wild Hart with the rest of the Blades, he knew all about the O'Brien family on both sides of the Atlantic. This was the son who'd married the McCafferty. Stone-faced, Liam put the pint glass down in front of Rory.

"Ta. You're Liam, aren't you?"

"Yeah. And you're Rory, aren't you? The jerk who blew a hole through my cousin's life?"

Rory casually scratched his chin. "That would be me, yeah."

"Don't forget he's also the one who treated his best buddy like shite," Teague Daly chimed in.

Rory couldn't believe it: Teague Daly, David Shiels, and Fergus Purcell, known as the Holy Trinity, were sitting in exactly the same seats they'd occupied the last time Rory had seen them. As a matter of fact, they were in the same seats where they'd been parking their carcasses since leaving school. It was as if they hadn't moved in ten years.

"Oh, yeah, that, too," said Old Jack disgustedly. "Put the boot in on Jake Fry, one of the best men in town." His contempt for Rory was now so fervent it was almost comical. "You're not fit to lick his boots. I can get them Fry brothers on you like that." He snapped his fingers. "Then where will you be?"

"I'll be standing right here, enjoying my pint."

"Not if they all came at you at the same time."

"Care to make a bet?"

Old Jack looked like he wanted to reach across the bar and throttle him. The only thing that held him back was the appearance of his wife, Bettina, her perfume announcing her entrance. Rory had forgotten about that: the cloying scent of the Lily of the Valley perfume she doused herself in. She'd packed on quite a bit of weight, too.

Jack gestured at Rory. "Look who's here."

"Well, you've got balls, I'll say that for you." Bettina sniffed, her face sour with disapproval as she looked him up and down. "What're you doing back here?"

Rory rested his elbows on the bar. "Jackson Bell rang me and said he wanted the football camp to be tip-top this year. Since I'm the one who founded the camp, he reckoned I'd be a big asset to him in terms of motivating the boys. I'm also helping my gran with some things she can't take care of on her own."

Bettina smirked. "And we're supposed to buy that line of bullshit, are we? It's quite obvious why you're here."

Rory took a sip of his pint. "I just told you why I'm here."

"Yeah? How about you pay a visit to Jake while you're here playing handyman? Apologize to him for fucking him over, if you'll excuse my language." Bettina cupped her mouth. "Best friends since they were five years old," she yelled to the pub at large. "But then Mr. Bighead here started playing professional hockey in New York, and all of a sudden, the likes of us aren't good enough for him. Isn't that right, Rory?"

Rory felt a pang of remorse. It was true; he had treated Jake like shit, ending the friendship without any explanation. But at the time, he couldn't stand the thought of appearing weak to his friend. He hadn't the guts to say, "Look, I just can't handle dealing with anyone from Ballycraig right now, okay?" He simply cut him dead right after he broke off with Erin.

It wasn't only the fear of looking like some kind of jerk-off that made him ditch Jake; it was the knowledge that Jake would have gotten in his face about what he did. The last thing Rory wanted to deal with was the truth. It was much easier to sever ties and convince himself that being an eligible bachelor and pro hockey player in the greatest city in the world was the life he was supposed to lead, not getting tied down before he'd even hit twenty-five.

"I will be apologizing to Jake," Rory replied politely. "Not that it's any of your business."

"I hope he spits on ya and tells ya to go to hell," said Teague.

Rory took a step toward his lumpy former schoolmate, and all of a sudden Teague's bravery fled. "What did you say?"

"Nothing," Teague muttered into his beer.

"Just keep your gums glued, you fat, waxy moron," said David under his breath.

He nodded curtly at Rory, who nodded back. He'd always liked David, and could never work out why he palled around with Teague and Fergus.

"I hate to tell you, Mr. Hockey Superstar, but Jake Fry would sooner kick you in the teeth than be mates with you again," Bettina informed him. "He might accept your apology, but he's changed a lot since you decided to come down off your high horse."

"We'll see." Rory's confidence had her shooting daggers at him with her eyes.

Rory took another sip of his beer. He hated to admit it, but something inside him was feeding off all the animosity being directed his way, making him feel cockier than ever. Which was why when Liam O'Brien planted himself in front of him with a menacing glare, Rory was unimpressed.

"Steer clear of my cousin. We clear?"

"As glass." He took his time downing more beer. If the folks of Ballycraig thought he was going to guzzle his pint and head out as quickly as he could, they had another thing coming. Feeling a bit congenial, he turned to Teague. "How's life treating you these days, Teague?"

"All right," Teague replied, still staring down into his beer broodingly.

"Yeah? What're you up to?"

"Same as usual," Fergus answered for him, talking more to his friend than to Rory. "Spongin' off his mam and dad and living on the dole." He patted his friend's hunched shoulder. "Buck up, Teague. It's nothing to be ashamed of. There's loads of people doing the same."

"Ah, shit off, the lot of yuz!" Teague snapped angrily, slamming his pint down on the bar and storming out of the pub.

"I see nothing's changed with Teague," Rory observed. "It just isn't Saturday night if he doesn't leg it out of here believing his dignity's been insulted."

"How about you leg it out of here?" said Bettina.

"It's a public house," Rory reminded her. He stood there fifteen more minutes nursing his pint, but finally he drained his glass and put his money down. "I'm looking forward to seeing you all again soon."

"Just you try it," Old Jack began to sputter. "Just you—"

Bettina stilled him with her hand. "Calm down, you old fool. Don't have a nervo."

Rory could feel them all watching him as he left. Ripping him to shreds the second the door closed behind him. *Rip all you want,* Rory thought. *But it's not going to get you anywhere.*

* * *

"Sandra?"

Erin's voice echoed nervously through what appeared to be an empty house. Ever since they were teenagers, each of them had had a key to the other's home. Larry hated it, of course, claiming it was a "gross violation of his husbandly rights." Sandra's reply to that was always the same: "Shove off." She wanted Erin to have access to the house "just in case," which meant if Larry was being a drunken jerk and Sandra needed someone to fetch the kids. Sometimes the mere threat of Erin's appearance made Larry back off; sometimes it made things worse. If the latter was the case, all Sandra had to do was pick up her cell and Larry was off like a shot.

Sandra's brood was gone, which was not a good sign. It meant Sandra had sent them off to her mother's. Erin surveyed the living room; nothing was broken and there were no half-eaten plates of food on the coffee table, which was good. It meant Sandra hadn't had to hustle them out in the middle of a boiling row. Erin proceeded into the kitchen. It was messy as usual, but nothing was broken. It was as she was walking back into the living room that she heard a groan from upstairs.

"Sandra?"

Another groan.

Erin tiptoed up the stairs. *Please, Christ, don't let that moron be there. Please.*

Fighting trepidation, she quietly opened the door to Sandra's bedroom. No Larry. But her friend was there, curled up in a little ball, her pallor gray and her eyes shut tight. "I have a terrible migraine," Sandra whispered as Erin perched on the edge of the bed.

"Yeah?" Erin asked, disinterested.

Sandra opened her eyes. "What's the matter with you?"

"What's the matter with me? You think I'm thick, after all these years? What did he do? You always seem to get migraines after he's pulled one of his stunts."

"You're wrong. He didn't do anything."

"What did he do? And you better answer me, 'cause I'm getting sick of asking."

Sandra looked chastised. "The usual: tearing me to shreds in front of the kids. I had Lucy bring the brood to my mam's."

"What was he even doing in the house, San?"

"He wanted to see the kids."

"Well, he sure did that, didn't he? I'm so sick of this."

"What?" Wincing, Sandra pushed herself up into a sitting position.

"You heard me. Year in, year out, it's the same old tune. Next I'm going to tell you he's a bastard, and then you're going to cry and say he doesn't mean it. Then Larry will come back and cry all apologetic, and you'll believe him because staying stuck is safer."

Sandra looked incredulous. "How can you say that to me? I'm your best friend!"

"Which is why I'm telling you the truth!" Erin was surprised to find herself trembling with anger. "You deserve better than this."

"Do I?" Sandra looked bitter. "I made my bed and now I have to lie in it."

Erin's voice shot up an octave. "Will you listen to yourself? You sound like half the old biddies in town, who stayed in the beds they made because the Church had them by the throat, making them believe they had to suffer. You can get out. There are ways out."

"You don't understand. I love him."

This was the line that always soured Erin's guts. She couldn't bear to hear it one more time. "WHY! He's a fat unreliable loser who treats you like shit and scares the hell out of your children. What's there to love? Is the sex really that good?"

"Go to hell, Erin."

"Right, I will." Pulse flying, Erin was almost to the bedroom door when Sandra called out.

"Don't go, please don't go." Erin turned back to find her friend's face crumpled with tears. "Don't hate me."

"I don't hate you, San." Erin sat back down on the bed, stroking Sandra's tangled hair. "I love you, which is why I'm tired of banging my head against the wall. D'you have any idea what it's like to see you this way? He's ground you down so badly over the years that you actually think you deserve the way he talks to you. I remember the way you used to be. Sometimes I see a flicker of it, like when you helped me through all the stuff with Rory. You were so strong. You and Jake."

"Because we were dealing with your life, not mine."

"Let's deal with yours, then."

Sandra looked at her warily. "You don't understand. I've got four kids. I can't just pick up and go."

"No, but you can make a plan to pick up and go, and then do it when the time is right."

"The kids'll go mad."

"Kids rebound. And it's not like he's even here most of the time."

Sandra lowered her gaze. "I know."

"Unless you let him move back in."

"No, no, he's not going to move back in," Sandra was quick to assure her.

Erin brightened a little. Maybe she was finally getting through. "Let's make a plan, then."

Sandra peered up at her with bloodshot eyes. "I'm too tired right now, Erin. I swear."

Fine, right, whatever.

Sandra looked at Erin sheepishly with a half smile. "I've heard that for the right price, Spats O'Toole can arrange for an 'accident' to happen."

Erin was appalled. "This is no time to make jokes!"

"Isn't it?" Sandra caught Erin's eye, and within seconds they were howling with laughter. A tried-and-true method to relieve stress. Let it out. Or hide it, whichever the case may be. Erin sometimes thought it was a mad thing for them to do, callous and inappropriate. And indeed, it was. But if it made Sandra feel better for a moment, that was all that mattered.

They wound down, Sandra swiping at her eyes. "Jesus, I don't think I've laughed that hard since Old Jack dressed up as Cher for that Halloween party."

"At least then we had the courtesy to go outside and laugh."

"Too true," Sandra agreed. She looked down at the duvet again for a long moment, then lifted her eyes to meet Erin's. "I swear I'll do something, Er. I'll call Social Services tomorrow."

"Good," Erin returned softly, even though she knew Sandra probably wouldn't. But maybe she was underestimating her friend. Maybe this time Sandra had had enough.

Erin playfully pinched the top of Sandra's hand. "You going to lie about all day like a queen?"

"No, of course not; I've too much to do." Sandra looked resigned as she swung her legs to the floor, rubbing her arms. "I'm freezing. Isn't it supposed to be summer?"

"You say that every summer."

"Summer: season of tearing my hair out," said Sandra grimly as she slipped on her robe. "All the kids home, moaning, 'I'm so bored, I'm so bored.' At least I've got Larry Jr. sorted."

"How's that?"

"He's going to the football camp."

"Really?" Erin knew it was stupid, but just the mention of the football camp made her stiffen. Football camp equaled Rory. Rory equaled pain. The moment passed.

"Apparently he's getting in because he's *underprivileged*." Sandra looked indignant. "Do you think he's underprivileged?"

"I don't. *Underprivileged* is quite a strong word."

"Thank you. He's got a roof over his head, food to eat . . ."

"I think they mean *disadvantaged*—like, you've no money to send him to camp or something like that. It's good he's going. It gives him something to look forward to every day, you know? Build up confidence."

"You're right. I suppose I didn't think of that. Well, he could be your spy if you wanted him to," Sandra needled as they headed downstairs.

"What are you on about?"

"Christ, you haven't heard? You must've been holed up all day and night yesterday with your nose pressed to the computer."

"What are you on about?" Erin repeated, growing irritated.

"He's back."

There was no question about who *he* referred to.

"Get out of it." Erin's mouth grew dry as she followed her friend into the kitchen.

"I've got it on good authority."

"Who?"

"Bettina," Sandra answered, looking proud that she'd been the one to tell Erin.

"Go on, then. What did she say?"

"She said the bighead came swaggering into the Oak like he owned the place."

Sounds like Rory, Erin thought.

"Said he's staying the summer to help his gran out with this and that. That he's gonna be helping out Jackson Bell at the camp. It's obviously a load of bull," Sandra continued, frowning as she took in the disaster area that was her kitchen. "He could hire someone to work on his gran's; he's got the money." She gave Erin a sly look. "You'd have to be stupid as a stone not to realize why he's really here."

Erin snorted. "Well, good for him! If he gets within a mile of me, he'll never play hockey again. My father will break his legs."

"He'll have help from all the men in town. Bettina said Liam told Rory that if he tried to come near you, he'd have his head handed to him on a plate. You know your cousin: he would do it."

"And what did Mr. Big-time Hockey Star say to that?" The thought of Liam threatening Rory was extremely gratifying.

"Bettina didn't say."

"Hmm."

Erin sat down at the table while Sandra put the kettle on.

"What are you going to do?"

Erin was annoyed. "What do you mean, what am I going to do?"

"You're bound to run into him."

"And when I do, we'll exchange pleasantries and go our separate ways."

"And what if he wants more than pleasantries?" Sandra pushed.

"Then he can go chase himself." Erin was tempted to take one of Sandra's cigarettes to calm herself. Her nerves were jumping. "I can't believe he has the gall to come back here."

"I know," Sandra agreed. "Especially when the reason is so obvious."

Erin frowned. "Will you stop banging on about that, please?"

"You know I'm right."

"All I know is he's the jerk who turned my life upside down, and if it wasn't for you and Jake, I'd be in the lowest level of hell. He's an idiot if he thinks I'd ever give him the time of day."

Sandra raised her eyebrows. "Seems to me you're getting very emotional about someone you claim not to give a toss about."

"We have a long history," Erin replied evenly. "It's not like that part of my brain has been burned out, you know. There's a thin line between love and hate. I used to love him. Now I hate him."

"You could always cross back over," Sandra said suggestively.

"And you could keep your yap shut." Erin looked at her in amazement. "Listen to you, talking about me crossing back over. I thought you hated him like poison. I thought you said if you ever crossed paths with him again, you'd tear his head off."

"I was just testin' ya. See how you would react." She gave a small yawn. "You do realize this is going to be Ballycraig's summer entertainment. You and Rory."

"That doesn't speak well of Ballycraig, then, does it?" Erin was working hard to hold her temper at bay. "It makes the village look like a pack of bumpkins."

"Nevertheless, I don't think you're going to be able to brush him off as easily as you think. Don't forget: I know you."

"Then you know I'm not a moron. Now can we change the subject?"

4

"The drainpipe needs fixin'. And I don't know what's wrong with the telly."

Rory took a deep breath so he didn't snap at his grandmother. His reception at the Oak was tepid compared to what he thought it was going to be. As always, Bettina was the one with the biggest balls, going after him about Jake. There was no gray with the lot of them: Erin and Jake were good, and he was bad. But that didn't mean he couldn't turn things around.

His assessment of the night ended abruptly with a sharp, painful twist of his right ear.

"Are you listening to me?" his gran snapped.

"Yes, for chrissakes." He rubbed his ear. She'd been doing this to him since he was a little boy. He'd hated it then, and he hated it now. "I promise I'll get around to it this afternoon, all right?"

"Why? What are you doing all day?"

"I told you, remember? I've got to go into town to finalize things about the camp with Jackson Bell, and then I'm going to check out the PJ Leary Walking Tour."

"That'll take all of two minutes."

Rory laughed. "Why do you say that?"

"He's not a native, is he? It's not like you can say, 'and here's where he went to school,' and 'here's where he wrote his first book.' There's nothing to see on the High Street. 'Here's where he took his first piss in the pub'? You'd do better just going up to his cottage and introducing yourself."

"Maybe," Rory mumbled. He was a huge PJ Leary fan. All the Blades were. Their secret started when they were on the road: when curfew kicked in, they'd all hang out in Eric Mitchell's room, where Eric would read the book aloud. Eric was great at putting on dramatic voices for each of the characters, maybe because he was married to an actress.

"How did it go last night, if you don't mind me asking?"

"How do you think it went?"

Rory 1, Ballycraigers 0.

"Did you have a drink or did Bettina chase you out right away?"

"Of course I had a drink."

"She was feeling merciful, I see." She paused. "Liam have anything to say to you?"

"Yeah, something about not coming near Erin. I wasn't really paying attention."

"Don't be arrogant, Rory. You know how much everyone loves Erin. I don't think you quite know what you did to her. If it wasn't for Sandra and Jake, the girl might have topped herself."

Rory was horrified. "Erin would never do anything like that."

His grandmother glared at him. "How would you know? People thought you'd never piss off on her, but you did, didn't you? I was mortified: *my* grandson, breaking up with the supposed love of his life on the phone!"

"What was I supposed to do!" Rory replied, guilt building inside him. "Fly back to Ireland to do it?"

"A real man would've. But not you. A coward, you were."

She was right.

"And a fool," she continued, on a roll. "So now you've got a case of 'you don't know what you've got till you lose it.' I'll be eager to see how that one goes. Now finish your tea and get workin' on that telly before you waste your time in town."

* * *

Never again. Erin was fuming as she got off the bus that ran between Ballycraig and Moneygall. Never again would she fold when her mother handed her a shopping list and, huffing and puffing as if breathing were a chore, told her, "My heart's acting up again. I can't handle the stress." Next time, she'd point out that her mother had never had a heart problem in her life, despite smoking and not having eaten a piece of fruit or a veg since the seventies. "Strong as a bull," her dad always said proudly. *More like full of bull,* Erin thought.

She was done being an indentured servant. Erin had placed an ad in the *Galway Independent* for someone to replace her as housecleaner and jack of all trades, room and board included. She was flooded with applicants. Her plan was to meet with applicants in Crosshaven, at a small caf there well known for its delicious bacon sandwiches. She'd bring her laptop with her and get some studying done in between interviews.

Erin dragged the upright shopping cart behind her. She hated the damn thing, with its squeaky wheel. She reminded herself she should be grateful. At least she didn't have to drag her clothes to the launderette like Sandra.

It was a cloudless day, the sky a blue tarp stretching over the world's head. *Now what color would you call that, Miss Art History Major? Powder blue. No, sky blue.* There was an infinitesimal difference between the two. But it was important, when it came to art, to describe things as accurately as possible, especially if one day you wanted to become a docent or a curator. Color choices could be a clue to the artist's mind. Somehow, Erin had known that before she even started working toward the degree. Many a time she and Rory would be out and she'd point at the pink streaks at sunset and—

Rory.

The bastard.

She tried her best to hide it from Sandra, but the news he was back in Ballycraig had shaken her. Reaching into her bag of clichés, she picked "out of sight, out of mind." Except it wasn't true. News of his return opened the door in her head called Rory, which was supposedly snapped shut for good. Now all sorts of emotions were loosed. She felt confused and overwhelmed.

Thankfully the bus stop wasn't far from the B and B. All she had to do was go down the High Street, turn right two blocks, and she'd be back at her own personal prison.

She said her hellos to Grace Finnegan, who was standing outside the grocer's, smoking a fag, and to Sandra's daughter Lucy, sitting on one of the benches outside of the pub with her "boyfriend." "He's got a face on him that would drive rats from a barn," Sandra had said, and it was true. Lucy looked mortified that Erin said hi to her. The only thing worse than being greeted by your mother was being greeted by your mother's best friend.

A small group of people were coming slowly toward her. Erin frowned. The PJ Leary Walking Tour. Knowing there wouldn't be enough room on the sidewalk for her and the loony devotees, Erin crossed the street, giving the group a quick once-over: a hip, young Asian man and woman dressed all in black. A middle-aged German couple dressed in matching hats. A pack of young, swarthy guys smoking. The usual group of avid Americans. At the rear was a handsome man who looked just like Rory.

Couldn't be, she told herself, even though she knew damn well he was in town. Erin ducked her head, continuing to check out the group surreptitiously. Shoot. It was him, all right.

Erin hastened her pace. Seeing him was like seeing a

ghost: it jolted her, cheated her of breath. *Three more blocks,* she thought desperately, beginning to feel shaky. *Just three—*

"Erin?"

She kept moving. If she stopped, she was affirming his question. But if she kept moving, there was a chance he'd think he'd just called out to someone who merely resembled her.

"Erin!"

Now he was jogging across the street. What was she supposed to do? Drop the grocery cart and run like hell? She was a deep-feeling person, but she was not a lunatic, at least not anymore. Appropriate cliché here: "time to face the music."

Erin halted, her right hand still gripping the shopping cart tightly, then she turned to him. An invisible fortress, impervious to pain, sprung up around her. If he stepped too close, he'd be massacred. She hadn't a hint of makeup on and her hair was pulled back with a scrunchie. Her jeans hung off her now because of the year she could barely gag down food, thanks to him. He looked shocked. He deserved to look shocked. He'd created the woman in front of him.

He was just about to open his mouth when the tour guide called out to him. "Mr. Brady? Will you be rejoining us or not? We're about to head to the cottage."

"I've got to pass!" he called back. "I'll be back tomorrow!"

The brevity of the exchange gave Erin a chance to look him over quickly. He still looked like Becks around the time his hair was buzzed and he did that ad for Calvin Klein. More color in his face, though.

That's as far as she got before Rory's attention was back on her. She waited. If he thought she was going to initiate conversation, he'd taken one too many pucks to the head.

"Hi," he said quietly.

Erin was unsmiling. "Hi."

"How are you?"

"None of your business." She resumed walking. But he wouldn't let it be.

"Erin." Her heart gave a tiny thump. She knew that tone,

the one that carried the mildest touch of entreaty. Once she would have melted. Now she just wanted to get away from him before she went rabid on him, howling out all her pain and grief while she tore him to shreds.

He repeated her name. Erin's shoulders drooped in defeat, but she kept on walking. "What do you want?"

"To talk to you."

"And so you have."

He was hustling alongside her. "No, I mean properly."

"As far as I can tell, this is proper."

"Erin, please." He put a hand out to stop the cart, but she jerked it away.

"Don't touch me, Rory." She quickened her pace, staring straight ahead. Almost there.

"All I'm asking—"

"Leave me alone, Rory."

"Erin—"

She glared at him. "Leave me alone, Rory."

She didn't care if she had to walk blocks and blocks past the B and B, repeating this over and over, if that was what it took to get him to leave her be.

Rory lapsed into silence, but he continued walking beside her.

"Christ, will you not even make small talk with me?"

"Leave me alone, Rory."

Erin quickened her pace even more. It felt empowering to tell him to leave her alone, but at the same time, she was so unnerved to be walking with him she felt like she might throw up. She'd truly thought she'd never see him again, except maybe when his gran passed and the family came back to Ballycraig for the funeral. Now here he was, trailing her down the street, thinking all he had to do was say her name and she'd fold. The man had a screw loose.

Erin?

Oh, Rory! How are you? I've been wondering what you've been up to since you messed up my life. Oh, come in, let's have a cup of tea and catch up. It's so good to see you again, you egotistical heartless wanker of a prat.

She was moving at a good clip, getting closer and closer to home, but Rory still trailed her. Erin couldn't help but wonder if he was so stupid that he was puzzled by her hostility. She couldn't believe he was going to be around all summer. She'd bet dollars to donuts (another cliché; she was going for the record) he was not going to back off.

Because Rory Brady never backed off. He kicked, fought, bulldozed; he did whatever he had to do to get what he wanted, whether it was playing for the NHL, or appearing in his hometown like the risen Christ to regain what he thought was rightfully his. Too bad the fool didn't know that the meek, love-sodden girl he once loved didn't exist anymore. Erin squared her shoulders and continued on her way.

*   *   *

Okay, so that didn't go exactly as planned, but it was the first time, Rory reminded himself as he turned around and started back toward town. "Piss off." Those weren't her exact words, but repeating "leave me alone" could be interpreted as the same thing.

He'd almost missed her. Standing in the cluster of tourists waiting for the PJ Leary tour to start, he was amazed by the variety of languages swirling around him. The tour guide looked like a nutter, dressed as the leprechaun queen character from the first book, but Rory supposed it helped create the mood. He handed over his euros, waiting as everyone else took their turn to pay. And that's when he saw Erin.

At first he thought himself wrong: this pale woman with long, lustrous black hair was far too thin to be Erin. But he'd know that slow, graceful pace anywhere. Without thinking, he called out her name. The woman quickened her pace. It was Erin for sure, trying to get the hell away from him.

He realized that now, but at the time, the thought never entered his head that she might not want to talk to him. He was too overwhelmed by the sight of her to create the simple equation: Erin + quickening pace = Go chase yourself, Rory Brady.

He jogged across the street to talk with her. The coldness in her once animated green eyes took him aback. Never had he seen such a look of pure hatred on Erin O'Brien's face. Just as disconcerting was the thinness. She'd never been overweight, but she'd never been all sharp angles that'd poke a man to death, either. She'd been soft and smooth-skinned, a carefree look on her face except when it came to her smothering parents or Sandra and the ball bag she'd married. Standing before him now, Erin's sweetness was well under wraps. Things had changed.

The minute he spotted her, he knew he'd bail on the walking tour. The chorus of voices that had initially caught his attention now sounded to him like a drone of bees he wouldn't be able to swat away.

Erin's frostiness hurt, but as he'd told himself, it was just their first encounter. He had the whole summer to make things right.

5

"Erin, I need to speak to you, love."

Erin hung her head in defeat at the sound of her mother's voice outside her bedroom door. It was close to midnight, which meant she wasn't here to discuss B and B business. Erin closed her laptop. She'd been reading about abstract expressionism. She particularly liked Jackson Pollock, those huge canvases with splashes of paint that looked chaotic but really weren't. As soon as she left Ballycraig, one of the places she wanted to visit was MOMA, to see one of these magnificent canvases in person.

"Erin!"

"I just need a minute." It was wearying, the way her mother still spoke to her as if she were a recalcitrant child who needed to be told twice she was wanted.

She opened the door just a crack, slipping through and locking it behind her before her mother could peep inside. Her mother hated the whole business with the lock. Weren't they family? What on earth could she be hiding? *My future,* Erin thought.

"What's up, Ma?" Erin's mood quickly turned to worry when she saw the distressed look on her mother's face.

She pressed Erin's shoulder. "Let's talk in the kitchen."

Erin followed her mother downstairs.

"Here, have a seat."

Erin sat, thinking to herself that if the kitchen gleamed any brighter, she'd be blinded. Her mother had always been a bit fanatical about keeping the kitchen pristine. A stray pea left in the sink didn't stand a chance.

Her mother pulled up a chair beside her, her expression grave.

"Ma, what's going on? Is it Da? Did something happen? Brian?"

"No, no, no, it's nothing like that."

"Then what?"

"This isn't easy for me," her mother began, massaging the back of her neck.

Erin's heart punched. "Are you sick?"

"No."

"Ma."

"Look, your da and I realize you're entitled to your privacy," her mother said with a grimace. "But we're not stupid. The locked door, you clacking away at that computer all hours." Her eyes grew watery. "We figured it all out."

Erin was confused. "Figured what out?"

"That you're looking at online dating sites."

Erin heaved a sigh of relief. Her mother could have a wild imagination when forced to fill in the blanks. For a brief moment, Erin was convinced her mother was going to accuse her of looking at online porn.

"I am."

Her mother blinked. "I don't understand. Why on earth would you do that?"

"Maybe I'd like to meet someone."

"If you're only looking at fellas online, then I don't understand why you need a lock on your door."

Erin contemplated banging her head on the table but knew it wouldn't do any good. "I need my privacy."

"But I'm your mother."

"The one who read my diary when I was thirteen!"

Her mother looked guilty. "I know, I know. I guess you've the right." Her mother tapped her nails on the kitchen table thoughtfully. "I could help you."

"Say again?"

"Look at fellas," her mother said, her voice growing animated. "If you found some you liked, you could run 'em by me, and I could give 'em the old thumbs-up or thumbs-down."

"I love you, Ma, but you've lost it."

"I've lost it? I'm not the one who refuses to take a good look at what's right under her nose. You need some guidance is what I say."

Erin groaned. "Not Jake again. Please."

Her mother pursed her lips disapprovingly. "It doesn't make sense to me. He's lovely, and what's more, he'd treat you right. Already has."

"I know that. But we work best as friends."

"Ah, you barely dated him."

"Because I didn't feel what you're supposed to feel."

"Relationships aren't all moonlit nights and roses, you know."

Erin was becoming prickly. "Really, Ma? Why don't you tell me more about relationships, since I've never been in one."

Her mother's expression remained serious. "Let me ask you something."

Erin sighed.

"Pretend—do not interrupt me, please—pretend you've never seen Jake Fry in your life. Ever. And then he walks into the Oak. What would you think?"

"I'd think he was handsome. So what?"

"And suppose he started to chat you up and asked you on a date. Would you say yes or no? Remember: you've never seen or talked to him before."

"Mam—"

"Yes or no."

"I'd probably say yes," Erin admitted.

"Well, that's what you need to do. Look at him with fresh eyes."

Erin was silent.

"D'you know how many women would give their eyeteeth for someone like Jake? He's a good man, and he loves you to death, that much is obvious. He was there for you when the chips were down."

"I know he's a great guy and all, but I just can't—"

"Get past that bastard Rory Brady," her mother cut in bitterly.

"That's not true and you know it."

"I know what I know, and it's a desperate woman looks to find fellas online when there are good men in her own town. Rory's turned you against all men in Ballycraig."

"You're addled. You know that, right?"

"I know what I know."

Erin grit her teeth. "I hate when you say that."

"You know what I think the problem is with you girls today?"

"I'm twenty-five, but go ahead, tell me."

"You're all for the action and adventure. You'd prefer a bloke who treats you like shite, because you're all caught up in the melodrama of 'he loves me, he loves me not.' You don't give a nice fella like Jake the time of day because there's no drama there."

Erin put her hands in her lap, digging her fingernails into her thighs. "Rory only turned out to be a shite in the end. You know that."

Her mother looked teary. "You should have given that one walking papers years before. For him to break up with you . . ."

"Can we please get off the subject of Rory? And before you say it, yes, I know, he's back in town. I saw him yesterday."

Her mother looked alarmed. "You did?"

"I was coming off the bus and he was taking the PJ Leary tour. He spotted me and said hello, I said hello, and he kept yappin' on. I told him to leave me alone, and he did. So you needn't worry about him trying to charm me."

Her mother looked dubious. "We'll see. He's got charisma, that one."

She began to rise from the table, but Erin asked her to please sit down. "You've had your say. It's my turn now."

"This'll be rich."

"It will and all," Erin shot back.

"Right, I'm sat down," said her mother, settling back into her chair.

"Why was I the one coming back from Moneygall with the groceries?"

Her mother furrowed her brows. "I don't understand."

"Yes, you do, you understand perfectly well. It should've been the person you've hired to replace me."

Her mother looked cornered. "I haven't had time to hire anybody. It's been busy. The summer . . ."

"It's going on months now," Erin pointed out plaintively. "Months. We agreed I would only be helping out for a short while, but I've started to feel taken for granted; you just keep piling more and more stuff on me."

Her mother stiffened. "I don't understand."

"First it was just laundry and making the beds. Then I started doing the shopping. Now you've got me vacuuming sometimes and baking the odd batch of scones." Erin pressed her lips together. "This is hard for me to say, but if you don't hire someone by the end of this month, I'm going to start interviewing people myself. I already put an ad in the paper and have had loads of responses."

Her mother pretended not to hear. "Darlin', I don't see what the problem is. Aren't you happy to be working with your family?"

"No," Erin said bluntly, regretting it immediately. She had to tread the boards softly. "I have other things I want to do in my life."

"Like what?"

"Get a college degree."

Her mother snorted dismissively. "Don't be daft."

Erin's insides felt like a dull razor was being scraped across them. "Why is that daft?"

"University is for snooty people. You know, like Aislinn's sister Nora."

"You had no problem with me taking courses when I was with Rory."

"Well, that was just a bit of fun, wasn't it?"

"No, it wasn't," Erin said sharply. "I've always wanted to make something of myself."

Her mother appeared mystified. "And what would you make of yourself?"

"Whatever I want." Erin tried to hold her temper back, but couldn't. Her mother's blatant insult cut her too badly to just sit there and take it. "Why is it that anything that doesn't fit in with your view of the world is 'daft'? I remember you saying Aislinn was mad because she took over her parents' sheep farm. You know what your problem is? You never encouraged us to reach. Me and Brian. You never encouraged us to dream, because you think that if you dream, you might get hurt. Sometimes that's true. I got hurt by Rory. But I learned from that: it's better to dream and get your bloody face kicked in than to play it safe and live in a very tiny world, never taking any risks."

"I see." Her mother's expression was cold as she stood. "Well, that certainly was an earful. Anything else while your tongue is in prime working order?"

"No. That's it."

"Sleep tight, then."

"You, too, Mam."

Erin remained at the table, listening to her mother's light footfall as she went back upstairs. Jesus wept. The woman could be maddening, not to mention downright bloody mean. Erin couldn't help but wonder if there was a bit of jealousy mixed in with her mother's put-downs. Maybe she'd wanted to cut loose once upon a time, but couldn't. She got up and turned off the kitchen light, suddenly yearning for sleep. A midnight discussion in the O'Brien house: this would count as an exciting night in Ballycraig, she supposed.

6

Sandra laughed so hard when Erin told her the story that tears were running down her face. Erin was laughing hard as well: once one of them started, the other always followed. San's booming laugh was one of Erin's favorite sounds in the world. All Erin had to do was hear it, and if she were in a bad mood, her negativity would vanish instantly.

"Oh, Christ," Sandra wheezed. "I've got to stop or I'm going to wet me knickers. Online dating? You?"

"I know. And even if I was, what would the big deal be?"

"Erin, your mother doesn't understand the Internet. That's part of the problem."

"You're right."

Sandra swallowed a deep breath, wiping away the tears sliding down her cheeks with the palms of her hands. "This one's going in the books. Especially the bit about her wanting to give the old thumbs-up or -down." She giggled. "They're like Holmes and Watson, your folks. Maybe they can solve the mystery of who stole the tea biscuits from Finnegan's Market."

"Don't be mean."

"I'm just saying."

Erin had "the day off," and as was usually the case, she spent part of it with Sandra. Sometimes she wondered if it was unhealthy that Sandra was her only female friend. It wasn't like they'd separated themselves from the other girls at school: they'd both drifted in and out of various cliques. But at the end of the day, no one measured up to Sandra in Erin's eyes, and vice versa. They'd probably wind up living together when they were old, two mad cows subsisting on crisps and tea in some dodgy caravan park somewhere.

Sandra leaned against the wall of the launderette, lighting a cigarette. "Don't tell me I'm ruining my health, because I know it." She took a drag and blew it out with force. "So your mam's still pushing for Jake?"

"Yeah," Erin said glumly. "Said I need to take a look at him with new eyes and all that."

Sandra took another puff, looking thoughtful as she blew a stream of smoke out the side of her mouth. "Mightn't be a bad idea."

"What? You're the one who said you couldn't picture him in bed!"

"I know. I do feel a bit guilty saying that, since he's a friend and all. But I was having a good think on it the other day."

"That's a terrifying combo, San, you and thinking."

"Shirrup. Here's the thing: There's something to be said for a fella who worships the ground you walk on, you know. A fella who's dependable and romantic and all that." Her eyes tracked a handsome, sturdy man down the street.

"Did Jake talk you into saying this to me?"

Sandra looked affronted. "Of course he didn't."

Erin remained skeptical. "Are you lying to me?"

Sandra's mouth formed a shocked *O*. "Of course I'm not lying."

"Then what accounts for the abrupt about-face?"

"I was thinkin' about me and Larry," she said in a melancholy voice. "What a right bastard he is. How my life might have been different if I'd kept me legs closed in school and held out for someone like Jake." She smiled sadly. "We could have double dated. You 'n' Rory and me 'n' Jake. It would have been brilliant."

"You could still marry a fella like Jake, easy. All you'd have to do is divorce the lummox."

"Thinkin' about it," Sandra muttered tetchily.

"What?" Erin said, trying to restrain herself from jumping up and down with glee.

Sandra's hackles went up. "Don't get yourself all worked up. It might not even happen. It's just . . . like you said, I've got to start thinking about the big picture. The kids."

"And?" Erin prodded.

"I went to the One Family place in Crosshaven, right? The one that gives free legal advice to women?"

"And?"

"They have free courses that train you up to get back in the workforce." Sandra tossed her cigarette to the ground, snuffing it out with the bottom of her well-scuffed sandal. "Not that I've ever really been in the workforce."

"Taking care of four children and Larry qualifies as work if you ask me."

Sandra smiled weakly. "Anyway, it seems it might be something worth thinking about. They have day care, too. I could bring Gina with me on the bus. Larry Jr.'ll be in football camp all day, and Oona's old enough to fend for herself, or I can talk with Becca Lafferty up the road about her spending time there, since Oona and her Britney are thick as thieves. I'd be home in time for tea."

"What about Lucy? She could help out a bit."

"Right. Twelve years old and climbin' out her window at night. I'm at my wits' end with that one. Truly."

"When do courses start?"

"Ongoing."

Erin paused. She didn't know if what she was about to say was madness, genius, or both. "I can help out a bit, you know."

"What the hell are you on about?"

"There's no reason I can't do a bit of your grocery shopping if you're so sure Lucy will be useless."

"She'd pocket the money, that one." Sandra shook her head emphatically. "There's no way I'd let you help out, Little Miss Goody-goody. You've got your own course to concentrate on."

"True," said Erin, plucking thoughtfully at her lower lip as she tried to think of other ways to help Sandra. She was finally taking the first step to get free of Larry, and Erin wanted to help facilitate that in any way she could.

"There's got to be something I can do."

"I know how you can help," Sandra said, shielding her eyes from the sun.

"How?"

"I need to put down an emergency contact in case Larry Jr. gets sick or hurt at football camp. I'm not putting his father down, that's for shit sure. Can I put you down?"

"Of course."

Sandra looked relieved. "That's a load off my mind."

"I just hope I don't run into Rory."

"You can handle it. Give him a good kick in the ball sack and be on your way."

"Shoulda done that when I saw him the other day."

Sandra shook Erin's arm. "You waited until *now* to tell me?"

"There's nothing to tell. He was taking the PJ tour and I was coming back from the shops in Moneygall, and didn't Mr. Eagle Eye spot me across the road and come running over."

Sandra was breathless with excitement. "What happened?"

"I told him to leave me alone."

"How did he react?"

"He backed off, miraculously."

"Ha! For now. He was just testin' the waters."

"Well, the water's freezing, I can tell ya."

Sandra gave a small grimace. "I hate to tell you, Er, but telling him to leave you alone is kind of lame-o, you know?"

"Why?" Erin asked crossly. "What should I have said?"

"I think 'go screw yourself till it falls off' would have been more effective, but that's just me."

"That's more your style than mine."

"How's he looking?"

"The same, I guess. I didn't really look." *You didn't really have to. "The same" meant handsome as hell.*

"He was always a looker," Sandra said with a sigh.

"Then you go look at him," Erin retorted.

Sandra looked surprised. "Don't have a nervo."

"I'm not!"

"Then why'd you go all sharp on me? Like it irked you I found him attractive!"

"It just bothers me that you can find anything good about him."

Sandra looked skeptical. "If you say so." She pushed off the wall. "Best go back and see if that old crow Edith Cruise is done hogging the dryers. It's just her and that dozy husband of hers. I don't see why she needs three dryers. I've half a mind to pull her stuff out of one of 'em."

"The last time you did that to someone, they tossed some bleach in one of your loads, remember?"

"Yeah, yeah. If I ever won the lottery, the first thing I would do is buy a washer and dryer. The second thing I would do is go for liposuction."

"You don't need it, but I know that's going in one ear and out the other." Erin hugged Sandra. "I'll give you a ring tomorrow, all right? Maybe I could come over, bring some pizza for us and the kids."

"You should be out and about, Erin. Not hanging with your married friend and her brood."

"There's no one to go out and about with."

"I bet Ja—"

"Shut it."

"Don't be tryin' to find Mr. Right online now," Sandra shouted as Erin started down the street. Erin grinned, looking back over her shoulder at Sandra. Sometimes they still acted as if they were twelve. And as far as Erin was concerned, there would always be comfort in that.

* * *

It was only a week later that Erin got a call from the football camp, telling her that Larry Jr. was "puking up a gale" and asking if she could please come get him. Sandra had started going for workshops and classes on Tuesdays and Thursdays to start out. They both knew that if Sandra leapt into the deep end and went five days a week, she'd be overwhelmed and quit. Going two days also allowed her to be home with the kids the majority of the week, arousing no suspicion in Larry. Erin was the only one who knew what she was doing, Sandra having decided not to tell any of her kids for now. Lucy and Oona thought their mam was at some playgroup with baby Gina. Sandra especially didn't want Lucy to know, because if she did, she wouldn't think twice about telling Larry in payback for some slight Sandra might have committed against her, real or imagined. Erin was pretty sure she and Sandra weren't as stroppy at that age as Lucy was.

It was Jackson Bell who'd rung her. For a split second, all she heard were the words *football camp* and her heart lurched. She promised she'd be there for Larry Jr.—or LJ, as he was now insisting on being called—in a few minutes.

Her intentions were admirable until she remembered, with some embarrassment, that she couldn't drive. She'd been meaning to call for driving lessons for months but hadn't gotten around to it, swamped in studies and housework. She remembered Rory trying to teach her to drive when they were fifteen, because her father wouldn't. The lesson with Rory had turned out to be a minor nightmare: he barked commands at her like a military officer, making her more and more nervous until she burst into tears.

She'd been an idiot to tell Sandra she'd be the emergency contact. What was she thinking? She felt badly for LJ, but she had no choice but to take the bus or to hire a cab, which would cost a ton. She couldn't run to the auto shop and ask her dad to give her a lift and back. Her father treated his Ford Fiesta like it was a Maserati: only he was allowed to drive it, not that he did much of that. He didn't drive it so much as admire it as it sat there parked in the sun, gleaming. She could plead it was an emergency, but all her dad would have to hear were the words "sick child," and that would be it.

Right. No time to waste. She started out the door, running smack into her mother.

"Where are you off to, looking like the Devil's on your heels?"

"Larry Jr. is sick. He needs someone to pick him up at football camp."

Her mother looked confused. "Why can't Sandra do it?"

"She's ill herself. Plus, she can't drive."

"May I point out that you can't drive, either?"

Erin was getting restless. "I was going to get a taxi."

"Are you out of your skull? Do you know how much that will cost?"

"But—"

"Ladies, ladies." Erin and her mother turned. Mr. Russell, the dapper, elderly permanent boarder, was right behind them, all dressed and ready for whatever it was he did all day since he retired from the Royal Mail. "Why raised voices on this cloudy morning?"

"I'll tell you why," Erin's mother said, fixing her daughter with a black look. "Erin has to go pick up Sandra's boy from football camp. He's ill. Unfortunately, my daughter seems to have forgotten she doesn't have a license to operate a motor vehicle."

"I can give you a lift."

Erin's face lit up. "Really? Oh, that would be wonderful, Mr. Russell. I'd pay you for the petrol."

"Don't be daft. It'd be my pleasure."

Erin's mother pasted a smile on her face. "That's really very generous of you, Mr. Russell." She turned to Erin. "When do you think you might be back?"

Translation: surely you can't expect me to do your chores.
"Don't know. Why does it matter?"

They locked eyes until her mother looked away. "No matter," she said, affecting a nonchalant tone. She regarded Mr. Russell. "Thank you again for chauffeuring my daughter."

"Think of it as payment for all those years you never moaned about the post being late." He offered his arm to Erin. "Shall we?"

* * *

Given that he was seventy-eight, Mr. Russell was quite a good driver. He could be a bit forgetful, and he did bang on a bit about working for the Royal Mail, but he'd had a hard life, what with his wife dying early and him never remarrying. He still managed to keep his sunny disposition, though. There was something to be learned from that.

No clear skies today; it was gray and drizzly. Larry Jr. was probably caked in mud; with this weather, the football pitch had to be dirt soup.

Erin knew she'd be seeing Rory. They hadn't crossed paths since their encounter on the High Street, but that didn't mean she wasn't aware of his every move. Everyone in town felt compelled to give her a Rory update, no matter how many times she politely informed them she didn't give a goat's arse. Even if she did want to keep track of Rory Brady's whereabouts—which she didn't—she certainly wouldn't let them know.

Mr. Russell turned into the dirt parking lot. Erin's eyes were immediately drawn to the shiny black Range Rover looking very out of place. Rory. What an idiot, rubbing his wealth and success in the noses of everyone who wanted his head on a pike.

"I can't thank you enough for the lift. I promise I won't be long fetching Larry Jr."

The old man looked a bit shamefaced. "A bit of a problem there. It totally slipped my mind I have an appointment in Crosshaven that I'm already late for. I won't be able to drive you back."

"No worries," Erin assured him, pretty certain she had enough cab fare to get herself and poor little Larry back to town. If not, Jackson would give her a lift. She got out of the car. "See you back home."

"Yes, I'll be home for tea."

Erin waved good-bye as he drove out of the parking lot, and started for the camp.

It hadn't changed much at all, except that the concrete building that housed the locker room/office "complex" had been given a fresh coat of blue paint. Two groups of boys were out on the muddy pitch with Jackson Bell and some unidentified teenage assistant. Which meant Rory was the one waiting inside with Larry Jr. Shite. Erin felt like a trespasser as she walked past the gaggle of boys, their heads' swiveling in unison to watch her before returning to their game. Jackson gave her a big wave. Erin remembered when it was Jackson himself who was a camper. Felt like it was a lifetime ago. It *was* a lifetime ago.

Erin pushed open the complex door, unable to stop a small smile of recognition as it squeaked as loudly as a mouse getting its tail stomped on. At least some things never changed.

She'd been right: it was Rory minding Larry Jr. in the office. He looked surprised to see her. Erin bypassed him and went directly to San's son, who was lying on a sort of makeshift futon. He was the color of milk.

"What's up, Larry?" Erin asked gently as she crouched beside him. "I hear you've been ill."

"My name is LJ now," he insisted weakly.

"Right. LJ. What's going on, love?"

"I've been puking."

"I've been giving him sips of water so he doesn't dehydrate," Rory put in.

Erin still wouldn't look at him. "Thank you."

She put her palm to Larry—LJ's—forehead. No fever. "What did you have for breakfast?"

Larry groaned. "Don't remember."

"I'm sure you can if you try hard enough," Erin coaxed.

"You promise you won't get mad at me?"

"Why on earth would I get mad at you?"

"Mam will when she hears." He looked at her pitifully. "Promise you won't tell her."

"I can't promise that. But tell me anyway. I have a feeling you're not the one behind this."

"It's Lucy's fault."

'Course it is, Erin thought. *Jesus, that girl.*

Erin steeled herself. "What did Lucy give you for breakfast?"

"Leftover fish pie, some ice cream, and a tin of peas."

"Oh, God." Erin covered her mouth so she wouldn't gag. "Did she feed that to Oona as well?"

"No. Oona told her she felt ill and went back to bed."

"Smart girl."

Rory came over, crouching on LJ's other side, where he began stroking the sick child's head tenderly. Erin looked away. It conjured up too many hours spent in conversation about having kids. She was unnerved by the tenderness of Rory's gesture. It was hard to completely hate a man who was kind to a child, even if that man was a prick when it came to women.

Rory's hand stopped moving but remained atop LJ's head as he addressed Erin.

"He felt ill when he came to camp, but he didn't want to tell anyone because he didn't want to miss out on practice." He looked down at LJ. "That was a silly thing to do," Rory chided softly. "Missing a day, even missing a few days, is no big deal. What if you had the flu? You would have gotten everyone else sick."

"But I was afraid if I didn't come, you'd put Frankie Dunlop in goal and you'd see he's better than me and I'd never be in goal again."

"Now that is pure madness," Rory assured him. "Haven't Jackson and I been rotating you all?"

"Yes, but I'm best in goal. My dad, he always said so."

Rory flashed Erin a quick look as if to say, *That feck is still around?* Erin gave a small shrug. She was not about to get into Sandra's business with Rory if she could avoid it.

Erin looked down at her patient. "Are you well enough to let me take you home, do you think?"

"I don't know," LJ said piteously. "I might need to have a good rest here for a little while longer. I'd hate to upchuck in your da's Fiesta, Erin."

Erin pressed her lips together to avoid laughing. The whole town knew about her father's obsession with his car.

"Guess what? We're going to have a big adventure in that department."

Some color leapt into LJ's cheeks. "What?"

Erin lowered her voice. "We're going home in a cab."

"A cab!" LJ exclaimed. "I've never been in a cab."

Erin smiled weakly. "Well, it'll be fun." She rose. "I'll just ring for it, shall I? Will you be all right for a few minutes?"

LJ nodded his head.

Erin walked into the hall and took out her mobile. Rory followed.

"Erin, don't call a cab."

She ignored him as she flipped open her phone.

"Don't call a cab," he repeated more emphatically.

"Why on earth would you think this is any concern of yours?"

"I have a perfectly good car sitting in the parking lot. I could run you and Larry—LJ—home, no problem."

Erin looked at him a moment before chortling with disbelief. "Sod off, Rory. I'd rather pluck my own eyes out of my head than get in a car with you."

"Yeah? What about LJ? You want him puking in a cab?"

Erin scowled. "No."

"So then let me do this for him."

"No. Not only do I not want our lives to intersect in any way, but I remember how you drive."

"I drive fine," Rory protested.

"Oh, yes, you drive great. I seem to remember a certain

someone nearly wrapping us around a tree after swerving to avoid some sheep."

"That was a long time ago. I'd forgotten about it. I'm surprised you remember."

"I remember lots of things. Like you wrecking my life. Did that one slip out of the ole memory box after too many pucks to the head?"

"Erin, I swear to God—"

"Spare me." She started toward the complex door.

"Where are you going?"

"I'm going to ask Jackson to bring me home."

"Jackson is in the middle of coaching."

"You two can just switch places."

"Erin," said Rory, raising his voice, "would you stop being bullheaded and just let me take you and LJ home? Do it for him, yeah?"

"Fine," Erin said grumpily. "As long as it's just for LJ. And I don't want you to say a word to me between here and Sandra's house. AND I'm sitting in the back with La—LJ."

Rory looked amused.

"This isn't amusing."

Rory held up his hands in surrender. "I know."

"Let's get this poor child home. And remember—"

"I'm nothing but your chauffeur. Got it."

* * *

"Thank you for the lift. I can walk from here, thank you."

LJ had looked a bit green when they'd started out from the camp, but then Rory engaged him in football chat and told him stories about New York, and he perked up a bit. What lad wouldn't, having a private audience with the great Rory Brady and getting a ride in his Range Rover?

A few times, Erin caught Rory looking at her in the rearview mirror, and she'd frown. What did he think? One potent look from his famous blue eyes and she'd come undone? Arrogant twit.

After thanking Rory for the lift, she took LJ inside. Lucy was there, legs dangling over the side of the sofa while she watched a repeat of *Father Ted*. She barely looked up as Erin gave her a piece of her mind about feeding her siblings. But then Erin spoke the magic words: "You do know that if I tell your mother about this, she'll take away some of your privileges, don't you?" The lackadaisical teen pretended not to care, but Erin caught the unsettled look that flickered across her face.

Erin wondered if she should stay until Sandra got home, but LJ seemed recovered enough to hop on to the computer. Erin rustled his hair, told him to ring her if he needed her, and left.

Rory's Range Rover was idling outside Sandra's house, the passenger-side window rolled down. "I'll run you home. Hop in."

"Hop yourself."

"C'mon, Erin; you're being ridiculous."

Erin refused to look at him as she started to walk away, Rory's car crawling along beside her.

"Get in. I'm going to keep shadowing you till you do."

"Really?" She pointed to a small rusted Toyota two blocks up. "How are you going to explain it to the owner when you just keep going and you smash into the back of his car?"

"I'll pay for repairs."

"God!" Erin spat out disgustedly. "Do you hear yourself? 'Look at me, I'm Mr. Smoothie. I've got money. I don't care whose property I destroy'"—she looked at him pointedly—"'or who I hurt, because I'm the great Rory Brady.'"

"It was a joke."

"Right." She couldn't believe his car was continuing to crawl beside her.

"D'you want me to beg? I will. Erin, please, please—"

"Shut up!" Erin snapped. Embarrassed, she hopped into the passenger seat and slunk down. "Happy now?"

"Yes." Rory stopped the car and looked at her. "Why're you sinking down like you've got no spine?"

"I don't want to be seen with you!"

Rory hit a button and the passenger-side window silently closed. "Suit yourself," he said, easing away from the curb. "But the windows are tinted. No one can see you anyway."

Erin reluctantly sat up straight. She hadn't really had a chance to take in the car while riding back from the camp, being more concerned with LJ. But it was beautiful. Leather seats, a GPS, and all that . . . and it didn't make a sound, just purred along. A rich man's car. She could just imagine what Old Jack and that lot were saying about it. The sheer jealousy of it must be choking them.

She hadn't really taken in Rory, either. As soon as she'd stupidly agreed to let him drive her and LJ, they'd gone directly to the car. He was in football gear: jersey and shorts. It showed off his physique, his muscled legs . . . and contrary to what she'd said, he was a good driver. Confident in everything. Erin used to wish some of it would rub off on her.

They were halfway down the road before Erin asked, "Where're you going?"

Rory looked at her oddly. "What do you mean, where am I going? I'm going to your house."

"I don't live on Bryant Street anymore, Rory. My parents sold the house and they're running a B and B now. But then you wouldn't know that, would you?"

"Actually, I do know about it. My gran told me. I'd just forgotten."

Erin softened for a minute. She loved Rory's gran. She felt guilty because she hadn't visited her since Rory dumped her. Talk about self-absorbed.

"Where is it, then?"

Erin hesitated, then told him, "Carmen Road."

"Two blocks from the High Street," Rory murmured, more to himself than Erin. "Makes sense."

Erin smiled sweetly. "Do you still know your way round town? It's been years since you've graced Ballycraig with your presence."

Rory glanced at her with surprise. "When did you get snarky?"

"Probably around the same time you kicked my teeth in."

Rory was quiet. Erin couldn't wait for the ride to be over. She was filled with an anxiety that wouldn't ease. If it kept on this way, she would explode.

She closed her eyes, the better to get hold of the roiling inside. It was the first time she caught a whiff of Rory's footballers' scent—sweaty, earthy—and it kicked something back to life inside her, a fast-moving array of images: watching Rory play football, she and Rory picnicking at the pond, she and Rory in a booth at the Oak, imagining their future while Erin got a little tipsy. Rory and—

"What're you smiling about?"

Erin opened her eyes.

"You were smiling," Rory repeated.

"So?"

"You were thinking about me. Us."

"Oh, of course. I was thinking about you. Because that's all that anyone in Ballycraig does: think about Rory Brady."

"You were thinking about me," he said lightly, "but if you want to deny it, I understand."

"You know what? The only thing bigger than your bollocks is your ego."

Rory laughed. "I'll take that as a compliment."

They pulled up in front of the B and B.

"Go around the corner," Erin demanded. "The last thing I need is my mother seeing this car and thinking some visiting dignitary has come to stay. Go round to Benton Avenue."

Rory did as she asked. She could picture her mother getting all wound up if she thought someone famous or rich might be coming to stay. Working herself into a frenzy. It wouldn't be good.

She turned to Rory as he pulled to the curb. "Thank you for the lift."

"We need to talk."

She knew this was coming. "Do we?"

Rory switched off the ignition. "I have something I need to say."

"I bet I can recite it by heart," Erin said bitterly. "'I'm sorry I hurt you, Erin. I never meant to. If I could take it all back, I would. I was just out of my head, being in Manhattan and all. I made a mistake, love. A big, big mistake. Can you forgive me and take me back?'"

"You've found me out."

Erin refused to look into his eyes. She knew Rory, and she knew he was sitting there looking smug as hell, thinking, *C'mon, you know you want to smile. You know you do.*

When she refused to react to his joke, he changed his approach. "Look, I know you wish I hadn't come back for the summer. But since I have, it would mean a lot to me if you'd let me do one small thing for you to make your life easier."

"And what would that be?" Erin asked guardedly.

"Let me drive you around." Erin had barely opened her mouth to respond when he rushed in with, "Hear me out. I don't know how you got up to the camp, but if it weren't for me, you would have had to take a sick child home in a cab. The other day when I saw you, you were dragging those groceries home from the bus. I've got this car. Please let me put it to good use."

"And what? Let you chauffeur me around?"

"Yes," Rory said plainly. "If you need to go to Moneygall to get groceries for your mother, I'll take you. I'll take you anywhere you need to go, anytime you need to go."

Erin was dumbfounded. "You've gone soft in the head."

"I've not," Rory insisted. "Think about it. It would make your life easier. I owe you at least that much."

"Charity."

"It's not charity. It's a small start at amends."

Her mind was a hodgepodge. "My mother will—"

"Sod your mother. She's always pushed you around. You can do as you please."

Erin knew he was right.

"And camp?"

"I can do as I please."

"I'll think about it," Erin muttered reluctantly. "But it's very doubtful I'm going to want to be trapped in a car with you on a regular basis."

"You've every right to feel that way. But don't let pride stand in the way of making your life easier. I need to do something for you, and right now, this is all I can come up with. Whatever you decide, the offer will be on the table for as long as I'm here."

7

Driving over to Jake's, Rory reflected on the progress he'd made with Erin two days before. He'd only managed to scratch the surface of her defenses, but it was a start. He'd been thrilled that they'd managed to actually have a bona fide conversation, even if Erin did hurl a few choice remarks his way. She could've said far worse. She probably wanted to. But that wasn't Erin. He knew her: deep down inside, there was a free spirit screaming to get out, but she was trapped in the role of dutiful daughter. Rory and Erin's mother had never gotten along. He understood why. In Mrs. O'Brien's world, daughters were supposed to take care of their mothers when they were old, and Rory was going to take her daughter away. She had to be thrilled that things had fallen apart between them.

Yet despite the difficulty Erin's mother had always presented, there was never any doubt that Erin loved her— loved her whole family, in fact. She was extremely loyal, a trait Rory had always appreciated. And she was kind, the kindest person he knew. Erin was the one who'd always stuck up for the kid being bullied on the playground, the one willing to risk being a target herself when some poor, smelly bastard was eating alone in the lunchroom. But she herself was never targeted, because she was well liked; having Sandra as backup didn't hurt, either. Everyone at school knew that if they dared look at Erin cross-eyed, they'd have to answer to Sandra, who could pack quite a punch.

Memories swirled round in his head like taunting ghosts as he recalled all those times he and Erin had laughed together. She'd always been able to make him laugh, and vice versa. It had helped defuse many a tense moment. They'd cried together, too. Rory never felt more himself than when he was with Erin. She always accepted him exactly as he was; she'd never once tried to change a single thing about him. Yet as open, honest, and caring as she was, Rory could never shake the feeling that he didn't know *her* completely. The mystery of that had always appealed to him. It still did.

Having started down the path to making amends, the next person on his list was Jake. Thinking about what a dick he'd been to his lifelong friend filled him with self-loathing. The last time they'd spoken was over two years ago. He hoped Jake didn't tell him to fuck off, but if he did, Rory knew he deserved it.

Jake was still living in the small house two miles down from Aislinn McCafferty's farm, which had once belonged to his aunt and uncle. Jake's older brother Alec was now living there as well. Rory didn't know how Jake could take it, especially since he and Alec worked together, too. Alec was a good bloke, but he was the most boring person on earth. It wasn't Alec's fault, Rory supposed, but that never stopped him and Jake from taking the piss behind his back. "Want to hear about my toolbox?" Alec would drone, and they'd be killing themselves with laughter.

Rory parked his Range Rover at the end of their drive, more out of guilt than anything else. He earned every penny he made playing for the Blades, and the only real luxury he was allowing himself this summer was the car.

He didn't care what everyone else thought, but there was a part of him that didn't want to be perceived as shoving his wealth under Jake's nose.

Rory started walking up to the house. The shitey old blue truck Alec had owned forever was there, bumping Rory's car guilt up to a whole new level. He felt better when he spotted the silver Civic on the other side of the drive, glowing metallic in the moonlight. That was new. It had to be Jake's. Alec would get by with a horse and trap if he thought he could.

He could hear Arcade Fire blasting on the other side of the door. He leaned hard on the bell; Jake was a famous one for not hearing a damn thing when he was into his music. Rory let his mind wander for a second, and in that second, the door opened. Jake looked at Rory. Rory looked at Jake. Jake punched him in the nose.

"Well, there's that taken care of, then," Rory joked lamely, grabbing the end of his shirt and pressing it against his nostrils to stem the stream of blood.

"You look pitiful," Jake announced. "Get in here." He looked disgusted as he pulled Rory inside.

The pain was excruciating. Not his nose. It was the pain of seeing his best friend in the world.

Jake gestured at the couch in the spartan living room. The place hadn't changed at all. "Sit down. I'll get some ice." He disappeared down the hall.

Rory turned down the music. His eyes scanned the living room for something, anything, that might be different. He wondered where Alec was, then wondered if he possessed the power of conjuring as Alec came bounding down the steep, carpeted stairs.

"Jake-o!" His mood was upbeat until he spotted Rory. "What the feck!"

Rory held up a hand in the hopes of warding him off for a moment. "He knows I'm here. As you can see, he's already greeted me."

"That's a shame," Alec sneered. "He should have torn your balls off and fed them to Deenie for dinner."

"Go on." Rory tilted his head back, pressing the tail of his shirt harder against his nose. A thin, metallic-tasting trickle of blood went down his throat. "Give me all you've got." *Which isn't much, you empty-headed sod.*

"I'm surprised Erin's father hasn't come round to your gran's and beat you with a tire iron," Alec continued.

"That would require asking his wife for his stones back, so forget that ever happening."

"I bet the Trinity would do it for him if he asked."

Rory snorted. "The three of them share a single ball. They take turns using it to get off their arses and buy a round."

Rory wished Jake would hurry up with the ice. He was a hockey player, so he could keep this trash talk up for days if necessary. But it was only a matter of time before Alec ran out of tough talk and returned to his usual subjects, like shears and Wellies. Rory decided he'd end the joust before Alec ran out of ammo by shifting gears with an out-and-out lie.

"I heard through the grapevine that the training of the new dog is coming along well."

Obviously relieved from the burden of coming up with more tough talk, Alec jumped at the chance to return to himself. "It is. Jupitus is going to be a champion herder. See, the thing about training herding dogs . . ."

And he was off. If Jake were in the room and they were still mates, they'd both be burning a hole through the floor with their eyes, trying not to laugh. Rory started to smile, then stopped. Hopefully he could fix things. Jake appeared holding a blue terry washcloth filled with ice cubes. He shoved it into Rory's hand.

"That should do it."

Jake stared at his brother.

Alec's brows furrowed in confusion. "What?"

"Can you get out of here? Rory and I have business to discuss."

"Oh. Right. I guess I'll go back up and watch telly." Alec suddenly seemed to realize that he should make some kind of final threatening gesture at Rory to show his brother he had his back. A blank look came over his face as he searched for something tough to say that he hadn't already said. "Watch yourself," was all he could manage, in a poor imitation of a growl.

Rory lowered his head so Alec couldn't see him smirk. "Thanks for the ice pack," he said to Jake.

"Well, I wasn't gonna let ya bleed all over my house, was I?"

"I can tell having Alec here hasn't improved your skills as a housekeeper."

"Yeah, well, we can't afford a cleaning lady like you, can we?"

Jake sat down opposite Rory. Their banter couldn't hide the anger in Jake's eyes. It was something Rory had rarely seen.

"Well?" Jake said eventually, leaning back as he laced his fingers behind his head. "You got something to say to me?"

"I do." Rory looked at his friend head-on. "I'm really sorry for what I did, mate. I'm a fucking arsehole." Rory gingerly pulled the flannel away from his nose. The bleeding had stopped.

He waited for Jake to say, "It's all water under the bridge." Jake had always been a forgiving soul. But his mouth remained clamped shut.

"Hey," Rory asked confusedly.

"Hey, what?"

"We all squared, then? Back to being mates?"

"You have got to be fucking kidding me. You think you can just appear in Ballycraig and everyone is gonna fall at the big hockey star's feet?"

"I wouldn't say no to that," Rory joked.

Jake was unmoved.

"Look, let me make it up to you, all right?" Rory asked, starting to feel a little desperate.

Jake snorted. "And how do you plan to do that?"

"How do you think? I'll buy you a couple of pints."

"You're a feckin' idiot, Rory."

"Tell me something I don't know. C'mon, Jake, let's get a pint."

"Yeah, all right. But it doesn't mean shite. It's just a chance for me to drink for free." Jake grabbed a faded red sweatshirt off the back of the chair. "Before we hoist a few, there's something you need to know."

"What's that?"

"Erin and I have gone out a few times."

Rory smirked. "Pull the other one, mate."

"Why would I lie?"

"To mess with my head?"

"Sorry to tell you, but you don't need me to mess with your head."

Rory remained skeptical. "You've gone out with Erin."

Jake pulled the sweatshirt over his head.

"You still going out with her?" Rory asked casually. It couldn't be. Erin would have shoved it in his face earlier in the day, wouldn't she? No. That wasn't her style.

Jake smirked. "Why shouldn't I go out with her?"

"No reason." There was no way.

Jake's voice was hostile as he asked, "You never change, you know that?"

"What the fuck does that mean?"

"It means you always think you'll win at everything."

"Generally I do."

"We'll see."

8

"*I hear Rory* was your chauffeur on Thursday."

Erin had been expecting this. She was sitting at Sandra's kitchen table, chitchatting as her friend casually buffed her nails. Erin had intended to tell Sandra about the "Driving Miss Erin" episode herself. But later, when she was up in her room prepping for an exam on surrealism, she realized LJ would tell Sandra the minute she got home from her course.

"Yes, Rory drove me and La—LJ—home."

She watched Sandra lift a hand to observe her handiwork. They were going to the pub tonight. One night a month, Sandra put aside being *mam* and was just Sandra in her own right. "Girls' night out," she called it, an old-fashioned moniker if ever there was one. In the past, Larry would stay home with the kids—if he was sober. But he'd always exact his pound of flesh, moaning and groaning as if he were doing Sandra the biggest favor in the world. Now that he was theoretically out of the house, Sandra's mother, Dot, was coming over to babysit. At Erin's urging, Sandra planned to ask her mam if she could watch Oona those two days a week she was at her course.

"Am I going to have to blackmail you to get the details?" Sandra asked, motioning for Erin to splay her own hands on the table so she could do her nails.

"You've got nothing to blackmail me with."

"Don't I? If you don't give the gories, I'm going to tell everyone you used to dance around in your bra and panties pretending you were Kylie Minogue singing 'Can't Get You Out of My Head.' Or what about your mad crush on that wrinkled old baldy, The Edge?"

"Shut up! That was for one month!"

"Well, it felt like ten effin' years to me, believe me." She gave Erin the evil eye. "I'm waiting."

"Tell me what Larry Jr. told you."

"LJ," Sandra corrected with a roll of her eyes.

"Go on."

"Nothing that has to do with you and Rory, I can tell you that." Sandra gingerly dropped the nail polish brush into the bottle. "He said he was dead ill, you came for him, you had no way home, and Rory drove you back to town in a big black fancy car, telling him all sorts of stories about New York."

"That's about all," Erin said flatly as Sandra coated her nails in Vibrant Violet. Erin thought it sounded like the name of a porn star.

"For Larry Jr., that was all," Sandra corrected pointedly. "A big black fancy car, huh?"

"Range Rover, tinted windows and leather seats and all that. No noise. You'd swear you were motoring along swaddled inside a cotton ball."

"Must be nice." Sandra was now painstakingly polishing the fingers on Erin's right hand. "Look, I'm getting a little cross here waiting for the details," she grumbled. "At this rate you'll be picking out my tombstone before you get round to them."

"Right, here's the riveting tale: I got a call from Jackson that your LJ was ill, and I wanted to get up there fast. I was going to hire a cab, but Mr. Russell was on his way out and gave me a lift up to the camp."

"He's a lovely old weirdo."

"Yeah, but he forgot he could only take me one way. So I was stranded. I was going to get LJ and me a cab back when Superman intervened."

Sandra leaned toward her. "What did he say?"

"Oh, that it was silly to take a cab since he had a car, blah, blah, blah. Then he started going on with 'let me at least do this one thing for you.'"

"As if one lift into town is gonna undo the destruction he's done in your life."

"Oh, there's more." Erin chortled.

Sandra looked thrilled. "What?"

"You'll love this. He said anytime I needed a lift—anywhere—I should just ring him and he'd take me wherever I wanted to go."

"You're jokin' me."

"I'm not. That's what he said." Erin shook her head. "Can you imagine?" She mimed flipping open her cell. "Hi, Rory, it's Erin. Yeah, I need to go down into Crosshaven because I've a yen for Chinese takeaway. Be here in five minutes."

There was a long pause as Sandra ran her tongue around her bottom lip thoughtfully. "Do it."

"Say again? I don't think I heard you right."

"Do it. Take the bastard for everything he's got. He owes you. Hit him up for rides. If you want to go up to Dublin to shop for a weekend, let him take you *and* pay for the lot. Anything at all you want, hit him up for it."

"I couldn't do that." But before the words were out of her mouth, she was having doubts. She imagined snapping her fingers and making Rory Brady do her bidding. Hmm.

"Did seeing him do your head in?" Sandra murmured sympathetically.

"A bit," Erin admitted reluctantly. "One minute I'd look at him and it was like a knitting needle was being driven into my heart, and the next minute there would be a bit of banter like no time had gone by. It was unnerving." Erin paused. "I hate him."

"You don't."

"I do!" Erin insisted.

"You want to hate him," Sandra pronounced, "but you don't."

"He's a bigheaded git, San. He thinks I'm such a push-over that all he has to do is say one mea culpa and all is forgotten."

"That's why I say you should take him for all he's got, the bigheaded ass. Let him go along thinking he's making progress with you, and then bam! You tell him to jump off the nearest cliff and that you want nothing to do with him."

Erin glanced away.

Sandra's grin was evil. "You want to do it, I can see it in your eyes. Nice girl Erin O'Brien showing Rory Brady and the rest of Ballycraig that she's grown a pair."

Erin shuddered. "I hate that expression."

"Such a delicate flower," Sandra teased. "I bet he'll be in the pub tonight."

Erin didn't respond.

Sandra completed Erin's last nail. "You're done. Just let it dry." She screwed the top of the nail polish onto the bottle. "Does he have his own teeth?" she asked abruptly.

Erin peered at her in confusion.

"I've heard all the blokes have their teeth knocked out in ice hockey. Did you notice if his teeth look fake?"

"I know he's got a few in there that are fake, but it's not like he's puttin' all his teeth in a glass at night. And what's this got to do with anything?"

"Just curious. Stand up."

"Inspection time, is it?"

"Yes." Sandra gave her the once-over. "Presentable. Your shirt should be a little tighter—you've got nice knock-ers. But other than that you look pretty hot."

"Ta."

"MAM!" Oona's voice cut through the kitchen, shrill as a siren. "GRAN IS HERE!"

"God, I hate when she yells. Puts my teeth on edge."

"C'mon. We'll face the Inquisition and then we'll be off."

Erin had always loved Sandra's mother. She was gruff, but she was also a laugh. Her house was a tip, which was where Sandra inherited her sloppy house genes from. Erin always preferred hanging around at San's rather than her own house. At Sandra's they could blast music and leave plates in the sink and not have to wash and dry them immediately. Sandra's mother didn't treat them like they were the world's biggest pains in the butt.

Sandra led the way into the living room. "Hiya, Mam."

"Hi, Mrs. Herbert." Erin kissed Sandra's mother's cheek.

LJ was hopping from foot to foot excitedly. "Gran brought a bat!"

Sandra fixed her eyes on her mother. "Wha?"

"A cricket bat! A bat!"

Sandra closed her eyes, speaking carefully. "Mam, why did you bring a bat over here to babysit?"

"You know damn well why," her mother replied in an exaggerated whisper.

Erin kept out of it. Good on Sandra's mam for bringing a bat over in case Larry decided to show up. On the other hand, it mightn't be a good thing for the kids to see their granny swinging a bat at their father.

"Gimme the bat, Mam," Sandra said under her breath. No one moved. "I said: Give. Me. The. Bat."

Her mother handed it over with a glare.

"Right," said Sandra, switching into her cheery mam voice. "You're gonna be good for Gran, right?"

"Yes," said Oona, playing with an iPhone.

"Where in the name of Christ did you get that?" Sandra demanded.

Oona didn't even look up. "Dad."

Erin and Sandra exchanged worried glances.

"I'm jealous," Sandra said to Oona. "I wish I had one of those. When'd he give it to you?"

"After school."

"After school." Enraged, Sandra hissed in Erin's ear,

"Thievin' bastard. Probably nicked it from Dixons in Cross-haven."

She ruffled her son's hair, smiling sadly as he jerked away. "You have one, too, you lucky thing? Did he give you yours after school as well?"

"Yep." Larry looked nervous. "He said not to tell."

"It's good you did," said Sandra. "Don't worry: I won't rat you out."

Larry the Bastard played on the boy's worship of him. Erin could picture it: Larry drooping his arm over LJ's shoulder and leaning in close, confiding in him with his boozy breath, saying, "Now I've got a present for ya, but it's a secret, okay? You can't tell a living, breathing soul. Ya hear?" What child is going to refuse a gift like that from his father in exchange for simply keeping quiet? Secrets, secrets, secrets. The Irish way. She ought to know: she was keeping secrets from her parents.

"Let's get going," Sandra said wearily. She turned to her mother. "Gina's in bed, obviously. These two can stay up late tonight, since it's Saturday."

"How late?" LJ asked.

"Gran will decide that." Turning to her mother, Sandra continued, "If Lucy comes skulking home with the bag of bones in tow, tell her that if he doesn't go, she'll be getting no allowance from me. As if that'll matter," Sandra said to Erin under her breath. "She'll just run to that no-good father of hers and boo-hoo it, and he'll give her whatever she wants so I look like the crap parent."

She sighed. "You have my cell number and the number at the Oak, right?" she checked with her mother.

"I do."

Sandra kissed her mother's cheek. "Thanks so much, Mam."

"Ah, you know me. A right sucker for punishment."

She looked at LJ and Oona sternly. "I better get a good report from Gran when I get home. Ya hear me?"

The kids nodded earnestly.

Sandra's mam smiled at Erin as she jerked a thumb in Sandra's direction. "Keep an eye on this one, will you?"

"Don't I always?"

Erin had no intention of getting even the slightest bit tipsy, since she wasn't much of a drinker. Sandra, on the other hand, sometimes needed a bit of looking after. She'd always been able to put away the pints. It embarrassed Erin sometimes.

They were out the door and halfway up the street before they realized Sandra was still holding the bat.

"It'll only take us a min to run it back," said Erin.

"Don't be silly. I'm bringing it with us to the Oak. That way if Larry comes in, he'll get the message loud and clear that if he messes with me, he'll be walkin' out with a head cracked open like a melon."

"Meanwhile, everyone else will think you're mad."

Sandra grinned. "And when have I ever given a toss about that in my life?"

* * *

"Jesus, Mary, and Saint Joseph. If I had false teeth, they'd be dropping to the floor right about now."

Old Jack's exclamation as Rory and Jake walked through the pub door together had the exact effect Rory knew it would: it killed conversation.

"You always were melodramatic, Jack," Rory said, enjoying the look on people's faces, especially the Trinity. He could hear their pea-sized brains working furiously: *What the hell is Jake doing with Rory? The feck's back in town less than two weeks and already Jake has let bygones be bygones? Jakers is a good sort, but this is sheer weakness.*

"You two kiss and make up?" Bettina asked dryly as Rory and Jake sidled up to the bar.

"Looks that way," said Rory.

"That's putting the cart a bit before the horse, mate," said Jake. Rory smiled tightly, ignoring the light laughter that came at his expense.

Rory nodded at Jack. "Two pints, if you please." He was feeling pretty good right now. The hometown crowd could hold grudges for decades, but now that they saw he and Jake were making amends, their hatred of him might loosen its grip. And once he and Erin were back together, well, he'd be back to being the pride of Ballycraig.

Jack plunked the pints down before Rory and Jake. "C'mon, then. We need a good story to cheer us up, especially after the way Galway got slaughtered today by Sligo. How did you lovebirds reunite?"

Jake smirked. "Didn't this one come knockin' at my door beggin' for forgiveness."

"I didn't *beg*," Rory corrected, mildly irked.

"God forbid the Great One beg," muttered Teague Daly.

Rory rounded on him. "First of all, there's only one Great One, and that's Wayne Gretzky. Second of all, you got something you want to say to me?"

Teague shrunk in his chair. "No."

"Didn't think so." Rory looked at Jake. "Mind if I continue the story?"

"Be my guest."

"I showed up. Jake punched me in the nose. We figured we could hash it all out over a few. Nothing a few pints can't solve, right?"

"Go tell that to my cousin," Liam called from farther down the bar.

He spoke his mind, Liam. Rory admired that. He had a sense that if the circumstances were different, and they were back at the Wild Hart in New York, he and Liam could have been great mates. Too bad his own treachery had made that impossible.

"I already have, in a manner of speaking," Rory told him. "I think it's great you want to protect her," he continued as he looked around the bar. "I think it's great you all want to protect her. But Erin can hold her own. Believe me." He grabbed the pint glasses, looking to Jake. "Grab a table?"

"Over my dead body," Bettina declared. "If you two end up rolling around in a good punch-up, I want to see it up close."

"And this way, you can all listen in on our conversation as well," Jake pointed out.

"As if we would," Bettina said indignantly.

Jake and Rory looked at each other and laughed.

"Go to hell, the both of ya," said Old Jack. He pointed a warning finger at Jake. "Watch your back, son."

"No worries. I can take care of myself, Jack." He touched his glass to Rory's. "To friendship."

Rory thought he detected a note of sarcasm. *Getting paranoid,* he told himself.

"To friendship," he echoed.

9

"What, have I got a booger hangin' from my nose?"

Erin cringed. She and Sandra had no sooner stepped over the Oak's threshold than their fellow villagers behaved as if they were watching a tennis match, eyes going from Rory and Jake . . . to Sandra and Erin . . . back to Rory and Jake . . . back to Sandra and Erin.

Sandra turned to Erin, exasperated. "Do I have a booger hangin' out or what?"

"San, you're carrying a bat," Erin murmured.

"Oh, Christ." Sandra lifted the bat, seemingly oblivious as to why people shrank back. "Don't worry: we're not here to harm anyone." She chuckled before flashing Rory one of the most threatening looks Erin had ever seen. "Well, maybe one or two people."

Sandra lowered the bat, and the bar patrons exhaled a collective sigh of relief. Erin refused to glance at the bar. The sight of Rory with Jake completely stunned her. She couldn't wrap her mind around it at all. She tugged on Sandra's sleeve. "C'mon. Let's see if we can find a seat."

Together they headed toward the back. The local band

were to the left of the old stone fireplace, winding down
from a well-known traditional reel; Sandra glanced at Erin
and put a finger down her throat as if she were going to
vomit. "Christ, if I never hear this song again in my life, it
won't be too soon."

Erin agreed, heart sinking as she scanned the room.
Every table appeared to be occupied. She was about to point
it out to Sandra when her friend lunged for a tiny table that
just that second was being vacated, beating out two middle-
aged, mildly drunk women whose puffy faces had clearly
seen better days.

"'Scuse me," one of them said in an unmistakable cock-
ney accent, "but that's our table, you fat cow."

Ever so subtly, Sandra began swinging the bat by her
side. "Excuse me: what gives you the right to think you can
talk to me like that?"

"San," Erin said quietly.

"This is our local," Sandra continued.

"Well, la-di-bloody-da," the drunker of the two said.

"You're damn right, la-di-bloody-da," Sandra retorted.
A standoff ensued. Sandra made a great show of looking
back and forth between the bat and the Brits.

"Fine, take your stinkin' table," said the bottle blond
who'd called Sandra a cow. "We were thinking of clearing
out of this piss hole anyway."

Noses up in the air, they walked away. The one time
they glanced back with matching sneers, Sandra gave them
the two-fingered salute.

"Ha!" Sandra crowed as they slid into their seats. "Pathetic,
those Brits."

"Sandra, you're holding a bat. What did you think they
were going to do?"

Sandra ignored her, looking around. "Not too many old
ones in tonight."

"*Strictly Come Dancing* is on, remember?"

"Oh, yeah."

Erin's parents were among the show's devoted follow-
ers. Often, when she was in her room studying, she could

hear it blaring from their TV. Sometimes she'd come in and watch it with them. It made her mother happy. It also helped Erin take her mind off the fact that she was home alone on a Saturday night.

She and Sandra had no sooner gotten comfortable at their hobbit-sized table than out of the corner of her eye Erin spotted Old Jack waddling toward them, his expression uncharacteristically grave.

"Evenin', ladies."

"Hey-o, Jack," said Sandra with a broad smile. "It's been a while."

"Too true." Jack held out his hand. "Gimme the bat."

Erin groaned.

Sandra looked offended. "What, you think I'm gonna club someone?"

"San, just give him the bat," Erin urged.

"It's not you beatin' on people I'm worried about," Jack explained. "It's some of the other elements here."

"Tourists?" Sandra mouthed.

Jack nodded curtly. "All I need is for a few of them to get pissed out of their skulls and grab it away from you, and I've got a real situation on my hands."

Sandra frowned. "That's never gonna happen. When's the last time there was a good punch-up here?"

"A month ago. Two of them PJ people were in their cups and got into an argument over whether the Salmon King could triumph over the Guardian of the Toadstool or some such nonsense. Before you knew it, they were throwing punches and crackin' each other over the head with chairs. If it wasn't for Liam, they'd have smashed the place to bits."

"All right," Sandra grumbled, handing over the bat.

"Thank you." He leaned over the table, looking like he was going to burst with a secret. "What d'you think of Frick and Frack over at the bar, hoisting a few?"

"Who?" Sandra asked innocently.

"Laughin' it up like the old days, letting bygones be bygones," Old Jack continued, looking for a reaction from Erin.

"Good for them," Erin replied flatly. It made perfect sense. Angry as Jake had been at Rory cutting him dead, it had always been plain to see that it pained him deeply, like being shunned by your own flesh and blood. She wasn't all that surprised to see them together, though she doubted Jake had welcomed Rory with open arms.

Old Jack looked disappointed with her answer. "Is that all you have to say about it?"

"Stop being a mixer, Jack," Sandra warned.

"Right, right." Old Jack sighed, knowing he wasn't going to get anywhere. "What can I get you two? Black Velvets?"

"Sounds good to me," said Erin.

Sandra agreed. "One of us'll be over in a few to pick them up."

"Good enough," said Jack. He held the cricket bat in both hands, weighing it, assessing it. "I think I might get one of these permanent."

"Just remember to hide it from Bettina," said Erin with a grin.

* * *

Jack gone, Sandra plunged immediately into the topic of the night.

"What do you think happened with Jake and Rory?"

"Obvious: Rory went and begged for forgiveness and Jake accepted his apologies."

Sandra looked disappointed. "I know. He's good at spouting the tough words sometimes, is Jake, but in the end, he's a big softie."

"I know."

"I hope he's making Rory crawl a bit."

Erin rested her chin in the palm of her hand and studied her friend's face. "You're very big on the crawling, aren't you?"

"Don't you think he should suffer at least a little bit for what he did?"

"Yes."

"Well, there you go, then."

Erin couldn't quite see the bar from where she and Sandra were sitting, and she was glad. She didn't want to see Rory and Jake together right now. The rapidity with which Jake forgave Rory made her feel petty. There was no way she was going to forgive him that quickly, assuming she forgave him at all.

"I'm parched," Sandra declared. "I'm gonna go tell Jack to hurry with our drinks. Be back in a tick."

*   *   *

"Good Christ, help me, here comes Sandra."

Rory steeled himself for what was certain to be the tongue-lashing of all tongue-lashings. Sandra wasn't just Erin's best friend; she was her protector. God forbid anyone said or did anything that hurt Erin in any way: Sandra would hand them their bollocks on a plate. Erin was the same way when it came to Sandra, which had always worried Rory. He was always fearful that one day, Sandra's husband was going to spew his filth at Erin the way he did at Sandra. Well, that would be the day that wanker met his Maker, that much was sure.

He could think of one positive to Sandra's ripping into him: it would help take his mind off Jake telling him that he and Erin had "gone out" a few times. What did "gone out" mean? A meal? A stroll? Just the thought of Jake being with Erin in any capacity beyond close friends set Rory's teeth on edge.

"Hiya, Jake," said Sandra. "Long time, no see."

"Ah, Aislinn's been working me to the bone."

"Usually does. You do get some time off, though, don't you? Time to relax, do a bit of wooing?"

"I do, yeah."

"Good on ya."

"Hello, Sandra," Rory said, striving to sound friendly. Maybe she wasn't going to ball him out. Maybe it would be the deep-freeze treatment.

Sandra barely looked at him. "Hiya, Rory," she replied

apathetically. She eyed Jake. "You two patched it all up, then?"

"In a manner of speaking," Jake replied obliquely.

In a manner of speaking? Rory puzzled. What the fuck did that mean?

"These things take time," Rory explained. "I was a right prick. I don't deserve his trust right off the bat."

"The only thing you deserve is to be run out of town on a rail," said Sandra.

"Can I get you a drink?" Jake asked politely.

"Erin and I already ordered, thanks. That's why I'm here. Waiting on two Black Velvets."

Rory smiled to himself. Erin had always loved Black Velvets.

"Maybe I'll go back to the table and sit with you two," said Jake.

"I'm sure Erin would love it," said Sandra, "especially since you two haven't been able to spend any quality time together as late."

"Maybe we could get a table for four of us," Rory suggested smoothly.

Sandra looked at him with contempt. "What're you going to do? Muscle those four fellas over there out because you want their table?"

"You know I'd never do that."

"All I know is you're a swine, Rory."

"I'll second that," said Liam, delivering Erin's and Sandra's drinks.

Sandra smiled. "What do I owe you, Li?"

"I've got it," said Rory.

"Sure, why not?" Sandra sniffed. "You've got the money."

"I'll get your next round, Sandra," Jake offered, in an effort to keep up.

Sandra smiled at him affectionately. "Thank you, Jake."

Before Rory even had a chance to lay his money on the bar, Liam pinned both he and Jake with an intense glare of displeasure. Sandra stood riveted to the spot. She had an avid look in her eyes that Rory knew oh too well: her gossip radar was on full blast.

"Listen to me, you two douche bags. I know there's nothing Ballycraig loves more than a juicy drama. But I'm here to tell you I've got about this much patience"—Liam pinched his thumb and forefinger together—"for cock blocking here at the bar. So do it somewhere else."

"Can we cock block over a game of darts?" Rory asked, tilting his head in the direction of the board. "The Yanks over there just finished up." He sipped his Guinness. "You up for a little game of darts, Jake?" he challenged.

Jake laughed. "You couldn't hit a cow's arse with a banjo!"

"What are we wagering?"

"The one who wins gets to take Erin to the fair in Omeath," Sandra blurted.

Jake regarded her with astonishment. "Don't you think you should check with her first?"

"She'll be fine. Everyone knows that Rory can't play darts worth a damn, Jake. And seeing the best man win will make me and everybody else in the pub happy."

Rory slid off his bar stool. "Bring it on."

* * *

Sandra was all hyped up when she returned to the table with Erin's Black Velvet. Erin assumed the crazed look on her friend's face was the result of her tearing Rory a new one in full view of half the village. But that wasn't it.

Erin leaned back, taking the first delicious sip of her drink. "Don't get cozy," said Sandra. "We're going over to the bar pronto."

"What for?"

"Rory's challenged Jake to a game of darts!"

"So what?"

"The winner gets to take you to the Omeath Fair."

Erin cupped her ear. "Say again? Because I could have sworn you just said the winner is taking me to the fair in Omeath. I must be going deaf, because that can't possibly be what I heard."

"It's true," Sandra said excitedly, oblivious to the displeasure in Erin's voice.

"And whose brilliant idea was this?"

"Mine."

Erin stared at her in disbelief. There were only a handful of times over the years that Sandra had done something that really cheesed Erin off. This was one of them.

She gulped her drink, more out of fortification than thirst. "You want to tell me why you've humiliated me in this way?"

"Hear me out!" Sandra guzzled so much beer Erin was afraid she'd choke. "Rory and Jake were trying to outman each other, and *Rory* is actually the one who issued the challenge."

"Rory couldn't play darts if his life depended on it."

"I know. Let me finish." Another long excited gulp had Sandra finishing her drink. "Rory wanted to know what the prize would be. And that's when I said the winner could take you to the fair."

"I see. So you just volunteered me up like some prize calf."

Sandra clucked her tongue in frustration. "You're not getting it. There's no way Mr. Cock of the Walk will win, and it'll bug the hell out of him being bested by Jake. He'll also hate that everyone will be rooting for Jake. It'll be good for him to eat a slice of humble pie."

"But then I still have to go to the damn fair with Jake!"

"Big deal," Sandra replied dismissively. "Tell him it's just as friends. But Rory won't have to know that, will he?"

Sandra's enthusiasm was not infectious. "How would you feel if I did that to you?"

"I'd be on the moon if two fellas were warring over me, and in public, too," Sandra retorted.

Erin felt guilty. "You think that, but—"

"No, I know it. So quit lookin' like a misery guts and let's go over there."

10

"Ah, the fair princess hath arrived!"

Rory noticed the deadly look Erin gave Old Jack as she and Sandra joined the small crowd gathering to watch him and Jake throw darts. He'd never been great at darts, but he was confident he could hold his own. Knowing Erin was watching would sharpen his concentration and push his adrenaline to the point of victory.

He caught Erin's eye. She was sober as a judge. He checked to see if she looked at Jake with the same indifference. She did. Thank God. Jake looked smug and relaxed. *I love you mate,* Rory thought, *but you'll be running back to cry into your mam's skirt tails when I'm done with you.*

Sandra sidled up to him. "This was a risky suggestion for you, Rory, knowing how much you suck. I admire you for that."

Rory was skeptical. "Really."

"No. I think you're a shite."

"Thanks, San."

Rory picked up a dart, feeling its weight as he pointed it between his thumb and forefinger in throwing position. In his mind's eye, he saw himself throwing darts again and again, each one hitting the bull's-eye. His aim would be fine.

Jake sauntered over to him. "Just in case you've forgotten, throwing an imaginary dart isn't like throwing a real one. Not only that, but you're not behind the ochre."

"I know I'm not behind the ochre," said Rory. He took a hearty slug of his stout. "What do you want to play? Around the Clock or Five-oh-one?"

"Five-oh-one," Jake replied with a smirk. "Seeing as that's the simplest."

Rory shrugged. "Fine."

Jake looked irritated. "You really think this is going to be no sweat, don't you?"

"Pretty much, yeah."

Jake shook his head, but there was a trace of affection. "Smug bastard."

"Have you ever known me to be any different?"

"Come to think of it, no. But things have changed round here. You'll see."

* * *

"C'mon, Jake! C'mon, Jakey!"

What had gone from a small crowd watching the darts match had become the night's entertainment for all as word quickly spread that the competition was for time with Erin. The excitement of the locals piqued the tourists' interest, even though none of them knew the backstory that made things so dramatic.

If one more person comes up to me and asks, "What if Rory Brady wins?" I'll scream, Erin thought. She'd always found darts boring as sin, but not tonight. Tonight, she was completely invested in the game, though for the life of her, she couldn't figure out why; neither of those two lunkheads were a prize to spend time with. Jake would try to get all wooey and she'd have to fend him off, and Rory would be all triumphant and smug. Forget Sandra's twisted logic: Erin knew that the big loser in all this was her. She glared at her friend, but Sandra was oblivious as she gabbed away with Bettina. Erin's eyes searched out the cricket bat. It was safely ensconced behind the bar.

"Way to go, Jake!"

Claps and whistles brought Erin back to the moment. Jake was kicking Rory's ass.

Rory looked unfazed, but Erin knew it was just a facade: beneath his unflappable exterior, he was annoyed. *Well, that's what you get. You screwed Jake over, and now he's going to get his own back, and in public, too.*

Erin took a sip of her second Black Velvet. Maybe the game would go on and on, and they'd wind up calling a tie with no definite winner.

Sandra was back, bumping her shoulder against Erin's. "This is getting painful to watch," she said gleefully.

"I'm not talking to you, remember?"

"C'mon, Er."

"Seriously." Erin was still peeved. "I can't believe you put me in this position. I don't want either of them and you know that."

"It'll sort itself out," said Sandra, her catchall phrase to soothe Erin. "Just look around you: people are lovin' it. I told you they would. Rory Brady brought low."

There was something satisfying about it, Erin had to admit. But at the same time, she found herself thinking: too bad his gran isn't here; at least then he'd have one person in his corner. She had to be getting tipsy, because if she were in her right mind, she'd never feel sorry for him.

The competitors took a much-needed break. Jake grinned at Erin, giving her a thumbs-up before heading to the bar. Rory was still standing behind the ochre, closing his right eye, then his left. He took a step back. He took two steps back.

"You're going to lose," Erin said, unable to stop herself from puncturing his ego just a tiny bit. "You know that, don't you?"

"It's not over till the fat lady sings."

He closed his right eye and extended his right arm in front of him.

"What are you doing?"

Trying to figure something out," he said distractedly.
"I think . . . maybe . . ."

"You were standing too close? Too far? Rory, you're a
terrible darts player. Face it."

"It's not over till I say it's over," he repeated stubbornly.

* * *

Ten minutes later the game resumed.

"I've fortified myself at the bar," Jake boomed, "so this'll
be quick and painless for you."

Rory had the first go. Two steps back, right eye closed,
throw. Rory reveled in the chorus of *ooh*'s as his dart hit
the double ring, instantly doubling his score.

He turned to Jake. "Your go."

"Watch and learn, son," Jake sniffed cockily, downing a
shot one of his admirers had bought him.

He picked up a dart and, without any contemplation at
all, hurled the dart at the board. Triple ring. Triple his score.
Fuck, thought Rory.

Jake accepted another congratulatory shot. "Your go."

Rory weighed the dart in his hand, then held it properly,
stabbing the air with it a few times. One step back, right
eye closed, throw.

Bull's-eye.

The atmosphere in the pub became charged. What had
seemed a foregone conclusion now looked like it might end
up being a real contest. Rory fed off the crowd's intensity.
He kept thinking of what his first coach in juniors told
them before big games: will beats skill.

"Don't get all puffed up," Jake warned before he downed
the shot.

"Back at you, mate."

Once again, Jake took no measure as he tossed the next
dart. Outer ring. Only twenty-five points. "Shit."

Rory pressed himself against the ochre, squinting hard.

"What are you doing, you eejit?" Old Jack snorted.

Rory didn't look at him. "Winning."

"Don't count those blessings before they hatch, boyo," Old Jack replied.

Rory threw and hit the twenty-five ring right next to the bull's-eye. Not bad, considering this wasn't his game.

"He must have put a curse on Jake when he was in the loo," Teague said to no one in particular.

"Could you stop being a moron for just once in your life?" Fergus replied.

Jake finished off his most recent pint and stepped up to the ochre. The smirk of just a minute before was gone; Rory had him running scared. He studied the board for a few seconds before throwing. Bull's-eye. The crowd went mad.

"All yours," he said to Rory, a wicked gleam in his eyes.

Two steps back, right eye closed, throw, Rory chanted to himself. His strategy worked again. Triple circle. Triple his numbers. He was breathing down Jake's neck, hard—and it was glorious.

"I'm tellin' ya," Teague said to Fergus, "he's got some fecked-up hoodoo goin' on here."

"The only hoodoo that's gonna be happening here is me willin' the cricket bat to fly across the room so I can smash your head with it," Fergus snapped. "Shut. Your. Gob."

Rory started picturing what a magnanimous winner he'd be.

He took a breath. Two steps back. Right eye closed. Throw. He hit a sixteen. Not his best effort, but he was still ahead of his friend.

"Your go."

No sooner had Jake hurled the dart than Bettina began screaming from behind the bar. "Look what you did, you effin' great idiot! Were you not paying any attention at all? You've missed the board completely and hit Vin Diesel square in the right eye! He autographed that picture to me special!"

There was an awkward silence. Rory couldn't believe Jake was so far off the mark. Clearly his "fortification" had been useless.

Old Jack's expression was chilly as he announced, "You've won, Rory."

"Yeah, but I didn't win fair and square, did I? Jake's a bit off his game right now. It's not fair to call me the winner when he's starting to feel poorly."

Jake plucked the dart from Vin Diesel's eye. "You won fair and square."

"C'mon, Jake—"

"No. You take this one, Rory. I'll take the next one."

"Good. I'll be able to practice in between."

"I'm not talkin' darts, you jerk. I'm talkin' a whole other contest of my choosing."

"Fine with me," said Rory. "As long as it's not herding sheep."

Rory chanced a glance at Bettina. She still looked beside herself, her expression so distraught it was as if Jake had hit the real Vin Diesel in the peeper. As soon as she disappeared down into the basement, whether to get supplies or weep in private, Old Jack looked at Jake in desperation.

"You best get her another pic of Vin."

"You can't even see the hole!" Rory pointed out.

"I know that, you know that, but every time she looks at it now, all she'll be able to think of is the dart in his pupil."

Jake frowned. "Are you shitting me?"

"I wish I were," Old Jack said grimly. "But it's my bollocks on the chopping block if she doesn't get a new picture."

"I'll get her one," Rory told Jake. "One of my teammates is pretty tight with him. It won't be a problem."

"I don't need your help," Jake snapped.

Rory was slightly taken aback by his old friend's vehemence, but he let it slide. "Suit yourself."

Jake checked his watch. "I have to be at work in three and a half hours. I'm gonna go." He patted Rory on the back. "Good game, mate," he said, reaching out to shake his hand, even though Rory could tell that what he really wanted to do was punch him.

"Thanks."

"Just want to say good-bye to the girls."

* * *

"Hail the conquering hero," Sandra proclaimed. "You're really gonna let Rory take this one?"

"I don't need his pity. Let him have it. I'll ground him into dust next time." He smiled at Erin. "What'd you think?"

Erin couldn't hide her disinterest. "It was all right."

"Next one'll be better, I promise. I'll ring you," he finished, loud enough for Rory to hear. Watching Jake walk away—with a slight stagger now after so much booze downed so quickly—Erin blew out a sigh of relief. The worst was over, at least for tonight. But of course, she was wrong. Rory was on his way over to take Jake's place.

Sandra raised her drink to him, but her expression was cool. "Congrats. One man's drunkenness is another man's glory, ay?"

"You're right. It wasn't a real win."

Sandra drained her glass. "Still and all, you got what you wanted, didn't you?"

"I think we should go," Erin said with concern. "I don't want to have to carry you into the house."

"You stay," Sandra replied. "I'll get a cab."

Rory offered her a lift.

"Oh, that's right, I forgot. You're Erin's chauffeur."

"Sandra." Erin was mortified.

"I wouldn't get in a car with you anyway," Sandra sniffed. She hugged Erin. "I'll walk. The air will do me good."

"You're not walking home alone. I'll have David go with you. Teague'll get lost and Fergus is still nursing his pint."

"As if David Shiels would leave them two to escort me!"

"He's a good sort, San. He's not like the other two."

"Maybe Liam could take me home," Sandra said, eyes lighting up. "I've never been on the back of a motorcycle before!"

"He's nowhere near done for the night," Erin pointed out.

Sandra deflated. "True. David Shiels it is, then." She hugged Erin again before zeroing in on Rory.

"You hurt her, you die," Sandra threatened.

"Too late," Rory said wearily.

Sandra waved good-bye to Erin, then made her way to the bar to talk to David, leaving Erin alone with Rory. *It just keeps getting worse,* Erin thought.

"Can I get you another Black Velvet?" Rory offered.

"No, thank you." Erin paused. "You know Sandra didn't talk to me about this contest, right? She just charged right in."

"You could have said no. But you didn't."

"And your point?"

Rory leaned in to her slightly. "I think you enjoyed it just a wee bit. It was like Lancelot and King Arthur vying for Guinevere."

"Don't be daft."

"I heard you were seeing Jake," Rory said casually.

"That's none of your business."

"That's where you're wrong."

"Stop being so oblique," Erin said curtly. "It's plucking on my nerves."

Rory looked humbled. "Look, here's the thing: You don't have to go to the fair with me. It's stupid for you to go if you don't want to."

Erin couldn't believe it: *he* was trying to get out of it, and it hurt her a bit. "No, a wager is a wager."

"I won by default. Jake was drunk. It really shouldn't count. So if you want to skip it, you've every right to."

"It's no problem," Erin insisted, acting like she was doing him a favor. "Anything I want, I'll make you buy it for me. Jams, breads, prizes. Anything I want."

Rory looked pleased. "Good."

"A few ground rules. Number one: don't try to hold my hand. Number two: if you think we're strolling around chatting, you're wrong. I'd like as little conversation with you as possible. Number three: I've no intention of wasting my whole afternoon with the likes of you. We're there for two hours, maximum. Are we clear?"

"What if I forget and I talk to you? It could happen, you know."

"Make sure it doesn't."

"Right," said Rory, looking like he was having a tough time keeping a straight face. "Guess I'll be off, then. Pick you up next Saturday around one?"

"Actually, I'll meet you at the fair. Say . . . two at the preserves booth," Erin answered, trying to sound lackadaisical.

"Right, then."

He strolled out of the pub.

chortled. "Oh, pin your teenage gluttony on me,
… ? I don't think so."

…as your fault when we got in those tiny bumper cars
…uldn't get out because I was too big for them."

… smiled wickedly. "I've got a picture of that some-
… you know. Them having to dismantle the ride."

…anging on to it so you can blackmail me some-
…?"

…elieve me, if I wanted to blackmail you, I've got loads
…her things at my disposal."

…o, you haven't thrown things out," Rory said softly,
… to touch her arm.

…rin jerked away. *What the hell are you doing, strolling
…n memory lane? You're not even supposed to be talk-
…to him.*

"No, I don't throw things away, Rory, unlike you. And
…mories are sweet, but that's all they are: memories. I'd
…reciate it if we could get back to wrapping this day up."

Rory cocked his head appraisingly. "I like this new you,
…nding your ground and all."

"I thought you said I'd become a hard one."

"More tough than hard, I'd say now."

"Go to hell, Rory. You make it sound like I let you push
all over the map."

"You did. And I didn't even think twice about it. Sorry
…that."

"Apology accepted."

Rory took one bite of his Mars bar and tossed it into the
…ish bin with a disgusted face. "I've eaten loads of crap
…y day, but that topped the list. How can you eat that?"

…Ah, what do you know?"

…Nothing about how your taste in sweets has changed,
…rently. What now? Home?"

…e was calling her bluff. Well, she'd call back.

…'d like to finish my candy bar, please. Then home—
…gh I would like to buy some jam and chocolate first."

…Vell, there's something I need to do, too."

…Vhat's that?"

11

Erin had always loved fairs. When she was small, there
used to be an annual summer fair in Crosshaven featuring
all the usual delights: pony rides, fortune tellers, a bouncy
castle. Her mother always thought the games of chance
were a waste of money, but her dad used to slip her and
Brian a few coins to play on the sly.

Arriving home the night of the darts game, Erin had sat
in her room for a long time, trying to sort out her feelings.
She was embarrassed by the secret thrill that ran through
her as she watched Rory and Jake go at it. At first, Sandra's
offering her up like a prize calf had maddened her. Sandra
knew Jake hadn't a snowball's chance in hell with her, and
the darts contest seemed cruel, giving him false hope
where none existed.

She found Rory's magnanimity in willing to forfeit the
match shocking. That he'd even suggested darts at all was
a stunner: he'd never been good at them, ever, at least not
compared to Jake. And if there was one thing that drove
Rory Brady mad, it was not being good at something.
Maybe he had really changed.

Erin caught a ride to the fair with Mr. Russell. The old man seemed especially excited about seeing one of the fortune tellers, while Erin was looking forward to the fried Mars bars, her favorite junk food.

She wasn't surprised when she arrived at the preserves booth to find Rory already there, looking semi-Yank in tight jeans, a striped green and yellow sweater, and white running shoes she'd never seen in Ireland. Christ, he really did look like David Beckham. And he knew it, too.

Rory grinned as he caught sight of her. Erin resisted the urge to smile back even as memories of fairs past darted through her mind. *That was then, this is now,* she scolded herself. Two hours, nothing more.

"Hiya. How was your ride over?" he asked.

"Fine. You?"

"Fine."

"Great. Well, now that that's established, what do you want to do?"

"It's what you want to do, Erin."

"But I'm the prize," she reminded him acidly. "It's about what you want."

She glanced around the market. It was getting so crowded that soon it would be hard to move. She wouldn't mind picking up a few jars of jam and some homemade choccies for her mam, but it was silly to get them now and have to carry them around. She'd buy them when they were done at the fair. Sandra's voice whispered in her ear: *Make him pay. Make him pay for everything.* Maybe she was foolish, but to Erin, the thought of snapping her fingers and ordering Rory about wasn't right.

Allowing him to drive her around was one thing. As he said, it was the least he could do to make her life a bit easier. But telling him he had to foot the bill for everything at the fair was bitchy. And immature.

"I don't really want to walk around the market," she told him.

"I did a once-round waiting for you. Your cousin Liam and his missus each gave me a champion glare when I

walked past, and I heard a couple o[f] muttering about 'putting the boot in.' charming place this can be for those o[f]

"Let's just get to the fair and get it o[ver]" with a heavy sigh.

"Oh, yeah, pure torture it'll be," Rory how much you hate fairs and all."

Erin gave him a dirty look. "Let's go."

She started walking, jostled by the crow[d] clear that it would be easier to forge a path lead. Funny: when someone as big and broad to get by, space magically opened for him. like that. Much to her chagrin, she still did.

* * *

One hour down, one to go. They'd gone on the T[ ] the Gravitron, and the roller coaster. Erin trie[d] Rory as little as possible, but it was hard, what being jammed together into small spaces. "It's fun you're ruining," Rory pointed out casuall[y] waited on the snaking line to buy a couple of bars. "I told you, you didn't have to honor the be[t] you did, why not enjoy yourself?"

Erin was silent. She hated that he was right.

Rory tapped her on the shoulder, pointing up Ferris wheel. "Remember that time we got stuck

"Vaguely," Erin lied.

"You wouldn't look down," Rory continued "and you were completely green around the trapped that high up. You were holding my ha[nd] I thought you'd crush my bones." He look[ed] "I know you remember it all, Erin, so don't don't."

Erin ducked her head sheepishly. "Right least I'm not the one who stuffed their face cotton candy they got a massive bellyache."

"That was because you kept buying it for m[e] the heart to turn you down."

"Come along and see."

Erin hung back a moment, then shrugged. "No skin off my nose," she said diffidently, when really, "come along and see" were words too enticing to ignore.

Rory led her to the long avenue of tented booths where the games of chance were. She saw herself and her brother, darting from game to game, competing. The sweet smell of the treats being sold, the swirl of the carnival music accompanying the surrounding tide of voices—it was still magical.

"Rory, what are you doing?"

"What do you think? I'm going to win you something."

"No need. I've decided I'd like to go home after all."

"Five more minutes won't kill you. Besides, I thought you wanted to buy some jam?"

"Can I point something out? You've always been awful at games of chance. Worse than darts."

"Maybe I've improved."

"Doubt it."

She ignored Rory's arrogant smile as they strolled past booth after booth. Eventually, they stopped at the shooting gallery. Hit one of the moving ducks with the air rifle, win a stuffed animal. The line was short, but it seemed to be moving quickly. All of the shooters were men determined to win a prize for their sweethearts. Rory took his place in line.

"You're a masochist, Rory Brady."

"We'll just see."

It was only a few minutes before it was Rory's turn. He slapped down a stack of euros, picked up the rifle, and, closing his left eye, took aim at the moving gallery of ducks. Three shots a game and he missed them all. And each time he lost, he put more money down.

"Rory, this is crazy," said Erin, beginning to feel self-conscious as the crowd of carnival goers around them began swelling, everyone wanting to see just how much time and money this big, handsome man was willing to go through for the small woman beside him.

Ten games. Twenty games.

"Rory . . ."

"He must love your arse," a gum-popping teenage girl caked in cheap makeup remarked enviously.

Rory heard her. "I do."

"C'mon, mate!" The crowd urged him on each time he lost a game. "You can do it."

Finally, he did, on his thirty-second game. Cheers went up, claps were pounded out. Yet despite paying a small, unnecessary fortune, Rory somehow managed to look gallant as he put the gun down and turned to Erin. "Pick your prize."

Erin, flushed and mildly panicked at being the center of attention, picked the first thing that caught her eye: a stuffed lamb. The carnival barker handed it over to her, his eyes glazed with boredom. "Who's next?"

Erin and Rory started to walk away from the booth so the next Romeo could take his shot at winning. Erin caught a few looks of envy coming her way. Suddenly, she felt ashamed for how horrible she'd been to Rory today. She owed him *something*.

"Thank you for the lamb," she said shyly.

"For Chrissakes, girl!" boomed a raucous male voice. "You can at least give the bastard a kiss!"

Rory was smiling beguilingly. "You heard the man."

Erin felt light-headed as she rose up on tiptoes to kiss Rory's cheek. Except it wasn't his cheek: Rory shifted his head so their lips met. It was over in the wink of an eye, but Erin couldn't deny to herself what was still there between them: desire as intense and electric as that first time he'd ever kissed her, round the back of the school one lunchtime. Anger hadn't dulled it at all. If anything, it made it sharper.

"There," Erin said, minimizing their contact. "You've won your prize, you've gotten your kiss, now let me go get my jam and choccies and we'll be done with it."

"How're you getting home? And don't lie."

"I was going to ride with Aislinn and Liam. I'm going back to their house for supper."

Rory looked alarmed. "Where, in the back of that death truck?"

"No! I'd be squeezed up front with them!"

"It's still a death truck. I don't want you in it." His expression was adamant.

"Oh, is that so? Has it not dawned on you yet that I couldn't care less what you want or don't want?"

Rory's brows came together and he rubbed his forehead as if trying to ward off a headache. "I'm just sayin' I don't want to risk anything happening to you. Besides, Liam and Aislinn won't be closing up shop for a few hours yet. What are you going to do? Hang about and help them sell wool?" He looked uncharacteristically tense. "Erin, please: just let me give you a lift home. We don't have to talk if you don't want."

"You promise?"

"I'll put tape over my mouth if it'll make you feel better."

"No need to go that far," Erin replied, alarmed that the thought of tape covering that gorgeous mouth of his struck her as a sin. There could be only one explanation for it: the sun beating down on her head was beginning to cook her brains.

Rory looked impatient. "Well?"

"I accept your offer."

"Good."

Erin couldn't see his expression as he turned away, but she knew a small smile of victory was playing across his lips this very moment. In Rory's mind, he'd won. It was sad how wrong one person could be.

12

Erin was having a lie down in one of the spare bedrooms in her cousin's house, surprisingly tired after the fair, when she was jolted awake by the sound of crockery smashing downstairs in the kitchen. She checked her cell: it was too early for Aislinn and Liam to be back from the farmer's market, which meant only one of two things: either Jake was rooting around down there, or Alec. Maybe both. She'd been so rattled driving with Rory that by the time he'd dropped her off at the house, she'd failed to even register the brothers' presence in the far south meadow. But judging by the annoyed look on Jake's face when she appeared in the kitchen doorway, she knew he'd seen Rory drop her off.

He was crouched on the stone floor, picking up the pieces of a large ceramic bowl. "Hey. Surprised to see you here."

"I'm having dinner with Aislinn and Liam. I saw no point in waiting around the fair for them to finish up, so—"

"You had Rory drop you here." He rose, carefully laying the broken pieces of bowl on the sideboard. "All it needs is a good glue," he said, more to himself than to her. His back remained to her as he asked, "How was the fair?"

"Crowded."

He didn't seem to register her answer as he headed for the sink, still not looking at her. He thrust his mud-caked hands under the running tap. "And did you have fun?"

"Not really."

"Glad to hear it. You would've if you'd gone with me."

"Rory offered to forfeit the game. You said no."

"He just wanted to look good."

Erin hesitated. "I think he might be trying to make amends."

Jake looked astonished as he glanced at her over his shoulder. "Are you defending him?"

"No. I just think you have to give him some credit for trying to fix things."

Jake dried his hands, then turned to her. "And how's he making it up to you, then?" he asked sarcastically.

He's going to drive me to Crosshaven next Tuesday afternoon. She couldn't tell him that. Jake could never match it, and Erin didn't want him to feel bad about himself, which was silly, since she didn't want either of them. "I don't think he's figured that out yet."

Jake changed the subject. "Good of you to come up here. Aislinn said it's been a while."

"Aislinn's talked to you about me?" Erin asked, surprised.

"Just in passing," Jake said offhandedly. "You know, mostly in the context of Liam, him missing you and all."

"Yeah, we haven't seen as much of each other as we used to now that I'm the unpaid help at the B and B."

"It's a good thing you're doing for your mam, Erin."

"I know." She was plagued with guilt. "But my mother doesn't seem to understand that it's not what I've planned for my life."

"And where are you in the planning process?" he asked softly.

"Smack in the middle. But I know one thing: I don't plan to live the rest of my life here, Jake."

"People change."

"Yes, sometimes they do," Erin agreed tersely, "but trust me on this. That's one thing I'll never change my mind about."

"If you say so." Jake held her gaze for a moment, then started back outside. "Enjoy your dinner."

Doubtful that's going to happen now, Erin thought grimly. But she'd try to keep a positive attitude nonetheless.

*   *   *

"I can't believe you talked to Jake about me."

Erin waited until she, Liam, and Aislinn were tucking into their rhubarb crumble before broaching the subject that had been niggling at her ever since she'd spoken with Jake. After he'd left the house, she was too wired to continue her nap and too restless to read. She decided she'd surprise Aislinn and make dessert herself. Aislinn wasn't fond of others messing about in her kitchen, but she seemed enormously pleased, which in turn made Erin feel more confident about bringing the subject of Jake up.

Aislinn looked blank.

"He told me that you'd mentioned my not visiting for a while," Erin clarified.

"I don't think that constitutes 'talking about you,' Er," said Liam. "At least not in the traditional sense."

"I can't see how the subject even came up," Erin replied.

"Why so tetchy?" Liam wanted to know.

"You know why," Aislinn said as she helped herself to more crumble. "The bet."

"Yeah, about the bet," Liam said carefully.

Here it comes.

"Don't you think you should stay away from Rory Brady?"

"I'd have kicked him in the balls by now," Aislinn declared matter-of-factly. "Would have done it the moment I clapped eyes on him."

"And that's why I love you, darlin'," Liam said fondly. "Because you're always ready to shoot on sight. You're like my very own Annie Oakley in Wellies."

"I've no idea who that is, but I'm going to assume it's not a complimentary comparison."

"An affectionate one." Liam dug heartily into his large piece of pie. "Seriously, Erin, what the hell? I can't believe you agreed to go to the fair with him. What did your folks say?"

Erin's anger reared its head. "For Christ's sake, Liam, I'm not some dozy little twit who doesn't know what she's doing! And I'm not a child who needs to let her parents know where she is every moment of every day. All I said was that I was going to the fair. Period. I'm a grown woman; I can do as I please."

"You're right," Liam agreed, backing off. "But I still don't see why you'd ever give that prick the time of day."

Erin took a sip of tea. "I'm milking him for all he's got."

Liam looked completely confused. "What do you mean?"

"He says he wants to make it all up to me—not that he ever can, mind. You've seen his posh car, right?"

"Nearly ran me over on my bike," said Aislinn.

"Well, I'm fed up to here"—Erin made a slashing gesture across her throat—"with my mam thinking that if she keeps me at the B and B long enough, I'll want to stay for good. I put an ad in the paper for domestic help, and I got a heap of responses. I'm starting to interview people this week in Crosshaven to take my place. Rory's going to drive me there and back."

Liam stared at her. "You have got to be shitting me."

"What's wrong with that?" Erin countered defensively. "He said he'll do anything to make my life easier. That makes my life easier."

"And that's it, then?" Aislinn snapped a finger. "He's forgiven?"

"He's not forgiven. He's nowhere near forgiven."

"Then what are the two of you going to talk about in the car?" Aislinn asked. "Football scores?"

"I'll listen to my iPod."

"Oh, that'll be comfortable," Liam mocked. "And what's he going to do while you interview people?"

"He can sit in the car and pick his nose for all I care. And before you say it, I don't care if it gets around town."

"Yes, you do," Liam retorted.

"Old Erin did. New Erin doesn't give a damn."

Liam looked worried. "This doesn't sound like you, Er."

Aislinn nodded approvingly. "Good for you, Erin, getting your own back. Playing the chauffeur is the least that wanker can do."

"Except that wanker wants her back," Liam said sharply.

"Like she said, she's not some dozy fool. She knows what she's doing."

Erin smiled appreciatively. "Thank you, Aislinn."

"However . . ."

Erin tensed. "However what?"

"I've never understood why you didn't want to give Jake a chance."

"Why didn't you want to give Alec a chance?" Erin shot back.

"Easy: because he's as boring as a bar of soap. Just because they're brothers doesn't mean they're alike. Jake isn't boring. I know that for a fact."

"I just don't have those kinds of feelings for Jake. Not only that, but he wants to live in Ballycraig forever. One day he'll take over his family's farm. There's nothing wrong with that, but it's not for me. Everyone has always thought that the only reason I was going to leave town was because I was marrying Rory, but they're wrong. I've always wanted to go out and see the world. And I'm going to." She hesitated. Should she tell them? They were both looking at her expectantly. "I'm finishing up that art history degree at Open University."

Aislinn looked intrigued. "What, the one you were taking on and off when you and Rory were together?"

"Yeah. I'm going to get my degree, and then I'm going to pick a city to live in and go."

Liam looked wounded. "Why didn't you tell me all this?"

"Oh, right. So you could tell your folks and it would get back to my folks? Not a chance!"

"I wouldn't have said anything!"

Aislinn gave her husband a withering look. "You have a mouth as big as a horse's."

"That isn't true."

"Yes, it is, Liam," Erin concurred.

"How are you paying for it?" he asked.

"How do you think? With the money I saved for the wedding."

Liam sat back in his chair, impressed. "Wow."

"Now you'll see why I've got to get my replacement up and going. Mam is going to curse me up and down, I know it. She'll accuse me of abandoning her when I finally leave town."

"Why?" Aislinn halted mid-chew. "She's not even fifty-five yet."

"I know. But sometimes she harps on about me marrying Jake and handing the B and B over to us when she's old."

"Talk about planning ahead," said Liam.

"No kidding. I think she's got the dress she wants to be buried in picked out already. It's at the back of her closet with a note pinned to it."

Liam sighed. "That's something my mother would do."

"That's what happens when you marry an O'Brien man," Aislinn needled Liam. "Stay married long enough, and before you know it, you start dreaming about shedding this mortal coil."

"It's a relief to tell you about school," Erin admitted. "I feel like I've been carrying a big secret."

"You have been," said Liam.

"And you're going to keep it, right?" Erin warned.

"Of course I will."

"Don't worry," Aislinn promised. "He knows he'll have to deal with me if he doesn't."

They all smiled.

13

"How was the rest of your weekend?"

Erin wasn't in Rory's car ten seconds before he started with the chitchat. It was a simple question. No harm in a simple answer, as long as he didn't interrogate her all the way to Crosshaven.

"Fine." She knew she was supposed to say, "And you?" but didn't. Her reticence didn't deter him.

"Do anything special?"

Erin knew he was fishing, despite his casual tone.

"Ate dinner with Liam and Aislinn. Jake was there." She wasn't lying: technically Jake had been there; he just wasn't present at dinner.

"That's nice," Rory replied evenly. "I stayed in with Gran and suffered through watching Mass on TV."

"Oh, God."

"Exactly. She was asking about you," he continued. "Said she hadn't seen you in ages. Not for a proper chat, anyway."

Erin battled guilt. "It's true."

"You should stop over sometime. If you give her fair warning, I can make sure I'm not there."

"Thanks." She pulled out her iPod. "I hope you don't mind."

Rory's eyes were steady on the road. "Of course not."

As it turned out, Erin was the one who minded. What an idiot she was, thinking she could ignore him sitting right beside her. The longer she tried pretending to gaze out with interest on the passing scenery and enjoy the music, the larger his presence loomed. She wondered if he knew how unnerving his proximity was to her. It was different from being at the fair with him; there she could distract herself with sights, sounds, the smell of food. But now it was just her and Rory. Alone. She stole a surreptitious glance at him. Relaxed as always, just motoring along.

Erin removed her earbuds.

"That was fast."

"We're nearly there, anyway."

Rory gave her a strange look. "Look, I haven't been here in ages and even I know that's rubbish."

"I'm nervous about these interviews," Erin admitted.

"Why? They're the ones in the hot seat, not you."

"Yeah, but I've never done anything like this before."

"Do you want help?"

Erin looked at him blankly. "I'm not understanding you here."

"I'll help you. I can be writing down all the answers while you fire away. Then you can look at your notes later."

"I'm not completely incompetent, you know."

"It's nothing to do with incompetence," Rory interjected patiently. "It's to do with making your life easier."

Listen to you, she thought, *Mr. Helpful.* But nothing about his expression or inflection rang untrue. He really was trying to do all he could for her, really was trying to atone in the hope of repairing the damage he'd done.

"How many are you interviewing?"

"Three today. I haven't set a day for the rest yet."

"Too bad you don't drive. I'd let you borrow the car— after I bought you a crash helmet."

"It wasn't my fault," Erin said under her breath, looking out the passenger window.

"Yes, it was," said Rory, sounding amused. "Every time you got behind the wheel, you tensed up."

"That was because you were barking commands at me!"

"I didn't want to die!"

Erin glowered at him. "Think what you want, but you were a terrible driving teacher."

"I might have been a little impatient," Rory admitted.

"A little? You snapped at me when I turned on the radio."

Rory frowned. "Now you're just exaggerating."

"I most certainly am not."

He glanced at her sideways. "Your father still won't let you behind the wheel of his precious car, eh?"

"No. He alone is allowed to pilot his Rolls-Royce."

Rory laughed, then casually continued, "And Jake never offered to teach you?"

"He did, but I was still recovering from the trauma of being taught by you."

"And are you recovered?" Rory inquired.

"Maybe."

It bugged her as Rory laughed again. She'd meant it as a dig, not a joke. Time to put her armor back on and show him that just because they'd bantered a bit, it didn't mean they were back on any sort of road to romance. To her mind, they weren't even pals.

Rory must have felt her coolness.

"So, after you do these interviews and hire the right one, what then?"

"Then my mother raises holy hell, talks about betrayal, and says she's not going to employ the person. I tell her that if she doesn't, or if she tries to make that person's life so hellish they quit, I will leave Ballycraig immediately."

Rory wasn't buying it.

"You would never do that. You haven't even told her you're doing these interviews."

"Because she'd make my life hell with the guilt. Better to ambush her."

"You'll still cave in. Admit it, love. Better to tell her all the facts, cut down on the stress. Your Achilles heel is your family. You're always the one that has to do the right thing. They've drummed it into you for so long, you've only now just gotten a grip on it."

"Then how do you explain the fact they were quite willing for me to move to America with you?"

"No, they weren't. Your mother hated the prospect of me taking you away. But she wanted you to be happy, so she backed off."

"Doesn't mean I'm still not moving."

"Erin, I was your ticket out of here," Rory said, slightly smug.

"Oh, saving the life of your country girlfriend, were you?" Erin snarled. "Assuming that without you, I'd have never left. You didn't think twice about dumping me, though, did you? So much for saving me. And PS—I didn't need you to be my ticket out of here, you bloody jackass. Once you broke things off, I realized I didn't need you to make my dreams come true. I actually should thank you for cutting me loose, because, in the end, it's been a gift. Now I do what I want to do for myself, without worrying about how to please or accommodate anyone else."

"Except your mother."

"I'm working on that, I told you. Some of us aren't hard-hearted: we don't just pull the plug on those we love and walk away."

Rory winced. "Touché." He was quiet for a long time. "You finishing up your course?"

"Yes. That's how I'm getting out of here. On my own."

"Then I can't see why your mother is putting up such a hullabaloo."

"Because she doesn't know. No one does except Sandra, Aislinn, Liam—and now you."

Rory smirked. "The wonderful Jake doesn't know?"

"I'm not discussing Jake with you, remember?"

Rory looked irritated as Erin turned to look out the passenger window, suppressing a smile.

"What're you thinking?" he eventually asked. "About how you might be able to forgive me?"

"Dream on."

"You've already started."

Erin turned to look at him. "You're maddening! You're truly maddening! You always have been, with your big mouth and your ego and—"

"That's why you hate yourself so much," Rory cut in confidently. "Because despite my being the biggest idiot on earth, you still have real feelings for me. It's there in the way you let down your guard so quick and chat with me. You want to hate me, but you can't."

"*Hate* is a strong word. I don't *hate* anyone. Not even you."

"Well, I do hate some things. I hate having these snatches of conversation. We need to sit down and just put it all out there. Clear the air between us."

Erin ignored him. "We're here. That's the caf up there. I'll ring you when I'm done."

"Are you sure you don't want any help?"

The look she gave him said it all.

"Right. Loud and clear. I'll be here when you're done."

* * *

Erin soon overcame her nervousness. The first applicant, a Mrs. Doyle, was lovely and soft-spoken, with loads of experience. There was just one problem: she was roughly the same age as her mother, who would feel threatened despite being the boss. There was no need to ask her, "Why do you want this job?" The Irish economy was in the toilet. Jobs were hard to come by.

The second candidate was only fifteen, a school leaver. She was sweet but had no experience, and given her age, Erin knew her mother would eat her alive. The poor girl wouldn't last a week.

Erin had a good feeling about the third candidate, Diana

Everett. She was thirty and no-nonsense. She had experience working in a B and B in Killarney, the undisputed
center of tourism in southwest Ireland. When Erin asked
why she'd left a good, steady job, she was blunt: "The pro-
prietor made untoward advances." Erin could see straight
off that Diana could hold her own against her mother if
need be.

Erin rose, shaking Diana's hand. "I'll be calling you
within a week with my decision. Thank you so much for
your time."

* * *

Erin was surprised when she walked out of the caf to find
Rory parked on the opposite side of the road, leaning
against the hood of his car, casual as could be, reading the
newspaper. Deep down, she was glad: the last thing she'd
wanted to do was ring him to pick her up, like a child need-
ing to be fetched from the cinema. Up until now, Rory was
the one who'd done all the mentioning of driving, and Erin
liked it that way.

As soon as Rory saw her, he folded the paper and opened
the car door for her. "Any luck?"

"A possibility." Erin cracked the window a tiny bit.
"What are you doing here? I figured you'd be shopping."

"I've always hated shopping, remember? Unless it was a
gift for you."

"Rory, don't."

He hopped in the front seat and started the car. "Remember that time I bought you those diamond studs? I thought
you'd skin me alive."

"I should have." Erin remembered it well. She'd burst
into tears, feeling unworthy of the gift, and lashed out at
him. Rory would have none of it. In the end, she accepted
the beautiful gift and apologized. They'd made up by having raucous sex in Rory's grandmother's living room while
she was in Crosshaven buying herself flannel nightgowns.
Rory eased the car away from the curb. "Let's take a drive."

"Let's not. I'm tired. Truly. And I have a paper to write."

"All right." He looked disappointed. "Maybe some other time, though."

"Are you soft in the head or what? The last thing I want is to go driving with you."

Rory looked at her seductively. "Too many memories, eh?"

"Go chase yourself."

"Rather chase you."

"Stop it." Erin was becoming genuinely irritated. This flirtatiousness was really getting out of hand. She felt herself softening toward him. Not good.

Erin picked up the folded paper. It was a copy of the *Sentinel*, one of New York's top tabloids. "Where did you manage to find this?"

"At the tobacconist, if you can believe it. The world is getting smaller all the time. I'm not big on reading the news online."

Erin thumbed through it, not really looking at anything, or for anything. *This is from New York,* she thought. *God, you're a simpleton.*

"Miss it?"

Rory hesitated a moment. "Yeah."

"You must be aching to get back there." *What if he says yes. Why do you care?*

Rory eased into traffic, if you could call it that. "Yes and no."

Cryptic Rory. No need to ask him what he meant. She wasn't thick.

"One of my mates on the team might be coming for a visit."

"Really?" This time there was no keeping the interest out of her voice.

"Do you remember me telling you about that Finnish bloke on the team, Esa Saari?"

"Not really." She was pleased that she didn't remember every little thing about him.

"I didn't like him at first. Totally egotistical. But he was cut down to size, and it turns out he's a nice guy. Anyway, he's all for a visit. Wants to relax for a week. He still plays football when he's back in Finland, so he might be a big help with Jackson."

"Is Jackson not doing well?"

"He can be a bit serious. He acts like the kids are going to be trying out for Man United next month."

"Larry—LJ—loves the camp."

"Nice escape from home, eh?"

"Sandra does the best she can," Erin said defensively.

"I'm castin' no stones. I know she loves those kids to death, but it would be better for them all if Larry pissed off once and for all."

"No kidding. I heard he's been dealing drugs with his brother, Lance."

"Oh, that's just great."

"I know," Erin said worriedly.

"Has Sandra heard about this?"

"If she does, she hasn't let on."

"Not good."

"Ya think?"

"Lucy's heading for trouble," Rory continued authoritatively, ignoring her sarcasm. "Going out with that thicko."

"I know. Sandra's worried."

"She ought to be."

"She's tried everything, but you know what adolescents are like. There's only so much she can do."

Rory chuckled. "Yeah, I know, having been one myself once." He glanced at Erin. "Sandra really hates my guts, doesn't she?"

"She's reason to, hasn't she?"

"Yeah, she does. I've always liked the way you two look out for each other."

"I don't think I'd be sitting here next to you if it wasn't for her," Erin said candidly.

"How does she feel about your plans to leg it out of here?"

"Don't say it like that. It sounds like I'm escaping from prison."

"Aren't you?"

Erin ignored him. "Sandra's sad about it. We both are. But we were prepared to be separated when I was supposed to—you know—"

"Marry me?"

"Mmmm," Erin supplied tersely. "She's all for my leaving. She knows it's something I have to do."

"I understand that feeling."

"I'm sure you do."

"Like right now," Rory continued, undeterred. "I have to be here to undo the biggest mistake of my life."

"You can't," Erin said plainly. "You can't just go back in time and fix things so you get the outcome you please."

"Can't I?"

"You show me no respect!"

Rory seemed to retreat, staring off into the middle distance, mindlessly tapping the steering wheel. Eventually, he looked at her. "You're right," he said bluntly.

Erin was shocked. She hadn't expected him to cop to it.

"I'm doing my best, Erin." The vulnerability in his voice surprised her as he tentatively put his hand atop hers. It was a gesture of simple connecting, a way of trying to convey to her his newfound humility. Out of sheer kindness, she let his hand linger there longer than she ought before carefully sliding hers out from beneath his. Rory looked at her questioningly.

"I was just trying to be nice, letting you put your hand on mine," Erin explained.

"Took your time taking it away, though, I noticed."

"Counting the seconds, were you?"

"Maybe." Rory looked restless. "Look, I'm not going to press the issue of you 'n' me right now. All I ask is that you have a good long think and be honest with yourself."

Which was exactly what Erin didn't want to do.

14

Most of the B and B guests were in the dining room when Erin got "home." Mr. Russell was there, of course, sitting at "his" table, the one nearest the kitchen. Since he now lived here, he had free reign to go into the kitchen now and then and ask for what he pleased.

Erin walked through, steeling herself for the showdown she'd be having in just a moment with her mother. But it wasn't her mam pulling scones out of the oven; it was her dad.

"What's happened?" Erin threw her bag on a kitchen chair and hurriedly shrugged out of her jacket.

"Calm yourself down, girl." Her father put the muffin tin on the stove top to cool. "It's nothing major."

"Then why are you here, Dad? What about the shop?"

"I left Geoff in charge for now. I'm just here until . . ."

He took the terrycloth gloves off his hands and began untying the apron.

"I got here, right?"

Her father looked shamefaced.

"Is that what she told you?"

"It's not a big deal, love."

"It *is* a big deal. When all those guests out there finish, someone is going to have to collect the dishes, put them in the dishwasher, wrap the leftovers, grab the napkins and tablecloths to go down to the laundry, polish the tabletops, vacuum, and set up the dishes for tomorrow morning.

"I can't believe she stuck you with that," Erin continued angrily. "You've your own busy business to run."

"It's women troubles and that," her father replied, waving his hand in the air vaguely. "Doubled over with the cramps."

Erin patted his shoulder. "Go back to the shop, Dad. I'll take care of the cleanup. Go."

"Are you certain?"

"I usually am."

"You're a good girl, Erin. Always have been."

It was time to test the waters. "Dad, I'm not going to be here forever, you know."

Her father smiled sadly. "I'm glad to hear it."

"Really?"

"Of course. That was never your plan. Rory Brady or not, it makes me happy to know you're sticking to your dreams." He took a deep breath. "Your mother's having a tough time of it."

"No kidding."

"Don't be snarky, now. You're her only daughter. I know she's trying to pour the guilt on thick, but that's only because she's scared. And sad, too, that neither of her kids will be close by."

"I wouldn't have been close by if I'd married Rory," Erin protested.

"I know, I know," he said, making a gesture that she should lower her voice a bit. "But that was different, see? You'd have someone there to take care of you."

"But I don't need anyone to take care of me!"

"We know that, but she doesn't. You know your mother's thinking is old-fashioned."

"I know. Remember she thought it was odd that Aislinn took over the farm when her dad died?"

"I do. But that's your mother." He tugged on the end of her hair the way he did when she was a little girl. "Cut her some slack, girl. She just wants you near."

"And does she think the way to keep me near is to work me like a slave?"

"I've told her the very same thing."

Erin was astonished. "You have?"

"Of course I have. Only a fool couldn't see she's deliberately draggin' her feet on getting a replacement for you. She thinks the longer she can get you to stay, the greater the chance you might get to like being part of the family business. Mad, I know. But mothers reach for these things."

"I was in Crosshaven today interviewing people."

Her father looked surprised. "And how did it go?"

"There was one woman who I thought could be a good match for Mam. But I've got some more lined up."

"Good for you." Her father moved to the stove top to see if the scones were cool enough to tip from the tin. "But you know what you're up against, don't you?"

"I do. I also know that whoever I bring in, Mam will try to make their life a living hell, until it dawns on her that if she fires them, she'll definitely be running this place on her own."

"That'll be a hard one on you, trying to turn her down." Her father turned the tray upside down, shaking out the scones onto a large tray.

"No kidding."

His expression was serious. "But I don't think you should fold on this one, Erin. Much as I'd love you to stay, I know you need to spread your wings. You've a right to do that. I'd rather you were happy miles away than unhappy right under my nose. Your mother just can't think straight about it right now, but she'll come round eventually. I'm a dab hand at getting her to see reason. You'll see."

Erin smiled. "I've noticed that, yes." Now that it was clear her father would champion her leaving town, she decided to tell him the entire truth.

"Dad, remember that course I started at Open Uni when I was seeing Rory?"

"You're finishing it up."

Erin was shocked. "How did you know that?"

"Because I know you. Once you start something, it drives you mad if you don't finish it. Correct?"

"Correct."

"It wasn't too hard to figure out. Besides, what beautiful, smart woman would spend hours locked away in her room? Though the thought of the online dating did give us a scare, I won't lie."

"And Ma hasn't figured out I'm studying?" She took the dirty muffin tray from her father and brought it to the sink.

"I think she knows that deep down, but she just doesn't want to deal with it. We'll figure all that bit out when the time comes, eh?"

Erin threw her arms around her father. "Thank you so much, Da!"

Her father held her tighter. "Anything for my girl. You know that."

"Anything? Can you teach me to drive your car?"

"Don't go pushin' it, now. Why don't you go say hello to your mother?"

"I will. And then I'm coming back down to clean up after tea. No ifs, ands, or buts."

"I promise." He checked his watch. "It's best I be getting back soon, anyway. See how Geoff is coming along." He winked at Erin. "It'll sort itself out. You'll see."

15

"This is incredibly stupid."

Rory had never had a problem stating his opinion, and he certainly wasn't going to hold back now, especially since the recipient was Jake. His friend had insisted they have another contest of his choosing, since he hadn't been willing to accept Rory's offer to forfeit the darts game. *More fool him,* Rory thought, thinking about the day he and Erin had spent at the fair. He could see her resolve slowly begin to crumble. Not only was the distrust in her eyes slowly fading, but her entire demeanor was becoming more relaxed. She wanted to hate him; that much was clear. But she didn't. Rory would never say this to her face, but she was a shite actress. Try as she might to tamp her true feelings down, they always managed to bob to the surface.

That wasn't to say that her newfound assertiveness was bluster. It wasn't. She'd found her voice since their split, which was a good thing, despite his horrible behavior being the catalyst. But toughening up and pure, true emotions were not mutually exclusive. When they got back together—

because they *were* going to get back together—it would be as true partners. It pained him when he realized how blind he'd been to his selfishness, thinking only of himself and assuming wherever he wanted to go, she would follow.

What was left now was to continue trying to regain her trust and to prove to her he wasn't a total asshole. In other words, he had to convince her that there was no fighting fate.

"A drinking contest?" Rory blurted out to Jake. "What's impressive about that? There's no skill in it that I can see."

"You're wrong. There's skill in holding it down, mate."

"What about being steady on your feet? Which you weren't by the end of the darts match."

"That's just because I'd had a few whiskeys as well."

"So we're battling to see who pukes first."

"Drinking contests are a tried-and-true Irish tradition," Jake replied contemptuously. "Or have you forgotten that?"

"Yeah, it's tried-and-true—if you're a drunk or some teenage twit who wants to impress his friends. And what are you going to do if you win?" Rory asked. "Take her to McDonalds in Crosshaven? I hear they've got a bouncy castle."

"You're about as funny as a nuclear explosion, Rory. If I win—which I will—it's none of your business where I'll be taking her."

"You're right," Rory agreed, though the truth of it got under his skin.

Rory peered in the pub window. The place was jammed. Not packed: jammed. Bloody tourists. Rory knew their presence was boosting the dying economy, but weren't the locals entitled to one place they could call their own? The Oak was the most sacred institution in Ballycraig, or it had been. Now it felt like just another pub.

Rory pushed the door open slightly, which required asking a bunch of people to please move so they could get inside. The charmed circle didn't budge. He asked again. No movement. Time to raise his voice.

"I've asked you nicely twice," Rory said ominously. "Don't make me ask again."

Annoyed, they turned to see who was so ballsy to make such a statement. Then, seeing Rory, they were suddenly able to make room for him and Jake to enter.

"Go feck yourselves," Jake muttered under his breath.

"And twice on Sundays." Rory looked at Jake in astonishment. "This is lunacy."

"It could be that Leary is here. I mean, it's always packed, but this is mental."

Rory felt like Godzilla stamping to the bar, his size and build a natural deterrent to anyone who was stupid enough not to take two seconds of their life to let Rory and Jake pass.

Waiting for them was the Holy Trinity, Mr. Russell, and PJ Leary. Rory froze.

"You all know PJ, right?" said Old Jack, looking bored, as if it were a question he'd asked a million times. His eyes caught Rory's. "Seeing as you look like you're about to shit your pants, I'd venture a guess that (a) you're a big fan, and (b) you haven't met him."

PJ turned around, shaking Rory's hand. "Nice to finally meet you."

Think straight. "Beg pardon?"

"I know all about you. The Wild Hart used to be my watering hole, remember? I still get all the dirt and read the papers online. Sounds to me like you're breaking some heads out there on the ice."

"And breaking hearts here," Liam added with a glare.

"Well, I know about that, too, of course, but it's none of my business."

Rory licked his lips, hoping his voice didn't break. "All the guys on the team are big fans. Your books keep us from going mad on road trips."

Old Jack yawned. "Here comes the part where the fan casually asks, 'Are you working on another one?'"

"Shut your gob, Jack," said Bettina as she walked by.

"I'm trying to," PJ answered, even though Rory hadn't asked. "I've got a bit of writer's block right now. Some ancient Druids have come back to life, and I'm not quite sure what to do with them."

"I'd have them reanimate the Irish economy," said Liam.

"That *would* take magic," said PJ with a heavy sigh. He regarded Rory with interest. "So, which of my books is your favorite?"

"Uh." All the titles flew out of his head for a moment. "I liked . . . *The Swans of Sligo*."

PJ looked delighted. "That one was the most fun to write."

"Oh, and why's that?" Old Jack mocked. "Did they give you piles of cash?"

"He gets piles of cash for all of them," Teague put in bitterly.

"They don't *give* me piles of cash." PJ's expression was chilly. "I earn it."

Old Jack's expression remained sour as he looked at Rory. "You make a nice tidy wage for yourself, too, from what I hear."

"Like PJ, I earn it."

"Damn right he does," said PJ, backing him up. He regarded Rory with the solemnity Rory knew well from hard-core sports fans' faces. "I'm going to try to get to New York sometime this fall. Hopefully I'll be able to catch a few Blades games."

"Well, stop by the locker room if you do. The guys'll freak out."

"Christ help me, grown men 'freaking out' over some book," Old Jack muttered, waddling off to get drinks for Rory and Jake. Obviously, Jake had told him about the contest. When he returned, he plunked down four shots of Jameson in front of each of them. Rory assumed bets had been placed.

PJ suddenly looked animated as he snatched a pen from his jacket pocket and, grabbing a napkin, began scribbling on it, talking to himself out loud. "Thought: send reawakened Druids to do battle with Thor, who has stolen King Brian Boru's magic boots. If—"

"Time to shut your piehole, PJ," said Old Jack. "We
don't need to hear you talkin' your gobbledygook; now it's
time to move on to what really matters." He looked deadly
serious as he addressed Rory and Jake. "I want to see some
serious bending of elbows, lads." He turned his attention to
his watch, looking as if he were counting down the seconds
to the day of reckoning. People's faces were frozen in
expectation.

"Right!" Old Jack bellowed. "Showtime!"

One, two, three, four. "Down the ole hatch," as Rory's
gran always said. Rory hated doing drams. They made it
impossible to savor the whiskey, to roll it round your tongue
and let the taste sink in. Instead, it was just throw it to the
back of your throat and grab the next one. There was still
some pleasure as the liquid blazed its way down to your
guts, but not as much as there should be.

Four more. A long time ago, Rory had been able to put
it away on a regular basis. It was part of being a college
jock, a badge of manhood. Those days were long gone.
Very occasionally, if there was something major to cele-
brate with his teammates, he'd get tanked along with everyone else. But by and large, he wasn't a heavy drinker. He
couldn't do his job properly if he was.

The world around him began to shimmer and vibrate.
He swore he could see every frenzied particle of air everywhere he looked. Rubbery legs. Jake was still going at it,
shooting the drams down so fast Rory didn't know how he
didn't puke. Which was what he would do if he didn't
bow out.

"I'm done." He held up his hands in a gesture of surrender that threatened his balance.

"C'mon! You've got to have more man in ya than that!"
Old Jack goaded.

"I might, but my idea of a good time isn't puking my
guts up in the street."

"All right." Jack looked disappointed. "You're the winner, Jake." Jake kept pounding down whiskey. "Jake, you
won!" Jack bellowed.

Jake downed his final shot, wiping his mouth with the arm of his sleeve before pumping his fist in the air. "Yeah! That's how a tried-and-true man of Ballycraig drinks!" He surveyed the empty shot glasses in front of Rory with disdain. "Eight? You could only put away eight?"

"Yup."

"You used to be able to put that away when you were eighteen, boyo, no problem."

"Well, I'm not eighteen anymore, am I?" Rory retorted. "The last thing I need is to get pissed out of my skull, fall down, and break a bone. Or two. I'm a professional athlete, remember?"

"How can we forget," said Jack.

"Actually, if the reports from back home are right, Rory's making his mark in the league, just like PJ said," Liam revealed reluctantly.

"Who told you that? That softie journo brother of yours?" scoffed Jack.

Rory saw how quickly the anger flared in Liam's eyes.

"I wouldn't talk about him like that, if I were you," Liam warned. "Not unless you want me to hand you your fat bald head on a plate." He glanced at Rory begrudgingly. "Quinn said you're kicking some ass out there on the ice."

"I'm trying," said Rory, with humility. "Maybe we'll go out for a beer after a game next time you're in New York."

"Maybe," said Liam with disinterest, walking away.

"So now what?" Jack asked, collecting the shot glasses.

"What'ya mean?" Jake replied. Rory couldn't believe he wasn't swaying on his feet.

"Arm wrestling?" Teague asked eagerly.

"Don't be a dope," said Fergus Purcell.

"It's a legitimate form of competition!"

"Yeah, if you're eleven and rowing over a bag of sweeties."

The usuals erupted in laughter. Teague went to slide off his stool when Bettina called out, "I'll give you five pounds if you don't go boo-hooing home to your mam, and you sit here and take the ribbing like a man."

Teague repositioned his ass on "his" chair. "Done."

Rory, still feeling a bit light-headed, stood up. "I'm off."

"Where?" Jake asked.

"Home. Why would I want to stay?"

"True," said Jake, "now that all the world knows you're a pussy."

There was laughter, but it wasn't mean-spirited. Rory held back a smile. It was clear as day that the old man and the others were slowly beginning to soften toward him, for which he was glad. Most people deserved a second chance. And even though Rory wasn't most people, he deserved his shot as well. No one was going to stop him from getting his.

16

"This is a blast, isn't it?"

Jake was grinning happily as he positioned his club behind the golf ball and tapped it, where it went straight into Bono's mouth. He pulled out the tiny piece of paper from his back pocket, carefully marking down another win. "Your turn," he said to Erin with a bright smile. "I never thought miniature golf could be so much fun."

Erin smiled thinly and lined up for her putt. When she got word that Jake and Rory had had another contest, and that Jake had won, her gut reaction once again was fury. How dare they act like she had no feelings in the matter, like she was some trophy to be boasted about and owned? Then she realized she couldn't blame them completely: she could have told Rory to get stuffed after the first competition, but she hadn't, and she'd be the biggest liar in Ballycraig if she didn't admit to herself that a tiny part of her was enjoying their little tournament. She got pleasure from knowing being with Jake tonight had to be eating at Rory.

Still, it was all wrong somehow. She shouldn't be here,

giving Jake some kind of false hope where none existed. But fair was fair: it wouldn't be right for her to have gone to the fair with Rory and not come out tonight with Jake. It would have hurt and humiliated him. At least that's what she told herself.

She couldn't imagine where he was taking her when they started out toward Omeath in his car. Erin wanted the old Jake back, the one who was purely a mate.

The ride over was more awkward than it should have been considering how long they'd known each other. Jake kept trying to pull the conversation to Rory. Erin didn't say anything. She didn't want to carve Rory up. In fact, Jake's bad-mouthing him got on her nerves a bit, especially since they were now "mates" again.

"Go on," Jake urged, standing behind her. "Tap lightly and you can't miss Bono's gob. Trust me."

Erin did as instructed but missed by a mile. "Ah, it's all right," Jake said consolingly. "I'll bet you dollars to donuts you get it through Saint Patrick's miter, no problem."

An Irish-themed miniature golf course. It had to be Alec who told Jake about it. Or Old Jack. The place was filling fast. Tourists, mostly older, blue-haired, sensible shoes. Click, click, click. Cameras. Who would want to take pictures of a miniature golf course? Ah, to each his own.

Toward the end of the game, Erin's apathy morphed into annoyance. Jake was letting her win. "I know what you're doing, and I don't appreciate it."

"What?" said Jake, coming over all innocent.

"Deliberately playing like shite. I don't need to win. You're insulting me by doing that. I'm capable of winning fair and square, and if I don't win, it's no big deal."

"I just thought it might boost your confidence a bit."

"Why would you ever think my confidence needs boosting?"

"I heard your mam is being a bit more demanding these days."

Her jaw set. "I don't want to talk about that now."

"Erin, I'm sorry." Jake looked distressed. "I didn't mean

to upset you. You know that's the last thing I'd ever want
to do."

"Jake, it's not that big a deal. Honest."

"Are you sure?"

"Let it go. I'm serious. If you'd really upset me, I'd let
you know, all right?"

Jake relaxed. "Okay, yeah."

"C'mon, let's finish this up."

"Drink after?"

"Sure," said Erin, forcing herself not to hesitate. She might
not want to be here, but that didn't give her license to be rude.

* * *

It was a gorgeous evening, with a delicious breeze and the
beginnings of a perfect sunset, soft as the muted blues and
pinks on an artist's palate. One thing Ireland did have
going for it were the summer nights.

They got their drinks and sat down at one of the picnic
tables outside the Hare and Hound. Jake tapped his pint
glass against hers, the tinkling sound reminiscent of a tiny
bell.

"To the future," he said.

Erin parted her lips slightly, then closed them again.
"Yes."

Jake looked around. "Place is fairly hopping."

Erin just nodded.

Jake tore open a packet of crisps. "Did you notice the
real golf course? That's new as well. Omeath is really starting to build itself up."

"Mmmm."

"Why would you ever think of leaving Ballycraig when
you've got this?" he joked, but Erin knew he really wasn't.

"This isn't why I want to leave Ballycraig," Erin said
gently. "You know that."

Jake shook his head. "I still don't think you're thinking
this through, Erin. You've got a great life right under your
nose, but you refuse to see it because of your tunnel vision."

Erin put her palm to her forehead, more to keep her

brains from exploding than anything else. "Jake," she began softly, "we've had this discussion before and it always ends painfully, with me trying to explain my dreams to you, and you encouraging me to make the safe choice. I don't want the safe choice. I want the choice that's exhilarating."

"And how exactly do you plan to finance your 'exhilarating' choice?" Jake asked bitterly.

"That's really none of your business, but since you're a mate, I'll tell you: I'm using money saved up from the wedding."

Jake took a long pull off his beer. "You're making a big mistake." There was no mistaking the appeal in his voice. "You could learn to love me. If you set your mind to it."

Erin started to choke up. "We've been down this road. You're breaking my heart. You deserve someone who loves you for you, not someone you think would appreciate you with time."

"And what if your dream doesn't work out?"

"Then I'll figure out something else to do. But coming back here is not an option."

Jake looked hurt. "You really hate it here so much?"

"I don't hate it at all." Erin didn't know how much longer she could stand going round and round in circles. "I just want a different experience of life. You ever feel like you belong to a place, the way you feel about Ballycraig? Well, my heart feels it belongs somewhere else. I'm not sure where, exactly, but I'll know it when I see it. Ballycraig isn't my soul home."

"And would New York have been your 'soul home' if you'd married Rory? Mmm? What if it wasn't?"

"It's still a city," Erin contended. "And it wasn't like he'd play hockey forever." She plucked a crisp from the bag. "There's no point in talking about that now, anyway."

* * *

"Hey, superstar goalie. Where's your brain today?"

Rory tousled LJ's hair affectionately, waiting for an answer. LJ wasn't the sort to let his mind wander, especially when he was in goal. But twice the kid had had his head in the clouds. Rory hoped to hell he wasn't fighting nausea due to some putrid breakfast his sister had cobbled together.

"Dunno." The tried-and-true answer any child gives when the opposite was true.

"Ah, don't give me that line of bull. Believe me, I notice when one of our top players doesn't have his heart in it."

"It's nothin'," LJ insisted.

Rory shrugged and started to walk away, waiting for LJ's voice to ring out behind him. And it did.

"Wait!"

Rory walked back to him. "You know you can talk to me about anything, right?"

LJ looked uncertain.

"Anything on earth," Rory continued. "And I won't tell another living soul."

"Not even Erin?"

"What's Erin got to do with it?"

"She and Mam talk about you all the time. They think we can't hear because of the telly, but it's dead easy to creep to the doorway of the kitchen and listen in."

"That's not very polite, LJ," Rory admonished, even though he wanted to promise the kid anything if he gave Rory gory details. "Sometimes people can't help themselves," he added sympathetically. LJ looked relieved. Yes, his face said, that is exactly what it was.

"So, they talk about me, huh?" Rory felt like the alpha dog in a large pack.

"You and my da."

Rory deflated.

"And what do they say about him?"

"I don't know."

"Probably just stuff."

"Yeah. Stuff."

LJ was looking at the ground, creating figure eights in the dirt with the toe of his trainer.

"It must be a lot of stuff if it's crowding your mind that way."

LJ paused. "It is."

"I could try guessing if you want. Like a game. Would you like that?"

LJ nodded.

"Right." Rory rocked on his heels, hands intertwined behind his back, as if he were pondering a difficult question. "Does it have to do with . . . your mam?"

"Yes."

"Does it have to do with . . . something your dad said to your mam?"

LJ nodded.

"Is it to do with . . . the house?" A nod, yes.

"You kids?" Yes.

"Does it make your mam cry when she talks to Erin about it?"

"Yes," LJ said, getting teary. "But sometimes they yell at each other. Mam and Erin. But they always make up."

"What did your dad say to your mam? If you don't mind me asking?"

"That she's a fat whore and she was stupid if she thought she could ever do better than him. He said"—LJ stumbled—"he said he'd take us from her. Mam said that was the stupidest thing she'd ever heard; he hasn't given any money for us in ages."

"And where were you when this was happening?"

"Hiding in the downstairs loo with Oona."

"And what else?" Rory swallowed hard, pushing down his fury. "Has he ever hit your mam?"

"No. Mostly he just curses her and breaks up the furniture. Then he goes off and, a few days later, comes back. He and Mam make up. She tells Erin it's all an act, her making up with him. That when she gets a job, she'll boot him proper."

"That must be hard to hear."

LJ just shrugged.

"Sounds like your da isn't very nice to your mam."

"He's dead mean!" LJ cried. "I hate to see Mam cry." He paused. "Sometimes Da yells at Erin if she's there. He tells her to get out and she tells him she's going to call the garda. He just kinda laughs and he says she better watch her step."

Rory struggled to keep his rage in check. "Phew! That sure is a lot to carry around, LJ."

"I know!" He looked relieved to have spilled it all out.

"Now can I ask you one final question?"

LJ rolled his eyes. "Yes."

"Is your sister still making you those awful weird breakfasts?"

"Yes," LJ replied, making a horrible face.

"Right. Well, we'll see if we can't do something about that."

LJ looked grateful. "Thanks, Rory."

Rory smiled. "You ready to go back out there and be the next Iker Casillas?"

LJ nodded. His demeanor had altered completely during the course of their brief discussion. Rory couldn't imagine what it was like to walk around keeping all that bottled up inside. His own home life had been fairly well balanced.

Something had to be done.

17

Rory knew a setup when he saw one, and Erin was pulling a good one: today she'd asked him to pick her up at Sandra's rather than have her parents give her a lift up to Aislinn and Liam's farm for dinner. He was sure it was to do with their previous conversation, when she'd accused him of having no respect for her. He'd admitted it, but he had a feeling that it wasn't enough for Erin, that perhaps it was time for him to face the full wrath of Sandra.

Rory was in a pretty good mood as he pulled up in front of Sandra's house. But that was before he stepped out onto the street and heard the shouting through the open window.

"You fuckin' slag! I bet half those kids aren't even mine! I've a good mind to punch you into next week, you cow!"

Rory lurched for the doorknob. Locked. Sonofabitch. "Touch Sandra again and you're dead, you coward!"

Erin. Jesus Christ. Rory took a step back, then threw himself at the door shoulder first, bursting in on the sight of Larry giving Erin a good slap across the face while Sandra sat sobbing on the floor, fingers pressing into her split, swollen lip. Instinct took over.

Rory grabbed Larry, spun him around, and shoved him against the wall. "You fat piece of shit."

Larry bared his teeth like an animal. "Who the fuck do you think you are—"

Rory didn't let him finish. He drove his fist into Larry's face.

As Larry fell to the floor, Rory jerked his head around to Erin and Sandra. "Go upstairs! Look after the kids!" Sandra hesitated. "GO!"

Erin grabbed Sandra by the wrist, yanking her up the stairs. The stinging red color of Erin's face was fading, but there was still terror in her eyes, and it was his job to erase it.

Rory turned back to Larry in disgust. The rage and adrenaline pumping through him was even stronger than when he was fighting on the ice. This wasn't another player who'd crossed a line. This was a coward who hit women. Who hit Erin. Rory jerked Larry back up to his feet by the lapels of his jacket, headbutting him square in the face. "I suggest you get the fuck out of here. NOW."

Larry crumpled to the floor again, groaning as blood poured from the gash to his forehead and his nose.

Rory pulled him up a final time. "Get the fuck out of here. Now." Rory dragged Larry to the open door and shoved him through it, slamming it behind him.

"I'm gonna get the garda!" Larry bellowed drunkenly from the sidewalk.

"Yeah, you go ahead and do that," Rory replied sarcastically.

Rory slowly scrubbed his hands over his face, pulling himself back together. The last thing he wanted was Erin and Sandra tiptoeing back downstairs, only to see the rage that was still flying through him. He could hear the kids crying upstairs, and the yen to pummel Larry again rose up in his gut. He knew he had to get away or he'd chase the bastard down and beat him to death right there on the sidewalk. He didn't move, knowing he couldn't just leave. He took a deep breath and slowly walked into Sandra's kitchen to wash Larry's blood off his knuckles and forehead.

Rory stuck his hands under the tap and then splashed his face, the rage in him ebbing away in time with his heartbeat, which was slowly returning to normal.

"Rory?"

He turned around. Erin was standing in the kitchen doorway, her lips trembling while tears trickled down her face. Rory quickly dried his hands and face with a tea towel, then held his open arms out to her.

"It's all right," he told her when she came to him and started sobbing against his chest. "It's all right; he's gone."

Rory held her tightly, hoping that his embrace was enough to convey the words he wanted to speak: *I love you. I will always protect you.*

Eventually, Erin's shoulders stopped heaving, and she stepped out of his arms.

"Thank you," she said stiffly. "For going after Larry and—you know—comforting me right now."

"I want to do more than comfort you, believe me," Rory said fiercely. "I want to hold you in my arms until you believe nothing like that will ever happen again."

"I do believe it."

"What the hell happened?" Rory asked disgustedly.

"He was drunk," Erin said numbly, walking toward the freezer. "Very drunk. Things escalated and he punched her. Then I tried to intervene, and he slapped me."

"Yeah, I was there for that bit," Rory spat out angrily.

Despite crying things out, Erin still looked dazed as she brought an ice tray to the sink, twisting it so the cubes tumbled out into the basin. "Thank God you came."

"Bloody right, thank God."

Erin grabbed one of the other tea towels on the counter, putting some ice into it. "I've got to go to Sandra."

"Erin." Rory stayed her, putting a hand on her shoulder. "Round her and the kids up; I'll take them over to her mam's."

"She's already said she won't go to her mam's. She's staying put."

Rory was shocked. "What? Can't you talk some sense into her?"

"Haven't I been trying to for years?" Erin snapped, looking again on the verge of tears.

"I know, love," Rory said gently. "I just thought that now that he'd laid a hand on her, maybe she'd come to her senses."

Erin suddenly looked exhausted. "It doesn't work that way. I wish it did, but it doesn't."

Rory couldn't shake his incredulity. "She's just gonna stay here, then?"

Erin nodded painfully.

"Well, you're getting the hell out of here, that's for sure," Rory declared.

Erin looked at him like he was crazy. "I'm not leaving her!"

"The hell you're not!" Rory thundered. "If she wants to stay here and risk another pummeling, that's her business. But you're not staying for that drunken asshole to come back and lay a hand on you when I'm gone!"

Love blazed up in Erin's eyes for a split second, but just as quickly it sparked out. If he mentioned it to her later, she'd deny it. But he saw it.

"I'm not leaving her, Rory," Erin said wearily.

"This is insane." He racked his brains. "How about this? I pack the lot of you up and take you to Aislinn's farm for a few days. You know she and Liam wouldn't mind."

"I told you, Sandra won't go."

Rory felt a surge of anger. "There's loyalty and there's madness. This is madness."

"She's my best friend," Erin reiterated plaintively.

"And you're my—"

"Don't." Erin swiped at her eyes, sighing with resignation. "I best call Aislinn and Liam and let them know I'm not going to make it for dinner."

"No, you know what? I'll tell them. I was going to talk to Jake anyway when I dropped you off, so I'll take care of it."

Erin looked unsure for a minute. "All right." She ducked her head shyly, then kissed him softly on the lips. "Well . . . thanks."

Rory nodded, wanting more and knowing it wasn't the time to try to take it. He also wanted to throw her over his shoulder and just get her the hell out of here. Christ, he wanted to get them all out of here. But Erin wouldn't see it as him wanting to protect them all; she'd see it as his not respecting her crazy insistence on staying here with her masochistic friend.

Rory left the house reluctantly. His first stop would be the pub. He was going to let Old Jack know what happened, asking him and any of the regulars who were there to keep an eye out for Larry. And then he was going to speak to Jake.

* * *

Rory hadn't been up to Aislinn's farm since he'd dropped Erin off there after the fair. Distracted by her nearness, he hadn't really taken in the changes that had occurred since he was last in Ballycraig. He was disappointed to see that some of its natural beauty was marred by electrical fences and No Trespassing signs. The Leary-ites. He could never imagine having to live like that.

It was a little after five, and the fields were cleared for a dinner break, or at least that's what Rory assumed. During the short ride from town, his adrenaline eased, but his anger grew. He took a deep breath and rang the bell. Aislinn opened the door.

"You have got to be joking me. What'cha want? A good beating from Liam?"

"I'm here to see Jake. And to tell you Erin can't make it."

Aislinn gave him the evil eye. "And why would that be?"

"Sandra and Larry had a dustup and Erin doesn't want to leave her alone." He didn't think he should give any more details.

He peered past Aislinn. "So is Jake about?"

"Let me go check and see if he wants to see *you*."

Tough nut. Always had been. She'd scared the hell out

of weaker men for years, but she'd never scared him. He'd always sensed her brusqueness was just a cover for deep emotional pain. He was glad she'd finally found happiness. Christ knew she deserved it.

"C'mon in!" Aislinn shouted. Rory slipped out of his muddy trainers and went to the kitchen. Jake was at the table with Alec. Liam was there, too. Aislinn was at the kettle. He was going to have to play nice for a few minutes and make polite conversation.

"Take that hat off," snapped Liam.

That was fast. "What?"

He gestured at the baseball cap on Rory's head. "The Yankees? This is a Mets family."

Rory took off the hat. "I bet you like the Islanders, too."

Liam turned to his wife. "Can you believe this shit?"

Aislinn looked at her husband questioningly. "You mates now?"

"What's up?" Jake interjected.

Alec was glaring at Rory from across the table. It was a useless gesture, but if it made the dullard feel as if he were somehow protecting Jake, Rory was willing to give him his macho moment.

Aislinn put a cup of tea down in front of him.

"Laced with arsenic, is it?" Rory asked.

"Worse. I laced it with guilt. And humility."

"Two flavors I'm very familiar with."

"Give over," Jake sneered.

Rory was unperturbed. "Ask Erin."

Jake looked ticked off, but before it developed into a pissing match, Aislinn was on it.

"None of this rubbish in my kitchen. Alec, come to the barn with me, we've to finish the dipping. As for you"—her expression was affectionate as she put an arm around Liam's neck in a light choke hold—"I'll try to make it down tonight if I can. Depends on how tired I am."

"Same old story," Liam teased. "I should get down there now, actually." He threw Jake a miserable look. "Bettina's still moaning about the hole in Vin Diesel's eye."

"Talk to Mr. Hockey Star here," Jake said sourly. "He said he could get one quick smart."

"You told me you'd take care of it," Rory pointed out.

"Well, I'm busier than I thought," Jake muttered. "So if you could call your mate, I'd be grateful."

"No problem."

"Must be nice to be so powerful."

"It doesn't take much power to get a Vin Diesel photo."

"And on that note," said Aislinn, "we're all on our way."

She, Alec, and Liam took leave of the kitchen, but not before Liam got another shot in at Rory. "The Yankees. Unbelievable."

Rory just smiled.

Now that everyone else was gone, Jake made a big show of yawning. "What's up, Rory? You want to go down to the pub, hoist a few, and get your ass kicked again?"

"Actually, I am here to talk about an ass kicking of another sort."

"What's up?"

"Feckin' Larry Joyce."

Jake groaned. "What about him?"

"Has Sandra never talked to you about any of the shit going on at her house?"

"No. She only talks to Erin. But everyone knows what's up."

"I went over there earlier to pick up Erin to bring her here," Rory started.

"Chauffeur duty?"

"Yeah, and there was a god-awful goings-on. Larry was off his head. I walked in just in time to see him slap Erin across the face. Sandra was on the floor crying; she'd already taken one to the nose."

Jake looked incensed. "He hit them both?"

"That's what I just said," Rory reiterated sharply, the anger in him rising again.

Jake must have sensed the reason for Rory's testy response, because he let it go.

"I roughed Larry up a bit and told him to get the hell out.

But Sandra won't leave, the daft thing. And Erin won't leave Sandra alone there with the kids. I've asked Old Jack to keep an eye out for him, but that's not a permanent solution."

"Fuck, no." Jake snorted. "Should we just kill him?"

"Don't be stupid. No, I thought we could have a nice chat with him, you know? Tell him how much we'd hate for the garda to find out about the little side business he and his brother are running."

"Well, if it's just going to be a chat, I don't know why you need me there."

"I need you there so he knows he can't just wait things out until I go back to the States."

Jake mulled this over. "True. Right. Let's do it."

"I knew you'd agree."

"I haven't seen the bastard in ages."

"Oh, he's a sight," Rory said, unable to hide his revulsion. "He's fat as Father Christmas and he still has that horrible rattling cough. He couldn't even walk the small hill to his brother's place without wheezin' and sweatin' like a man on death row. Death on two legs, that one is."

Jake turned circumspect, tapping his index finger against the tea saucer. "How're San's kids?"

"They're great, but their home life is shit, same as it's always been."

Jake drained his tea. "I could never understand what she saw in him, anyway."

"Well, you wouldn't give her the time of day."

Jake scowled. "What?"

"Don't play like you don't know. She had it bad for you all through school. But you didn't even see it, because you were too busy having a crush on Erin."

"You're pulling this out of your ass, mate. Seriously."

"Guess Erin was making it up all that time." The incredulous look on Jake's face made Rory laugh. "Christ, I can't believe what a thicko you are."

"Fuck off out of it, Rory. You're pulling my tits on this one."

"Ask Erin."

Jake looked skeptical. "She goes from a crush on me to getting knocked up by Larry Joyce? Talk about doing a one-eighty."

"Yeah, well, sometimes people make bad choices. You know San. She's never believed she deserves better, with that mother of hers—"

"What a nutter," Jake agreed.

"You ask me, getting knocked up was her way to get out of that mad house. Eight kids, and her watching them half the time."

Jake narrowed his eyes. "You better not be blaming me for the path she took."

"Don't be an arsehole. I'm just sayin' things could have been different for her if you weren't so busy staring at Erin's tits."

"Fuck off, Rory."

Rory ignored him. "You wanna do this or not?"

"'Course I do."

"Well, then, we'll set a time to do it." He paused. "There's just one thing."

"There's always just one thing with you, Rory."

"We don't boast about it. Let everyone come up with their own reasons why that loser pulled a runner. There's no need for people to know we had anything to do with it."

"Yeah, yeah, yeah," Jake replied, beginning to chafe.

"Boring you, am I?"

"No, I have to get back to work. Some of us do have to do that, you know?"

"As a matter of fact, I do know," Rory fired back. "And so do you."

"You look like an arse in that baseball cap, you know."

"Ta, Jake." Rory stood. "I'll ring you when I know the lay of the land."

"And I'll ring you when I've figured out the next competition."

Rory groaned. "Give it up, mate. It's getting sad."

"You're the one who couldn't hold his drink."

"Right, fine, if it'll stop you harping like a nagging old woman, one more contest. One." He shook his head. "I don't know why we're even bothering with this. It's clear she doesn't want you."

Jake laughed loudly. "Oh, and she wants to be with you, does she? One stuffed animal won at the fair and she's all for bearing your children? Watch you don't trip over that ego of yours and break your neck, Rory."

"I'll do that." Rory went out the front door, Jake out the back. Him and Jake taking care of the Larry problem. It just might be the way to mend things.

18

Two nights later, Rory was buzzing with adrenaline as he and Jake went to "chat" with Larry.

Rory knew from Erin that Larry was parking his fat arse in front of his brother Lance's TV. Jake learned from Bettina that it was definitely true that the two brothers were dealing dope from the house. Larry was there most nights, since Lance held down an actual job as a night watchman at the mall in Moneygall.

Rory and Jake parked at the head of the narrow street and then quietly strolled up to Lance's two-up, two-down, identical to every other house on the road. They knew someone was there, the flickering kaleidoscope of colors from a TV lighting up the lace-curtained windows like a blaze. Rory peeked through the flimsy lace. "He's there."

Jake rang the bell. No answer. Again. No answer. Again. But this time a nasty voice from inside boomed, "Feck off!" Rory and Jake looked at one another and kicked the door in.

"What the fuck?"

Presented with two large men looking angry, Larry put

his hands up immediately. "Take whatever you want. Seriously. I'll even show you where the shit is. Just don't kill me."

"No one's here to kill you," said Rory in a voice meant to soothe a child. "Although I should have when I had the chance."

Larry started up out of his chair, but Rory shoved him down. "You're sitting for this one."

"Fuck you."

"I suggest you do what Rory says," said Jake, nodding his head approvingly as he inspected the nasty cut on Larry's forehead, a souvenir from when Rory had headbutted him.

Larry muttered a few indistinct curses beneath his breath, but he stayed put on the chair.

Rory stood directly in front of him, arms folded at his chest. He towered over the sickening coward, intimidating him, which was just the way he wanted it.

"Here's how it's going to go: you're going to get the hell out of Ballycraig."

"Mind your own feckin'—"

Rory grabbed his face. "Shut up." He released him with a shove.

"As I was saying," Rory continued congenially, "you're outta here. Sandra is going to get a protection order. The school is going to get a protection order. If you ever go near her, the kids, or Erin again, they're gonna find your body in the Dumpster behind the Oak, mate."

Larry gave a phlegmy laugh. "You threatenin' me? The minute you leave here, I'm calling the garda."

"I thought you did that last time," Rory taunted.

"I know people in the garda," Larry continued, trying to sound menacing.

Rory laughed in his face. "I bet you do, arsehole. How many times have they nicked you for petty stealing? Drunk and disorderly conduct? Eh? We're not fucking about here, Larry," Rory said, stone-cold serious. "You disappear by morning or we drop a dime on you about your and Lance's little sideline."

Larry stared up at them stupidly. "Drop a dime?"

"We'll tell the garda you're dealing drugs out of this place," Jake said with exasperation. "Got it?"

Larry nodded, glaring.

"No." Rory grabbed him by the collar. "We want to hear you say you've got it."

"I've got it," Larry muttered.

Rory released him with a shove. "Good. Glad we're clear." He turned to Jake. "We done?"

"One more thing. Think on this," Jake said to Larry, his smile glittering with malice. "I've more brothers than you've got brain cells, so don't even think of trying to pull something stupid. They'll hunt you down like a dog. I'd leave Ballycraig as soon as possible if I were you."

Larry's eyes were beady with hatred, but he kept his yap shut.

Rory turned to Jake. "We ready?"

"I think so."

"Have a nice life, you piece of shit," Rory sneered, then spat on the floor. Jake did the same. No more words were needed. As they strolled out of there, Rory was confident about two things: one was that Larry was leaving and Sandra, her kids, and Erin were safe; the other was that he and Jake were solid. Two victories down, one to go. He was going to score a hat trick if it killed him.

19

Erin had finished tidying up the dining room at the B and B when someone leaned hard on the front door buzzer. Maybe Mr. Russell had locked himself out again. It had been happening with alarming frequency. Erin put down the dust rag in her hand and opened the door. There was Sandra, looking like a wild-eyed thing.

Erin pulled her inside. "What's the matter! Did that bastard come back? Is it one of the kids?"

Sandra looked around, agitated. "Can we talk?"

"You even have to ask?" Erin could feel her stomach begin to shrink into a cold, hard stone as she led Sandra into the kitchen. Bloody Larry. She knew he'd weasel his way back into the house. That jerk could talk the Queen into giving him the crown jewels.

"Sit, honey."

Sandra sank into her chair like a sandbag, limply holding out a crumpled piece of paper to Erin. In childish scrawl, it read:

Sandra,

> *I'm sorry for what happened.*
> *I think it's best I go.*
> *I love you and always will.*

> *Your Larry*

Erin folded it neatly and handed it back to her friend. *Finally,* she thought.

"You've got to talk to Rory," Sandra said frantically.

"Whatever for?"

"I'm sure this has to do with him giving Larry what for in the living room. He's chased him off."

"Good." Erin moved to put the kettle on, but the sound of Sandra's wail put a stop to that.

"Ssh," Erin hushed, closing the kitchen door. "There are guests here, remember? All we need is tourists thinking a banshee lives here, and my folks will lose a boatload of business."

"I'm sorry." Sandra's lower lip was quivering.

"It's okay. You can cry. Just keep it down a bit."

"This is all Rory's doing," she accused.

"I doubt that," Erin said tersely, even though her gut told her otherwise. "Rory might have been the one to set the wheels in motion by defending us, but you and I both know Larry was going to pull a runner sooner or later. I just wish it had been sooner."

Sandra was staring vacantly out the back window. *She thinks her life is over,* Erin thought. *But really, it was just beginning.* She'd realize that eventually.

Erin poured the tea and grabbed a box of Jacob's Cream Crackers from the cabinet. It was just San, no need to put them on the plate.

"Right," Erin said, tearing open the cellophane with her teeth. "Tell me what happened."

"I woke up before the kids the way I usually do, right, to make their breakfast. And I'm coming down the stairs, and this white envelope was on the floor that someone had pushed through the letter box. My first thought was, 'Oh crap, don't let it be from the council saying they're gonna turn the water off.' My heart was in my throat, Erin. I swear to God.

"So I picked it up, thinking, 'What the—' And I opened it"—her eyes started brimming again—"and there it was, the note from Larry." Tears ran freely down her cheeks.

"And there's no part of you that's glad he's not going to come round anymore and terrorize you and your kids?"

Sandra wasn't hearing her. "You have to find out what Rory said to him when we were upstairs," she pleaded.

"What does it matter?" Erin was about to tear her own hair out by the roots. "We don't know where he's gone, and even if we did, I would never speak to you again if you went chasing after him. I mean that. You should be thanking Rory! I don't even want to think about what could have happened if Rory hadn't walked in."

Sandra looked distraught. "What am I gonna tell the kids?"

"Sandra, they know he hit you. They're not idiots."

"He's still their father."

Erin grit her teeth. "Fine. Tell them he's found work somewhere."

"Work? Not bloody likely."

"You know, there are some positives to this," Erin said cautiously.

Sandra scowled at her. "Oh, really? What's that?"

"Well, for one thing, you were thinking about getting away from him anyway, taking classes and all that. But he's gone and done it for you. And you don't have to worry anymore about him coming home drunk, or not coming home at all. Or *hitting* you. Or belittling you in front of the kids and chucking furniture about. Or trying to win the kids' affection with iPhones."

"Wonder how he managed to afford those," Sandra muttered.

"You know how: either he stole them like we thought, or

he bought them with drug money. Things can only go up from here, love."

Sandra burst into tears again. "But I love him! What am I going to do without him?"

Erin lost her temper. "San, I'm trying to be as supportive as I can, but you seem to have forgotten that Larry hit me, too! Who would he be hitting next if he stuck around? Your kids?"

Sandra's voice trembled. "I'm so sorry he did that, Erin."

"It's not your fault. But if you really give a damn about your family and friends, you'll set your sights on building a good life for you and your kids without that prick."

"I'm just scared," Sandra whispered.

Erin brushed a tear from her friend's cheek. "Scared of what, love?"

"Scared of happiness. I don't know how to be happy."

"Yes, you do. You've just forgotten how. I'll help you figure it out, okay?"

Sandra looked at her pitifully. "Promise?"

"Promise. Cross my heart and hope to die."

"Stick a needle in my eye."

"If I die before I wake."

"Ask the Lord my soul to take."

They'd been saying this to each other since they were kids, and saying it now helped lighten the mood.

"See, it's a little better already, isn't it?"

Sandra nodded wearily. "It always is, girl. I don't know what I'd do without you."

* * *

A few days after Larry Joyce disappeared, Jake rang Rory up, asking if he could stop by after supper. Rory was surprised, but happy. He'd had the feeling that handling the Larry situation together wasn't just about the two of them making sure the wanker never terrorized his family again; it was a way for them to bond, despite their competition for Erin's attention.

His gran was bustling around the kitchen as if Leonardo DiCaprio, her favorite actor, were coming over.

"Gran, it's just Jake, all right? You don't have to make sure there are three types of biscuits on the table. Jake'll eat whatever you put in front of him."

"It's my house and I'll do what I feel is proper."

"All right, all right."

Rory joined her at the kitchen counter, tearing open a pack of McVitie's Dark Chocolate Digestives. "I suppose you want these on a plate."

"Take a wild stab at the answer, son."

There was a knock at the back kitchen door and then Jake came in. "Hiya, Gran."

"Jake! If it's not the man himself. What're you doing, knocking on the door? You're family; you can come and go as you please."

Jake smiled and gave her a big hug. "It's good to see you." He looked sheepish. "I mean, visiting and all."

"I'm glad you're here," said Gran. Rory waited for her to get a little dig in at him, but none came.

"Now," she said, face glowing. "We've got digestives, shortbread, scones, and cream crackers, so don't be shy."

Jake looked over her head at Rory in amusement. "I guarantee that a good lot will disappear, believe me."

"I've got Barry's or Lyons for tea."

"Barry's."

"There's a good lad."

Jake had always been good at chatting with Rory's gran, which was no surprise: she'd known him since he was five. When the tea was ready to be served, his gran poured three cups and Rory brought the big plate of biscuits to the table.

"There you are." She looked at Rory, the tiny tea cup in her hand trembling a little from age. "If you need me to break ya apart before you crack each other's heads open and sawdust goes tumbling to the floor, just give me a shout. I'll be in the other room watching the telly."

Rory gave her the thumbs-up. "Got it."

His gran shot him a look of warning. Rory knew that

look: *act like a jackass and you'll be getting an earful from me, mister.* His ears should have been elephant-sized by now, that's how many earfuls she'd subjected him to over the years.

He sat down opposite Jake. It didn't feel weird so much as formal.

"I feel like we're two mafia dons at a sit-down."

Jake smiled at that as he reached for a digestive biscuit. "I suppose it is a sit-down, in a way."

"Is it? You've got your brothers stationed outside the door to burst in at any moment?"

"If I asked them to, they would."

"I know." Rory took a big gulp of tea. "C'mon, mate. What's eatin' at you?"

Jake let out a groan. "Threatenin' Larry like that."

"What?"

"I keep waiting to feel guilty, interfering in San's life that way without her knowing, but I don't."

"'Course you don't. The fecker deserved our threats, and more. If you ask me, he's lucky we didn't beat him within an inch of his life."

"Yeah, I know." Jake mulled this over as he dipped his biscuit in the tea. "The thing is, Rory, it sort of made me feel like we were brothers again, you know?"

"I feel the same way."

"I still hate your bloody guts, mind you. But now you've come back for a bit, I can see you know you ballsed it all up with Erin. I figure I can hate your guts but still be your mate. That's how I feel about my brothers, after all."

"I know I fucked up. But you can see I'm trying to make things right."

"I know. There's just one thing more to get straight between us: Erin."

Rory regarded him warily. "What about her?"

"Much as I would like it to be otherwise, I know I don't have a piss chance in hell of winning her. Not only does she want the opposite of everything I do in life, but she's still in love with you."

Rory went very still. "Why'd ya say that?"

"Cut the fake humility, you pompous twit. You know she is. I think there's a difference between a good life and a happy life. And what'll make Erin happy is getting out of Ballycraig and being with you."

"You're right."

"You wanker! Fake some humility just to make yourself a tolerable mate, would ya?"

Rory was trying to come up with something snappy to say. But he was at a loss, and so he resorted to what he and Jake always fell back on at times of emotion.

"Fuck you, you stupid shite, you just told me to cut the fake humility," he said, grinning broadly.

"And fuck you, too, you gobshite," Jake responded reflexively, breaking into a laugh.

He bit into a biscuit. "She's yours," he admitted. "Always had been, always will be. But I swear on my mother's grave, if she takes you back and you mess her around, I will hunt you down like a dog, Rory, and beat you within an inch of your life."

"I know." He grabbed a shortbread from the plate. "Mates?"

"Mates."

Jake turned gloomy as he took a bite of his biscuit. "It's back to online dating for me, I guess."

Rory frowned. "What are you on about?"

"In case you haven't noticed, there's not a huge bevy of girls to choose from here."

"You're a moron."

"What? Who's here? Old Grace Finnegan? Those two batty twins in Crosshaven who go everywhere together?"

"What about Sandra?"

"Oh, right. Yeah. Sandra. Are you out of your fuckin' mind? For starters, she's Sandra."

"What the hell does that mean? She's your mate. You like her."

"I know. But she's got a lot of baggage. And a house full of kids."

"You've always said you wanted some."

"Yeah, my own, not prefab." Jake shook his head in disbelief. "Sandra."

"Sorry. I just thought: good-looking woman, you've known her for ages, happy living in Ballycraig, and all that."

"Appreciate the thought, mate, but it's back to tapping the keyboard for me, at least till the right one comes along."

20

Sitting in the small caf in Crosshaven, Erin tucked her cell away in her bag, elated. She'd just gotten off the phone with Diana Everett, who'd accepted the job at the B and B. Diana would definitely be able to hold her own against Erin's mother. The problem would be the rubbish her mother would heap on her, not Diana. It wouldn't matter that she'd taken advantage of Erin's good nature for months now. She wouldn't be able to see past Erin's "betrayal," interviewing prospective employees behind her back. Erin had warned her, and her mother hadn't wanted to listen. Well, she had no choice but to listen now.

Erin had taken the bus into Crosshaven because she was in no mood to study at home. Her mother was in one of her manic spells, which was likely to result in multiple unwanted knocks on Erin's door. Normally it would be Rory's "job" to drive her, but she knew he was taking his gran for a checkup with Dr. Laurie. She almost enjoyed the bus ride, being able to read or eavesdrop if she wanted. It almost made her wish she'd hung on to her old job at the jewelry store. Almost.

Nursing her second cup of tea at the caf, she opened her laptop to do some studying for one of her final exams. She'd handed in what she thought was a well-written final paper on the sculptor Louise Nevelson. Nevelson had been flamboyant, self-confident, and brave in a way Erin dreamed of being. Her work challenged Erin, which was one of the things she liked about it. Erin had never been challenged in school.

Erin still found herself in the grip of panic sometimes. Art history: what a stupid, useless degree to get. As if there were loads of jobs for art historians out there. She'd almost chucked it all in except that one night, she and Sandra had ordered in Chinese, and when Erin cracked open her fortune cookie, the tiny slip of paper inside said, "Do what you love and the rest will follow." Ridiculous as it was, Erin took it as a sign, especially when the first song she heard on Pandora the next morning was Tom Petty's "Runnin' Down a Dream." Maybe the universe was trying to tell her something.

Erin wasn't sure how long she sat absorbed in her studying. All she knew was that the sight of Rory strolling through the door caught her completely by surprise.

"What are you doing here?"

"Picking you up."

"How did you even know I was here?"

Rory tapped the side of his head. "Radar."

Erin rolled her eyes. "How's your gran?"

Rory grimaced. "Fit as a fiddle, if a fiddle had cataracts and was losing its hearing."

"Oh, no." Erin squelched the instinct to reach out and squeeze his hand in a gesture of consolation.

"Ah, it's not that bad." Erin knew he was minimizing things. "She'll get cataract surgery and a hearing aid, and she'll be good as new. At least now I know she won't be asking 'WHAT?' every two minutes. It's beginning to drive me spare."

Erin laughed.

"I've always loved your laugh," Rory confessed with a

big smile. "Like crystal running down a . . . oh, feck it, you know I'm not a poet."

"You certainly aren't." Erin steered the conversation away from herself. "How long is she going to have to wait, your gran?"

"For what?"

"Her operation and her hearing aid."

"She's not waiting," Rory replied indignantly. "I'm bringing her to private doctors in Dublin. None of this National Health runaround."

"Good idea," Erin said, remembering how her brother had once had to wait two years for his elective hernia operation. She could still see Brian walking around with his hand on his abdomen, looking like he was trying to hold his guts in.

Rory picked up one of the laminated menus on the table and started looking it over. That's when Erin noticed the knuckles of his right hand were still scraped. The pieces came together in a flash.

"You ran Larry out of town, didn't you?"

Rory smiled slyly. "Maybe so."

"Don't come over coy. I know you did. He'd never leave otherwise."

"Jake and I had a little chat with him, yeah."

"'Chat'?"

"We didn't throttle him, if that's what you're worried about. We just conveyed to him that if he enjoyed breathing, he might want to leave town for good."

"Why was it you and Jake took care of it? Not just you?"

"We both agreed he had it coming. Plus, we didn't want the weasel thinking he could sneak back into Ballycraig once I went back to New York."

"I don't know whether to be appalled or impressed."

"I'd say 'impressed.'" Rory laughed delightedly. "Look at you. Your eyes are so wide with wonder you look like a kid who's just seen Father Christmas."

"I feel like I have."

"You can't go telling Sandra."

"She suspects it already, but even so, why would I ever do that?"

"How's she doing?"

"Holding up," Erin replied matter-of-factly, fiddling with an empty sugar packet on the table. "Saying she loves him and wondering how she's going to face life without him."

Rory cocked his head inquisitively. "And who do you love?" He covered his eyes with his palm. "Wait, wait, I think I know."

"Shut your gob."

Rory pulled his hand away. "Why? Because my gob speaks the truth?"

"Your gob speaks a load of rubbish."

Rory rose and leaned across the table, rubbing his nose against hers. "You're almost there," he whispered. "I can feel it."

Erin pushed him back down into his seat. "You're so annoying."

"I know. But seeing as how I saved you and your best friend, I think the least you can do is give me a little kiss."

Erin leaned over, aiming for his cheek, but Rory pushed his chair back so he was out of range. "Oh, no, no, no. Not one of those chaste Catholic school kisses." He smiled wickedly. "I'm talkin' a real kiss."

"Yeah, you've mentioned that already." Erin knew she wasn't going to win this one. *Well, it's nothing,* she thought, a quick skim of her mouth over his and she'd be done. She paid her bill. Rory was waiting for her at the caf door, looking all smug as he held it open for her. Twit.

"Let's just get this over with, shall we?" Erin said briskly as she started up the street.

Rory made a serious face. "Oh. I agree completely. It's a horrible chore. The sooner it's done, the better."

Halfway down the street, Erin realized she had no idea where she was heading to. Well, Rory Brady would just have to forget about his kiss.

He pointed across the street at a fish and chips shop.

"Maybe they'll let us use their basement. Nothing more romantic than locking lips surrounded by bushels of spuds."

"You're an idiot."

Rory shook his head disappointedly. "I can't believe you've forgotten."

"Forgotten what?"

"Come on."

He took Erin's hand, twining his fingers through hers. He'd always been a good hand-holder, Rory, his grip firm and protective.

It all started coming back to Erin as they approached the jewelry store where she used to work. The alley. The long, narrow, brick alley between the jewelry store and the tobacconists next door. She couldn't count the number of times they'd snogged there, especially when they were teens.

"Remember now, do you?" Rory asked, leading her down the alley.

He stopped at the end, casually leaning up against the wall with his hands deep in the front pockets of his faded jeans like he was some bad boy, his expression one of cool composure.

"You think you're some kind of rock star, don't you?" Erin's sarcasm was purely a cover for the exquisite anticipation sparking inside her.

"C'mere."

Rory held out his hand. Erin hesitated, pretending the last thing she wanted was to be in his arms but was somehow managing to force herself. She squirmed. He was holding her too tight, then not tight enough. "I don't know what you think you're doing," she said with a huff. "Because if you think you're going to get anything beyond a simple—"

Her sentence was swallowed up by a rough kiss. It was familiar, yet gloriously new. Erin hadn't realized she'd parted her lips until Rory's tongue touched hers. She knew this taste. The technique. And then, where a few seconds ago her senses had been adrift, she realized what she was doing and who she was doing it with, and jerked her mouth from his.

"There," she said, trying to regain the upper hand. "You got your kiss, now let's go back to Ballycraig."

Rory looked genuinely bemused. "What are you so afraid of?"

"Do you really need to ask that?"

"Yeah. I'm thick. Tell me."

Erin tapped her chin thoughtfully. "Maybe, just maybe, I'm afraid of getting my teeth kicked in again. Just maybe, mind."

"How long do you want me to keep groveling? Forever? Because if that's what you want, so help me God, I will."

"Don't. This has been madness, me getting rides from you. What was I thinking?"

She made her way back onto the sidewalk, tears stinging her eyes. What must he think of her? Stupid Erin, so-easy-to-manipulate Erin.

"Where're you going?" Rory followed, keeping pace with her. It felt like a bad déjà vu.

"Where'd ya think? To catch the bus."

Rory groaned. "Don't be ridiculous. I swear I'll never touch you again, all right? Or put you in a position where you have to kiss me. Okay?"

Erin wasn't buying it. "Really."

"Yeah."

"Let's just forget this happened."

Rory looked angry. "You know what, Erin? I'm tired of pretending things never happened. Things are happening, and for a reason, too. You still love me. But here you are, wasting all this precious time we could be together."

Erin turned on him. "Until when? When you leave at the end of the summer and dump me?"

Rory's whole body was tense with frustration. "I'm not going to dump you. I love you. I didn't come back here for my gran. You know that. Everyone knows that. I came back here for you. Everyone deserves a second chance, don't you think?"

"You're doing my head in, Rory. Truly."

"Isn't that a sign you care?"

"You have to back off," Erin said testily. "I need to think."

"Of course."

She wasn't looking at him, but she could feel his elation: it felt like bright, golden beams directed right at her. "I'm going to take the bus back to Ballycraig. Like I said, I need space right now. To breathe. You've no need to wait with me."

"I understand."

He walked her over to the bus stop, then gave her one of those chaste Catholic school kisses he'd mocked earlier. She watched him go, a little bounce in his step despite the chilly drizzle that was starting to fall. So sure of himself. Cocky bastard. *Don't put the cart before the horse, mister,* Erin thought.

21

Erin had the entire bus ride back to Ballycraig to think about Rory. She tried puzzling it out as if it were a math equation. *You like Rory's kiss, ergo you still like Rory. You gab with him like you're old pals, ergo you still like Rory. You sort of like being fought over, ergo you still care about Rory, because you always want him to win. You're afraid of letting your heart loose again, because you live in mortal terror Rory will crack it into a million tiny bits, ergo he affects you, ergo you still love him, ergo goddamn ergo.*

Erin tried to imagine what it would feel like taking him back. Would it feel like coming home, or would it feel like stepping off a cliff?

It was close to five when she got home. Five meant doing the laundry and making up the beds. But not tonight.

"Well, look what the cat's dragged in," her mother said, not without affection, when Erin walked into the kitchen. "And where have you been, if your own mother is allowed to ask?"

"In Crosshaven. I found the woman who's going to replace me. Her name's Diana Everett and she's got loads of experience. I think you'll like her."

The stillness was killing. Erin had never seen someone's face turn so red so fast. Red as a fire truck, it was, with the purple veins faintly pulsing in her mother's temples taking the place of the flashing lights. *Well, I warned her.*

Her mother seemed to be cemented to the spot beside the open dishwasher. "Mam?"

"How dare you? How bloody dare you?"

Erin's hackles went up as soon as her mother said "bloody." Her mother rarely, if ever, cursed.

"I told you ages ago I wasn't going to be here for good," Erin pointed out calmly. "I also told you that if you didn't start interviewing people yourself, I would do it."

"You've no right!"

"And you've no right to keep me on here months and months! I've been a good sport about this! No—more than a good sport! I've been a wimp. So don't start giving me the old rubbish about loyalty! Most parents would want their children to go out into the world and do what makes them happy."

"I just want to protect you, Erin!"

"Protect me or hinder me?" Erin took a deep, frustrated breath. "Look, just because I want to go out and do things doesn't mean I don't love you or that I'll never come home. That's silly."

Her mother looked smug. "Have you figured out yet where exactly it is you're going?"

"Yes. Away. You have to be willing to take chances in life."

"I'm all for taking chances—"

"You aren't—"

"If you've got a sensible plan in place."

"I do have a plan."

"What's that?"

"I'm finishing up my degree online."

"Online?"

"Yeah, on the computer. The one I'd been doing in bits and pieces. That's what I've been doing upstairs: studying. Art history."

"Jesus, Mary, and Joseph, I thought you'd knocked that thought out of your head," her mother said, looking appalled.

"Why would I do that?"

"I just thought it was something you were doing to keep yourself occupied while Rory wasn't here. That once you got married, you'd drop the whole thing."

"I did. For a while. But when I was right in the head again, I thought: 'I want to do it, and I need to do it, so I'm doing it.'"

"And there's hundreds of jobs waiting out there for you, sure," her mother drawled.

"No," Erin replied with a defiant tilt of the chin. "But I'll work till I find one."

"Doing what?"

"I'll work at a B and B," she said dryly. "God knows I've got more than enough experience."

"And when will you be leaving to start this mad idea of yours?"

"I don't know exactly."

"But until then—"

"Until then, you'll be meeting Diana Everett on Thursday. I'm going to show her the ropes Thursday, Friday, and Saturday. She can start next Monday. I told her she'll have Sundays off, as is customary. I also asked around to find out what a decent wage is, and that's what you'll be paying her."

Her mother was flabbergasted. "You can't do this."

"Then you find someone else between now and Thursday," Erin replied with a shrug. She walked out of the kitchen, her heart rapping against her ribs. There. She'd done it. And with any luck, it wouldn't be undone. But with her mother, you never knew.

* * *

It had been a dead ballsy thing to do. Then again, Rory had never lacked for balls.

The lip-lock in the alley with Erin left him frustrated. Two steps forward, one step back. *More like four steps back,* he thought ruefully. He knew she still cared. To even say to him, "I need space," proved that. It was a helluva long way from, "Leave me alone, Rory." One of the hard things about it was the time being wasted. If they got back together now, they could enjoy the rest of the summer together. If they hadn't mended things by the time he had to go back to New York, he didn't know what the hell he'd do. The only person he could think of to help him out was Sandra. If that wasn't a testament to his desperation, nothing was.

Standing at Sandra's door, he was happy to find himself face-to-face with LJ, even if LJ did look a bit apprehensive.

"Hey, mate. How's it going?"

"All right," LJ said suspiciously.

"Is your mam home?"

"Yeah." He looked worried. "Did I do something wrong?"

"'Course you didn't. Why on earth would you think such a thing? I just need to talk to her about Erin, is all."

LJ ushered him into the chaos of his home. Lucy wasn't there, thank Christ. Last time Rory had seen her, she was sitting outside the Oak with a gaggle of friends. They were passing around a cig, thinking they looked so sophisticated.

Oona was nowhere in sight, either, which disappointed him a bit. Last time he'd seen her, she was all sharp elbows and knobby knees, prone to mad fits of giggling. A terrifically smart thing, she was madly in love with Nicky Byrne of Westlife. Made sense: she was a little girl, and little girls liked crap music.

Reggae music was blasting away in the kitchen as the stomach-rumbling scent of frying chips wafted his way. Second best smell in the world, the first being the soft scent of Erin's skin.

"I'll tell mam you're here."

"Ta, LJ."

He'd barely had a chance to look round before Sandra appeared in front of him, her eyes cold as marble.

"Hiya, Sandra."

Sandra nodded curtly. "Rory."

"I was wondering if I might have a word."

"C'mon," she said stiffly. LJ started walking into the kitchen with them but stopped when Sandra lightly touched his shoulder. "Just grown-ups for now, all right, love?"

LJ's shoulders sank, but he obeyed his mother and sulked his way back into the living room, his face a pout. Rory winked at him; that seemed to cheer him a bit.

In the kitchen, he was shocked by the sight of a pink-cheeked, black-haired toddler sitting in a booster seat at the table, happily chomping away on mash and peas. He knew San had had another baby, but this was the first time he'd actually seen her.

"Who's this, then?" The baby was cute: all Sandra, no Larry.

"Gina."

Rory slid into the chair next to the baby. "Hiya, Gina. I'm Rory."

"I don't know why you're telling her your name, seeing as you're never going to see her again."

The baby offered him a spoon full of mash, but Rory turned it down. "It's your dinner, love. You eat it all up, like a good girl."

Sandra was unsmiling. "What do you want, Rory Brady?"

"Need to talk to you about Erin. First things first, though: how are you?"

Sandra's voice was clipped. "I'm fine."

Okay, so the theme of the evening was going to be "Back off, Rory." He understood. But it wasn't going to stop him from getting what he came for.

"So . . . Erin?"

Sandra went over to the stove, giving the frying chips a good stir before turning up the burner beneath the ancient chip pan. "Nothing to talk about, as far as I can see."

"This isn't easy for me, San."

"Good."

"But you're the only one I can talk to about this."

Sandra turned to him. "Go talk to Father Bill. Maybe

he'll make you say ten decades of the rosary for penance and then you can piss off back to New York."

"Could you cut the show short? You know I wouldn't come round here buggin' you if I didn't think it was important."

"Go on, then," Sandra returned with a smirk. "I need a good laugh."

"I know Erin still loves me."

"Why? Because you saved her from big bad Larry Joyce?"

Rory bit down hard on his tongue to stop himself from saying something he might regret. *Keep to the issue of Erin,* he told himself. *Sandra's life is a muddle and she's not thinking clearly. Stick to Erin.*

"Mock all you want, but you know Erin loves me, too. Even though she hasn't come out point-blank and said it; I see it in her eyes and in her body language, I feel it in her kiss . . ."

Sandra looked shocked. "You kissed her?"

"No, she kissed me." Technically, that was true.

"What did you do? Hold a loaded pistol to her head?"

"I'll ignore that comment. You know I've been driving her—"

"I'm her best mate, you flaming eejit. Of course I know. What do you want?"

"You know what I want."

The chip pan was beginning to smoke. Sandra turned the burner down low. "And what the hell do you expect me to do?"

"Tell her she should give me a second chance."

"Oh, you've got to be kidding. Even if she still loved you, you think I'd plead your case after what you did to her?"

"Biggest mistake of my life," said Rory gloomily.

Sandra snorted. "I'll say it was."

"At least I'm admitting it and trying to fix it."

"That's nice. But it doesn't make you a good man. Because you're not."

"If I'm so horrible, then why were you so keen on the competition?" Rory asked in puzzlement. "I mean, you had to know that if I won, she'd be spending time with me."

Sandra reddened. "I was a bit tipsy that night."

"No kidding."

Gina was banging her spoon against her plate. "I'm done."

"Down you go, then." Sandra helped her off the booster seat. "Go sit with LJ."

Sandra gave him the once-over now that it was just the two of them. "All right, I'll give you that one about the contest. But there's a world of difference between that and my telling her I think she should forgive you, when all you've done is wreck her life."

"I'm talking about second chances here. You forgave Larry over and over. That bastard didn't get just a second chance; he got twenty feckin' chances, if not more. And don't tell me it's different because you were married and had kids."

For a second it looked like Sandra might fly at him. But whatever flare-up of temper she felt in that moment, she held back, because she knew he was right.

"I heard he pulled a runner," Rory said softly.

"Don't pretend you had nothing to do with it." Sandra put on a devil-may-care look. "Anyway, what of it? It was bound to happen eventually, right? Larry Joyce, King of the Scum."

"I wish it had happened sooner."

"Oh, do you, now? Why, because you give so much of a damn about me?"

"You've been Erin's best friend forever. You've been there for her, no matter what. You deserve better than what you've got, San. A better life, a better man."

"Not going to find one of those, am I?" she replied sarcastically. "Unless I order one in the mail."

"There are good men in this town."

"Father Bill doesn't count."

"Jake?"

"Jake?" Sandra looked at him with contempt. "The same Jake who's competing with you for Erin? Yeah, okay, I'll take Erin's castoffs. Sure. Why not?"

"That's not it at all and you know it. Didn't you have a bit of a case for him in school?"

Sandra was incredulous. "That was yonks ago, Rory. I've no interest in him beyond him being a good mate. Have you gone soft in the head?"

Rory shrugged. "I dunno. I just thought two good-looking, single people who've known each other forever, who get along and want the same things—"

"Shove it up your arse!" Sandra snapped indignantly. "You think I need your matchmaking help? Keep your bloody nose out of other people's business."

She marched over to the stove, twisting the burner beneath the chip pan off. "I'm still not seeing why you'd think I'd go shaking a tambourine about, singing your praises."

"Because you love her and you want her to be happy. You and I both know she can't have the life she wants in Ballycraig. There's no future for her here. She wants to get that degree and leave, but she also wants me. You give your stamp of approval and it's done. Your word is like law with her.

"Look, I'm not expecting you to do anything that's truly against your conscience. If telling her to give me a second chance is something you just can't stomach, I understand. Seriously."

Sandra was quiet as she pulled two plates out of the cupboard and began setting the table. "I do want her happy," she said. "I want that more than anything in the world." She looked at Rory. "But I'm not sure you know what you did to her. Truly."

Rory flinched. "I do know. That's why I'm swearing to you that will never happen again. The man that did that to her was a total shite. I'm not that man anymore. I'm doing the best I can to prove it."

"I know you are," Sandra muttered reluctantly.

She dumped the mountain of chips on a big plate and

brought it to the table. Rory could tell from her expression that she was right on the edge of caving in, and he waited.

"Right," she said resignedly. "I'll talk to her. But I'm not pushing her, you got that?"

She clapped her hands loudly. "LJ! Oona! Tea!"

LJ came racing into the kitchen, groaning when he looked at the kitchen table. "Chips? Again? All we eat is chips!"

"Some people don't even have that," Sandra replied edgily.

Before Rory could even open his mouth, Sandra wheeled on him and mouthed, "NO!"

Rory nodded with resignation. There was no reason for her to play proud with him. He, Erin, and Jake had all helped her and the kids out over the years. Did she think he was such an idiot that he'd give her cash in front of the kids?

Gina toddled in and Sandra picked her up, swinging her around and blowing a big raspberry on her cheek. "You silly little monkey. Who's Mam's silly little monkey?"

LJ slouched down miserably in his chair.

Rory gave him a surprised look. "What's with the face? You don't like chips?"

"We have them all the time."

"That's good! Have you never heard of carbohydrates? Go look it up on your computer when you're done eating. Carbs are really important if you want to play sports. Really important."

LJ perked up a bit. "Really?"

"Yeah, really! Why would I lie to you?"

LJ looked at his mother. "Is it true?"

"'Course it is," said Sandra, as if it were something everyone knew. "Why'd ya think we've got chips coming out of our ears? I want you to be doin' well at the football camp."

LJ broke into a wide grin and began heaping chips on his plate.

"I'm just going to see Rory out now. I'll be right back."

"Thanks for talking to me, San," said Rory when they reached the front door.

"I'm not that cold of a one, am I?"

"'Course you're not." There was a moment of awkwardness. "Look, don't bite my head off when you hear what I have to say, all right? But if I can ever help you and the kids out in any way, please let me do it."

Rory waited for the verbal blast. Instead, Sandra, ever proud, looked like she was struggling to hold back tears. "Thank you, Rory."

"It's no problem."

"Would you like to stay for tea?" Sandra asked quietly.

"Thanks, but I'm set."

Sandra opened the door. "Well, thanks for stopping by." Her voice held out a small touch of promise. "I'll see what I can do."

22

"*Rory told me* that I should tell you that I think you should take him back."

It was a gorgeous Saturday morning, the sun having decided to make an appearance. There was still dew on the grass, along with a small, refreshing nip in the air. Erin had taken the opportunity of grabbing Sandra for a breakfast by the pond, thanks to a rare alignment of the planets known as "Gran wants to see her kiddies." The kids were at San's mom's house, and now Erin and she were sitting on an itchy old army blanket not far from the water's edge, with a pile of egg sandwiches and a vacuum flask of tea between them.

"Can I hear that again, please?" Erin asked. "I've not got enough tea in my brain to process what you just said."

"One minute," Sandra garbled as she took a bite of her sandwich. "Rory said—"

"Wait. Back up the lorry. When did you see Rory?"

"He came round to mine on Thursday."

Erin was skeptical. "Rory came round to yours."

"No, I'm a big fat lyin' sow! Yes, he came round to my house."

"For what?"

"What d'ya think, you daft cow?"

Erin closed her eyes. "Okay, okay, so paint me the picture."

"I'm painting you nothing, Erin. I'm just going to tell you what happened. If you want to add 'There was a purple halo round Rory's head,' you can do that. But don't ask me what he was wearing or how did he look or any of that."

Erin frowned, disappointed. "Go on, then."

"So, he came round. Shocked to shit, I was. I knew it couldn't be about LJ, because if it was, he would have rang up and we'd have had some meeting up at the camp."

"Right."

"In he comes. No beating around the bush with that one. He says, 'I know Erin loves me, you know she loves me, please talk to her and help her to see reason.'"

"Reason!" Erin tore off a piece of her sandwich roughly and threw it into the pond at the duck who wouldn't stop staring at her.

"He didn't exactly use the word *reason*."

"What did he say, then?"

"Look, it's all a big gobbledygook of words in my head," Sandra replied, flustered. "But the upshot was that if I thought he was a changed man, and if I knew that you loved him and that being with him would make you happy, I should be honest and tell you so. The end."

"Not *the end*." Erin swallowed a bit of sandwich. "Since when have you ever done someone else's bidding?"

"Jesus wept, Erin, it's not bidding." Sandra licked some dripping butter from her fingers. "It's bringing the truth out into the light."

"Yeah? And what truth would that be?"

"That you still love him—and don't even try to protest, because we share the same brain, girl."

Erin downed a gulp of sugary tea. "Right, so he tells you I love him, and you think I love him, so then what?"

"He realizes he was a dick, and he swears he's changed his dickish ways."

"Do you believe he's amended his dickish ways?"

"For Christ's sake," said Sandra in exasperation, "would you let me finish one sentence before you leap at me like some deranged creature?" Erin glared at her. "Thank you.

"As I was saying," Sandra resumed pointedly, "it was all about the dickish ways 'n' that. And I was holding my ground. But then he said something I couldn't respond to, because of the truth of it: he said everyone deserved a second chance, and I should know all about that seeing as I forgave Larry loads of times."

Sandra fell silent. Erin studied her friend's face: she looked so fragile sitting there, a worn out little girl with tired eyes, staring out at the gentle ripples of the pond's surface.

"I know you miss him, San." Erin put an arm around her shoulder. "I know it's tough."

"It is, even though I know he's a prick." Sandra took a long drink of tea. "But the thing is, Rory was right. People do deserve second chances."

"Even Rory Brady?"

Sandra frowned. "Even him." She lifted her face up to the sun, wiggling her toes and taking a deep breath. "God, I'm freezing my tits off."

"Me, too," Erin confessed with a small shudder.

"We're tough, though. We can stay."

"I agree."

"Right. Here's my big finale, Er: I do believe he's well and truly sorry for what he's done, and I do know you still love him."

"I haven't said I still love him," Erin gingerly pointed out.

"You don't have to!" Sandra bellowed. "This is me you're talking to, remember? You love him. Okay?" Her voice was so loud a flock of birds scattered.

"I love him, I love him, calm down."

"You and your semantics and technicalities—oh! Oh! Christ, I'm an idiot! How could I forget? Rory said you kissed him. Is that true?"

"We kissed casually. It was no big deal."

"Then tell me all about it."

"Well." Erin pictured a smaller, hysterical version of herself running around her brain, arms flapping, screaming, *Help get me out of this!* "We were both in Crosshaven, and we passed the jewelry store."

"The alley." Sandra's eyes lit up dreamily. "It was like you were strolling down memory lane. There was the store, and the alley, and it all came flooding back."

"In a way, yeah," Erin replied uneasily. "It wasn't like a snog or anything. It was just one little kiss. No rockets and all that."

"Frenchie?"

"SANDRA!" Erin's cheeks were burning.

"It was a Frenchie," said Sandra, pleased with her detective skills. "What happened next?"

"I told him it was madness for me to have been getting rides from him, and that it had to stop. He kept pushing, and finally I said that I needed time to sort everything out."

Erin lay back on the blanket, closing her eyes. "I do still love him. But I'm scared. If he did that to me again, I don't know what I'd do."

"Well, what's your heart telling you to do?"

"Forgive him."

"Then do that," Sandra said simply.

Erin lifted her head. "Really?"

"Yeah, I know it's a risk. But what's the alternative? Pretend the feelings between you two aren't there? You're a different woman than you were two years ago, Erin. And judging from what we've seen so far, he's a different man—listening to what you have to say, being considerate of others, willing to admit when he's made a mistake. He doesn't think the world revolves around him anymore. I think you should forgive him."

"All right. I just hope you're right."

23

"You've got to be kidding me."

Two weeks after her conversation with Sandra, Erin decided it was time to have *the discussion*. Instead of looking forward to it, she was anxious about it, even though she knew there would be a positive outcome (unless Rory had suddenly gone mental). It made her feel vulnerable, which is why she had put it off until now.

She'd rang him, surprised when he picked up on the second ring. His gran had him doing chores. He couldn't get together until later in the day because she was insisting the legs of the kitchen table were uneven, and she wanted him to even them up. He knew damn all about sanding, but he'd done as she asked. Now they were even worse.

"Glad you rang," he said, relief in his voice. "The only skilled carpenter I know died two thousand years ago. Clearly, we're in no way related."

"We need to talk," Erin told him calmly. Rory agreed to pick her up later, saying he had a surprise for her. And now here they were on the Copley Road, one of the old country roads rarely traveled anymore, and he was dangling his car keys in front of her face, saying he was going to give her a driving lesson. The hedges on both sides were overgrown, but not so badly the road was undrivable. There was no chance of being interrupted, that was certain. But a madman coming out of the woods with a machete and hacking them to bits? That, she wasn't so sure of, considering how isolated it was.

Rory jangled the keys. "C'mon, then."

"I told you I wanted to talk."

"We will. After I give you your first driving lesson. It's been eating at me, you saying I was a bad driving teacher when we were kids. I think we were both very young and uptight. It's different now, so I thought we'd have a go. C'mon."

Erin's anxiety turned into a full-out case of nerves as she exchanged places with Rory. She turned the ignition and the car purred to life. Her foot barely touched the pedal.

"Go on, then, adjust the seat. There's a switch on the right side." Erin felt butterfingered as she felt for the switch and the seat slowly moved forward. Rory clapped.

"If that's going to be your attitude, we're ending this lesson right now," Erin huffed.

"Relax. You've got to relax."

"I am relaxed."

"Right," Rory said dryly. "You're relaxed. Next, adjust your mirrors. You do the rearview mirror manually, see? You want to make sure you can see behind you. This panel between us has the switch to control your side-view mirrors. You want to see a little bit of the side of the car, but mostly what's going to be alongside you."

Erin started to adjust the side mirrors. "Don't watch me."

"Whaddaya mean, don't watch you? This is a lesson, remember?"

"I think I can handle adjusting mirrors without your supervision."

Rory looked up at the car ceiling, whistling. "Let me know when you've got that done."

"You're the biggest arse God ever made. I just want you to know that." It took her all of a few seconds to adjust the mirrors.

"You can stop whistling the Bee Gees 'Stayin' Alive' now," she told him.

Rory looked at the side-view mirror of the passenger seat. "Good job."

"Stop making me feel like I'm five and I've just completed a drawing of an apple or something!"

"I'm trying to encourage you!"

"All you're doing is making me annoyed with you, which makes me more nervous."

"Apart from giving you instructions, I'll keep my piehole shut. Would that make you happy?"

"Very."

"Now. Put your hands on the steering wheel at ten and two. Imagine the wheel is a clock. Ten and two."

Erin put her hands at ten and two.

"Time to drive."

Erin panicked. "What, now? The first time out?"

"What did you think? We were gonna practice adjusting mirrors all afternoon?"

"I don't know about this."

Rory leaned over and caressed her cheek. "You'll be fine."

Erin closed her eyes for a moment, relishing his touch. "If you say so."

Rory clapped his hands together enthusiastically. "Now. Keep your foot on the brake, and see the stick shift here? Put it in drive—but still keep your foot on the brake as you do it, yeah?"

Erin nodded. Her right hand gripped the wheel while her left sought the stick shift. She could hear her heart whooshing in her ears. *You're not an idiot,* she reminded herself. *If that fat dosser Teague Daly can drive, then you should be able to grasp it in no time.*

"Now," Rory continued ever so authoritatively, "take

your foot off the brake and put it gently on the gas pedal. Then push down slowly on the gas pedal with your foot. Slowly mind. And you'll be driving forward."

A nervous wreck, Erin did as Rory instructed and the car began to move forward.

"Keep it going. Just aim straight."

Erin slowly motored up the old road. She was shaking a bit, but she was driving.

"Right. I want you to stop now, so put your foot on the brake."

Overwhelmed, Erin pushed her foot down hard and she and Rory rocked forward, then back.

"I said *gentle*!"

"You didn't! You just said 'put your foot on the brake'!"

"I thought it would be *obvious* that if you gently tap the gas pedal to go, you would gently tap the brake pedal to stop. Put it in park."

Erin leaned her head against the steering wheel. "I knew this was a bad idea."

"What are you on about? It's a good idea. You just have to loosen up. Here, this'll help. Fresh air." He hit a button and the car windows rolled down. "This time, keep going forward slowly till I tell you to stop."

Erin put the car into drive and slowly crawled up the road. She was just gaining in confidence and picking up a little speed when some overgrown brambles smacked her in the face through the open window. Panicking, she hit the gas rather than the brake and they were flying.

"Brake!" Rory yelled.

Erin was too shaken to stop.

"Erin, stop the car. BRAKE!"

She mashed down on the brake pedal, hard. This time she and Rory jerked forward and back with even more force.

Erin's leg was shaking as she put the car into park.

"Um. Okay. Okay." Rory's voice was kind but impatient at the same time. "That's all right—those brambles smacking you in the face was unexpected. But that's what good driving is all about: keeping alert, keeping aware, concentrating on what you're doing. My da gave me a golden piece of advice that still applies to this day: assume that everyone else out on the road is a jackass who doesn't know what the hell they're doing. It works."

Erin was still shaking. Rory took her hand and kissed her palm. "I know it's scary the first time out, but you can do this."

"I know I can. I just get so overwhelmed, and it doesn't help that I'm sitting here thinking, 'He thinks you're a twit.'"

"I don't think you're a twit," Rory insisted. "I just think you need to relax. Tense drivers aren't good drivers, Erin."

"You should put together a driving handbook for twits," Erin said bitterly.

"I could put you on the cover if you like," Rory offered. He pointed at her face. "Ah. Don't think you can hide it from me. I see a smile coming on. Oh, she's fighting it, but her mouth isn't listening. The corners are curling up . . ."

Erin broke into a grin.

"There it is! The smile I love."

She turned to him. "Rory." The safety belt was cutting into her shoulder.

Exasperated, she undid it. "I really think we should talk."

"Me, too. But not sitting here in the car. Let's take a walk. I'll find a nice old brick wall covered in moss you can crash into."

"I'd forgotten what a wisearse you could be."

"Anything else you need to be reminded of?" Rory asked seductively.

"Maybe," Erin murmured back.

There was no mistaking the dark gleam of desire in Rory's eyes as he got out of the car and came around to open the door, extending his hand like a true gentleman to help her out of the car.

She was no sooner free of the vehicle's confines than Rory pulled her into his arms. The hug, so heartfelt and fierce, felt like home. She'd forgotten how safe she could feel here. Rory tilted her chin up and their eyes locked.

"I love you. I know I don't deserve it. But a life without you is unimaginable, Erin. Please take me back."

Erin's eyes slowly drifted shut as she savored the fervency of his words, as seductive as anything he'd ever said to her over the years.

"I love you, Rory." Saying the words aloud made her feel like a prisoner who'd just been set free. "God help me, but I do."

"Thank God," said Rory, bending to kiss her mouth. Erin had forgotten that desire could be coated in sweetness. But once that sweetness melted away, what was left was a hunger that wasn't easily satisfied.

Erin felt reason slowly crumble as Rory's kisses grew more possessive. It spurred Erin's own boldness as she tore her mouth from his to nip at his neck. Rory's low groans incited her to do more. And so, ever so gently, here and there, she bit him.

"I want to make love to you," he whispered huskily. He grabbed her chin and clamped his mouth on hers, greedy and demanding, pulling her closer to him than she ever believed possible. No boundaries. They were just brilliant silver molecules, combining and recombining, binding them together forever.

"Hang on," he said, eagerness in his every move as he opened the back door of the car with a seductive smile. "What do you say? Seems a waste not to use it, seeing as it's so roomy and all."

"Oh, I agree completely," Erin said solemnly as Rory backed her up to the open car door. Prickles of mad anticipation hit her skin as she lay down, the cool black leather a lovely, gentle shock.

Rory paused a moment, silhouetted by the sunlight pouring through the open door. It looked as though he stood in the center of a blazing fire. The silhouette disappeared as he carefully climbed atop her, his mouth seeking hers like a parched man seeks water. His mouth moved to her throat, then to the sensitive spot at the base of her neck, his kiss turning gentle as he put his lips there again and again. She'd been to this place with him before, but it felt different now, more real. *I know this man,* she thought in amazement, *every inch of him, every scar, every freckle. The way he moves in bed, and the way he moves when he walks.* Simple things a woman would notice about a man she loved, and would never forget. The press of his body on hers, his knowing just where to kiss her and how, filled her with such passionate love for him she thought she might burst into tears.

Rory lifted his head, staring into her eyes. He wanted her badly. She knew that look, the one that magically conveyed lust and love at the same time, overwhelming her. It was as if her senses were working overtime, trying to make up for the time lost. His burning skin and the intense gaze. The scent of clothing that had been dried out on the line in sun and fresh air. Rory.

She couldn't stop staring at him. It was as if he were a breathtaking piece of art that had come to life, enrapturing her completely. Gently, she took Rory's face in her hands and pulled his mouth down to hers. *Familiar but new,* she thought again, the hunger on both sides reaching an entirely new level. Heat was building inside her, not incrementally but in huge leaps. She could tell it was the same for Rory.

Erin was fighting for breath, trying to keep at least a semblance of a clear head. She wanted to remember every detail of these moments. But Rory, pressing into her hard, was making it impossible. Erin had put her hands up his shirt so that her palms could play over his back. She knew she should be patient, but she couldn't be. There would be other times for slow, sensuous lovemaking. Right now, all she wanted was for Rory to fuck her.

"I want you inside me now."

"Are you sure?"

"Yes," Erin said with a guttural groan.

Rory sat up astride her, hurriedly tearing off his T-shirt

before helping her rip off hers. The sight of her in her bra seemed to tantalize him.

"I'm sorry, love," Rory said, leaning forward. "Just a minor detour."

He roughly pushed her bra up and clamped his mouth down on her nipple, hunger biting through her as he suckled, blew on them, then teased them with his tongue. He was hard against her; Erin reached down and began rubbing him through his jeans. "Don't," he whispered huskily. He returned to her breasts, teasing with his teeth and lapping with his tongue. *So good,* she thought. *God.* The fire was building in her as her breathing grew faster and faster, little moans escaping from her throat.

"Yeah," Rory groaned, lifting his head momentarily to graze her earlobe. "I want you to come for me."

It was more than Erin could take. The minute his tongue returned to her nipple, she was bucking against him, screaming ecstatically.

"Now you," Erin said, pushing some hair from her face. "Fuck me like you mean it. Fuck me like a man."

Rory's reply was a whispered, "Oh, yeah," as he slid down her body and stood up in the space of the open door. He pulled off his shoes and socks, then hers. There was a rough impatience in his fingers as he leaned forward, tugging down her jeans and panties.

Rory hurriedly unbuckled his belt and fly, kicking himself free of his jeans and briefs. He parted her legs roughly and then thrust into her, hard. Erin drew her legs up, feeling herself on the verge again as Rory thrust away inside her.

"Faster," Erin begged, pressing, squeezing, wrapping her legs around his hips as tightly as she could. "I told you to fuck me. Do it."

Rory groaned again but he did as she asked, slamming into her again and again as she screamed with delight as the second wave of orgasm broke over her, sending her into another ecstatic freefall. It was too much for him to take. His hips began pumping wildly as he panted. And then it

happened, him crying out as he lost all control and aban-
doned himself in his frenzied climax.

Rory Brady. Hers again for eternity, she was sure of
that now.

                          *   *   *

"I suppose this isn't a very dignified sight, two naked people
in the back of a car, my feet dangling off the seat. My bare
arse alone would send them screaming away."

Erin laughed, holding Rory tight. After they'd made
love, they'd lain together quietly for a long time. No need
to try to read each other's mood. They were just Erin
and Rory, the way it always had been, the way it always
would be.

Erin playfully slapped his rump. "You've a magnificent
arse."

"Yeah, that's what my teammates are always telling me
in the locker room. 'Rory,' they say, 'that is one helluva
freckled white Irish ass you've got there.'"

"They're just jealous."

"You're probably right." He pushed himself up on his
elbows, looking down into her face with a mischievous
grin.

"What would you do if Father Bill came along right now
on one of his chastity patrols?"

"Die of mortification."

"D'you remember that time he burst into one of Sandra's parties like he was the snog sheriff come to arrest us
all?" Rory launched into an imitation of the wheezy self-
righteous priest. "'Don't think I don't know what you've
been up to! Don't think God doesn't see your filthy ways.'"
Rory shook his head in pity. "Poor bloke. He's probably
never had any in his life."

"I just remember Sandra's mam walking in and Father
Bill standing there, looking all triumphant until she said,
'What the hell are you doin' in my house? You bloody
Nosy Parker. Leave 'em alone! They're just kids; let 'em
have some fun.'"

"Isn't that when Sandra—"

"Yes. Let's not talk about that."

"Right." Rory nuzzled Erin's neck, sending bolts of pleasure through her. "Can I assume we're back together?"

Erin was nonchalant. "Yeah. I guess so."

Rory lifted his head in surprise. "That wasn't very enthusiastic."

"I'm teasing you." Erin slapped his butt again.

"I knew that."

"Did you? How?"

"Because you're lying beneath me naked as the day you were born, after practically deafening me with your screams."

Erin was mortified. "Beg pardon?"

"I'd forgotten how loud you are," Rory rolled on, clueless.

"I am not!"

"Well, sometimes you are," Rory amended.

"So are you!"

"I love this," Rory said, playfully biting the tip of her nose. "Our first post-sex spat."

"Not a spat. A disagreement."

"Ah." He became reflective. "So we're agreed? We're back together?"

"I already told you we were!" Erin shifted her weight beneath him so that she didn't feel quite so pinned. Despite being on his elbows, Rory was a big man. Still, she wouldn't change being beneath him for anything.

To her great surprise, Rory looked relieved. "There's that settled, then."

Erin was mildly insulted. "Do you think I'd sleep with you if it didn't mean we were back together?"

"No. Not your style."

"Exactly."

"Say the words, though. Say, 'I love you, Rory.'"

Erin's eyes began to fill up. "I love you, Rory," she whispered.

"And I love you, Miss Erin O'Brien. I swear to God, I will do everything in my power to love you the way you deserve to be loved, to protect you from harm, to never hurt you, and to make you happy. I'm not a perfect man, I know. But I'm the man who loves you."

"I'm so happy," said Erin, sniffling as she wrapped her arms around his neck.

"I feel like I've just said my wedding vows," Rory joked.

"I know."

"We'll figure out soon when to do them for real, yeah?"

"Yeah."

It was really going to happen, Erin thought deliriously. They were going to marry. There really was such a thing as fate.

"Not that I don't love lying atop you in the backseat of an SUV, but I'm thinkin' we might want to get dressed and resume your lesson."

"No," said Erin resolutely. "No more lessons for today."

"I think I'll drive back into town buck naked."

I dare you, Erin wanted to say. But she knew Rory would take the dare.

"I'll walk, then."

"Ah, you're no fun." He slithered down her body till he was standing, and took her hand, helping her out of the car.

"Ballycraig's Adam and Eve."

Erin smiled. Perfect day. Sun, and the lazy hum of bees, which she'd failed to notice before. And Rory's beautiful body in the sunshine. She changed her mind.

"Go on. Drive into town starkers."

Rory looked pleasantly surprised. "Seriously?"

"Seriously. Who's going to see you? The windows are tinted."

"I'm not driving back into town starkers by myself. I want my naked queen beside me."

"All right," Erin agreed. Every day, little by little, she was chipping away at the good-girl facade. It dawned on her that their split really had helped her in many ways. She hadn't really felt like a woman before the split. She'd still felt like a girl. Rory Brady's girl. Now she was her own person. She didn't need to be with him to feel complete.

Naked, laughing their heads off, they headed back into town.

"This is so daft. I love it!"

"We used to do stuff like this all the time," Rory reminded her, squeezing her bare thigh. "And we're gonna keep on doing it till we're old and gray."

"Promise?"

"Promise."

24

Nothing could steal Erin's joy as she let herself in to the B and B through the kitchen door, or so she thought until she saw Diana Everett sitting at the table, stiff backed and poker-faced.

"Hey, you all right?" Erin asked, even though she knew the answer.

"No. We need to talk."

Erin sat down. "What has she done?"

"What hasn't she done?" Diana said bitterly. "My workday never ends. She keeps coming up with more and more things for me to take on. She thinks I'm her personal slave. I know she's a tough nut, but if I didn't know better, I'd swear she was trying to break me."

"She probably is," Erin agreed gloomily.

Diana looked at Erin uncomprehendingly. "But why would she do that? I'm not a mad egotist, but I think she's lucky to have me."

"Oh, believe me, she is."

"Then why is she doing what she's doing?"

"Because she mistakenly thinks that if you quit, I'll rush in to help again."

"And if I do quit?"

Erin's heart sank. "Please, Diana, don't. I swear I can make things right. Just give me a chance to talk to her."

"Fair enough. One chance. But if it doesn't work, I'm afraid I *am* going to have to quit, Erin. Life's too short, if you know what I mean."

"I do," Erin said. "If you're done for today, then go. I'll handle my mam. Truly."

"Thanks so much."

"Things will be better when you come in on Monday, I promise. Now off with you. Go enjoy the sunshine while it's still here."

* * *

Erin waited until the evening to have *the chat* with her mother. She'd had a feeling all along she was going to have to do this, even though Erin had told her mother flat out that she wasn't going to ever come back to work at the B and B. Her mam was banking on Erin's guilt kicking in. Too bad that particular well had run dry.

Her parents were in their cozy flat, watching the latest episode of *Time Team*. Her father was already slack-jawed and asleep in his recliner, as was often the case. Her mother sat on the couch in her puffy pink bathrobe, sipping Horlicks.

"Hello, love," she said to Erin quietly. She gestured at the telly with her mug. "You've come in just in time for a new one. Mick and Phil think they might have found the remains of an eleventh-century monastery in Sark. Tony is skeptical. Of course."

"Mam, all they ever seem to do is find remains of monasteries."

"That's not true."

"I need to talk to you."

Her mother patted the empty space beside her on the

couch. "Sit. We'll have a good chat at the commercial break."

"No, now," said Erin, taking care to be firm but not bossy. "You know I wouldn't bother you during *Time Team* if I didn't think it was serious. Just record it; you can finish watching it later."

Her mother picked up the remote. "I'm not really sure how to work this thingy."

"Hang on." Erin took it and set the DVR to record the rest of the show.

"There we go."

Her mother looked anxious. "Are you sure that works?"

"Trust me, it will, okay? You should just have Da teach you. It's simple."

"Ah, I've got enough clogging up my brain without adding all that technology to it."

"Suit yourself."

Her mother rose, following Erin downstairs to the kitchen. As always, Erin was creeping down the steps quietly, so as not to disturb any of the older guests who might already be in for the night.

"Cold in here," her mother said, rubbing her arms as she sat down. She was right—it was a bit chilly. Erin turned up the heat.

"Better?"

Her mother took a sip of her Horlicks. "Yes. So what's the big hullaballoo?"

"It's not a hullaballoo. It's a mystery."

"Oh, I like mysteries."

"Well, you won't like this one, trust me."

Erin sat down beside her.

"Here's the mystery. Why are you trying to drive Diana to quit when I've told you I'm not going to replace her?"

Her mother pulled a face. "I don't like her."

"What's not to like? I saw how hard she worked when I was showing her the ropes, and so did you. She even had that letter of recommendation from the last B and B she worked at."

"She's not family," her mother maintained stubbornly.

"Dad's apprentice isn't family, either."

"That's different."

"How?"

Her mother got defensive. "I don't know, but it is."

"That's not a very good answer." Erin was suddenly thirsty and went to the fridge to get some ice water. "Could you give me a better one?"

Her mother sighed. "I told you ages ago. Your da and I bought this place as a family investment. It should be family running it."

"And I told you ages ago that I had no intention to stay in Ireland."

Her mother shook her head obstinately. "I'm still not getting that one, Erin. If you just took your eyes off your studies a minute, you'd see—"

"I'm back with Rory."

"Please tell me I'm getting all addlepated and I didn't hear that."

"We're back together. We're getting married. We're going back to New York at the end of the summer."

"I didn't raise you to be stupid. That boy—"

"He's not a boy; he's a man. And I'm not stupid."

"What fool would take Rory Brady back after what he did to you?"

"A forgiving one. One who believes everyone deserves a second chance."

"And what if he does it again?" Her mother looked anxious as Erin slid back into her chair.

"He won't."

"You don't know that. A leopard can't change its spots."

"Really? So Da still gets off-his-face drunk every weekend?"

It was dangerous territory, Erin knew, but she needed to go there to make her point. For years her da was a heavy weekend drinker. *Say the word, Erin, don't pussyfoot around it. Alcoholic.* It finally came to an end when he got in a fist-fight with her brother and near demolished him. The next day her father had stopped drinking completely. He never touched another drop.

"That's different," her mother repeated.

"No, it's not, and you know it." She put her hand atop her mother's, surprised by how loose and dry the skin felt. "Why can't you just be happy for me?"

Her mother's expression was hard. "Family should always come first."

"I disagree," Erin replied, shocked to find a sense of nervousness creeping in. "I love my family, but not at the price of my own happiness."

"Your father's going to go mental when he finds out you're back with him."

"I don't think he will, because he knows about second chances and he cares about my happiness."

"And what's that supposed to mean?" her mother snapped.

"I know you love me," Erin replied, choosing her words carefully. "That's never been in doubt. But you haven't always liked the choices I've made, because they're different than choices you've made. Just because I want something different from you doesn't mean I look down on what you do. It's not a judgment or a rejection of you."

"I don't know as that I agree," her mother said stiffly as she rose. "Would you mind if I got back to *Time Team*, love? I know you recorded it for me to watch later, but I'd like to see how it all works out before I go to bed."

"Go on," said Erin, giving up the fight.

"'Night, love."

"'Night. Don't forget: I meant what I said."

Her mother didn't reply. Whether her mother didn't hear her or was pretending not to hear, Erin didn't know. All she knew was that she couldn't keep twisting her guts into knots over it anymore.

* * *

"I expect to see Noah floatin' by," Sandra joked.

"I know," Erin agreed. She knew the rain would come eventually. This was Ireland, after all. But she was expecting the usual gentle rain, not these great lashings of water pouring down from the skies.

They were in Sandra's living room, which was surprisingly clean. "What happened here?"

"Bored one night. Told Oona I'd give her five euros if she helped me out. She's golden, that one."

"LJ, too, when you think of it."

"I know. He's a good lad, all things considered. He's gonna be dead depressed when camp is over, but it's given him confidence to try out for the football team at school.

"Before you ask, Lucy is at her boyfriend's. That's going to end badly, I can tell you. I wouldn't listen to my mam for shit, and now look where I am."

"She's younger than you were, San. It'll all sort itself out in the end."

Erin tried to hide her amazement at the dusted shelves, the kids toys all tucked up in one corner, the clean rug. It reminded her of when Sandra first married that moron: she was so concerned about being a "good" wife. That faded fast, and a good thing, too.

Sandra flashed a look of indignation. "You're a mean one! That text you sent me—'Hot sex in the car. Back together, more later'—was downright cruel! I sat here all weekend champing at the bit for the details, so you better start talking."

Erin told Sandra about the driving lesson, which had Sandra dying with laughter. She was more sketchy about the sex; she didn't think Sandra needed to know every detail, just the general stuff about how Rory was as skilled as ever.

Sandra looked envious. "You lucky cow. I might as well sew up my nethers. I doubt I'll ever get any again."

"Don't be such a drama queen. Doesn't suit you."

"You want it plain? I'm an unemployed woman with no job and four kids. What bloke is gonna want to poke that? Answer: none."

"I'm not gonna try to convince you of anything different, because it just goes in one ear and out the other."

Sandra looked tired. "Don't mind me. I'm just in a bad place right now, what with Larry and the money stuff and all that crap. Even this free course . . . yeah, I'm learnin' and all, but I don't quite have a job yet, do I?"

Idiot. Idiot. Idiot. Idiot. You're an idiot, Erin O'Brien. "You've got a job right now if you want it."

"What the hell are you on about?"

"At the B and B. The woman there now can't handle my mam. She's going to quit this week. I can feel it. You should take the job. My mother knows you, she trusts you, and we can work it out so you're only there three times a week. Or whatever you want." Erin was getting excited. "This is so perfect! I can't believe I didn't think of this before! I'm such a twit."

Sandra pursed her lips. "Hmm. It's tempting, I'm not going to lie. There's just one stumbling block as far as I can see."

"What's that?"

"Your mam knows me, but she doesn't like me."

Erin frowned. "That was when we were younger and she was jealous you were my best mate. She's gotten over it."

Sandra looked doubtful. "If you say so."

"I do. Look, you know your way round my mam, just like I know my way round yours. We've both been handling them for years. Plus, there's the added benefit that my mother very much cares about what other people think. If she fires you, a lot of people in town won't regard that kindly, will they? Everyone knows about Larry and the mess he caused even before he legged it out of here. It's perfect. Seriously."

Sandra looked thoughtful. "I'd want weekends off to be with the kids."

"We might have to work around that. Would you be willing to work Saturdays, at least?"

Sandra hesitated, then nodded. "I would."

"We're all set, then."

"Slow down, girl! I do need time to mull this over!"

"C'mon, San," Erin implored. "This is so, so perfect."

"I'll give it serious consideration, I swear. Let's get back to you and Rory. Foregone conclusion you're back with him, then?"

"Yeah."

Sandra looked sad. "Off to America."

"I know. But I was going to do that anyway." The sadness in her friend's eyes was contagious. "It's not like I'll never come back. My parents are here. You're here. I'll visit every year."

"Depending on how much money you make, and how many days you get for your holidays, when you find a job," Sandra pointed out despondently.

"Exactly." God, her exams were just weeks away. She really had to hunker down.

Sandra managed a tease. "Well, I hope it takes this time with you and Rory. I don't think I can go through this a second time."

"Nor can I. You decide about the job, and then I'll talk to my mam and get this sorted. In the meantime, let's go out and have some fun when Gina wakes up."

"Ooh, what do you have in mind?"

"Exotic trip to the green grocer's."

"Count me in, sister."

25

Rory stood in front of a long, rectangular glass case filled with engagement rings and wedding bands. He was at Morgan's, the jewelry store where Erin used to work. He decided that since they were making a fresh start, he'd ask Erin to marry him again. He brought Sandra with him to help pick out a ring. He still had the original ring he bought that he'd never given to give her, but when he mentioned it to Sandra, she looked at him like he held the title for Stupidest Man on Earth. "New start, new ring," she'd declared adamantly. "Sell the one you bought first time round quick smart, believe me. You don't want it hanging round, sending out bad vibes."

Rory was confused. "Since when did you care about energy and vibes and all that shite?"

"I saw a show on the telly. It was amazing."

Sandra's eyes scanned the row of rings. Rory found the selection overwhelming; two minutes and his eyes were already becoming blurry.

Sandra tapped a luridly purple fingernail atop the glass case. "Can we see that one, please?" She was pointing to a ring with a huge, square cut diamond. The saleswoman smiled and obliged. Rory remembered Erin saying how much she hated helping men looking for engagement rings. "You'll be standing there for hours," she said, "and you have to smile the whole time." Her jaw would hurt by the time she was done.

The saleswoman handed Rory the platinum ring with the big diamond in the center. He had to admit: it was magical, especially when the light hit it. But it wasn't Erin.

"Don't think so. That diamond's way too big."

Sandra looked at him like he was mad. "What are you on about? It's a gorgeous ring. She'd love it."

"No, she wouldn't. It's not her."

"I can show you a similar style with a smaller diamond flanked with some baguettes," the saleswoman said helpfully.

Rory handed the ring back to her. "That would be lovely."

Sandra stared at him. "Look, I'm her best friend, right?" she said to Rory under her breath. "I know what she'll like and what she won't."

"She wouldn't like that," Rory maintained stubbornly.

The saleswoman delicately selected a ring from three cases down, bringing it to Rory. It had a similar square cut diamond, but with three little diamonds inset on each side.

"That's nice," Rory murmured to himself. He held it out to Sandra. "What d'you think?"

Sandra inspected it as if she were a jeweler looking for flaws invisible to the naked eye. All she was missing was a jeweler's loop.

"Nope." She handed it back to the saleswoman, whose face was frozen in a polite smile. Rory felt bad for her, knowing how she'd feel by the end of the day.

Sandra began perusing the case again, while Rory found himself beset by memories: he remembered picking out a simple gold, heart-shaped locket for Erin when they were seventeen, as well as the time the two of them were in here, pretending to shop for engagement rings.

"I know the ring I want!" Rory burst out. He racked his brain, trying to remember it perfectly. "It was white gold . . . and the diamond was round but it kind of looked like a star . . ."

The saleswoman smiled. "I know the one you mean." She moved down two cases and delicately plucked a ring from the red velvet foam it was cradled in. "Is this it?"

Rory's heart flipped. "It is."

How many times had Erin returned to that ring again and again when they were in here? Yet when he was in New York, he'd never even tried to find this simple ring. The ring he'd picked out for her was, in retrospect, a bit too flashy. He remembered how much he wanted her to be impressed that he was making enough money to buy her a ring like that. What a jerk.

But this was definitely the ring she'd always wanted. "She loves this ring," he said, passing it to Sandra. "What do you think?"

Sandra's eyes began to fill up. "I think it's perfect," she whispered. She handed the ring back to Rory, who, feeling all aglow, passed it back to the saleswoman. "I'll take that, please."

"May I help you with anything else today?"

"Yeah," Rory said, smiling at Sandra. "What's your fancy?"

Sandra looked mystified. "Whaddaya mean, what's my fancy?"

"It means I want to buy you something. Can't have Erin's best friend walk out of here without something for herself, eh? Think of it as a token for all you've done for us, San. Please."

"You don't have to do that, Rory."

Rory squeezed her shoulder. "I know that. But I want to. Go on and have a look round."

It made Rory happy that Sandra was allowing him to do this for her. She eventually showed him a simple gold tennis bracelet.

"It's yours," he said.

When he put it on her wrist, she burst into tears. "That was the loveliest thing anyone has ever done for me. Truly."

"You deserve lovely things, even if you are an old bag. You can help me figure out where to pop the question on the ride back."

26

"I can't believe what a great football player you've turned into, LJ. Truly." Rory and the boy were sitting together beneath a tree a few yards from the football pitch. It was the last day of camp, and Rory was delaying packing up the equipment for as long as possible. To him, the end of camp had always meant summer was truly coming to a close.

Rory tousled LJ's hair. The morning and afternoon sessions had been combined earlier in the day, playing a match against each other. The afternoon team won, but there were no hard feelings. Still, LJ looked gloomy.

"You're gonna try out for the school football team, right? You're certainly good enough."

"You think so?"

"What did I just tell you? You're brilliant, LJ."

"I kinda wish my dad had seen me play," he replied sadly.

"Maybe one day he will."

LJ shrugged. "Maybe." He traced a finger in the dirt. "I wish you didn't have to go."

"I know. But I've got to go back to work."

LJ looked thoughtful. "That's why I want to play professional football."

"Why's that?"

"Because being an athlete—it's not really work."

Rory near killed himself laughing. "Not work, eh? I think you'd be surprised at just how much work it is."

"I'd like to see you play," LJ offered shyly.

"You can see me playing on YouTube, you know."

"Yeah, but those are old games."

"Well, I'll see if I can't work something out so you can watch some of them right while they're happening."

LJ's mouth fell open. "Stop the lights!"

Rory just smiled. *Stop the lights?* That was a new one.

"Can I come visit you?"

"Sure, you can all come over whenever you'd like."

"Mam's dead sad Aunt Erin is leaving."

"It's hard to leave a good mate behind. How's it goin' round your place?" Rory casually asked.

"All right, I guess. Sometimes Jake is there. He's okay."

"Hey, he's more than okay. He's my best mate, remember? So you better be dead nice to him."

LJ's expression turned dramatic. "He saved Lucy's life!"

"Did he?" Rory had no idea what the hell he was talking about.

"Yeah. You know how Lucy, like, gets pissed out of her skull sometimes with her mates and then pukes and pukes?"

"Eh, right," Rory replied carefully. *Twelve? She and her mates get pissed and they're twelve?*

"Well, loads of 'em end up puking in the High Street. They just lie there in their sick and sometimes their mates just leave 'em there.

"Well, Lucy did too many alcopops with her mates, and she was stumbling in all drunk and that, and she fell and was just lying there on the sidewalk."

"Back up: who gets the girls alcopops?"

"Older girls and guys."

Fuckin' great, thought Rory.

"Jake was coming out of the pub and he picked her up off the ground. And she puked in his car. And she was crying and moanin', 'Oh, don't tell me mam,' and all that. And Jake told her, 'My lips are zipped if you stop doing this shite, because you're breakin' your mam's heart and I don't like it one bit.' And he took her to Gran's till she stopped pukin' and then she took a shower at Gran's and then Jake drove her home. Mam was asleep and Lucy went up to bed and Mam never knew."

"How do you know?"

"Gran told me, and she told me not to tell anyone else. She says she likes Jake and he's a good sort. So Lucy didn't die because of Jake."

"That is one amazing story!" Rory marveled, going wide-eyed with admiration for LJ's benefit. "And how's Lucy been since then?"

"Good, I think."

"That's a relief."

"Yeah."

Rory flashed an impish smile. "I've got a bit of a surprise for you. You might not like it, though," he teased.

"Oh, I'm sure I will," LJ replied eagerly.

"Right, then hang on a mo'. I'll be back in a minute."

Rory jogged to his car, grabbing LJ's present from the passenger seat. He had a feeling LJ would go mad over it, but you never knew with kids.

He sat back down next to LJ and handed him the plain white box. LJ's cheeks were flushed as he hastily tore the top off, pulling out the garment inside. Rory could tell by LJ's awed expression that the boy was overwhelmed by the New York Blades jersey that had his own name on it.

"Feckin' hell!" LJ exclaimed, then quickly corrected himself. "I mean, wow!"

"'Wow' is right. If your mam heard you using that language, she'd send you back to the dark ages to punish ya, with no phones or computer or anything."

"I won't. I won't say it again," LJ promised fervently. He

stood up, slipping the jersey over his head, waiting for Rory's approval.

"Fierce," Rory said. "No one'll mess you about when you're wearing that, believe me."

"It's the best gift I ever got, honest. I'm gonna wear it home. I'm gonna wear it every day."

"You better wash it now and then."

LJ's unabated enthusiasm struck a sentimental chord. Suddenly Rory was back in tenth grade in Boston. He was playing on the third line for his school's hockey team, but he didn't care. He had his first hockey jersey, with his name on it. It was as wonderful as when he'd gotten his first football jersey as a small boy, maybe even better. He remembered feeling invincible, and that was what he wanted for LJ: an unshakable sense of self-confidence. If Jake wound up with Sandra, the kid couldn't lose.

"All right, sport, we've got to make tracks."

LJ wrinkled his nose confusedly. "What?"

"It's some kind of old American slang for 'Okay, we've got to hit the road.'"

LJ looked crestfallen. "I wish we didn't have to."

"Look, you'll be seeing me again before I leave to go back to America, LJ! It's not like this is the last time!"

"Good," LJ said, relieved. They both stood. LJ seemed anxious.

"What is it?"

He couldn't make eye contact. "Can I give you a hug, Rory?"

"'Course you can. Why would you ever ask me a silly thing like that?"

LJ lifted his eyes to him. "Da always said men don't hug each other. Except when they win football matches."

"That's the biggest load of buggery bollocks I've ever heard in my feckin' life, son."

LJ laughed delightedly hearing Rory's bad language. Then he threw his arms around him. "I'm gonna miss you, Rory."

"I'll miss you too, mate." Rory was getting choked up. "But we can Skype, yeah?"

"Yeah." LJ broke the embrace, his grin wide as he held his arms out in front of him, admiring his jersey. "All right, Rory," he declared. "Let's make tracks."

* * *

Rory was surprised by how sad it felt saying good-bye to all the kids at camp. He couldn't help but wonder what would fill the hole in their lives now that the school term was looming. His hope was that they'd all have a go at trying out for the school football team, even though he knew they wouldn't all make it.

Rory made a mental note to congratulate Jake on getting Lucy in hand. Sure, he was blackmailing her, but as long as it didn't hurt anyone, Rory saw little harm in it. He just hoped Lucy kept to it.

The bells above the front door of Erin's da's shop jingled as Rory stepped inside. When her father came out from the back, he looked surprised to see Rory, but not unpleasantly so.

"Hey, Mr. O'Brien. I was wondering if you had a minute."

"Sure, sure." He called to his apprentice to mind the shop for a few minutes. The minute they got outside, Erin's da made a beeline to Rory's car, walking around it, admiring it, kicking the tires. It was as if he couldn't help himself.

"Nice."

"You want to drive it?"

Erin's father waved the suggestion off. "No, no, I couldn't possibly."

"Why not? I know you like fine cars. One spin around town, c'mon."

"All right."

Rory tossed him the keys, and after making the necessary adjustments, Erin's da pulled away from the curb, steering the car slowly up the street.

He was silent for a few moments. "Rides like a dream."

"Doesn't it?"

"And these seats—smooth as a baby's arse."

"Yup."

"I like the tinted windows. No one knows who you are."

Rory got great pleasure seeing how happy Erin's da looked driving around in the car. It was on the tip of his tongue to offer to buy one for him, but he thought better of it. That would look like sheer bribery.

They took four or five spins round before Erin's da pulled up in front of his shop.

"Don't suppose you have time for a pint?" Rory asked.

"I wish I did." There was a small, awkward pause. "What can I do for you?"

Rory cleared his throat. "A few things." He'd been memorizing a script in his head, though he didn't know why: rehearsed words always flew right out of his mind when the time came for a face-to-face chat.

"First off, I want to apologize for how I treated your daughter. I was a total prick."

"Go on."

"I was all dazzled by being in Manhattan, and I lost my way for a bit."

Erin's da looked skeptical. "And now you've found it?"

"Yes, sir, I have." Rory felt like he was standing in front of his old headmaster, defending himself against one stupidity or another he'd committed.

"I've always liked you, Rory. Surely you know that."

"I do. I mean, I did."

"But I'm not going to lie to you: when you ripped my girl's heart out, I was ready to hop the next plane to the States, get a gun, and shoot you square in the head. That's how angry I was."

Rory's shame felt like a poisonous snake, wrapping round and squeezing the life out of him. "I can imagine."

"I'm not sure you can, actually."

Rory bowed his head.

"Now, here's the thing. Erin is a smart girl. And she's

gotten tough, too. I trust her instincts. So if her gut is telling her you're worth a second chance after all you've put her through, then I stand behind her decision."

"Thank you, Mr. O'Brien," Rory said humbly.

"But I want to make one thing perfectly clear: if you dare hurt her again, I will break your feckin' neck like a twig. Are we clear?"

"Totally. Absolutely, sir."

He nodded approvingly. "I'm glad you came and talked to me."

"Me, too." Rory swallowed. Who was this nervous twit who'd invaded his body? "There was one more thing I wanted to talk to you about, Mr. O'Brien."

"Mmmm?"

"This is totally arse backwards, I know. But with your permission, I'd like to marry your daughter."

Erin's dad cleared his throat, looking like he didn't know what to say. Rory knew he wouldn't say no, having already told him he trusted his daughter's instincts. But Rory still wondered what was running through his mind as they sat there in silence.

"Rory." Mr. O'Brien's voice was shaky. "I can't tell you what it means to me that you've come to ask me that question."

"I swear to you, I will love Erin the way she deserves to be loved, and I will never, ever hurt her. She will always be safe with me; I will always take care of her. You have my word."

"Then, yes, of course, you may marry my daughter."

"Thank you, Mr. O'Brien. Thank you so much."

Erin's father's eyes glistened as he tossed Rory's keys back to him. "Welcome back to the family, Rory."

*   *   *

Rory racked his brains all night, trying to decide where he should do it. The next morning he asked his gran over pancakes. "Where did Grandda propose to you?"

"Propose to me? He never proposed to me. After we'd

been seeing each other for a while, he just said, 'I suppose we should do it, then.' And I agreed."

Rory felt bad for her. "That's not very romantic."

His grandmother looked puzzled. "It was fine. No one in his family or mine had a pot to piss in."

"Well, let's say we've got a time machine, and you can go back in time and have Grandda propose to you in a proper way. Where would you want him to do it?"

His grandmother shrugged. "Anywhere would do."

"Gran." Rory kneaded the back of his neck in frustration. "I'm asking for help here. Pretend you're twenty or whatever age you were when you and Grandda got married. You love this man. Where do you want him to ask you the most important question of your life?"

His gran actually went starry-eyed for a few moments. "At the end of Mass. We'd go to Mass together the way we always did, and then in my fantasy everyone would leave, and it would just be me 'n' him in that lovely, quiet place, with the light flooding in through the stained glass windows."

"What would be your second choice?"

"What, my first isn't good enough?"

"Gran, I haven't been to Mass in ages, in case you hadn't noticed. I can't just walk in there like a hypocrite and ask her to marry me." *Not that that's where I'd even think of popping the question, anyway.*

"Why not? Erin still goes to Mass sometimes. Not a lot. Not as much as she should. As long as one of you still does, I don't think God would mind you lingering there."

"Second choice, Gran. Please."

"Honestly, is your head filled with rocks or what? What about that old rowan tree on the edge of the Purcells' property? That's romantic."

"I broke my collarbone there."

"You're trying, son, did you know that? Very, very trying."

Rory winked at her as he put a piece of pancake in his mouth. "Must be why you love me so much."

His grandmother playfully lashed his shoulder with a tea towel. "Go on with yourself."

"Thanks, Gran."

"You're welcome. Now hurry up and finish your breakfast so you can hang that new shower curtain for me, please. I've been begging for a month."

It'd been three days.

"I'm on it."

27

"God, it's been ages since I've been here." Erin settled down on the ground under the huge rowan tree a few miles out of town. It was impressive, close to fifty feet tall, with a broad trunk and sturdy spreading branches. The tree seemed to have its own gentle soul, which was why generations of Ballycraig children had been taught that if you sheltered beneath its branches, it would be protection from faeries.

The tree sat high on a magnificent hill, round and green, overlooking the village. Another vague memory came into sharp focus: Erin and her brother fighting over the last biscuit during a family picnic. Her mam had wisely taken the Solomon approach, breaking it in two.

Rory stood, hands on his waist as he slowly turned in a circle, looking every inch the master of all he surveyed.

"Bring back any memories?" Erin asked, loving the way the breeze tousled his hair.

He turned to her. "Apart from breaking my collarbone when I was a kid? Yeah. I think the last time I was up here might have been with you."

Erin was pleased he remembered. "It was. That summer between your junior and senior year of university."

"Thought so." He closed one eye, scanning the land like a surveyor. "There," he said, pointing two hundred yards away. "We had sex there."

"I thought men didn't remember things like that."

"They do when the sex is amazing."

Erin kicked off her sandals, fluttering her toes in the cool air. It was so relaxing, being up here with him and away from worries like exams and whether or not her mother could drive even Sandra mad.

"I remember the pictures you showed me when you were at university: all those waterfalls and countryside, that big lake. I thought, 'It's as lovely there as it is here.'"

"Yeah, Ithaca's pretty great." Rory sat down beside her. "I'm sorry you never got to see it while I was going to school there. I'll bring you there when I've got a break in my schedule. I promise."

She laid her head on his shoulder. "I would love that."

He stroked the back of her hair. "You're sure you can leave all this behind?"

Erin slowly lifted her head and looked at him. "Rory, all I've ever wanted to do is leave this. Not that I don't love it, mind, but you know I've always wanted to live somewhere else." A sick feeling was creeping up on her, and as much as it scared her to ask what he was getting at, she had to. "Are you getting cold feet?"

Rory pulled back slightly so he could look her fully in the eyes. "Are you jokin' me?"

"Cut me slack, will you please? I've been floatin' on air about us getting back together, but when you say things like that, it makes me worry that you're not sure you want me to come back to America with you."

"That is probably the maddest thing that's ever passed your lips."

"Oh, I'm sure I've said madder things than that. Maybe not to you, though."

"Ah, so you've got secrets."

Erin laughed with amusement. "Oh, yeah, that's me from head to toe: an international woman of mystery."

"I'm so sorry," Rory said abruptly, deep pain lining his face. "For all of it."

"Where's all this coming from?" Erin asked softly.

"Just now. The fact that you could even doubt I want you with me. It kills me, the way you still don't completely trust me—" He broke off, overcome by emotion.

"Rory." Erin cupped his cheek in her palm. "I do trust you. I just had a momentary lapse. I appreciate so much that you realize how badly you broke my heart. But it's in the past now, love. You've got to stop beating yourself up over this. I want to look forward, not back, unless it's memories of the good times."

"Which I'm sure is the main reason you're willing to give me another chance," Rory ventured.

"Not the main, but it did help that there was a shared history between us I could look back on. Ultimately, though, it's about more than memory. It has to be." She ran her finger along the side of his cheek. "I was never able to really hate you. Distraught as I was, the world still felt out of step without you. Now I feel like all the pieces fit." She halted, blushing. "God, I must sound like I'm on *EastEnders* or something."

"You sound lovely." He rested his forehead against hers. The mind meld, they'd always called it. *My thoughts are yours and yours are mine, same as our hearts.* It went all the way back to their teenage years, those words.

"I want you to close your eyes," said Rory.

Erin lifted her head, looking at him suspiciously. "Uh-oh."

"Uh-oh, what?"

"Uh-oh, I'm not too sure about that."

"Uh-oh, I want to propose to you, and if you say yes, I'll give you a ring, you daft woman."

Erin's lips parted in shock. "Oh."

"Yeah, 'Oh,'" Rory replied, amused. "I suppose I can't do it now I've spoiled the surprise."

"No, no, do it," Erin implored, twining her fingers through his.

"You sure? Because—"

Erin cupped his neck, roughly pulling his mouth to hers. "I'd forgotten what a windbag you could be."

"I know. I know. All right, then, close your eyes."

Erin closed her eyes, then opened one. "Why do I have to close my eyes? Don't you want to gaze into them as you pop the question?"

"Yeah, I guess I do," Rory replied, brows furrowed in confusion. "It's obvious I've thought this out all backwards, because I'm nervous."

"*You* nervous?"

"Yes, it does happen once every ten years or so." His lips moved slightly as he murmured to himself. *He's so adorable,* Erin thought. He would hate to hear himself described this way, but it was true. When he did things like this, she saw the handsome teenage boy she'd fallen for.

His lips stopped moving, and he looked at her with such tenderness and longing that Erin felt her heart tumbling.

"First, I need to get down on bended knee." He winced slightly as he positioned himself in the classic will-you-marry-me pose.

"Are you all right?"

"Yeah," Rory said dismissively. "Hurt my knee two seasons ago. Sometimes it gives me a bit of trouble." He checked his stance. "I'm pretty sure you have to be standing for this to work."

He was right. Erin stood in front of him.

Rory fished in one of his front pockets, pulling out a small, square, blue velvet box. The anticipation. *Miraculous,* she thought, *that it's come back round to this.*

"I think you're supposed to give me your left hand."

Erin extended her hand to his. There was something comical to his directing the action step-by-step. Touching, too. There was no sign of the swaggering egomaniac here. Just a man and a woman with a past, wanting to step into the future.

Rory cleared his throat. "Erin Margaret O'Brien, will you do me the great honor of—"

"Yes!"

Rory laughed. "Can I finish the sentence, please?"

"Sorry," Erin said sheepishly.

"No need to apologize, love. I just want to do this proper."

Erin nodded, her left hand trembling in his.

"Erin Margaret O'Brien," he began again. "Will you do me the very great honor of becoming my wife?"

"Yes," Erin whispered, beginning to weep.

"Then—oh, shite, I was supposed to take the ring out of the box so it was ready to slip right on your finger if you said yes. Let's do it again."

Erin wanted to tell him to take a deep breath and relax, as but intuited it would only make him more nervous.

"Okay." He removed the ring from its home, holding it in his right hand as his left again took hold of hers.

"Third time's the charm, right?" He swallowed, his expression so sweetly vulnerable it transformed Erin's anticipation into something deeper.

"Erin Margaret O'Brien." He took a deep breath. "So far, so good. Will you do me the great honor of becoming my wife?"

Erin paused a moment to let the beauty of the words sink in. "Yes," she said, pure joy winging through her.

Any trace of anxiety that had Rory in its grip vanished as he slipped the ring onto her finger.

"It's beautiful," said Erin, overwhelmed. It caught the light perfectly, a rainbow of colors reflecting every facet of the ring. She held her hand out in front of her. She recognized it from all those trips to the shop years before. It was magical. Real. Hers.

"It's our ring," she whispered. "From when we used to pretend."

"It is. I'm glad it's still your taste," Rory laughed. "I brought San with me to help pick it out. It was like bringing Elizabeth Bloody Taylor."

"That's San."

"I bought something for her as well. A tennis bracelet. You woulda thought I'd bought her the Hope Diamond."

"That's so lovely of you, Rory."

"It felt like the right thing to do."

"It was."

Rory took her hand, examining the ring closely. "I don't want you to ever take this off. Ever."

"Why would I want to?"

Rory gave a small grimace as he sat down on the blanket, Erin following suit. He lay back, his fingers entwined on his chest as he gazed up through the branches of the tree. "I'm trying to figure out how I only broke my collarbone and not my neck."

"Charmed life." Erin lay down beside him. "When I was little, my mother told me the branches of the tree would protect me from fairies."

"My gran said the same thing," Rory recalled.

He rolled toward her, his fingers running a lazy trail up and down her arm. Erin embraced the feeling, shuddering a little. She laughed softly, touching his cheek, losing herself in those blue eyes that had always held the promise of love.

A trace of a smile played at the corners of Rory's mouth. He leaned toward her, kissing the tip of her nose before moving on to each of her cheeks, and then finally her mouth. His lips on hers were tender as a caress, sweet as if this were the first time they'd kissed; it felt that innocent and new. Erin cupped her hand against the back of his head, sliding her fingers back and forth over the soft prickle of his buzzed, blond hair.

"I love when you touch me," he murmured, his body pressing into hers. "Nothing else in the world compares to it. It feels like home."

Erin smiled, putting her mouth to his lips. Home. That was the word for Rory. He was her home. She didn't have to hide with him, or put on a show, or worry that she wasn't enough for him. He came back for her. Nothing else needed to be said.

She pulled back, smiling at him. "I love you."

"That's convenient, seeing as how you agreed to marry me," Rory replied playfully. He grabbed her and pulled her on top of him, drawing her into an intimate embrace. Erin closed her eyes, reveling in the feeling of the sunlight hitting her face, the breeze trifling over her body.

"May I kiss you again, miss?" Rory asked.

The question sent a steady thrum of warmth through Erin as she nodded yes. This time, Rory's kiss was more demanding, the feel of his tongue effortlessly sliding between her lips inducing a potent sense of intoxication. She couldn't lie: Rory had been this good girl's drug of choice since she was a teenager. She adored the familiar terrain of his skin, the way he gently held himself atop her so she could run her hands up and down his muscled back. Even when they'd been apart, she'd been able to conjure every inch of his body and how it felt atop her, beside her, inside her.

Rory rolled them so he was now the one on top, his gaze beating down on hers, full of months—years—of pent-up desire. Erin wrapped her arms around his neck, the thought entering her head: *You're hanging on to him for dear life.* Because she was.

Rory had started showering every inch of her face with soft, well-placed kisses. Erin giggled, then closed her eyes, knowing how the tenderness would soon give way to intensity. She loved when his lips brushed her earlobes, when he bestowed quick, tiny nips there. And her neck—it had always been one of her spots. All Rory had to do was deliver a small bite here and there, and fever shot through her. He could do anything he wanted to her now. Anything.

He sat up, the hard press of his legs against hers as he straddled her arousing her even more. He was sloe-eyed as he slowly unbuttoned his shirt, one she'd bought him years back—denim, but it was faded and soft now. Her breath caught as he removed the garment. Such a *man*, was all she could think. Muscular and trim, no trace of the football-playing schoolboy she'd fallen for back when she was fifteen and he was all lean and bone. This was the body he'd always aspired to, and now he had it: the cut biceps, the firm stomach. God, the solidity of him.

She brought her hands up to his chest, opening her palms, fingertips pressing the warm flesh. Rory closed his eyes and smiled, giving a small moan of delight. She could feel him getting hard, and stopped pressing his skin just for a moment to fully appreciate it.

Rory leaned forward, burying his face in her neck. "I love you," he said, his hot breath making every nerve in her body tingle.

"I love you, too," she breathed. She took one of his hands, brought it to her breasts. Rory raised his head and began undoing the buttons of her shirt, leaning forward to take a small bite of her shoulder when it was bare. Erin shuddered. "I love when you do that. I've always loved it."

He helped her peel off her shirt, then unfastened her bra, and soon that was gone, too. The excitement, coupled with the chill, had made her nipples hard. And when Rory lowered his mouth to them, his teeth tugging and his tongue flicking, Erin felt herself beginning to disintegrate. Groaning, she rocked her hips against him, shocked by how quick her body was to shudder from this small increase in contact.

"Shall I make love to you?" Rory asked, his breath cool as he blew on her heated skin.

"You shall," murmured Erin.

She could see from the dark of Rory's eyes that he was fighting for control, fighting to keep it slow as he undid her jeans and gently tugged them free of her legs, along with her panties. He kissed her low on the belly, pushing the heat pulsing through her to the surface. She wanted him now, and pulling her knees up, she wrapped her legs around his hips, carefully thrusting against him, each slow buck of her body against his exciting him more and more.

"I can't take this," Rory groaned. Erin released him from her grip, desire roaring through her head as she watched him stand and hurriedly remove his pants and briefs. That's when she felt everything inside her coalesce into one furious, vibrant hunger.

"Rory . . ."

He settled back atop her, Erin gasping with pleasure as he slid inside her and began moving. It was slow at first, beautifully, torturously slow. He increased the tempo bit by bit, so carefully Erin was in agony. Even so, she would never trade it for the slow build of heat that was curling through her body, the anticipation of how it would all end.

Rory was breathing hard, moaning, his own mounting pleasure evident in every move he made. Erin tightened and flexed her inner muscles around him; that's when his expression changed to something more driven, a craving. He began moving faster, thrusting himself deeper, whispering secrets and endearments in her ear that only the two of them knew. It wasn't only the deep passion of the movement that finally pushed her over the edge into rapture; it was knowing this was *it*, finally, she and Rory, the way it was always meant to be. The way it always would be.

* * *

They lazed together in the sunshine for a long time, occasionally murmuring and stirring to kiss or to rearrange tangled limbs. Erin didn't know what time it was, nor did she care. All that mattered was the man holding her.

Rory lifted his head with a smile. "One of these days we'll do it indoors, I promise."

Erin laughed delightedly. "I don't care where we do it. Being with you is all that matters."

"I'll remind you of that when we row."

"We'll never row again."

"You know what? I think you're right."

28

"First you twist my arm into letting Sandra work here, and now this."

Erin ignored her mother's latest stab at martyrdom as she helped her set the small kitchen table in her parents' flat. It was Sunday, two weeks after she and Rory had gotten engaged, and he and his gran were coming round for tea. It didn't take as much strong-arming as expected, thanks to her father. "This is what she wants. We're civilized people, are we not?"

It had shocked Erin; usually her father retreated pretty quickly when her mother started getting worked up. This was proof he was truly on her side.

It'd been killing Erin to keep quiet about the engagement, but she knew the only way to handle telling her mother was for she and Rory to announce it together. She'd been itching from day one to show her folks the ring: it had been hard to put it away in the bureau and not wear it. Her ring finger actually felt naked without it.

Erin folded the napkins, placing them around the table.

"Thanks for making soda bread," she said gratefully, hoping it might help to shake her mother out of her mood.

"Well, Rory likes it, doesn't he?" was her mother's sour reply.

Erin's fingers braced the table. "I told you: I'm not having this. Either you keep a civil tongue in your head or I'm off."

"I don't know what's happened to you, but I don't like it one bit."

Erin came over to the counter where her mother was slicing bread and hugged her from behind. "What's happened, Mam, is that I'm not a little girl anymore."

"Well, I don't like it very much, I'm telling you."

Erin kissed her cheek. "I appreciate the honesty."

"He better be on time," her mother muttered under her breath.

"Of course he'll be on time."

Erin's father walked into the kitchen, giving her mother a big smacky kiss on the cheek. "How's it going, my girl?"

"Oh, it's going," she replied dryly.

Erin's dad gave her a wink.

"I see we've got a lovely collection of tea cakes," he commented.

"Mam thought it would be better to have a tea and cake kind of thing, and I agree."

"No, this is grand," her father noted. "This way Rory and Fiona can leg it out of here if the dragon lady appears."

"You better watch yourself," her mother said. Erin knew she wasn't joking.

At precisely four p.m. the doorbell rang. Erin hadn't had the least bit of nerves all day, but now that the moment was actually here, her heart did what it wanted, racing in her chest.

She walked downstairs to open the front door. There was Rory, looking dead handsome as always, and his gran, her hair looking freshly set, the short gray waves frozen into place.

"Hello, love." Rory's gran gave her a hug.

"I'm so glad you're here, Gran," Erin said.

"I'll bet you are," she replied mischievously.

"Hi," said Rory, discreetly kissing Erin as he closed the door behind them. "What's the temperature?"

"Cool, but I think we can achieve a thaw if all goes well."

Rory held out a box of Cadbury chocolate. "Mixed assortment. She likes these, right?"

"Loves them," Erin concurred. "You're halfway home already."

Gran had toddled off to inspect the B and B dining room.

"Very nice," she commented approvingly "Not too posh." She turned to Erin. "Looks like your parents did a good job here."

"Gran," Rory said in a low voice. "We're here for tea, not to go snooping around the B and B."

"The family flat is upstairs," said Erin. "Shall we?"

Rory paused at the steps. "Gran, are these too steep for you?"

His grandmother looked at him disdainfully. "My old legs work fine."

"All right. Up you go, then."

"Don't look so nervous," Rory whispered to Erin as they slowly followed his gran up the stairs.

"Do I?"

"You know you do. The color's draining from your gorgeous face. It'll go fine."

"I know," replied Erin, hoping Rory's saying so would make it so.

Erin hadn't had unrealistic expectations. She hadn't expected her parents, her mother especially, to embrace Rory with open arms. But she hadn't realized just how chilly the reception would be. Her mother barely thanked Rory for the choccies. Thank God he'd had the foresight to bring his gran along.

Formalities over, the five of them crowded round the table to talk over tea and cakes. Erin's parents and Rory's gran had a brief discussion about how deadly boring Father Bill's sermons had been of late.

"So, Rory Brady," her mother finally said. Full name. Not good. "Will you be leaving town soon?"

"End of summer," Rory said politely, taking a sip of tea. "I've got training camp."

"In New York. Yes. I remember." She turned to her husband. "You remember that, don't you? How Erin was going to join him over there when he was in training camp?"

"Don't be doing this," Erin warned. "I'm not joking, you."

"Doing what? Exchanging memories?"

Rory's grandmother gave her mother a frosty glare. "Don't be a mixer."

"I don't know what you're talking about."

"You do, which makes you a liar as well. You're not being very Christian, Bridget, if I might say so."

"Crap," Rory said under his breath. "C'mon now, let's not be slinging barbs. Especially today."

Erin's mother glared at him imperiously. "And what's today?"

Rory looked at Erin, whose hand was shaking as she pulled her engagement ring from her pocket and slipped it onto her finger. Nervous as she was, there was no stopping her beaming. "Rory's asked me to marry him, and I've said yes."

Rory put his arm around Erin. "I'm the luckiest man in the world."

Rory's gran clasped her hands together excitedly. "Now, this is lovely news! Lovely. True love always finds a way, eh?"

There was no response from Erin's mother, but her father got up and kissed her.

"Congratulations, love." He shook Rory's hand. "Congrats."

"Thanks," he said, looking grateful.

Erin's dad returned to his seat.

"Isn't it good news, Bridget?" he prodded his wife.

"What? That my daughter is a fool?"

Erin's guts clenched. "I told you not to do this."

"I'm just speaking the truth." She looked at Rory's grandmother with disbelief. "Don't tell me you're happy about this."

"And why shouldn't I be?" Gran had a defiant look on her face. "Rory knows he did wrong, and he set it right. He loves your Erin, and she loves him. Get over yourself, Bridget. It's not all about you."

Mouths fell open in shock, but Gran clearly didn't care. "I'm sorry, but I had to say my piece. I'm not going to sit here while you slag my grandson off."

"Nor am I," said Erin.

"Oh, so Fiona Brady can say her piece," her mother said indignantly, "but I can't."

"Go ahead," Erin challenged. "Say your piece."

Beneath the table, Rory was stroking her hand soothingly.

"You've hurt her once," she said to Rory, "and I'm worried you'll hurt her again."

"That's legitimate," Rory agreed. Erin's mother looked surprised to be agreed with, even more surprised that it was Rory who did it.

"Let's say she marries you, and you take her to New York, and then you break her heart. And there she is, having given it all up for you, with none of her people around her, no support system, nothing. Just a slap in the face from you."

Erin was getting steamed. "First off, I'll be getting my own work in America. Second off, I'm not the innocent I was two years ago. I'm clear headed and I know what I want. And if, God forbid, something happens and I—or we—need help, we've got Liam's branch of the family nearby."

"The American O'Briens." Her mother sniffed disdainfully. "I think you're making the biggest mistake of your life, marrying Rory Brady."

"It's not about you, Bridget," Rory's gran repeated.

"Listen," said Rory calmly, stepping into the fray. "Your fears are absolutely justified, Mrs. O'Brien. But I swear to you, I love your daughter, I've learned my lesson, and I will never, ever hurt her again."

"Fancy words," Erin's mother sneered.

"I'm not going to sit here and listen to you tear down my grandson," said Gran, raising her voice.

"Gran, leave it," Rory warned quietly.

"This girl's been quiet as a church mouse most of her life because of you," Gran continued. "I, for one, am glad she's getting away from you, Bridget. Maybe it'll teach you a lesson."

"Gran," Rory hissed.

Erin's mother turned to her father. "Are you going to let her talk to me like this?"

"She's got a point," her dad said quietly.

"Was I not open to letting her go the first time he was going to take her to New York?"

"That's only because you wanted to show off a bit," Erin said. "'Look at my daughter with the famous hockey player.'"

"I never!"

"You also thought I couldn't take care of myself," Erin continued, "so it was good Rory was there. Well, I can take care of myself, and I wasn't put on this earth to please you. I love Rory, and that's the end of it."

"You think so, eh? If you go off and marry him, you'll never set foot in here again."

"Bloody hell, Bridget," said Erin's dad. "Have you gone batty or what? Don't make threats you might regret."

"I stand by what I say. I refuse to watch her ruin her life."

Erin stood up. "So you're saying it's you or him?"

"That's right. Him or your family."

"Then I choose him," Erin said fiercely. "And you're a stubborn, blind old fool to think I'd choose otherwise. You want to cut me off? Fine. I'll be round here tomorrow to collect my stuff."

Her mother just shrugged. "No skin off my nose."

"She doesn't mean it," Erin's father assured her. "She's just being melodramatic."

"I do mean it," Erin's mother countered emphatically.

"And so do I," Erin replied. "Rory, Gran, I think we should go."

Gran shook her head, looking at Erin's mam as if she were contemptible.

Rory stood, his hand still entwined in Erin's. "I'm sorry you feel that way, Mrs. O'Brien. I thought we'd be able to let bygones be bygones. I'm sad you've put Erin in this position. She loves you very much."

"I do," Erin said tearfully. She kissed her father on the cheek.

"She'll get over it," he said under his breath.

Erin's mother let her kiss her, but not before giving a small flinch.

"Thank you for having us," said Rory's gran. "I was wondering: might I take home some of the soda bread, since I didn't really get to have any?"

Rory looked mortified. "Gran." He looked at Erin's dad apologetically. "Sorry about that."

"Don't be daft. We've got an uncut loaf in the kitchen." He fetched it and gave it to Rory's gran.

"Thank you," she said again.

"Yes, thank you," said Rory.

"At least we got something out of it," Gran muttered as they headed down the stairs.

"I'm so sorry about this," Erin said.

"There's no need for you to apologize," Rory said.

"I second that," said Gran. "Now let's go back to mine and have a proper tea."

29

"*It'll blow over,*" said Aislinn.

"She'll get over it," said Liam.

"She'll come to her senses," said Rory.

Erin felt not the smallest spark of hope as she sat at Liam and Aislinn's kitchen table. After the tea debacle, she'd gone back to Rory's gran's with them. Gran sliced soda bread, Rory soothed, and Erin cried, more out of frustration than devastation. She knew her mother might be unpleasant to Rory, but it had never crossed her mind that she would issue an ultimatum. What made it all the more shocking was that she was delusional to think that put in that position, Erin would choose family over Rory. It was a ridiculous challenge, especially since her dad had, in his quiet way, backed her. Why did her mother not respect her decision, or notice that Erin had gotten out from under her thumb? Her mother claimed it all came from a place of love and protection, but Erin knew otherwise and had even called her on it: it came from a place of sheer selfishness and fear, maybe even envy.

There was no sense in her spending the night at Rory's

gran's, as there was no place for her to sleep. Erin loved his gran, but she much preferred going up to her cousin's place, where she'd have her own room. Tomorrow, she'd go round to the B and B to fetch her things, then return to her cousin's to hunker down in earnest for exams. Truth be told, they were the farthest thing from her mind right now. Concentrate on the difference between baroque and rococo? What a joke!

"What if she doesn't?" Erin asked, looking round the table. "What if she doesn't come round?"

"Once she realizes she could lose you forever, she will," Rory assured her.

"Look, if you think it will help, I'll go over and try to talk some sense into her," Liam offered.

"Absolutely not," Erin said resolutely. "This is between me and my mother. Thanks for the offer, Li, but I can fight my own fight on this one." She took a sip of tea. "Trouble is, she's stubborn as a mule. You've really got to back her against a wall to get her to see things your way."

"You've backed her into the ultimate wall," said Rory.

Erin cradled her head in her hands. "Christ, I hope she doesn't take it out on Sandra."

"As if," said Rory. "Sandra'll snap her in two."

"Plus, if she fires Sandra, she'll have no help at all," Aislinn pointed out.

"True."

"You can't cave on this, Erin." Aislinn's voice was firm. "You know that, right?"

"I do," said Erin. "It just makes me sad that if she doesn't come round, she might not be at our wedding."

Aislinn looked delighted. "Wedding! And when would that be?"

Erin looked at Rory blankly. "We haven't really talked about it yet, have we?"

"No, we haven't." Rory shrugged easily. "Whenever you want, Erin."

"I can't even think about it right now, to be honest. I need to get my exams out of the way first."

"It'd be great if you had the wedding here," said Liam. "On the farm."

"Or anywhere nice in Ballycraig, really. It would save money," Aislinn chimed in. "Then you wouldn't have to worry about flying your folks over, and San, and your nan, Jake . . ."

"Look, seriously, you're doing my head in talking about this," said Erin. "One thing at a time." She remembered something. "Isn't your Finnish friend coming tomorrow?" she asked Rory.

"Yup. Esa."

"It's a good idea, having him stay here," Erin said to Rory. "No chance of my mam giving him a hard time because he's a friend of yours."

"Here for a week, right?" Liam checked with Rory.

"Yeah. Getting a bit of relaxing in before the season starts."

"We'll show him a good time," said Liam.

"He's pretty easygoing. He won't be a problem."

* * *

"This is where you grew up? No wonder you were so happy to leave." Esa had just gotten the tour of Ballycraig's High Street from Rory. The remark rankled, even though Rory knew it was a joke. Esa knew his story full well: how he left Ballycraig when he was fifteen and eventually left Erin, too, not wanting to be strangled by his roots. But now that he was back for the first time in years, and seeing clearly for the first time in a long time, Rory could appreciate the village he'd grown up in, where everyone watched each other's back and the pace of life was relaxed. The pace had livened up a bit now with the PJ tourists, but it still couldn't be termed brisk.

"What's your beef against my hometown?" Esa had gotten in late last night. Erin had told Rory she was already in bed when Esa arrived and gone in the morning by the time Esa got up. Something about watching Gina for a bit. So his fiancée and friend still hadn't met yet.

"It's very tiny," Esa continued. "Really tiny."

"Not like bustling Helsinki, is it? What did you do for excitement: watch ice melt?"

"Pretty much. When do the leprechauns come out?"

"Feck off, Saari."

They both laughed out loud, prompting a large number of female heads to turn in their direction.

"Can't believe they're all giving you the once-over," he told his friend.

"Now it's my turn to say 'fuck you,'" Esa replied. "You should be used to this by now: the women wanting me."

"I thought you were still seeing that model Kayla."

Esa frowned. "I ended that. She was stupid."

"Lookin' for something meaningful now, are you?" Rory ribbed.

"When the right one comes, I'll know. At least I won't have to resort to a mail-order bride like Torkelson."

"C'mon, have some pity for the guy, will ya? She got her damn green card and took off, but not before robbing him blind, I might add. And he fell for her. That's the heart-breaking bit."

"What an idiot."

"Yeah, but he's our idiot."

Esa's attention was drawn to the tourists lining up across the street for the Leary tour. "I want to take the tour."

"Be my guest."

Esa looked surprised. "You won't come with me?"

"No. That's for losers."

"Oh, so you already took it?"

"Twice, actually."

Esa had the shortest attention span on earth. Now he was watching a buxom redhead go into Finnegan's. "Cute," he remarked.

"Jailbait, I reckon."

"Her ass is too big. Why do Irish women all have such big asses?"

"Excuse me?" Rory was deeply offended.

Esa backpedaled. "Not all. Some. I'm sure Erin doesn't have a big ass."

"Even if she did," Rory replied crossly, "I wouldn't care. Better that than holdin' a skeleton in my arms."

"Hmmm. You might be right," Esa conceded. His head turned again, lowering his sunglasses for a better look at a leggy blonde blatantly staring at him. "I'll meet Erin tonight?"

"Yeah, down at the Oak. It'll be me, you, Erin, and Erin's best mate, Sandra."

Esa pushed his sunglasses back up. "Is she hot?"

The question caught Rory off guard; he'd never really thought about San that way.

"She's pretty. But she's seeing someone." At least, that's what he could glean from Jake spending so much time with Sandra. Jake had been uncharacteristically quiet about it.

"Why isn't he going to be there?"

"He'll be joinin' us later. In fact, he works up at the farm with Aislinn."

"Five people. That must constitute a crowd in this town."

"Shut up, you Finnish prick. I'll show you around a bit more and then you can go on your pathetic tour."

30

Erin would never tell Rory this, but Esa Saari was one gorgeous specimen: hair so thick and black it almost had that blue sheen, and eyes such a deep blue that Erin was sure he was wearing a pair of those fake-colored contacts.

They were down at the Oak: her, Rory, Esa, and San. Jake was running late. Erin couldn't wait to see him and San together, even though San insisted they were still just friends. But her eyes glanced away a little when she said it, a big tip-off she was lying.

Erin's eyes were burning from sitting in front of her computer most of the day. After a quick hour watching Gina, she'd gone round to the B and B to fetch her things. Liam had been nice enough to drive her into town so she could load her things into Aislinn's truck. Her guts were twisting when she went inside, but her mother was nowhere to be found.

She didn't have too much stuff, so she and Liam were done in a flash. She thought her mam might show her face, even if it was just to scowl at her, but no. It hurt Erin more than she cared to admit.

Old Jack glided over to the table, all smiles.

"Evening all." He shook Esa's hand. "Nice to meet you. Who are you?"

"Jesus, Jack. You could be a bit more polite," said Rory. "This is my teammate, Esa. He's here for a week to blow back, relax."

"Another hockey player, eh? Maybe we can get some more of you to come over and form a proper Irish hockey team."

Rory laughed. "In your dreams, Jack. I know you've got one or two club teams here now, but the truth is, you'll never tear an Irishman away from the football pitch."

"What can I get you all?" He looked at Erin and Sandra. "Black Velvets for you two, that much I know. Rory?"

"Know what? I think I'm going to branch out tonight. I'd like a pint of India Pale Ale."

Jack looked at Esa. "You?"

"What's your strongest stout?"

"Russian Imperial."

"I'll have that, then."

They had a few minutes to chat before Rory and Esa went to the bar to fetch the drinks. Esa was extremely solicitous, asking Erin and Sandra loads of questions about themselves and their interests. He was flirting mercilessly with Sandra, who was lapping it up. The minute he and Rory excused themselves to get the drinks, Sandra gave Erin a conspiratorial pinch.

"Frickin' hell, he looks like he dropped down from heaven," Sandra whispered.

"He's certainly turning on the charm with you," Erin noted.

"Jealous, are we?"

"Go chase yourself. I have Rory."

"I'm liking the charm. It's been years since I've had a man stare at my titties like that."

Doesn't Jake? Erin wanted to ask, but kept quiet. She changed the subject.

"How you getting on with my mam?" Erin asked.

"The dragon knows better than to go after me," Sandra boasted.

Erin put her hand to her chest, relieved. "I was hoping that would be the case."

"She should have been in the army, your mam. Good at barking the orders. But I get it: the place has to run like a well-oiled machine, doesn't it? Still and all, she's dead pleasant with the guests."

"I know. I think she really is happy running the place. Not that she'd admit it."

"She's always been one to get up on the cross when it suits her. She'll get over it, by the way."

"So you say. You look really great tonight, San."

Sandra looked pleased. "Do I?" She took a deep breath. "It's so lovely to be here and not have to worry about what I'll come home to. The kids haven't really been asking too much about Larry, except LJ. I told him his dad had to go away to where the jobs were, but he's not stupid; he knows I'm lying through my teeth. But he's content to leave it there for now. Thank God for your Rory, and Jake, and Jackson Bell: he's finally got some positive male role models in his life." She looked down at the gleaming gold tennis bracelet on her left wrist. "I never thought I'd hear these words out of my mouth again, but he truly is a good sort, your Rory."

"I know," said Erin. She looked at him at the bar with Esa. They were chatting with Liam. *Never thought I'd see that,* she thought to herself.

Rory and Esa wended their way back to the table, Esa handing them their drinks.

Sandra was positively flirtatious as she accepted her glass from him. Erin hadn't seen her bat her eyelashes like that in years.

Esa took one slug of the stout. The sour look on his face took Erin aback.

"This is disgusting," he said to Rory.

"You're a wuss."

"You have no taste buds."

"Excuse me while I get something cold."

"Finns," said Rory in mock disappointment. "They're such prima donnas." He turned back to the table. "Let's get our Irish on. Show him how it's done properly."

* * *

Rory was pleased with the way the evening was progressing. Esa was pouring on the charm, his charisma undeniable. But Rory could see he was even spinning a net around Erin, which cheesed him off. When Sandra and Erin excused themselves at one point to go to the loo, Rory told him to pull it back a bit. Esa needled him about being jealous, asking again and again how serious Sandra and her boyfriend were.

"She's got four kids and has no intention to leave Ireland," Rory snapped.

"So?" Esa laughed. "That doesn't mean she can't have one night of unforgettable passion."

"That's not her style. Trust me."

"Maybe it is now that she's met me," Esa needled.

It took Rory a while before he noticed Jake standing at the bar, glaring at them. At first he thought he had to be mistaken; why would Jake look pissed off? He focused. Nope, it was definitely Jake, and he was definitely glowering. Rory excused himself and walked over to his friend.

"What're you doing over here?"

"Assessing." He tilted his head in the direction of Rory's table. "That's your mate, eh?"

"Yeah. C'mon. We're having a right laugh."

"Don't think so."

Rory was puzzled. "What's gotten up your arse?"

"Your mate really seems to be pourin' it on with San."

"Jealous, eh?"

Jake raised his pint glass to his lips, his eyes still locked on Esa. "Look at her," he said angrily as the women returned to the table. "All gooey-eyed, even lookin' like she enjoys him checking out her body."

"If it bothers you so much, then come sit with us. Defend

your territory." Jake turned to him. The glaring hadn't stopped. "For fuck's sake, Jake. Stop being such an idiot." He said it so loudly Bettina turned from where she was pulling some stout. Rory could tell from the look of intense concentration on her face that she was all ears now, so he lowered his voice.

"Come over to the table," he repeated. "You're my best mate. I want him to meet you. He's just being nice, making her feel good. And like I said, if it bothers you, defend your territory. Show her you want to take it to the next level. Now. Tonight. Even if it's something small."

"All right," Jake capitulated, still frowning.

* * *

Erin, Sandra, and Esa were already feeling good after a few drinks, so there was not the slightest bit of tension when Jake joined the table. That is, until Esa continued mesmerizing Sandra. There was no mistaking the antagonistic look in Jake's eyes. Erin and Rory exchanged worried glances, but behind it, Erin knew they were both glad Jake had finally seemed to realize that Sandra and he both wanted the same thing: a good, happy life in Ballycraig.

"I can't believe you were married and he let you go," Esa marveled as he gazed deeply into Sandra's eyes. He turned to the rest of the table. "Can you?"

Erin grimaced. "Actually—"

"My husband was a drunken loser," Sandra supplied.

"I'm glad he's not here to make you unhappy anymore," Esa continued. "You deserve happiness."

"Yeah, she does." Jake sneered. "You gonna give it to her?"

Sandra looked at Erin with wide eyes.

Esa looked at Jake, puzzled. "Does it bother you that I'm being attentive to Sandra? Is it something you're not capable of doing yourself?"

"You better feckin' watch yourself, mate."

Esa looked at Sandra. "You've been having a good time tonight. Am I right?"

"You're right," Sandra said. She touched Jake's arm. "It's just harmless fun."

"Is it?" Jake snapped.

Sandra looked perplexed. "What the hell has gotten into you, Jake?"

"It bugs me, okay?" His voice was forceful. Impressive.

"What for?"

"Because I don't like you flirting with him, right?"

Sandra turned to Erin. "Are you hearing this?"

"Look," said Jake, "I've realized a few things."

"Oh, what's that?" Sandra retorted. "That you're out of your gourd?"

"No. That what I want is a woman who wants the same things I do: a life here in Ballycraig."

Esa looked at Erin and Rory. "Perhaps we should leave."

"No one's goin' anywhere," Jake declared. "I don't care who hears what I have to say."

Sandra's expression was skeptical. "So you want a life here in Ballycraig. There are loads of women here who want that."

"I don't want to see them. I want to see you."

"God Jesus," Sandra slugged down some of her drink. "This is doing my head in."

"Why?" Erin asked. "You two have been hanging out a lot, right? Plus, you had a mad crush on him at school."

Sandra shot her a murderous look. "That was a hundred years ago."

"Feelings can be revived," said Erin. She leaned against Rory. "Look at us."

Esa stood. "This is degenerating into a soap opera. I really think I should leave."

Jake stood up, looking at Esa with contempt. "Think you're better than us, don't you?"

"Jake, c'mon," said Rory. "There's no reason to go down this path."

"Don't you?" Jake pressed Esa.

"It was harmless fun," Esa said, looking bored. "Sandra herself said so. Just chill."

Jake took a swing, aiming to punch Esa in the face. Esa deftly sidestepped the punch, grabbed Jake's wrist, and twisted it hard enough behind his back to force Jake back into his seat. It all happened so fast that no one else in the pub seemed to have noticed.

"Jake!" Rory snapped. "What the fuck are you doing?"

"Showing this arrogant asshole where he can put it."

Esa slowly released Jake's wrist with a look of condescension. "Tougher men than you have tried that and failed, and they weren't drunk at the time. Let's chalk this up to your having too much to drink. I'm staying up at the farm. I think it best if we avoid each other." He turned to the table, smiling graciously. "Sandra, Erin, it was very nice to meet you. Rory, I'll give you a call tomorrow."

Erin looked at Sandra as Esa left the pub. Rather than looking horrified, Sandra actually looked tickled.

"Sorry about that," Jake muttered.

"Yeah, me, too," said Rory angrily. "He's one of my mates, Jake. There was no reason for you to be a *total* dick to him. You're gonna apologize to him at the farm tomorrow, yeah?" Jake was silent. *"Yeah?"*

"Yeah, I'll apologize." He looked at Sandra. "You look very pretty tonight," he said quietly. And that was all it took.

31

My head's gonna explode.

It was early the next morning. Erin had promised her-self that no matter how hungover she was, or how late the hour, she would stick to the new schedule she'd set for her-self and get up at seven to study. She'd grown used to study-ing in the evening, but morning was when she was at her most alert.

She was tempted to ignore the alarm when it went off, but she didn't. She wasn't hungover so much as exhausted. She quickly padded downstairs to make tea. The house was quiet. Liam and Esa were still asleep. Aislinn had been working for at least two hours now. Erin silenced the tea kettle before it had a chance to scream, then crept back upstairs to her room with her cuppa. She checked her phone; no messages from her mother.

The estrangement hurt more every day, though Erin hated to admit it. It made her feel like her mother held all the power. But Erin was determined not to bend.

Two hours had passed with her glued to her laptop, answering mock exam questions like, "Which female artist

painted Marie Antoinette's portraits?" She much preferred
working on practice essays in her specialty area, modern art.
Those were a joy to write. The closer it drew to the days of
her exams, the more doubtful she grew. What if this really
was a stupid field to have picked? What if she never got a job?

Her half-finished cup of tea had gone stone-cold, and
she wanted to make a new one. She opened her bedroom
door at precisely the moment Esa Saari opened his.

"Hello," Erin said politely. The evening had ended
oddly: Jake driving Sandra home, Rory driving her home,
even though both houses were within walking distance of
the Oak.

"Hello," Esa returned courteously. "I was going down
to make myself some breakfast. Would you like to join me?"

"Sure." What Erin wanted to say was that she really
needed to get back to studying, which was true. But then
she thought: *this could be a good opportunity for him to
get to know me as myself, not just Rory's fiancée.* She just
wished she were wearing something a little more attractive
than yoga pants and a sweatshirt.

Esa quietly followed her down the stairs. Once in the
kitchen, Erin could hear the sound of Aislinn herding her
flock nearby.

"I can't believe Aislinn is already out there," said Esa.
Erin noticed he didn't mention Jake being out there as well.

"Farmer's hours," Erin replied.

"My maternal grandfather was a farmer. Reindeer."

"Reindeer," Erin mused. "I never really thought about
them actually being raised somewhere." She had a disturb-
ing thought. "Do you eat them?"

Esa looked amused. "Yes."

"All right, let's change the subject. I don't want to think
about someone tucking into Rudolph."

Esa gestured at the fridge. "Is it all right if I just—"

"Of course. I'm sure Liam and Aislinn told you to take
what you'd like."

"They did. I just wanted to make sure they weren't just
being polite."

"No, Aislinn would have let you know if you couldn't help yourself to anything in the fridge, believe me. I'm making myself some tea," Erin told him, turning on the kitchen tap. "Would you like a cup?"

"Actually, not to be a pain in the ass, but do they have any coffee?"

"Oh, loads. Liam prefers coffee to tea." She pointed to the coffeemaker. "Coffee and filters are in the cabinet above."

"Thank you."

The atmosphere felt a bit awkward. Erin found it mildly disconcerting, but she assumed it would pass once they actually sat down over breakfast.

Esa opened the fridge, peering inside. "Hmmm. Eggs. Also some apples, some muffins . . ." He turned around to look at her. "If I make eggs, will you have some?"

"Sure. And I'll have a muffin, too. With lashes of butter." She wasn't about to squash down her appetite because he was used to bone-thin models.

Esa nodded, pulling out ingredients. "First, I have to make the coffee. If you don't mind."

"Esa, look. You don't have to be so deferential. I thought we got past formalities last night."

Esa ran his hand through his hair, looking apologetic. "I know, but I feel like an intruder. I didn't mean to cause problems last night."

"Jake was the problem, not you."

"I thought: harmless flirting."

"Well, Sandra did, too."

"It was fun. She's a good-looking woman, and she seemed to be enjoying it."

"Jake will be apologizing sometime today, I guarantee it. He realizes he went a bit mad."

"I hope so. I'd hate to have to snap his neck. It would make things very awkward between me and Rory."

Are all hockey players arrogant? Erin wondered. She couldn't tell if he was joking or not. He wasn't smiling, which meant he had to be serious. So macho, so early in the morning. Rory was probably the same way.

Despite his confidence, however, Esa was going about making the coffee all wrong. If anything happened to the coffeemaker, Liam would go mental. Erin had no choice but to intervene.

"No so much coffee," she called over to him. "The carafe can't hold it. You put that much in for a carafe that size, and you'll be drinking mud."

Esa peered at the coffee basket. "You're right." He scooped some coffee back into the airtight storage container. "Rory seems very happy," he noted, sitting down at the table.

Erin was thrilled. "Does he?"

"Yeah. He's been a miserable bastard the past year. Now I see why."

Erin blushed, and then she fished. "Rory really didn't get serious with anyone while we were split up?"

"He wasn't a saint, Erin. But he wasn't a dog, either."

"That's good to hear."

Esa looked at her curiously. "What if he had been? Would you still have taken him back?"

"I think so. But I honestly don't know."

"It's hard to believe he didn't grow up playing hockey. He's a very talented athlete."

"I've never seen him play."

Esa looked shocked. "What?"

"I've never seen him play hockey. In person, I mean."

"You'll love it. I'm better than he is, of course," Esa said, "but he's pretty good. He's been a real asset to the team."

The coffeemaker hissed its completion. "Tell me about you, Erin," said Esa, pouring himself a cup.

She suddenly felt shy. "I'm sure Rory has told you loads of things."

"He has, but I'd like to get to know you myself." He brought his coffee to the table. "For example: Rory says you're getting a degree in art history?"

"Yeah." Another blush made an appearance. "Probably crazy, I know."

"No more crazy than trying to make it as a professional athlete," Esa pointed out with a smile.

"I suppose."

"I envy you, going to university. Maybe I'll go when I retire. I don't know. There are lots of subjects I'm curious about, but I don't have the time right now because I'm pursuing other things."

Erin ventured a tease. "Like models and parties?"

"Ah, my reputation precedes me," replied Esa with a boyish grin.

"It does."

"I like having fun. Who doesn't? But I won't do that forever." He took a big sip of coffee. "One day I'll meet the right person and surprise everyone by turning into a mature, responsible adult. But until then, I'll have a good time."

"Good for you," said Erin. She liked Esa. She got the sense that for whatever reason, he didn't want people to know he had any emotional depth.

"And you?" Esa inquired. "Are you having a good time?"

The question took her aback. She had to think about it. "Not in the sense you are, larking about and all that. But I'm having a good time in that I'm back with the man I love, and hopefully, I'll eventually be doing the thing I love. It's been a long time coming."

"Don't tell Rory I said this, but he's very lucky to have you."

"Yes, I know." They both laughed.

"I look forward to getting to know you better, Erin, when we're all in America."

"Me, too, Esa."

"Now let me make you some eggs, Finnish style. But I promise: no reindeer sausage."

32

"Still being a stubborn old bat."

Erin and Sandra, who had baby Gina on her lap, were sitting in the field behind Saint Columba's school, the one that served as the playground when school was in session. Oona was jumping rope with three friends on the small strip of blacktop running beneath the classroom windows. LJ was at a friend's house. Lucy was earning a few bob helping San's mother clean her house.

Despite her better judgment, Erin had asked Sandra if her mother had mentioned her at all. She thought: she had to have, even if it was just to casually ask Sandra if she was okay. But she hadn't.

Sandra adjusted the straw hat on her head. She told Erin that she'd just read an article on the damage direct sunshine could do to your face, the way it could age you. She didn't want to wind up looking like a shar-pei when she was old.

"Look," she continued, "I can tell she's dyin' to ask about you. She'll say, 'Sandra,' and then she'll pause and say, 'Nothing. Forget it,' and walk away. I think it's killin' her, this rift. Same as it's killing you."

"It's not killing me!" Erin protested.

"Oh, give over. How long have I known you? Differences or not, you love her to death."

"It's not killing me; it's hurting me, more than I thought it would. Is she really willing to let me go off to America without mending things?"

"Have you talked to your da?"

"Yeah, on the sly. You'd think we were having an affair, he's so tense on the phone. Even though he usually rings from work."

"What does he say?"

"Same as you, but nicer. That she's stubborn, she's always been stubborn, and I should know that. Honestly, sometimes I don't know how he's stuck it for this long."

"Love, maybe?"

"Oh, listen to the great romantic here."

Erin took Gina onto her lap, then reached into Sandra's oversized shoulder bag for a comb. Gina loved it when Erin brushed her fine, short hair.

"You should come round bath time," said Sandra, watching Erin and her daughter. "Screams like she's being murdered when I try to comb her hair."

"That's 'cause you're her mam," replied Erin in a stage whisper. "My combing her hair is special."

"I'll try to remember that next time I'm worried the garda are going to bust into my house because they think I'm killin' me own child."

Erin's gaze drifted to Oona and her friends jumping rope. "Did we ever jump rope? I can't remember."

"I think we did, for a short while, with that mad little witch, Amy MacFadyen. But then we stopped, remember, because her mam went all Jehovah's Witness-y, and she told us we were going to burn in the fires of hell if we didn't convert."

"I remember now." She gently ran the comb through Gina's bangs. "A lot of hell talk."

"It was big in those days, hell. Now kids think hell is having their phones taken away."

"Suppose you're right."

Erin closed her eyes, letting the breeze play over her face. "I can't believe summer's almost over."

"I can't believe you'll be leaving soon."

The catch in her friend's voice prompted Erin to open her eyes. Tears were welling up in Sandra's eyes, which could cause a chain reaction. Erin clenched her jaw tight, the only way she knew to hold tears back. She was afraid if she gave in to it, they'd sit there like two weeping fools and scare Gina. "It's not like I'll never be back," she pointed out to Sandra. "And maybe you can come over for a visit."

"Oh, right. And how am I going to do that? Ask Peter Pan if I can cadge a ride on his back?"

Gina began to whine, and Erin put the clip Sandra had brought along in her hair. "Maybe you and Jake could come over together."

"Knew that was coming."

"Well?"

"Well, what?"

"Last night was quite the about-face."

"Tell me about it." Sandra took a bite of her biscuit. "It made me feel weird all over. We've been hanging out, yeah, but now, to hear him say he wants to see me . . . I don't know."

"He's a good bloke."

"Question." Sandra seemed mildly vexed. "Why was it all right for you to say, 'Oh, Jake, no way, I can't think of him that way,' but I can't?"

"Because I never fell out of love with Rory. And because Jake and I never wanted the same things." She nudged Sandra in the ribs. "You liked Jake warning Esa off you. Admit it."

"It was a little flattering," Sandra conceded.

"You two looked dead cozy by the end of the night."

"We were both a bit tipsy."

"Right."

"Listen, Erin: whatever happens with me and Jake, I'm

not leapin' into it. I've got to get my family and myself sorted first."

"Unless he properly courts you," Erin replied with a wicked grin.

"Christ, I should have run far and fast from you in Infant school while I still had the chance." San eyed Erin with affection. "I say this with nothing but love: time for you to butt out."

"I'm butting, I'm butting," Erin promised. She knew San as well as she knew herself: if Jake kept on it, Sandra would fold pretty fast. She was desperate for respect and companionship. Jake would give her both, and more.

A cry rose up from Oona, and both she and Sandra tuned in immediately. "What's up, sweet?" Sandra called. "You skin your knee?" Oona nodded. "C'mere, then, and I'll stick a plaster on it, and you can go right back to playing." She turned to Erin, shaking her head. "It's something every minute."

"Yeah, and you love it."

Sandra cocked her head thoughtfully. "You know, I do. Jesus wept, listen to me; do you hear me? I'm starting to sound like someone who's happy."

"You deserve it, San."

"And so do you."

33

"*I don't know* why you want me to come along." Erin and Sandra were in perfect step as they headed down to the Oak. Sandra was meeting Jake for a drink, and she wanted Erin along so she could "objectively" assess Jake's level of infatuation. Erin thought it was a foregone conclusion, but Sandra was so insistent, and so excited, that Erin couldn't turn her down.

She wished Rory were here. The minute Esa had left two weeks ago, he'd packed his things and gone up to Dundalk, where there was a rink. Esa's level of fitness had jarred him. because it showed Rory how much he himself had slacked off. He told Erin he'd be skating every day until his legs turned into rubber and his muscles screamed for mercy. He refused to start training camp with even the slightest hint of physical weakness.

"Now here's what you look for," Sandra instructed, side-stepping a melted ice cream cone on the pavement. "If his eyes dart away when I'm talking, that's not good. It means I'm boring the teeth off him and his mind is elsewhere. But if his eyes hold mine, then he's truly keen."

"Sandra, you already know he's truly keen. Besides, that's just common sense you're spouting. It's not unique to romantic relationships."

"Just do what I say, right?"

"I'm on it, bossy pants."

Sandra was always buoyant on Friday nights: that's when she got her wages. Erin had given up asking how her mother was. Erin thought that with each passing day, the pain she was feeling would abate just a tiny amount. In fact, the opposite was true: her mother's silence ate at her more and more, a gnawing pain she couldn't contain.

"You're buying the first two rounds, right?" Erin teased as the pub came into view. Sandra was proud to be able to contribute more to the bar tab than in the past. Who paid for what didn't matter to Erin either way. The important thing was that San was happy.

"Christ, I hope that Jarlath Fields isn't in there." Sandra groaned. "You know, that gooey-eyed slip of a thing who's helping out Grace at the greengrocer? Caught him looking at my arse the other day."

"He's quite the arse man, from what I hear."

"Man?" Sandra chortled. "He's twenty if he's a day. He'd best watch himself: if I catch his eyes going southward again, he'll find his voice going up three octaves. I'll take my mam's cricket bat to him."

"I can't believe Jack and Bettina still have it behind the bar."

"Mam doesn't need it now that Larry's gone."

"Too true." *And the gobshite better not come back.*

They pulled open the pub door. It took Erin a split second to process the shouts of "congratulations" being blasted her way. But then she realized: it was a surprise graduation party. And there, standing smack-dab in the middle of the crowd, grinning at her like a fool, was Rory.

"I . . ." She was gobsmacked. Truly. Sandra was beside herself with excitement.

"You really didn't suspect a thing? Truly? Not even a beensy-weensy bit?"

"Why would I?"

"A Black Velvet and an Academy Award for me," Sandra shouted out to Rory. She gave Erin a friendly push. "Go on. Give your man a big, wet, sloppy kiss. He's the one that put this thing together."

Erin threw her arms around Rory's neck amid cheers and whistles, the soundtrack to so many pub events. "I can't believe you did this!"

"Why? Am I that bad of a fiancé?"

"Don't be daft." Erin's eyes were swimming in tears. "No one's ever done anything like this for me before. Ever."

Rory was beaming. "As soon as the idea struck me, I knew I had to do it." He crushed her to him. "I'm so proud of you, *macushla*."

"Thank you," Erin whispered.

"Okay, enough of this 'Oh, boo-hoo, I love you, Rory' claptrap," called Old Jack. "I don't know about anyone else here, but I'm in the mood for one feck of a party." The roar of approval was near deafening. "By the way, it's an open bar, courtesy of Wayne Gotti over here." He pointed to Rory.

"I think you mean Wayne Gretzky," Rory corrected.

"Gotti, Gretzky—who gives a damn? All I care about is that our girl knows how proud we are of her. The bar is officially open."

* * *

The liquor flowed and there was no pause in the laughter. After playing a string of traditional Irish tunes, the band decided it was time to play Cliff Richard's classic "Congratulations," a staple in the UK and Ireland for over forty years. Everyone in the pub joined in. Erin couldn't count how many times she'd sung that song at birthdays, wedding receptions, engagement parties, communion parties, and baptism parties. Everyone seemed disappointed when the song came to an end.

"God, I love that song," Sandra said with a sigh, looking at Erin fondly. "D'you remember when my gran learned to play it on the uke?"

"I do. And I remember your granddad breaking it in two because he couldn't take it anymore. It was the only song she knew."

"Never tried anything musical again, my gran."

Everyone at the table laughed. Erin beamed at Rory. "I know I'm starting to sound like a broken record, but this is dead brilliant. You must've pulled it together pretty fast."

"Simple as pie," Rory boasted. "One call to Bettina and the whole town knew within a day."

"Things like this. I'll miss them."

"People do get to know each other in New York, you know. Sometimes whole groups of them."

"Don't be cheeky." Erin glanced about. "I wonder where Aislinn and Liam are."

"Liam said they'll be along soon. Said Aislinn is feeling a bit under the weather."

Erin felt a surge of excitement. "Maybe she's—?"

"Don't ask me. And don't ask her, either. If she is, she'll tell us in her own good time."

Erin felt her eyes welling up again. "No one's ever thrown me a party before."

"I'd dispute you there," said Sandra. "Your parents threw you a sweet sixteen party."

Embarrassed, Erin covered her mouth with her hand. "God, you're right."

"I was upset I couldn't be there because it was during the school year, remember?" said Rory.

"I can't believe I forgot."

"Cut yourself some slack," said Rory. "You've a lot on your mind right now—including planning our wedding."

Erin's pulse skipped. "Can I assume—"

"As soon as we figure out our schedules, you can ring Father Bill so we can secure a date."

Erin leaned over, hugging him tight. "You're the best."

"Whatever the bride wants, right?"

"Where should we go on our honeymoon?" Erin asked breathlessly.

"Hey, let's nail the wedding plans down first."

"Go troppo," Sandra suggested.

Erin looked at Rory hopefully. "I have always wanted to go troppo, you know."

"Yes, I do know. Sometimes I think I remember more things about you than you do!"

"I wouldn't be surprised." Erin rose. "Be back in a mo'."

She felt a bit wobbly, making her way to the loo. It was from the champers. Erin liked the way the bubbles sometimes tickled her nose as it went down, and it went down a lot smoother than she expected. She had a nice buzz on. It felt good.

Christ, don't let the loo be crowded. She hated standing there in a line with her bladder filling. But maybe it was just her night all round: there was no line as she pushed open the bathroom door.

Her mam was leaning close to the mirror above the sink, applying her signature coral lipstick.

Erin's feet were nailed to the floor. If someone pushed open the door behind her, she'd be hit squarely in the ass and find herself sprawled on the cracked tile floor. Her mother caught sight of her and halted mid lipstick application. Erin saw her hand trembling as she put the lipstick back in her purse. Erin waited, pulse pounding away in her throat. Finally, her mother slowly walked toward her.

"I am so, so sorry, lamb," she whispered, holding her arms out. "Please forgive me."

Erin burst into tears and flew into her mam's arms.

"I love you so much," her mother continued, choking up. "Stupid, that's what I am. Missin' out on all this time with you." She pulled back, pressing her lips softly to Erin's forehead. "You can't imagine how much I've missed you. I've been kicking myself for being a fool, but you know me: I'm a stubborn old nag."

Erin hiccupped, trying to slow her tears.

"One day your father said to me that I'd better think hard about the stand I'd taken, because you'd be off to America soon, and that'd make it harder than ever to patch things up. Then he pointed out what a pity it would be, me missing your wedding and all. That did it: my stupidity came rushing back and bit me on the arse. It said, 'You'd better go to her, Bridget, or you're going to lose your girl.' So here I am."

Erin swiped at her eyes. "I'm so glad. You don't know. This thing was killing me."

"Me, too. God, the tears. And still I wouldn't bend. 'Pride goeth before a fall'—isn't that what it says in the Bible? Well, I fell, all right. I just hope you can forgive me."

Erin took a tissue out of her pocket and dabbed at her mother's wet eyes. "How you could ever think I wouldn't forgive you is a mystery to me."

"I haven't been the most pleasant creature to be around."

"I know."

Her mother looked caught off guard, then smiled. "It's all going to be good from now on, Erin, I promise you that. I can't wait to help you plan your wedding—that is, if you don't mind."

"You can help," Erin warned, "but—"

"I know, don't go criticizing and that. So help me God, I won't."

"Good." Erin paused. "How'd you get in here without anyone seeing you?"

"People did see me. I just walked in as if it was no big deal and no one seemed to give a toss. Except Bettina. She was right on my tail comin' in here. I told her to please keep her gob shut about it until I'd talked to you. Now that things worked out the way I hoped they would, she'll be grabbin' a megaphone to tell the whole world."

"Where's Da?"

"Driving Mr. Russell to see his sister in Clifden, since his car is in the shop. Apparently she's got a nice place on the Sky Road. They fight like cats and dogs, though. It'll be a miracle if he lasts the weekend."

"I can't believe Da's letting Mr. Russell's bony arse cheeks touch the seat of his car."

"I know. But sometimes people can surprise us, no?"

Erin smiled happily. "They can. And when it's the people you love, that's the best."

* * *

Erin and Rory were snuggled up tight in Erin's room at Liam and Aislinn's. The party had run very late—three a.m.—but everyone seemed to enjoy it right down to the last minute. Erin was sure Jack would have kept the Oak open all night if people wanted, but seeing as three was way past the legal time for last call, keeping it open till the sun began peeping through the windows would have been pushing his luck a bit.

The evening had gone too quickly. She'd been flying high before she and her mother made up, but afterward, the night was pure bliss. Erin was certain she could never, ever be happier. Surrounded by those she loved, she felt both cherished and invincible. She just wished her brother, Brian, could have come from Liverpool. Rory's gran was missing, too. "Too tired," she'd told Rory. "Besides, she knows I'm proud of her."

"Feels like sinning, the two of us here in this bed," said Erin, nestling closer to Rory.

"I know. But you know how Gran feels about premarital sex."

"Same as my parents. If not letting us sleep together under the same roof allows them to maintain their fantasy of chastity, it's really no big deal."

Rory looked amused. "They've been maintaining the fantasy for years." There was awe in Rory's eyes as they held hers. "It was wonderful to watch you tonight."

"What are you on about?"

"The way your happiness just lit up the room. What's the word? Incandescent. That's what you were. Gran would say you were filled with the holy light."

"She wouldn't be saying it right now if she knew the unholy thoughts chargin' through my head."

Rory propped himself up on one elbow. There was arousal in his eyes. "Why don't you tell me some of them?" He gently nipped her earlobe. "Better yet, why don't you show me?"

Erin kissed him with great gentleness, her entire body slowly coming to life even though the kiss was more that of careful courting lovers than two who knew each other intimately, both inside and out.

Rory kissed her back, but there was nothing chaste about it. His lips pressed against hers were hard, demanding. Erin eagerly succumbed, her tingling body her confessor.

He drew her as close as he could. The embrace. It was solid and reassuring, yet unmistakably possessive at the same time. She wound her arms around his neck, held on tight. She was all his. He took his mouth from hers, softly pressing his mouth to her throat. She was beginning to get breathless, that old familiar feeling of ease and desire. He knew just where she wanted to be kissed and how. *I remember,* his body was telling her. *I remember everything.*

His kisses became more teasing, more challenging. Erin grabbed his face hungrily, claiming his mouth with hers. Rory drew her to him even closer, no hiding his greed, his cock twitching against her thigh. Reaching down with one hand, Erin wrapped her hand around it and began pumping. He flexed his body against her, his heavy breath begging. He put a hand on hers. Slowed it down. He made her tighten her grip ever so slightly, but slowed the rhythm. Rory's groans of pleasure were making it harder and harder to ignore what she wanted. She draped a leg over his hip and ground herself against him, knowing he'd be able to feel her wetness there.

Rory smiled at her wickedly. "Trying to tell me something?"

Erin smiled seductively and pulled him atop her, drawing her knees up toward her chest. She wanted him deep.

Rory took her arms, pushing them high over her head. She was prisoner, but just for a moment. When he pushed inside her, her hands broke free. She had to touch him while he moved inside her. Caress him. Spur him on by digging her nails into his back. But he wouldn't let her. He grabbed her by the wrists and, once again, pulled her arms over her head.

The thrusting turned rougher. She liked the way he held her down. He asked her if she wanted it hard. She did. Erin began shivering uncontrollably as Rory hammered himself into her, his eyes never moving from her face. She knew he wanted to see the moment when it became too much for her. She succumbed mere seconds later, gasping with pleasure as her body shuddered, the aching inside subsiding.

Her breath was coming hard and fast as she arched against him. No verbal incentive needed. Rory slammed into her mercilessly, driven by the old need to devour. When he could take no more, he groaned and, with one final thrust of his body, left his senses behind.

34

"*Ah, screw Crosshaven* and Moneygall. The only place to be on a Saturday night is the Oak."

Rory's toast as he touched pint glasses with her, Jake, and Sandra was dead-on, Erin thought. The four of them had gone to a Moneygall pub and a Crosshaven pub the week before, just for a change of pace. Neither came close to the Oak, though. The bar offerings were the same, but both were dominated by a sense of commerce that the Oak lacked. The warmth felt slightly contrived, the bands a little too slick. It was as if both places were created to cater to tourists who imagined that this was what an authentic pub experience might be like. Erin and Rory knew there had to be a true local pub hidden somewhere in those towns, but they couldn't find it.

Even though the Oak was getting its fair share of tourists these days, Jack and Bettina had always had a take-it-or-leave-it attitude. It was that no-nonsense approach that helped make the Oak, the Oak. No one gave a toss that Chuck Clayton really couldn't carry a tune for his life, or that the Holy Trinity would die on their stools, bodies slumped over the bar, or that all the tables in the place wobbled, and had for years. The Oak belonged to them, the people of Ballycraig.

Erin looked around sentimentally and sighed deeply. "I've not even gone and already I'm dreamin' about when I'll be comin' back to visit."

"And when will that be?" Rory asked, sounding slightly irritated. They'd been going round and round on the issue.

"You tell me," said Erin. "I mean, you've got to be back in training camp in September, and I have to look for a job . . ."

Sandra's face fell. "Will you not be home for Christmas, at least?"

"'Course we will," Erin said.

Rory looked at her a bit crossly.

"We'll try our best," she corrected.

Erin and Rory had at least worked this much out: they'd try to spend Thanksgiving with his parents in the States, then come back to Ballycraig for Christmas, if they could work around the Blades' schedule. Her uncle Charlie and aunt Kathleen were thinking of coming over for the holidays as well, which would send her da and Liam over the moon.

"Maybe when you're back, we could go up to Dublin one day and look at wedding dresses," Sandra suggested eagerly.

"I think that's the best idea I've heard in a while," Erin declared. She and San shopping in Dublin . . . it would be brilliant.

Rory sipped his lager. "Who's on babysitting duty tonight?" he asked Sandra.

"Lucy, if you can believe it. Something must've happened to shake that girl up, because she's been as good as gold."

"Maturing, I'd say." Erin cast a surreptitious glance at Jake. Rory had told her what Jake had done.

"She's broken up with that weasel as well."

"Thank Christ."

They were having a good-natured argument over the singer Adele (Rory and San hated her, Erin and Jake thought she was pretty damn good) when a tall, thin, well-dressed woman entered the Oak. Her wavy bobbed hair was shining, and she carried herself with sophistication. At the bar, she seemed to fall quickly into conversation with Liam, who was jawing away with her like he'd known her for years.

"I wonder who that is," Sandra said, giving her a thorough once-over. "Dead classy. Really put together. So what's she doin' here?" she joked.

They all laughed.

A few minutes later, the woman appeared at their table. "Hi. I just wanted to introduce myself: my name is Wendy Dann. I'm a literary agent here from New York to talk to PJ Leary. I know Quinn O'Brien pretty well, which is why I thought I'd stop by the table." She smiled shyly at Rory. "He told me there was a player for the New York Blades in Ballycraig as well."

Rory grinned. "That'd be me." He held out his hand. "Rory Brady."

Wendy gave Rory the once-over, which annoyed Erin. "It's a pleasure to meet you."

"Big fan, are you?"

Wendy blushed. "I'm new to it, actually. My boyfriend—ex-boyfriend, actually—was a big Blades fan. We split up and here I am, hooked on hockey."

"My heart's breakin' for ya, love," said Sandra, drinking down more of her Black Velvet. "Truly."

Erin gave her a dirty look. She didn't want this Wendy thinking that Rory's people were coarse and snide. As if Rory seemed to care; his attention was still focused on Wendy.

"I can't believe you know Quinn. I've never seen you two bendin' the elbow at the Wild Hart."

Wendy smiled discreetly. "We usually tip elbows at literary parties." She leaned in closer to Rory. "He hates those parties, but he's shopping a book around."

"Now that is a prime piece of blackmail," said Rory. "Thanks for the tidbit."

"You're very welcome."

Sandra jerked a thumb in Erin's direction. "Hey, since we're talking about Quinn and Liam, it might be nice, Rory, if you point out that Erin here is their cousin."

Wendy smiled at Erin. "Are you? That's lovely."

Erin just nodded, like some kind of tongueless fool. She felt like a lower life-form compared to this Wendy, who was dressed so simply yet so stylishly, while here she was in nothing but faded jeans and an old concert T-shirt, not a lick of makeup on her face. Then there was Wendy's voice, so confident and low. Were all Manhattan women like this, so smooth and charming? If so, she was royally screwed. The worst part was, she could see how taken Rory was by her.

He grabbed an empty chair from a nearby table. "C'mon, Wendy, join us."

Wendy looked put on the spot. "No, really, I couldn't."

"Don't be daft. Sit down."

Sandra shot Erin a distinct look of displeasure. It wasn't hard to figure out why: Jake's eyes were glued to Wendy's breasts.

Sandra smiled at Rory sweetly. "Might be nice if you introduce us all."

"Well, Sandra here is the impatient one," Rory said pointedly.

Wendy smiled. "Nice to meet you."

Sandra said nothing.

"Don't be like this," Erin whispered. "Just be polite. Play along. Hopefully she'll go away soon."

"I feckin' hope so."

"This bruiser over here is my best mate, Jake," Rory continued with pride.

"Are you a hockey player, too?"

Everyone looked at one another.

"God, I'm sorry, I've obviously made some kind of mistake," said Wendy, looking embarrassed. "It's just—you're so big like, like Rory—I assumed—"

"I was an athlete?" Jake finished for her smoothly. "Don't be embarrassed. A lot of people make the same mistake."

"Christ on a bike," Sandra marveled. "I've heard some whoppers in my day, but that about takes the cake, Jake Fry." She looked at Wendy. "He's a sheep farmer."

Wendy looked impressed. "I've never met one before."

Jake turned to Sandra smugly. "You hear that?"

"Would you all button up for a minute so I can introduce my lovely fiancée to Wendy?" Rory put his arm around Erin. "This is Erin, who is, as previously mentioned, related by blood to both Liam and Quinn O'Brien, as well as a host of other O'Briens both foreign and domestic. For some reason, she wants to marry me."

Wendy smiled at Erin. "Congratulations! When's the big date?"

"We're not sure yet."

"Well, let me know. I know some fabulous wedding planners in New York."

Sandra stared her down. "She's got a wedding planner: me."

Wendy looked surprised. "You're getting married here?" she said to Erin. "Well, if you change your plans, let me know. There are so many amazing places to hold a wedding in New York."

Rory looked mildly sentimental. "Yeah."

"A friend of mine just got married at The Lighthouse at Chelsea Piers," Wendy went on, as if Erin would know, or should know, where the hell that was. "It was really beautiful."

"I'll bet."

Erin could feel herself beginning to sink into a mild panic.

"One of the blokes on my team got married at, uh, now let me think . . ." Rory snapped his fingers. "Central Park Boathouse. That's it!"

Wendy put her hand to her chest with a small swoon. "That place is so romantic."

Erin shot a look of warning at Sandra, who she knew was gearing up to say something.

Sandra scowled at her, but at least she got the message. And maybe Rory did, too: he changed the subject from places to tie the knot to hockey.

"I'd never peg you for a hockey fan," he said to Wendy.

"Nice choice o' words," Sandra said under her breath.

Wendy ignored her. "I'm glad we returned to the subject of hockey." She touched Rory's shoulder. "I wanted to ask you something."

"What's that?"

"Do you think you could comp me for the season opener? My nephew will be in town, and I haven't been able to get us tickets."

Rory shrugged. "Sure, no problem."

"Thank you so much," Wendy said gratefully. She paused, biting her lower lip. "One more thing. If it's not too much."

"Here comes the part where she asks Rory to be the father of her child," Sandra said in a stage whisper.

Wendy again pretended not to hear.

"Would you be open to being interviewed for a book? One of my clients is putting together a proposal about foreign players in the NHL, and I thought you'd be perfect for it."

"Sure." It was obvious Rory was eating up the attention.

"Great." Wendy dug into the pocket of her blazer and handed Rory one of her cards. "Call me when you're back in New York. We'll meet for a drink."

Erin tried to ignore her heartbeat's madly increasing tempo. She was trying to think of something witty to say to Wendy. Something that would show her why Rory had picked her above every other woman on earth to marry. All she was coming up with was a big fat blank.

Rory looked around the bar. "Has PJ stood you up?"

"Not exactly. I'm here to poach him."

"Poach him?" Jake asked, his gaze still locked on her chest.

"I'm hoping to steal him away from his current agent. I think I can make him a lot more money than he's currently making. *A lot* more. I want to talk to him about that."

"He'll shoot you if you just show up unannounced," said Jake.

"No, Aislinn will shoot her," said Erin.

"We've already talked over the phone; he knows I'm a friend of Quinn's. He told me to stop by anytime, so I think I'm going to head over there in a bit."

"You're golden if Liam has put in a word for you as well," said Rory.

"Do you need a lift?" Jake offered solicitously. "It's on my way home. It'd be no problem."

"Thanks, but I've already got a lift."

Erin raised an eyebrow. "It's not Liam, is it?"

"Dear God, no. You couldn't pay me to get on the back of a motorcycle. Especially on these unlit country roads." She twisted in her seat, pointing to Old Jack. "No, he said he'd help me out."

There was a split second of silence, and then everyone round the table collapsed into fits of laughter.

Wendy looked irked at not being in on the joke. "What's so funny?"

"First off," said Rory, "he drives a jalopy. If you hit a bump, the doors might well fall off. Second, he owns the bar. You'd have to wait until after closing time for him to take you."

"And third, his wife would kill you," said Jake. "I'll gladly take you," he repeated, trying to look and sound gallant. "It's no problem."

"Are you sure?" asked Wendy. "I really don't want to be any trouble."

"Yeah, but see, here's the thing, Miss Wendy," said Sandra, tilting her head back as she finished her Black Velvet. "You're already trouble. You're flirtin' with my man, Jake, who's one second away from drooling on himself because he finds your boobs so magnificent, and you're flirtin' with Rory here, who's engaged. Not once have you asked

me or Erin what we do for a living. Suppose it doesn't matter, ay? We're not big and handsome. We can't further your
career, and we're not powerful enough to get you freebies.
We're invisible to you, two simple Irish country girls." She
looked at Wendy with unconcealed loathing. "Why don't
you just take your bony arse back to the Big Apple, because
I, for one, am tired of looking at it. You've taken what
started out as a great night, and you've turned it into total
shite."

Stunned silence crashed down all around them. It was
impossible to move, or speak. Finally, Wendy rose. "I'm
sorry," she said softly. "The last thing I wanted to do was
cause any trouble for anyone." She looked around the table.
"It was very nice to meet you all." She smiled at Erin.
"Congratulations on your engagement."

"Thank you."

Wendy walked slowly back to the bar.

35

Sandra drained the dregs of Erin's drink. "I can't believe the nerve of that one."

"I can't believe your nerve," said Jake, looking mildly embarrassed.

"What're you on about?"

"Sandra, you tore the woman to pieces!"

Shocked, Sandra turned to Erin. "Did I?"

"A little bit."

"A lot," Jake countered.

"Well, she deserved it! There she is, flirtin' up a storm, and what do you and your mate here do? Lap it up like two schoolboys! 'Oh, I'll drive you home, Wendy!' 'Oh, yes, Wendy, I can get you free tickets!' The woman thinks she's the end-all and be-all!"

"You're just jealous," Rory countered.

Erin turned to him. "Not jealous. Insulted. What do you think it was like for me, the two of you chatting away about places to have *our* wedding?"

"She acted like Erin and I were below her!" said Sandra.

"That's not true," Jake mumbled. "But answer me this: why

were you allowed to flirt right under my nose with Esa, and I can't flirt in front of you?"

"Because it doesn't work that way."

Jake scowled. "Who says?"

"I say. In Sandra world, it doesn't work that way. And if you don't like it, you can stuff it, Jake Fry."

Erin leaned over to Rory. "She's a bit tipsy. I think I should take her home."

"I agree."

"Well, I'm with Sandra," Erin announced. "The night's turned to total shite, and I, for one, don't see any point in sticking around." She tugged on a strand of Sandra's hair. "Let's call it a night."

"Fine with me," said Jake, looking away.

Sandra rubbed her temples. "Okay. I'll admit it: I might have had a little bit too much to drink. I'm sorry."

"You can turn into a nasty cow after a few, darlin', I hate to say it," said Jake, turning around to take her hand. "It worries me."

Sandra looked touched. "You're a sweet one, Jake. I won't ever flirt with another if you promise you won't, either."

Jake kissed her hand. "Deal."

Sandra suddenly looked weary. "God, I could fall on my face right here. I can't believe I have to work so early in the morning."

"I thought you didn't work Sundays," said Erin.

"Ah, your mam needed a spot of help. And before you get in my face and tell me she's starting to work her manipulative charms on me, I want you to know I volunteered. It's only a bit of polishing the silver and that, things that it's getting hard for her hands to do. Foldin' some linen and stacking it in the upstairs linen closet. She doesn't like to get on that step stool, and I don't blame her. And, yes, she is paying me."

"Glad to hear it."

"I suppose you two're staying?" Sandra said to Rory and Jake. "Continue your adventures with Miss America?"

"Yeah, Jake and I are gonna stay for just a few more and

then we'll go," Rory answered, ignoring the Miss America crack.

"You're already weaving on your feet, Rory," Erin said worriedly.

"I know. But we're making up for lost time. You know me, Erin: if I'm too drunk to drive, I won't, and neither will Jake."

"Good."

He squashed her in a big bear hug. "I love you, Erin."

"And I love you, Rory. I'll call you in the morning, love."

* * *

"One crack over the head. Two, at the very most. Problem solved."

Erin heaved a sigh of disbelief as she and Sandra headed out of the Oak into the darkness and drizzle. The door had barely closed behind them and already San was blathering about the cricket bat and how many wallops it would take to bring Wendy to her knees.

"You've a real violent streak in you, you know that?" Erin folded her arms across her chest to keep warm. She'd forgotten to bring a jacket, and the drizzle was chilly. "I think if you could commit a murder and get away with it, you would."

"Damn straight I would. And there's no need to guess who the victim would be."

They both chuckled.

"God, I couldn't stand that woman," Sandra continued vehemently.

"Really? I couldn't tell."

"Right, I'll admit it: I behaved badly. I may have been a bit harsh on her."

"A bit? They could use you to break prisoners!"

"But I didn't like her attitude. What I said was true, Er: she never asked us what we did. Who we were. Yeah, she showed a little interest in your wedding for about five seconds, but then it was back to Rory. It was like we were invisible."

Erin swallowed. "I know."

"And just because she wasn't sticking her tits under their noses doesn't mean she wasn't flirting with our men. Did you see Jake, fallin' all over himself to give her a ride? And Rory looking so pleased with himself because she wants him for some feckin' book project? Talk about having powers to bewitch men. Made me want to puke."

Erin put her face up to the rain. She thought, *If I start to cry, San won't know.*

"You know what makes it worse?" Sandra prattled on. "That self-confidence. I mean, a slag, right, she's only got one thing to offer. A bloke can put a bag over her head and get on with it."

"Sandra!"

"I'm sorry, I'm not gonna lie. But a woman like that—well, she's got loads of ways to keep a fella interested, doesn't she? Both in and out of the sack."

Erin felt a lump thickening in her throat. "I suppose."

"I kept thinking about that show, *Sex and the City*—you know, where the women were all smart and smooth, with great clothes? Perfect-looking? *That's* what she reminded me of." Sandra paused. "Cow."

Erin's chest began to ache. "Can we please change the subject before I get sick?"

Sandra laughed. "Will do."

Erin wished Sandra was sober. If she was, she wouldn't be talking like this. She'd realize that everything she was saying was like plunging a dagger in Erin's heart, making her feel more and more inadequate. There was no way in hell she could ever compete with Wendy Dann, or any other New York women. Tonight had just confirmed it.

36

Until her parents had taken over the B and B, Erin had been fond of Sundays. The family went to Mass, then headed home to make a big afternoon dinner. It used to be the way every churchgoing family did things, but the tradition was dying as fast as church attendance in the country was dropping off. Ballycraig was one of the few villages that could still fill up the pews, but everyone tacitly knew (apart from Father Bill, apparently) that it wasn't the homilies they were coming to hear; it was the cake hour after Mass, where everyone exchanged gossip.

After walking home with Sandra, Erin had gotten a call from Liam, telling her he was leaving the Oak early because he felt like shite, and if she wanted a lift back to the farm rather than crashing at San's, which was quite noisy, he'd swing by and pick her up. It worked out perfectly. She really hadn't wanted to sleep at San's, nor had she wanted to go back to the pub and horn in on Rory and Jake's bonding. Sleeping at the B and B was out. She felt bad that Liam seemed to be in the beginning stages of a wicked cold, but it helped her out.

Sandra rang her a little after noon, asking her to stop over. Erin had nothing on today, since her parents were visiting her mam's younger sister, Josie. They saw each other twice, maybe three times a year. Her mam always came home in floods of tears because they fought, and then for two weeks afterward there would be lots of angry words sizzling down telephone lines. Then it would blow over.

"Hiya."

Erin used her key to get in. The scene she came upon was the usual one: Oona at the computer and LJ watching a football match on TV. No sign of Lucy or Sandra.

"She's in the back garden," LJ said flatly, eyeballs glued to the screen.

"The back garden? Are you sure?" Last time she'd seen San's back garden, half the plants had met their maker, and a colony of sunflowers and mint had taken over.

"Yep."

Erin headed through the kitchen to find Sandra sitting on the back stoop, smoking a cigarette. There was a swath cut through the jungle.

Erin urged her to shove over and sat down. "You're going to start gardening?"

"Fuck, no. I just wanted to cut a path to the back fence. Oona's gone all green and wants to get a composter."

"Jake cut it through for you?"

"Nah." Sandra took a puff off her cigarette. "Mam let me borrow her machete."

"Her machete? What is it with your mother and objects that can kill, San? It's getting a little scary, if you don't mind me saying."

"I don't. The cricket bat was to crack Larry's head if it came to it, as you know. She uses the machete to protect herself in the house."

"From who? Pirates? Where on earth did she even get it?"

"That's what I don't know, and to tell the truth, I don't want to ask." She handed the fag over to Erin, who took a puff. Somehow, it still felt illicit when she and San smoked together. It was great: God knows there were few things illicit these days.

"Where's Miss Gina?"

"At Mam's."

Sandra sounded off: not quite her usual wisecracking self. She looked pensive.

"You okay?"

"No."

"Tell me what's going on, San."

Sandra looked pained. "I was at your Mam's dead early this morning, like I said I'd be last night."

"Yeah?"

"I was on the step stool at the end of the second floor, putting linens away, being dead quiet and all so I didn't wake anyone."

"And—"

"I saw your Rory coming out of one of the bedrooms."

"Are you out of your mind?"

Sandra looked on the verge of tears. "Erin, honest. Why would I tell you something like this if it wasn't true? You're my best friend. I'd never want to hurt you."

A thundering began in Erin's head. "There's no way."

"I know what Rory looks like! He was creepin' down the hall guilty as a cat, leaving the room of that New York smoothie."

"Couldn't be him," Erin insisted.

"Jesus God," Sandra said, wrapping an arm around Erin's shoulder. "I swear on the heads of my kids."

"It doesn't make sense," Erin replied. The thunder in her head was turning sharp and painful. *I knew it,* she thought, trying not to let the hysteria she was beginning to feel overwhelm her. *I knew that was the type of woman he really wanted.*

"Maybe it was one last hurrah," Sandra suggested gently. "Or something like that."

"Before what?" Erin retorted. "He gets saddled with his unsophisticated fiancée? He's the bastard who wanted me back, not the other way around. He's spent all summer trying to regain my trust, and now he does this?" She choked back sobs. "I knew I wasn't enough for him!"

"Stop being daft." Sandra twined her fingers through Erin's. "It's got nothing to do with you, and everything to do with him."

"That's hard to believe." She paused, trying to get her thoughts in order. "One last hurrah. That's the only thing that makes sense." She felt mildly nauseous as she looked at Sandra for confirmation. "Right?"

"It's gotta be that, love. Nothing else makes sense."

"Unless seeing her reminded him of what's available back in New York."

Erin put her head in her hands, succumbing to her misery. "I can't believe I have to go through this again." She looked down at her engagement ring. "I'm stuffing this down Rory's throat if anything happened."

"No, you're not! Did you know women are under no obligation to return an engagement ring to a fella when she breaks things off? Or come to think of it, even if it's him who breaks things off. That ring was a present to you. Sell it back to the effin' jewelers. Or have it redesigned and call it your 'Go feck yourself, Rory Brady' ring."

Erin sniffled, managing a small smile. "You've always been able to make me laugh. Even when some wanker turns my whole life to shit. Again."

"It's his life that's turnin' to shit, girl. Mark my words," Sandra lit another cigarette. "I'd cut his dick off with my mam's machete if I could."

"Maybe she'll let me borrow it," Erin replied glumly.

"Look, you know I'm here for you in whatever way you want me to be. If you want me to go with you when you kick him in the pants, I will. Anything."

"Thanks, Sandra."

"Now what, Er?"

"Now I throw up, square my shoulders, and walk over to his gran's cottage."

"And then you come back here, right, and we'll pal around with the kids, yeah? Get your mind off that loser."

"Yeah," Erin whispered. She was afraid if she succumbed to the waves of tears building inside her, she'd never be able to stop.

Sandra hugged her. "I'll be here."

"I know. Right now, it's the only thing keepin' me going."

37

"Thanks for the ride, Da."

Erin wasn't sure where to go or what to do when she left Sandra's. Her first impulse was to walk to Rory's gran's cottage, but it quickly became apparent, even though she was in a state of increasing devastation, that confronting Rory with his gran there was completely inappropriate. It wasn't like she could ask her to leave.

The Oak was out as well, for obvious reasons. Ditto Aislinn and Liam's. She had to see him alone. She walked up and around the streets surrounding the High Street for a while, alternating between feeling dazed and feeling like she was being flayed alive. Finally it came to her: she'd meet him at the rowan tree, private enough for her to scream her guts out at him. He sounded baffled when she told him she didn't need him to pick her up because her dad would be driving her there. But ultimately, he didn't question.

Her mother was near delirious with joy when Erin showed up at the B and B unexpectedly to catch a ride with her dad. "Now, don't tell me you can't be here for tea later," she gently admonished. "You and Rory both." Erin smiled weakly, assuring her she'd try to do her best.

Rory was already there when they arrived, sitting against the thick trunk of the tree. The sight of him canceled Erin's devastation, replacing it with black rage. She knew that if she couldn't contain it, the unleashed energy of it would decimate him. Maybe it was his turn to see what annihilation felt like.

"Rory's gonna drive you home, yeah?" her father checked.

"Yeah, Da. No worries." She was fibbing: after Rory left, she was going to walk down to the road and call herself a cab.

"All right, then. Here, give your old man a peck on the cheek." Erin complied, trying hard not to burst into tears as the crushed child within her silently begged, *Da! He hurt me! Go hurt him, please!*

"Right, off with you now. Give my love to Rory."

"I will." Erin was reminded of working at the jeweler's as she flashed her father her best fake smile. *Best get used to it. There'd be no real smiles today.*

The closer Erin got to him, the more the dark energy inside her pushed, desperate to burst out. He was a liar, a cheat, a selfish bastard. How could he have this kind of lack of respect for her? He had a happy smile on his face she wanted to slap off.

"Hey, you." Rory stood up to hug her.

Erin's face hurt as she forced a second fake smile. "Hey, you, too." When he leaned over to kiss her, it took every ounce of energy and self-restraint she had not to shove him away and tell him to go screw himself.

Who the hell did he think he was? Who the hell did he think she was?

"How's your morning been?" he asked.

"Fine. Yours?"

"All right." He rubbed a spot above his right eye. "Though I do have a bit of a headache. Me and Jake tied one on. Had more than a few after you and San left, I have to confess."

"Uh-huh."

Erin folded her arms across her chest, staring out over the graying horizon. Clouds were moving in. What a cliché. Maybe Rory would get hit by lightning. She could only hope.

Rory looked concerned. "You okay, Er?"

"I'm fine." She couldn't look at him.

"You just seem in a bit of a black mood."

"You'd be in a black mood, too, if you found out your fiancé slept with another woman."

"I don't understand."

She whirled to face him. "Don't play the innocent. It doesn't suit you. It never has." Look at him, she seethed, pretending to be mystified. "Look, I know what you did, right?"

He looked even more confused. "Er . . ."

"Oh, cut the shit, pretending you don't know what I'm talking about! How dare you insult my intelligence this way!"

Rory was blinking confusedly. "What way?"

"You know, you scumbag!"

"Jesus Christ, Erin!" Rory seemed alarmed. "I've no idea what you're on about! I swear to God!"

Erin sighed wearily. "You want to play this sad little game? Fine." She took a second to unclench her jaw. "Sandra saw you sneaking out of that New York agent's room at the B and B early this morning, Rory. She was loading up the linen closet and she saw you creep down the hall. Care to explain that to me?"

"Sure." He actually had the balls to look relieved. "Neither Jake nor I were fit to drive by closing time. So we sat on the benches outside the pub just talking—and near puking, I might add—until I felt clearheaded enough for me to drive him home. Around sunrise, this would be."

Erin crossed her arms and said nothing, so Rory continued.

"Anyway, I'm driving back to gran's, and who do I see limpin' on the side of the road but Wendy Dann, looking like five miles of bad road."

Erin frowned. "Right."

"Seems she'd been 'chatting' with PJ all night"—he gave Erin a significant look—"and he wanted to drive her back to the B and B, but she told him no, she wanted to walk back into town in the lovely, early-morning Irish mist."

"Stupid twit," Erin said under her breath.

"Well, she tripped in a hole along the way and twisted her ankle. I wanted to ring Doc Laurie and take her there, but she insisted on going straight to the B and B. I drove her there, I carried her up the stairs to her room, and then I left. I guess that's when San saw me."

"What a tidy little tale," Erin said sarcastically. "Tell me: did you tuck the little darlin' in as well?"

"Only if you define 'tuck in' as helping someone with a badly sprained ankle into her room."

"Was her ankle so bad you couldn't fuck her standing up?"

"I didn't fuck her at all!" Rory snapped. "What is it that you don't get?"

Now he had the gall to start losing his temper, which made Erin even angrier.

"You know what I get? That you're a lying wanker. It's coming in loud and clear."

Rory looked astounded. "Do you really think I would do that to you? After returning to Ballycraig to win you back? What'd be the point in it?"

"Maybe you wanted one last hurrah before you hitched up with your old Ballycraig albatross."

"And if I did want a 'last hurrah,' as you call it, do you think I'd be thick enough to fuck someone under your parents' roof? I can't believe you could even think this of me. Sandra runs to you tellin' you half-arsed tales, and you believe her."

"Because it's such a normal thing for her to see," Erin replied sarcastically. "You creepin' out of the B and B in the early morning."

Rory's mouth was set in a hard line. "I just explained to you what happened."

"Yeah, and you're banking on my gullibility to get you off the hook. I'm not that timid, accommodating mouse who worships you and thinks everything that comes from your mouth is the Golden Word of God." Erin laughed scornfully. "I don't blame all of this on you; it's partially my fault for being so stupid as to give you another chance. I should have known this could never work. Not after you've been living in New York all this time."

"You're talking complete shit, Erin. I wish you could hear yourself."

"And I wish you could have seen yourself! The way you looked at her, and how easily you fell into patter about this place and that place around town! The polish of her! I could never measure up to that!"

"Who the hell is measuring?" Rory yelled plaintively. "This is all in your head!"

"You really seemed to want a life with me. Now I see you're still the same selfish bastard! I can't spend my life with someone like that. I won't. I gave you another chance, and you blew it."

Any warmth that had been in Rory's eyes was fading. "I'm gonna say this once, and then I'm not gonna say it again: I'm not lying to you. I've never slept with another woman behind your back, and I'm not now. If you stop a minute and think, you'll see what I'm telling you happened makes sense."

"Yes, it does fit together very nicely."

Rory tipped the aviator sunglasses perched atop his head down onto his nose. "I've explained to you what happened," he said in a controlled voice. "If you don't want to trust me, or believe me, well, that's up to you. But I'm not gonna stand here and go round and round on this."

He started down the hill. Erin was furious as she watched him go. He was betting on her running after him, all, "Rory, Rory, I'm sorry, how could I ever doubt you?" That was the way things used to work in the past when they'd have a bad argument. Rory would always cut the discussion short and walk away, thus ensuring he carried all the power with him. And Erin, frightened little Erin, would scamper after him, terrified that in her stupidity, she had finally said or done the one thing that would make him see who she really was—a loser—and she would lose him for good.

Not this time.

38

"They'll love this."

Erin stood next to Liam at his kitchen table, watching as he loaded up a large canvas tote bag with sandwiches, vacuum flasks of tea, and a nice big chunk of buttered brown bread. Usually Aislinn and Jake took their lunch break at the house. But today, since it was so nice outside, Liam had decided he'd bring lunch out to them. Erin, still living there, thought it was a lovely thing of him to do.

She hadn't talked to Rory in three days, which was fine with her. She doubted she'd ever speak with him again.

The opening bars of "New York, New York" bleated from Liam's cell phone.

"Fuck." His expression clouded, but he picked it up anyway.

"Is everything all right?" Erin mouthed.

"Hang on a minute." Liam covered the mouthpiece. "Can you bring their lunch up the hill? It's Jack. Something's gone wrong with one of the beer distributors and he sounds like he's on the verge of a breakdown. I need to go down to the Oak."

Erin started outside, Liam's angry voice fading the farther she walked from the house. Erin knew Aislinn would be cheesed off that Liam was going down to the Oak— again. She often made the sarcastic comment that it was getting to the point where if Old Jack had a hangnail, he'd ring Liam to come into town to tear it off for him. From what Erin could see during the time she'd been under their roof, Aislinn was right.

Jake and Aislinn were up in the high north pasture. Often they worked different fields, but today they were both working with Jupitus. Actually, it would be more accurate to say the three of them were working with Jupitus, since Deenie was there, too. Wherever Aislinn went, so went Deenie. The older dog was sitting next to Aislinn, looking like a contest judge as she watched the younger Border collie with Jake. Deenie was half human, half dog. Aislinn waved her arms, whistling the command for the young dog to return to her side. Jake followed. Both he and Aislinn looked pleased to see Erin.

"This is a lovely surprise," said Aislinn. Deenie started nosing the tote bag containing the food. "Hey! I taught you better manners than that, miss! Lay down."

Deenie gave Aislinn a dirty look but did as she was told. Jupitus was already laying down beside Jake.

"Liam meant to surprise you, but Old Jack caught him on the blower."

Aislinn looked angry. "That's it. I'm giving that Jack a mouthful if it's the last thing I do. Liam works damn hard. He's allowed to have a few bloody hours to himself a day." She rose and started down the hill. "Start without me."

"He's in for it now, Old Jack," said Jake.

"He does seem to ring Liam a lot."

"He's getting old and needs help, but he's too proud to admit it." Jake peered into the tote bag. "There's loads of food here. Why don't you stay?"

"Nah, that's all right."

"Ah, c'mon. Here, you won't even have to deal with the

dirt." He took off his jacket and spread it out on the ground. "There you go. Sit yourself down."

Erin really had no pressing need to be anywhere, so she sat, watching as Aislinn closed in on the house. Jake handed her half a ham and Swiss sandwich. Erin held her breath, waiting for the sound of Aislinn blasting Old Jack, but there was silence. She must've changed her mind on the way down the hill, not wanting to stress Liam out even more.

She took a bite of her sandwich, washing it down with a sip of tea. It was a bit weak; after all this time, Liam still hadn't gotten the hang of brewing a decent cuppa yet.

"Good sandwich," said Jake.

"I was just thinkin' that."

"Bad tea," he continued.

"I was thinkin' that, too." They laughed.

"He didn't sleep with that woman," Jake said casually, a non sequitur if Erin ever heard one. "He was beside himself that you could even think that. He was all for going round to Sandra's and giving her what for."

"For what? Something she wasn't supposed to see?"

"He wouldn't do that to you, Erin. Think hard."

Erin opened her mouth to protest but was stopped by the larger realization that Jake had just defended Rory. Not that they were still rivals in any sense of the word, but hurtful barbs were still occasionally thrown, most of them having to do with her.

Erin sipped her tea slowly. *He wouldn't do that to you.* That's what her first intuition had been. But her internal compass was broken.

"Why should I believe him?" she asked Jake quietly.

"Maybe it'll help if I fill you in on some other details of the night." He took a hearty bite of his sandwich. "I'm sure he told you we got a bit pissed."

"Yeah."

"I'm talkin' lying-down-on-the-street-singing pissed."

"That's bad."

"Yeah, it is." Jake smiled sheepishly. "Around five, Bettina was awake and took pity on us. She took us inside and made us some coffee. Instant, but still.

"Rory drove me home. When I talked to him later that morning—well before you went feckin' batshit on him, thanks to Sandra—he told me about that Wendy woman twisting her ankle. Rory wanted to take her to Doctor Laurie, but she was too embarrassed to go because she'd spent the night with PJ, and she didn't want to look like a slag. So Rory helped her out and took her straight back to the B and B."

Erin regarded him with suspicion. "How do I know you're not covering for him? How do I know you and he didn't concoct this big bullshit story to explain why Sandra saw him?"

"Number one: as I already told you, Rory would never do such a thing. Number two: men are thick as planks. We don't have the brains to concoct a story that good even if we wanted to."

Erin said nothing.

"He'd never do that to you," Jake repeated firmly. "He never fooled around behind your back before, and he wouldn't now."

"How do you know?"

"I'm his best mate. He treated me like shit, but he admitted he was an asshole and a coward, and we've worked it all out. He's not a prick anymore."

Erin didn't know what to say.

Jake, still sweaty from his chores, ran a cloth over his face. "Look, men don't come runnin' to each other spilling their guts once a day, like you and Sandra do. For Rory to talk to me about this shows how upset he is. He said it was worse than taking a puck to the mouth, the way you immediately jumped to the worst possible conclusion."

"Sandra jumped to the worst possible conclusion, too! So would any woman!"

"Yeah, and then their fella would tell them what really happened, and that would be the end of it," Jake countered, tilting his head back to chug from his vacuum flask. His sideways glance was quizzical. "So?"

"So yourself. Think about it from my side, Jake. In walks this beautiful sophisticated woman—one who you were trying to impress, by the way, with your baloney about being mistaken for an athlete and all that—and within seconds she and Rory are speaking the same language. One I don't know and will never know. And she's talking in a way I'll never talk, and carrying herself in a way I'll never carry myself, and I know I can never be that for him. Ever."

Jake looked frustrated. "He doesn't *want* that. Why can't you see that?"

"He's on a different level than I am now."

Jake rolled his eyes. "That's rubbish."

"Don't tell me he hasn't had women like this fallin' at his feet for years."

"Look, Er: the man's not a priest. I'm sure he had a few good tumbles while you two were split. But that's all they were: tumbles. All he's ever wanted was you. He told me that. Even when you were apart, he thought about you endlessly. He knew he fucked up. It just took him a while to admit it to himself.

"Fix it," Jake urged. "In your gut, you know he's not lyin'. Don't let some crazy notion you've got in your head wreck it all. Go talk to him."

39

"Right, so we agree: from here on out, nothin' but trust."

Erin twined her fingers tighter through Rory's. "Agreed."

She'd felt a right twit going back to him, having to apologize for her assumption that the minute he saw a sophisticated, available woman, he'd jump at the chance. More than her lack of trust, which was insulting to him, it showed how immature she could still be, and how inadequate she still felt, despite proclaiming otherwise. She knew part of it had to do with those last few years, but it was wrong to blame it all on him.

"I can't believe how hot it is tonight."

They were lying on a blanket beneath a canvas of stars that looked freshly painted: the sky was as black as spilled ink, the stars sharp and bright as fine crystal. *Soaking it all in*, Erin thought. *There are couples all over Ireland doing what we are tonight, relishing the solitude and beauty, the perfect atmosphere it creates for unhurried talk and ease.*

She was bursting to tell him the good news. Rory was on his back, his fingers laced behind his head, gazing skyward peacefully.

"Rory, I've got some important news."

He turned his head to look at her. "Yeah?"

"I've gotten an internship offer at the Guggenheim in New York. It doesn't pay much, but it's a start."

Rory broke into a delighted grin. "I'm so proud of you. You were afraid to do it, but you took the leap anyway. Not everyone has the bollocks to do that, love."

"I know. But there's nothing in life that says just because you worked your arse off, things are going to go your way."

"No, there isn't. That's called justice, and unfortunately, it doesn't always seem to exist." He lifted her hand to his lips and kissed it softly. "But justice or not, I promise you our lives will be good. I promise."

"Rainbows and unicorns all around, is it?" Erin teased.

"Only in the baby's room."

Erin's eyes filled up quickly. "To hear you say that . . ."

"We always said we wanted kids."

"We did. I'm just glad you've not changed your mind."

"The only thing I've changed my mind about is being a self-absorbed prick."

Erin turned onto her back, her gaze skipping from star to star as she held Rory's hand tightly. "Tell me again about New York. About the flat."

"It's a bit small, but we can get a bigger one. It's high up enough that we won't hear the noise on the street, and we've got gorgeous views of the city. It's also close to a subway stop."

"An underground stop, you mean."

"Right. I've got a few pieces of furniture . . . you'll probably hate them. But we can worry about all that later."

Erin's stomach was flipping. She thought carefully. "I've been doing some thinking about the wedding."

Rory pushed himself up on his elbows, looking at her excitedly. "Yeah?"

"About when to have it. What do you think about over Christmas?"

Rory deflated. "We talked about this. I don't know what

my schedule is going to be like. We don't play on Christmas, but I don't know how much time off I'll have."

"I don't care."

"What?"

"I don't care if we're only here for three days. I want to get married over Christmas, in the town where everyone has known us most of our lives. It's what I've always dreamed. I don't care when we have a honeymoon."

"Well, that's it, then," Rory said easily, standing up and brushing off his pants. "I think that's doable, even if it means flying in on Christmas Eve and flying out on Boxing Day."

Erin hopped to her feet and threw both arms around his neck, giving him a powerful kiss. "It's going to be wonderful."

"It's going to be Father Bill marrying us," Rory said with a groan.

"It's going to be wonderful," Erin repeated. "Just wait and see."

40

"Christ, he's a natural. I don't know why it didn't dawn on me sooner that he'd be goddamn great at all this PR shit. Irish! You've all got the gift of gab, right?"

Erin smiled weakly and returned to watching the same thing the Blades head of PR, Lou Capesi, was: Rory talking to Hugh Grant. She was glad she wasn't with him right now; she'd be so nervous her drink would be shaking in her hand. Still, watching him with the handsome actor rankled a bit: technically, she and Rory were supposed to be at the London-held party together. But it wasn't exactly working out that way. One minute they'd be together, and then the next someone would "need" Rory for something, or Rory would excuse himself "for just a minute" as someone motioned him over. The minute would turn into two, three, many. Erin knew Rory: he was all about being a good sport and a team player. If someone needed a quote, or wanted to do a quick Q and A, or snap a photo, he had no problem accommodating them.

The Blades, as well as the league, had called and asked him to come to this charity party in London to help raise the league's stature in the UK, and to help promote the upcoming exhibition games. Erin wasn't happy, even though he'd insisted on bringing her with him and arranging a few guided, private tours for her of the Tate and Tate Modern. The problem was that Rory always went above and beyond because he loved it: the attention, the hobnobbing, the "it-ness" of it. He looked so happy, so vibrant and alive. He was in his element, and she was way out of hers.

He wasn't totally neglecting her. Whenever someone came over to them whom she didn't know (which was pretty much everyone), Rory would proudly introduce her and try to get a pleasant conversation started. Sometimes it worked. But very often it didn't, the other person ignoring Erin completely as he or she drew Rory into deep conversation about sports or Manhattan. And once Rory was drawn in deep, forget it.

"You havin' a good time?" Lou asked.

"I am," Erin answered.

Lou frowned. "No, you're not. Can't bullshit a bullshitter. I know how you feel. I hate these fuckin' parties. There a necessary evil, though. I didn't want to come here, but the league insisted someone be here to push Rory into the right conversations. As if he needs much pushing." He drained his martini glass. "That soccer player Rory looks like, Beckham?"

"Yeah?"

"He's over there if you want to meet him." Lou indiscreetly pointed at Becks where he stood across the VIP tent. "You ever hear him talk? He sounds like a mouse. I mean, yeah, the guy is a great athlete, right? And the women love him. But it's hard to give him his full due when he sounds like Mickey."

Erin pressed her lips together, trying not to laugh out loud.

"And his wife? *Madonn'*, someone needs to order that woman a pizza. So thin you can see her ass bones? It just ain't right."

This time Erin did laugh, and the sound, miraculously,

caught Rory's ear. He said something to Man United's Wayne Rooney, and then he was back with her and Lou.

"Christ. Sorry about that."

Lou scowled. "About what? Did you talk to Simon Cowell about donating to the Blades Children's Fund?"

"For chrissakes, Lou, it was the first time I met the guy. Besides, I'd really like to spend a little more time talking to Erin, if you don't mind."

"I do mind," Lou said brusquely. "You're great at this shit, and if there's one thing the NHL needs, it's players who are great at this shit. They all seem to love you, Rory. I don't care who tugs on your sleeve: if they're famous and not dangerous, talk to them. Talk to everybody. You get it? Erin, blame me for all this, not him. Okay? Now I gotta find something real to eat, pronto. None of this finger food bullshit."

Erin heard Rory curse Lou under his breath as he waddled away.

"Quite the character, eh?" Rory looked apologetic as he leaned over and kissed her bare shoulder. "I'm sorry about this. I knew it was going to be a big-deal party; I just didn't know how big deal. I—*shit*."

Erin looked around. "What?"

"See that guy over there beckoning us over? The one with the slicked-back hair and kind of rubbery face?" Erin nodded. "That's Ken Taggart. He's the chairman of the English National Ice Hockey League. I really should go talk to him." He cocked his head hopefully. "Come with? It won't be long."

"No, you go. I'll just be in the way."

"No, you won't."

"Rory, go," she said, which was the last thing she wanted.

Rory searched her face. "You sure?"

"Go. I'm tired. I'm just going back to the room. I'll be fine."

"I won't be too late," said Rory. "I promise."

* * *

Christ, he's a natural. Irish. You've all got the gift of gab.

Lou Capesi's words reverberated in Erin's head as she returned to the hotel room. *I must have been born in another country,* she thought, *because if there's one thing I don't possess, it's the gift of gab. Never will, either.*

She unzipped her dress and peeled off her Spanx, hoping that if her body were able to relax, her mind might follow. But it didn't. She felt miserable at the party, watching Rory glide smoothly from clique to clique, bringing smiles to people's faces, making them laugh. She knew it was all part of his job. She also knew that when he was exercising that part of his personality, she ceased to exist for him. She wasn't like him—wasn't like that—and she never would be. At first he'd say, "It's okay," but eventually he'd become annoyed, and then he'd flat-out start to feel she was holding him back, this silent albatross of a wife who was such a terribly shy bore at parties. She'd become a liability. There was no way she was going to let that happen.

She pulled on the clothes she'd arrived in, threw all her things together in a bag, and then, opening the safe in the room, took some money for herself. She left a note in the safe, telling him she'd pay him back. She wrote another and left it on the bed, telling him she loved him, but that he'd be better off without her. He mightn't be able to see that now, but give it one season back in New York, and he would.

Finished, she went downstairs to the lobby and ordered a cab to take her to Heathrow.

41

"I never thought I'd be so happy to see your busted cabbage of a face, Rory Brady."

Rory was relieved when he pressed Sandra's doorbell and not only did she answer it right away, but she almost disconnected his arm pulling him inside, she was that glad to see him.

It didn't take a rocket scientist to figure out Erin would go straight to San's when she got back to Ballycraig. When he'd gotten up to the room and read her notes, he'd wasted no time. He threw his stuff in a bag and caught the next flight from Heathrow to Galway, glad that he'd left the Range Rover in the airport's long term parking lot. He was having nonstop conversations with Erin in his head all the way back to Ballycraig. Explaining. And doing his fair share of wondering, too.

It was one of those boiling, end-of-summer days when the air was as stagnant as that of an old classroom. Unfortunately, the only relief in Sandra's house was a small plastic fan on one of the end tables. Honestly, Rory didn't know how she could stand living without air-conditioning.

"She just ran into town to pick up a few things for me at the shops," San told him. "Here, let me get you a glass of water, then I'll give you the quick low-down before she gets back."

Rory nodded, picking up a copy of the newspaper to fan himself with. Something was different. Then he realized: the room was tidy as a pin. Maybe working and being free of that prick bag Larry had lifted San's self-esteem.

"Here you go." Sandra handed Rory a glass, pressing her own to her forehead. "This is murder. Any ideas I have ever had of going troppo for a holiday flew out of me head today, I can tell ya that much."

"San, please." Rory couldn't hide his desperation.

"She showed up here at around ten this morning, gobsmacking me, as you might imagine. I thought: Jesus, this isn't good. But she still had her ring on, so I figured it couldn't be too bad."

Rory gulped down some water. "Was she crying?"

"Nope. She looked more blank than anything. She came in and just plopped down on the couch and told me all about you goin' to do the PR and that."

Rory braced himself. "Well, why did she pull a runner? Does she think I was out whoring or something?"

"Feck off. She still trusts you. No, she started talking about seeing you in your true element and all this shite. How happy you were flittin' about shaking hands and all that."

"It's part of my job!"

"I know, I know," Sandra soothed. "Calm down." She pressed the cold glass to her cheek. "She's getting cold feet. For all her talk about a new life with you in New York, she's scared to death about leaving home."

Rory grimaced. "I thought that might be part of it."

"You know Erin: sometimes her way of dealing is to just cocoon herself." Sandra's gaze shifted guiltily. "Look, I'm sorry about the trouble I caused between you two about you leaving the B and B so early that morning. I should've kept my piehole shut. But my first instinct was to protect her."

"I appreciate the apology," Rory murmured.

The front door opened. "San—"

Erin halted.

"Don't give me that trapped look," said Sandra, pulling no punches. "You knew he'd come after you. So don't you dare turn tail, especially since you're holding my bag of groceries."

"Jesus, you could have let me at least put the groceries down before bludgeoning me," said Erin. She handed the bag over to her friend, but it was Rory she was looking at. "I thought you had another day of PR activities," she said coolly.

"I did. But I told Lou I couldn't be there, because this is more important. Believe it or not, the fat bastard agreed. The way I see it, this is what's going to happen: we're going to fix this, then I'm going to pack and say my good-byes to everyone in town. Then I'm going to fly to New York, where you're going to meet me in two weeks."

Rory surprised himself, the authoritarian sound of his voice, the inflexibility of his words.

Erin looked taken aback. "You're being a bit pushy, don't you think?"

"That's all I've got time for, Erin. Take it or leave it."

"Not here." She looked at Sandra apologetically. "Do you mind if we go?"

"Don't be a daft cow. Get out of here."

"Where do you want to go?" Erin asked Rory.

"Somewhere air-conditioned."

"Only place I can think of is the B and B. Or the church."

Rory looked skeptical. "The church is air-conditioned?"

"She's not jokin' you," said Sandra. "The place is still packed, but the average age of the parishioners is sixty, and they're startin' to get a bit wobbly when it's warm. The younger ones don't even want to go in the summer, especially if their parents are taking a break from it. It's Father Bill's way of trying to hold on to what he's got, I guess."

Rory wasn't pleased, but it didn't seem they had much choice. "Saint Columba's it is."

"You could go to confession while you're there, Rory," Sandra said playfully. "Get rid of all those black marks on your soul."

"We can't have Father Bill having a stroke now, can we?" Rory replied. He turned to Erin. "Shall we?"

* * *

Erin hadn't been inside Saint Columba's in quite a while. The old pews were nicked but still shone, thanks to the cleaning woman, Mrs. Kendall, who buffed them with lemon cream and beeswax every Monday. The tile floor was spotless, too. Looking down at it reminded Erin of the brisk *click, click, click* of the women's heels every Sunday. Colored light streamed through the stained glass windows, while up front, rows of red votive candles flickered beneath a statue of the Virgin Mary. Above the draped altar hung a crucifix. Erin always avoided looking at it; the gruesome, twisted body of the man nailed to it always upset her.

They chose the pew closest to the back doors in case they needed to make a hasty escape from Father Bill. The man yammered so much he could make a dead man rise up just to tell him to button it.

"I'm sorry about the PR situation," Rory began. "It was the exception, not the rule. It won't be like that all the time."

Erin folded her hands in her lap, embarrassed. "I know. I just sort of short-circuited. I watched you at the party and saw how much you enjoyed all the mingling and hobnobbing, and I thought, 'He's in his element.' You didn't even seem to mind being pulled away for conversations all that much. Lou said you were a natural."

"Yeah, I'm sure he thinks it's the stereotypical Irish-gift-of-the-gab thing." He touched her cheek. "Don't you think I'd rather have been with you?"

"I don't know," Erin despaired. "I really don't. I was at the party and all I could think was, 'I don't belong.'"

"As I said, that party was an exception. However, you had better get used to parties like that if you're serious about the art world." Erin was mildly taken aback, which

amused Rory. "What did you think, you'd hide in the basement of a museum archiving things? You'll have to be out
there, at gallery openings and new exhibits and all that.
Did you never think of that?"

"Of course I did," Erin lied, somewhat irritated.

"You can't just run away because something frightens
you."

"Are you calling me immature?"

"You are when it comes to this."

"I just felt trapped, Rory." Her throat felt tight. "All of a
sudden, it seemed to be happening so fast. I know I've always wanted to leave Ballycraig, but that was overwhelming."

Rory looked crestfallen. "You didn't enjoy sightseeing
or the art tours?"

Erin grabbed his hand. "No, no, I loved all that," she
assured him fervently. "Like I just said, I was overwhelmed."
Rory started stroking her hair tenderly. "The past few days
are the only time I've ever been out of Ireland. You know
that. And so—"

"Joining me in London was both good and bad," he finished for her, pulling her close.

"Yeah. I've been slinging around this bravado, and now
that everything I've ever wanted is all coming together, I
realize how sheltered I really am, and you know what? I'm
scared witless." Her lower lip began trembling. "I'm the
same wimp I always was."

"That's not true."

"Yes, it is." They held each other close for a long time.
Erin heard the church doors open behind them and stiffened. But it was just Teague's mother, come to light a votive
candle and say a few prayers. If she noticed her and Rory,
she gave no sign.

Rory kissed her hand. "Here's what I think we should
do. I'm going back to New York. You stay here until you've
got your mind all sorted. I don't care if it takes you more
than the next two weeks. Take a month. Take a year. You
come to me when you're ready. I'll still be there waiting.

I'll always be there waiting for you. There's no way I can be happy if you're not happy, too. I mean that."

"Rory—"

"I mean it." His hands were on her shoulders, eyes searching hers. "This time it's about you, Erin."

Erin began to cry. "I love you so, Rory Brady. You know that?"

"I do." He gazed around the church. "You know what I'm going to do right now? I'm going to light one of those votive candles and say a prayer for us."

Erin's jaw dropped. "I don't know if you can do that."

"Why not? I was baptized here and I'm getting married here as well. I've a right to light one candle."

Erin nodded. "All right."

Her eyes tracked him to the front of the church. She pictured the two of them standing there with radiant looks on their faces, while the pews behind were overflowing with relatives and villagers looking on as she and Rory exchanged wedding vows. The image filled her with a sense of joy and happiness she could barely put words to. She'd waited a long time for this.

42

"*Yo, Bono: I'm* really getting tired of looking at your ugly mopey face."

Rory gave Eric Mitchell the finger as they pushed tables together in the back of the Wild Hart. He'd never fully enjoyed hanging out there because it was run by Erin's uncle Charlie and aunt Kathleen. Erin's aunt was a pro at getting off a good crack or two underneath her breath. It was a marvel she and Bettina weren't related.

Now that he and Erin had reunited, this branch of the O'Briens were okay with him, albeit warily. They had all spent the past two weeks keeping an extra eye on him, all except Quinn, who told Rory he believed people's relationships were their own business.

There were six of them hanging out tonight: him, Eric and Jason Mitchell, Esa, Ulf, and Sebastian.

Rory lowered himself down into his chair with a grimace. They all did. Practice was killing them. Last year Rory had thought, *Ah, I'll be used to it by next year,* but he wasn't. He never would be, which was the point. No matter how great you might be doing on the ice, you could always do better—at least according to Coach Dante, nicknamed "Mikey the Merciless" behind his back.

"He's right," Ulf chimed in, backing up Eric's statement. "Mope, mope, mope over Erica."

Rory rolled his eyes. "Erin."

Her uncle came over from the bar, smiling sympathetically. "How's training camp going, fellas?"

Ulf groaned. "Hell, as usual."

"That's because you're getting old," said Sebastian.

"No, it's tough." He pointed at Rory accusingly. "It doesn't help that he's about as happy as a priest at a swinger's party."

Erin's uncle looked pleased about that. "'Course he doesn't look happy: he's parted from my beautiful niece."

"She is beautiful," Esa concurred.

Erin's uncle scowled at him. "Hey! I'll thank you to keep your Finnish eyes to yourself."

"Just looking, no touching."

"Feckin' A, you're not," said Rory.

"A good Irishman always defends his turf," said Erin's uncle. He folded his arms across his barrel chest. "Usual all round?"

Six nods of the head.

"Any food?"

"I could eat," said Ulf.

"What a surprise," Jason drawled.

"I'm hungry as well," Rory confessed.

"Yeah, me, too," said Sebastian.

"Good pot pies tonight," said Erin's uncle. "Fish and chips as well."

"We'll all have both," said Esa, looking around the table for confirmation. Everyone agreed.

"Good boys," said Erin's uncle, heading into the kitchen.

"He's a good guy, your uncle," said Ulf, watching him make his way to the kitchen.

"He's my fiancé's uncle, Ulfie."

"Well, he's still a good guy," Ulf insisted with a sulk.

"You say that every time we're in here, you dolt," said Eric.

"Back to Mr. Happy," said Esa, addressing Rory. "You need a wild night out, Bono. Revelry."

"Revelry is the last thing I need."

"Afraid you'll stray?" Esa asked, arching an eyebrow.

"Afraid I'll be bored to death."

"It's only been two weeks, Rory," Esa continued. "You act like it's been years."

"If your fiancée was Erin, wouldn't you feel that way?" Rory challenged.

Esa squirmed a bit. "Well . . . "

"So shut your gob, then."

"What is she again?" Ulf asked. "A painter?"

The Mitchell brothers exchanged looks.

"Can you believe two women have married him?" Jason asked his brother.

"No shit," said Eric.

"The last one doesn't count," Ulf growled.

"Cut him a break tonight, guys, will ya?" Rory implored. "He's still in mourning."

Ulf narrowed his eyes. "You mockin' me?"

"I swear to God, I'm not!" Rory looked around the table at his teammates. "I'm not!"

"I know," Esa said. "That's what makes you so sickening."

Conversation masked the sound of rumbling bellies. Rory's mates were right: he was being a bit of a mope. He had to put things in perspective: yeah, things weren't exactly how he'd pictured them to be, but it wasn't forever.

"Ho. Ly. Shit."

Esa punched Rory's shoulder. "Look who's coming out of the kitchen to serve us dinner."

Rory turned. It was Erin, carrying a large platter of food. Rory pushed himself out of his chair so hard it fell over as he started hustling toward her.

"Let the girl at least put the tray down," said Erin's aunt, appearing at the door of the kitchen with a second platter.

Rory strained impatiently in Erin's wake as she made her way to the Blades' table.

"Hiya, fellas," she said with a friendly smile as she started unloading the food.

"Would you ever hurry up so I can throw my arms around you?" Rory cried.

"I'm goin' as fast as I can."

Finally, *finally*, the tray was empty.

Erin looked around, confused, not knowing where to put it, till her aunt plucked it out of her hands. "I've got it. You can hug her now," she informed Rory.

Rory picked her up, swinging her around. He was laughing like a fool, near delirious with love and disbelief.

Erin was laughing, too. "Put me down! You're going to give me vertigo!"

Rory put her down, still not quite believing his eyes.

"Shall I pinch you so you know I'm real, then?" Erin offered.

"A kiss might be better."

Rory thought her natural shyness would kick in, but she threw her arms around his neck, kissing him so passionately he was the one who began to feel self-conscious.

Her aunt coughed loudly. "Enough of that, now."

They broke apart. Erin couldn't stop grinning. She looked like a kid who'd gotten every single thing she'd ever wanted in her life. "Surprised?"

"What do you think?"

"Surprised me, I can tell you that," said her aunt. "Am I correct in assuming you will not be sleeping under my roof tonight?" she asked Erin politely.

Erin blushed. "Yes."

"I thought as much."

Erin kissed her aunt on the cheek. "Thanks so much for keeping my secret, Aunt Kathleen. I'll be round tomorrow."

"Good. I'm going to go tell your uncle that he can ring your mam and dad now to let them know it all went off without a hitch. They've been on pins and needles, especially your mam."

"That doesn't surprise me."

Her smile was affectionate as she hugged Erin. "Welcome to America, love."

* * *

"Well, that was deliciously primitive."

Erin was lying in Rory's arms, so relaxed she thought she might just float away on the breeze. It had been comical, the two of them trying to stay a decent amount of time at the pub with Rory's teammates when, really, all they wanted to do was head back to Rory's and tear each other's clothes off. But the universe seemed intent on putting a few more obstacles in their way first: It was pouring when they got outside, so it took them eons to get a cab. When they finally got back to Rory's flat, he couldn't find his key. Turned out it was deep inside one of his skates. But for a moment there, they thought they'd have to troop back to the pub.

Their clothes had come off pretty damn quickly, which was fine with her. Sometimes sex was meant to be slow and exquisitely torturous; other times, it was meant to be raw and frenzied. This was one of those times when wildness lay waste to your senses.

"I like that word, *primitive.*" Rory mused. "It conjures up images of cavemen."

"You are a bit of one, you know." Erin loved the thin sheen of sweat on his face and gave his cheek a small lick.

"How'd you reckon?"

"You're macho, always have been. Not much of a decorator, though."

Rory looked offended as he propped himself up on one elbow. "What'd you mean by that?"

Erin chortled as if it were self-evident. "Rory, you're still living out of boxes. We're on a mattress on the floor!"

"So? I know where everything is."

"Well, I don't. First thing tomorrow, I'm giving this flat a good cleaning."

"Wrong." He took her in his arms and flipped her so she

was lying on top of him. "First thing tomorrow, you're going to make love with me before I go to practice."

"Deal."

"I can't believe you're really here," Rory marveled. The amazement in his voice made her tingle, not only because it was obvious he really was glad she was here, but because it confirmed what she'd known the minute he'd flown out of Galway: her life *was* meant to be lived right by his side.

THREE MONTHS LATER

"Da, being allowed to sit in your Ford Fiesta is the best wedding present any girl could ask for."

Erin couldn't contain her joy, grinning at her father as they cruised down the High Street to Saint Columba's church. Even though she knew the car wouldn't be an issue, she liked teasing him anyway. Her mother was in the backseat, fussing with her hair and generally looking nervous.

She'd taken the internship at the Guggenheim, and it had led to a job. When she and Rory got back to New York, she'd start at the museum as a trainee archivist.

Thank Christ for Sandra, she thought. Were it not for her, it would have been near impossible to plan the wedding from afar. San had arranged the flowers, the photographer, and the music, running stuff by Erin via e-mail, phone, and Skype. Since Sandra was the only one standing up for her, Erin told her friend to go to Belladonna Bridal in Galway City to pick out any dress she pleased. Rory's bank account was large enough to give both of them free rein to create the day Erin had long dreamed of.

Rather than have the reception at the Oak, she and Rory had opted for the parish hall at Saint Columba's, which was now also miraculously air-conditioned thanks to an anonymous donor whom everyone suspected was PJ Leary. Erin's parents insisted on taking care of the catering ("Best in Galway City") and Jake had picked the band.

There were so many things about today that were making

Erin happy. Not just that she and Rory were finally going to
be married, but that her aunt Kathleen and uncle Charlie
were here, as well as Rory's parents. Jake was standing up
for Rory. Esa had flown over for the wedding, while the rest
of the team was watching the wedding on closed-circuit
TV at the Wild Hart.

Erin hadn't felt the least bit nervous until now, when she
and her da pulled up in front of the church, and there were
familiar faces standing outside waiting for her arrival,
including the Holy Trinity.

* * *

She'd chosen a simple vintage wedding gown, opting for
light champagne pink over the traditional white. Tea
length, with a delicately ruffled hemline, it was exquisite,
with subtle floral embroidery at the bust and at the bottom
of the scalloped shoulders. She'd never pictured herself in
a wedding dress with a capital *W.* It wasn't her style; plus,
she was too petite to carry it off.

As she started up the church steps, Teague reached into
a paper bag, but David quickly grabbed his wrist. "Not now,
you stupid bastard! You throw the confetti afterwards."

The idea of confetti amused Erin: the reception was being
held a few feet away. Standing at the back of the church,
she began to tear up unexpectedly. The early-evening light
shining through the stained glass windows made the chapel look magical. Pink and white roses adorned the altar,
matching Erin's bouquet of pink and white rosebuds. The
chapel was packed. One look at the crowd and Erin's mother's lower lip began quivering.

"None of that now," her father chided affectionately.
Erin's brother and his wife were already sitting up in the
left front pew. Erin and her parents were just waiting on
Sandra, who'd insisted on getting to the church early to
make sure everything was perfect, and to put the fear into
Father Bill if he somehow managed to make a hash of
things.

Erin was just about to ask her da to go check and see if

everything was okay with Sandra when Erin spotted her tiptoeing down the left aisle of the church.

"Sorry," she whispered, joining them in the vestibule. "Just getting my last fag in. Don't worry: I popped a mint." She blew a stream of breath at Erin. "Is it okay?"

"Gorgeous," Erin teased.

Sandra kissed Erin's parents on the cheek. "Look at you two. You look lovely, Mrs. O. And you, Mr. O—if you were twenty-five years younger, Mrs. O over here'd be havin' some stiff competition."

Erin's mother scowled, but her da enjoyed the compliment.

"Everything's a-okay," Sandra told Erin. "Rory's as twitchy as a man trapped in a bag of fleas, but he'll be all right.

"Jake's a bit nervous, too." At this, Sandra's eyes dropped demurely.

"Yeah, I'll bet he is," Erin said slyly.

Sandra kept reaching out to touch her dress. "You look so beautiful."

The lovely, gentle organ music had stopped as Jake and Rory appeared on the altar. If Rory was nervous, it didn't show on his face; he looked happy and confident. In fact, it was Jake who was looking a bit peaky.

Erin and Rory had decided they didn't want a traditional wedding march played as Erin walked up the aisle; so when the sound of Nat King Cole's "Unforgettable" came floating out of the speakers, people looked confused. But it only took them a few seconds before they all grew misty-eyed.

Sandra headed up the aisle, beaming, which obviously wasn't lost on Jake, who beamed back.

"It's time," Erin's da said quietly. She'd asked both her parents to give her away. She took a deep breath, then nodded.

Afterward, Erin would have no memory of the walk up the aisle, or of her parents kissing her and sitting down. There was only one person in the church, and it was Rory.

She'd dreamed of this day for years, and now that it was here, she realized just how pale one's imagination could be. The intensity of the love she felt for this man was so overpowering it was almost indescribable. It was almost as if she'd been spending years dreaming in black-and-white, but now that it was finally here, the real event was in Technicolor.

Time didn't exist: there was no fast or slow, just the two of them, the words, the connection. They finally belonged to each other, heart and soul. And nothing would ever, ever tear them apart again.

Go ahead. Try…

Just a Taste

By *New York Times* bestselling author

Deirdre Martin

Since his wife's untimely death, Anthony Dante has thrown himself into his cooking, making his restaurant, Dante's, a Brooklyn institution. So far, his biggest problem has been keeping his brother, the retired hockey star, out of the kitchen. But now, a mademoiselle is invading his turf.

Stunning Vivi Robitaille can't wait to showcase her taste-bud-tingling recipes in her brand new bistro, Vivi's. Her only problem is an arrogant Italian chef across the street who actually thinks he's competition.

The table is set for a culinary war—until things start getting spicy outside of the kitchen…

11

Erin had always loved fairs. When she was small, there used to be an annual summer fair in Crosshaven featuring all the usual delights: pony rides, fortune tellers, a bouncy castle. Her mother always thought the games of chance were a waste of money, but her dad used to slip her and Brian a few coins to play on the sly.

Arriving home the night of the darts game, Erin had sat in her room for a long time, trying to sort out her feelings. She was embarrassed by the secret thrill that ran through her as she watched Rory and Jake go at it. At first, Sandra's offering her up like a prize calf had maddened her. Sandra knew Jake hadn't a snowball's chance in hell with her, and the darts contest seemed cruel, giving him false hope where none existed.

She found Rory's magnanimity in willing to forfeit the match shocking. That he'd even suggested darts at all was a stunner: he'd never been good at them, ever, at least not compared to Jake. And if there was one thing that drove Rory Brady mad, it was not being good at something. Maybe he had really changed.

Erin caught a ride to the fair with Mr. Russell. The old man seemed especially excited about seeing one of the fortune tellers, while Erin was looking forward to the fried Mars bars, her favorite junk food.

She wasn't surprised when she arrived at the preserves booth to find Rory already there, looking semi-Yank in tight jeans, a striped green and yellow sweater, and white running shoes she'd never seen in Ireland. Christ, he really did look like David Beckham. And he knew it, too.

Rory grinned as he caught sight of her. Erin resisted the urge to smile back even as memories of fairs past darted through her mind. *That was then, this is now,* she scolded herself. Two hours, nothing more.

"Hiya. How was your ride over?" he asked.

"Fine. You?"

"Fine."

"Great. Well, now that that's established, what do you want to do?"

"It's what you want to do, Erin."

"But I'm the prize," she reminded him acidly. "It's about what you want."

She glanced around the market. It was getting so crowded that soon it would be hard to move. She wouldn't mind picking up a few jars of jam and some homemade choccies for her mam, but it was silly to get them now and have to carry them around. She'd buy them when they were done at the fair. Sandra's voice whispered in her ear: *Make him pay. Make him pay for everything.* Maybe she was foolish, but to Erin, the thought of snapping her fingers and ordering Rory about wasn't right.

Allowing him to drive her around was one thing. As he said, it was the least he could do to make her life a bit easier. But telling him he had to foot the bill for everything at the fair was bitchy. And immature.

"I don't really want to walk around the market," she told him.

"I did a once-round waiting for you. Your cousin Liam and his missus each gave me a champion glare when I walked past, and I heard a couple of spare Fry brothers muttering about 'putting the boot in.' I'd forgotten what a charming place this can be for those on the outs."

"Let's just get to the fair and get it over with," Erin said with a heavy sigh.

"Oh, yeah, pure torture it'll be," Rory teased, "knowing how much you hate fairs and all."

Erin gave him a dirty look. "Let's go."

She started walking, jostled by the crowd, but it became clear that it would be easier to forge a path by letting Rory lead. Funny: when someone as big and broad as Rory wanted to get by, space magically opened for him. She'd used to like that. Much to her chagrin, she still did.

* * *

One hour down, one to go. They'd gone on the Tilt-A-Whirl, the Gravitron, and the roller coaster. Erin tried to talk to Rory as little as possible, but it was hard, what with them being jammed together into small spaces. "It's your own fun you're ruining," Rory pointed out casually, as they waited on the snaking line to buy a couple of fried Mars bars. "I told you, you didn't have to honor the bet. But since you did, why not enjoy yourself?"

Erin was silent. She hated that he was right.

Rory tapped her on the shoulder, pointing up at the large Ferris wheel. "Remember that time we got stuck at the top?"

"Vaguely," Erin lied.

"You wouldn't look down," Rory continued undeterred, "and you were completely green around the gills, being trapped that high up. You were holding my hand so tightly I thought you'd crush my bones." He looked amused. "I know you remember it all, Erin, so don't pretend you don't."

Erin ducked her head sheepishly. "Right, I do. But at least I'm not the one who stuffed their face with so much cotton candy they got a massive bellyache."

"That was because you kept buying it for me and I hadn't the heart to turn you down."

Erin chortled. "Oh, pin your teenage gluttony on me, will you? I don't think so."

"It *was* your fault when we got in those tiny bumper cars and I couldn't get out because I was too big for them."

Erin smiled wickedly. "I've got a picture of that somewhere, you know. Them having to dismantle the ride."

"Hanging on to it so you can blackmail me someday, eh?"

"Believe me, if I wanted to blackmail you, I've got loads of other things at my disposal."

"So, you haven't thrown things out," Rory said softly, going to touch her arm.

Erin jerked away. *What the hell are you doing, strolling down memory lane? You're not even supposed to be talking to him.*

"No, I don't throw things away, Rory, unlike you. And memories are sweet, but that's all they are: memories. I'd appreciate it if we could get back to wrapping this day up."

Rory cocked his head appraisingly. "I like this new you, standing your ground and all."

"I thought you said I'd become a hard one."

"More tough than hard, I'd say now."

"Go to hell, Rory. You make it sound like I let you push me all over the map."

"You did. And I didn't even think twice about it. Sorry for that."

"Apology accepted."

Rory took one bite of his Mars bar and tossed it into the rubbish bin with a disgusted face. "I've eaten loads of crap in my day, but that topped the list. How can you eat that?"

"Ah, what do you know?"

"Nothing about how your taste in sweets has changed, apparently. What now? Home?"

He was calling her bluff. Well, she'd call back.

"I'd like to finish my candy bar, please. Then home—though I would like to buy some jam and chocolate first."

"Well, there's something I need to do, too."

"What's that?"